Waiting for the Day

LESLIE THOMAS

Waiting for the Day

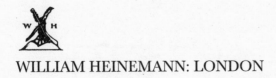

WILLIAM HEINEMANN: LONDON

Extract from 'Actors Waiting in the Wings of Europe' from *Collected Poems* © Keith Douglas.
Reprinted by kind permission of Faber & Faber Ltd.

Published in the United Kingdom in 2003 by
William Heinemann

3 5 7 9 10 8 6 4 2

William Heinemann
The Random House Group Limited
20 Vauxhall Bridge Road, London, SW1V 2SA

Random House Australia (Pty) Limited
20 Alfred Street, Milsons Point, Sydney,
New South Wales 2061, Australia

Random House New Zealand Limited
18 Poland Road, Glenfield
Auckland 10, New Zealand

Random House (Pty) Limited
Endulini, 5a Jubilee Road, Parktown, 2193, South Africa

The Random House Group Limited Reg. No. 954009
www.randomhouse.co.uk

A CIP catalogue record for this book is available from the
British Library

Papers used by Random House are natural, recyclable products
made from wood grown in sustainable forests. The manufacturing processes conform
to the environmental regulations of the country of origin

Typeset in Baskerville MT by SX Composing DTP, Rayleigh, Essex
Printed and bound in the United Kingdom by
Mackays of Chatham Plc, Chatham, Kent

ISBN 0 434 01143 6

'The hour of our greatest efforts and actions is approaching . . .
The flashing eyes of all our soldiers, sailors and airmen must be
fixed upon the enemy . . .'

Winston Churchill
Broadcast, March 1944

'Actors waiting in the wings of Europe
we already watch the lights on the stage
and listen to the colossal overture begin'

Keith Douglas
Collected Poems, 1943

'Flasks of hot tea and jam sandwiches were collected for use on the
flight . . .'

Private Ron Gregory, paratrooper
who dropped over France on D-Day

Sixty years have gone by since the D-Day invasion of northern France by Allied forces in the Second World War.

This story is for everyone who remembers those times and everyone who may want to know about them.

Chapter One

Nearly six hours late the wartime train dragged west, the night bone cold, the land black; its windows were masked and inside each compartment a weak blue light lent an eerie shape to the lumped passengers. Some stirred but, from the old, labouring steam engine to the slowly rocking guard's van at the back, men, mostly soldiers, and a few women, lolled and lay as though they were already dead in battle.

It was two nights before Christmas 1943 and in the shapeless country through which the train crawled there were more than a million men, sleeping with their tanks, guns, planes and ships, waiting for the day to invade, to liberate, German-occupied Europe. It was still almost six months away.

Paget was in the window corner of what was still called a first-class compartment, its seats threadbare, its woodwork rattling. It was reserved for officers but at that bleak hour the shadows surrounding him were anonymous. He looked at the luminous dial of his air force watch, its small glow just enough, as he stood, to reflect in the glass of one of the framed seaside photographs fixed to the wall in front of him. He looked more closely; there was a beach and a pier but he could not read where it was. All in the past now, anyway, over four years ago.

In the opposite seat was a sweating major who had earlier been taking measured swigs from a big silver whisky flask, burping on each one, but who now sat, head hung back, mouth open, with the flask in his lap like an empty trophy. There were two other army men, strangers perhaps, but leaning against each other as if for assurance; a khaki chaplain was snuggled against an officer of the women's Auxiliary Territorial Service. Both the padre and the fat-legged female were snoring, she boisterously, drowning his refined wheezings.

Paget opened the door carefully. There was a small aperture like a sniper's slit in the blacked-out windows of the corridor and he put his eye to it. The glass was cold on his cheek and outside was dark as an unending tunnel.

There were two civilians in the lavatory, ministry men judging by their bulging briefcases, slumped one each side of the pan, the blue light spectral on their faces. He tried not to disturb them, but they had become accustomed to intrusions and rose, hardly opening their eyes, and stumbled into the corridor dragging their briefcases with them. When he had finished and pulled the chain they went back.

He saw how congested the train was. Men wrapped in great-coats were lying in the smoke-choked corridor, heads to boots, their kit piled on their bellies or pushed as pillows below their heads. Between them beer bottles were scattered like expended shell cases, one rolling hollowly with the movement of the train. There were fragments of food, a shattered meat pie, half a sandwich, and cigarette stubs and packets: Players, Capstan, Craven 'A'. Each compartment was occupied by many more passengers than intended, crammed on the seats, sprawled between them and stretched out in the luggage racks. A female leg in a thick service stocking dangled over the side of one rack. In another compartment one of the racks had just partially collapsed on to the sleepers and they were cursing and spitting, trying to disentangle themselves. A soldier with a shoulder flash reading 'Norway' had his face plunged into his hands, laughing or crying.

As Paget neared the guard's van the train jolted and the engine, not for the first time, wheezed to a stop. A window was lowered and someone put his head out. It seemed the steam from the locomotive froze white on the midwinter air. A voice shouted: 'Shut the bleeding thing!' The man who had opened the window closed it forcefully and grunted: 'Christ only knows.' Paget wondered if Christ did.

There was a layer of human beings in the guard's van. Behind them he could make out packages and some piled newspapers pushed into one section segregated by a rope and a net. In the central dim light he could see the guard bent face forward on his swivel chair against a shelf, his cap like a bowl, his face in it. Paget climbed over to him.

'Could the driver be persuaded to stop at Crockbourne?' he asked. The guard roused, blinked, and put on his cap. His Great Western Railway badge glimmered. In wartime everybody had some sort of badge. 'GWR,' said the guard, seeing Paget's glance. He tapped it. 'God's Wonderful Railway. Was once. Will be again when the war's over.' He looked at Paget's squadron leader's rings. 'I had a boy in the air force,' he said.

He pushed his cap away from his forehead. 'Crockbourne? I don't see why not. We've stopped everywhere else.'

Paget said: 'If we go on to Taunton I'll have to hang around two hours to take the local train back.'

'You will, sir.' The man opened the timetable but did not refer to it. 'Crockbourne in about . . .' He took a turnip watch from his waistcoat. '. . . well, say half an hour. If we're lucky.'

He sniffed. 'It's all that heavy stuff, tanks and that, going down to Devon. They've even got Yankee locomotives in Newton Abbot yards. Gurt great things. Cow catchers on the front. Never thought I'd see that, not in England.'

'Half an hour then,' said Paget turning and stepping across the nearest sleeping men.

'Thereabouts, sir. I'll come back and give you a call.' There was only one first-class coach.

'Second compartment,' said Paget. 'There's a vicar and an ATS woman jammed in the corner.' The train began to move.

One of the soldiers in the guard's van had helped himself to the *Daily Mirror* from the pile behind the net. He pushed his face close to the page in the poor light. He was small and grained although he was only thirty.

'Those are private property,' the guard pointed out. He moved to retrieve the paper which the man put behind his back. ''Ang on now,' the soldier said. 'Oi can't see proper to read the bloody thing anyway. Not in 'ere.'

A tall and bulky soldier hunched next to him, head protruding from his greatcoat like a dopey tortoise, lifted his black-ringed eyes and said: ''Ow much has that Jane got on or off?'

''Ardly a stitch,' said the first man, opening the paper to the cartoon. The big soldier gave a grunt. 'Still not showing everything.'

The guard peered over the top edge of the paper. 'She's not allowed to show all she's got till the war's over,' he said. 'I 'eard it's a Government order. Stops the fighting man getting overexcited.'

The undersized soldier closed the page. 'We're *allowed* to get a bit excited,' he grumbled. 'It's a free country, they can't stop us. There's nothing in King's fucking Regulations about not getting excited, is there?'

'It's dirty women, that's what Churchill's afraid of us doin',' said the second soldier wisely. 'Getting weakened. Under the Emergency Powers, Defence of the Realm, and all that stuff you ain't allowed to do.'

'Like blowing whistles,' sniffed the guard as if it were a personal affront.

Somebody groaned for them to shut up and the guard wandered back to his ledge. The smaller soldier called after him: 'Who did he think he was then, when he's 'ome? That blue job.'

The guard responded cautiously: 'He's a squadron leader.'

'So 'e can stop the train where 'e likes, can he?'

'He's an officer.'

'Got some cushy desk job, I bet. Be the same after the war.'

The guard went out of his van, timing his steps to the roll of the train. 'Bleedin' squadron leader,' said the small soldier. 'He's all right. Never mind us.' The big man next to him said: 'You'm from

4

Coombebury, ain't you? Your name's Blackie. I went to school with you.'

'Ron Blackie,' nodded the small man. He manoeuvred himself to stare into the other's face. 'Miss Billips's class,' he said.

'Big Lips we called 'er, di'n we.' A smile of memory, probably the first smile on the train that night, broke on his rough face. 'Or big tits more like.'

The smaller man concentrated on the indistinct features. 'Oi 'member you,' he said. 'But Oi don' 'member your name.'

'Warren. Called Bunny.'

Blackie gave a nod. 'Course. Got you now. We took your trucks off in the playground one day, di'n we. And all the maids in the school was there. All laughing at your dick.'

Warren sniffed. 'I don't forget that.'

Blackie said: 'And you was wearing your mother's knicks.'

Warren sounded ashamed: 'It were cold, bloody cold, that winter, and my old girl didn't 'ave the money to buy me no underpants, so I wore her bloomers. She tried putting newspapers in but they kept falling out. After the maids and all you others laughed, I put up with freezing my balls off.'

'None of us 'ad anything then,' remembered Blackie. 'Bugger all. No money.'

'No underpants,' said Warren, still sadly. 'Things'll never be as bad as that again. So they tell us.'

Blackie sniffed. 'We'll see. Not the first time the working class been told lies. There's money around now, 'cos of war work and that. There's blokes in Plymouth clearing the bombing, patching up, and that, taking 'ome *six quid* a week.'

Warren nodded. 'And we're in this mob, likely gettin' our 'eads blown to bits, for seven bob.'

Blackie said: 'You up on Salisbury Plain?'

'Aye, right up on it. You as well?'

'Like you, right up on the bastard. We went to Portsmouth last week, one of these embarkation drills, 'orrible and wet, but it weren't bad when we got off duty.'

'We're close on Salisbury,' said Warren. 'There's a bus. You can go to the pictures and watch them Yanks climbing all over the girls in the back seats.'

Blackie said reflectively: 'Oi 'ad quite a nice shag, Wednesday down Portsmouth. Five bob. Outdoors, mind.'

Warren mused: 'Five shillings. That's a lot for a bunk-up, open air. Not that I'd know. I never got anything left, 'ardly enough for a pint of old and mild.'

'Pompy was full of soddin' Yanks as well, and the navy. You could scarce get into a pub. But she was all right, nearly young, if you know what I mean. We went at the back of a shop, stood up in some sawdust.' He leaned forward confidingly although none of the men around them stirred. The guard was in the corridor. 'I put my greatcoat round us both and . . . and she weren't wearing nothing underneath.'

Warren leaned. 'Not a stitch?'

'Not even a bit of 'lastic. And d'you know what she said for me to do?'

'No. What?'

Blackie's voice fell to a whisper. 'She had these stockings on, from some Yank, I 'spect, and she got me to put the money in the tops of her stockings. Half a crown one side and half a crown the other.'

'That's . . . like, romantic,' said Warren wistfully. Then he said: 'You goin' home to the wife?'

Blackie knew what he meant. 'Aye, but she blows hot and cold, mostly cold. I got her a nice Christmas present, though. When that tart went off she left 'er scarf and it's a good 'un. Suit my missus.'

Paget was fitfully dozing when the guard slid open the door. The ATS officer raised one large eye and regarded the intruder belligerently: 'Are we never going to get there?'

'One day, lady,' responded the guard. 'Or one night. Soon, I 'spect.'

He said to Paget: 'Crockbourne next stop, sir. Five minutes.'

Paget took his case and overcoat down from the rack and put on a pair of knitted gloves. The artillery major woke and made to drink from his empty flask. He peered down the neck and then glanced suspiciously about him. Since Paddington scarcely a word had been exchanged in the compartment but now, as he left, the woman wished him a Merry Christmas and the padre, keeping his eyes closed, added: 'And a holy one.'

The engine steamed into the dark and freezing Crockbourne station at five in the morning. As Paget climbed down to the platform some of the servicemen who had woken were attempting to sing, defiantly, tunelessly:

> *'She's a big, fat cow,*
> *Twice the size of me.*
> *She's got hairs on her belly*
> *Like the branches on a tree.'*

He shut off their song as he slammed the door. The engine eased away with a melancholy toot and for some reason, like a boy, he gave a single wave. He could scarcely see the station name board, restored now after being taken down during the time when a German invasion was feared. It had been kept in the waiting-room.

As he walked the frost made each footstep sound like a gunshot. He knew the door through the vestibule by the ticket office would be locked but he tried it anyway. It was. He felt stiff and chilled even in his RAF topcoat. Taking it off he flung it over the station fence and threw his case after it.

In the dark he tripped over a bucket on the platform and it clanged as it rolled. He picked it up and placed it upside down on a bench next to the fence and, with the bucket rocking under his feet, awkwardly clambered over.

''Alt! Oo be that?' It was more like a squeak than a challenge. 'Oo goes there?'

The bucket had tipped as Paget climbed and now it clattered noisily along the platform beyond the fence. He stared into the gloom and down the barrels of a shotgun pointed at him from twenty yards by a thin and shadowy man.

'Put that gun down,' ordered Paget. 'I'm an RAF officer. Can't you see?'

'You'm could be in disguise.'

'Well, I'm not.'

Reluctantly the gun barrels were lowered and Paget stepped closer and leaned towards the face framed by several woollen balaclavas. 'You're Skinner, aren't you?'

'Hughie Skinner,' agreed the man in a pleased way. 'An' you'm be Mr Paget from Ash Lodge. Mr Paget's son, that is.'

Some dead rabbits hung over the bicycle handlebars. 'I'm 'Ome Guard,' said Skinner. 'But right now I bain't in uniform.'

'I thought the Home Guard had Sten guns these days.'

'Been out after a few bunnies for the pot.' He went to the bicycle and detached a dangling rabbit. 'Maybe your good mother would like one for Christmas.'

Paget hesitated but then held out his hand and nodded his thanks. In wartime you never knew when a rabbit might come in useful. 'Somehow I've got to get home,' he said. 'I'll have to ring Wilks. He might come out even at this hour.' He turned towards the dark telephone box by the booking-hall door.

'Phone don't ackle, Mr Paget, sir,' said Skinner. 'Been bust a fortnight. Nobody to come and mend it, so they says. You could ride on my crossbar but I don't reckon this old shaker would stand it.' He paused thoughtfully. 'But I tell you what I'll do, I'll pedal down to Wilks and turf 'im out. I know for sure 'e's got some juice. They Yanks 'ave give 'im some.'

Skinner creaked off into the icy night. Paget put on his coat and his cap and went into the phone box for some kind of shelter. In the dark cold everything was tranquil. He could make out the winter tracery of the great trees creaking over the station yard. They used to collect conkers below them after school. He and Margaret had enjoyed their first kiss one peacetime evening under the summer leaves. What had happened to Margaret? What had happened to him? To all of them?

After twenty minutes he gratefully heard the taxi coming, rattling through the dark, and picked up his case as Wilks brought the Austin, its headlights only slits, around the corner.

Wilks was an old man swathed in coats and scarves, his face barely visible. 'Mr Paget,' he said. 'Welcome home, sir. Skinner got me out of bed. But it's all right, part of the war effort.'

'Thanks, Wilks,' said Paget, putting his case in the car and climbing into the warm leather seats in the back. 'That train should have been here at eleven thirty last night.'

''Ow they 'ope to invade France if they can't get the trains right, confounds me, sir. Good job I 'ad some petrol.'

The engine grunted and they turned a crunching circle in the station yard. 'Gave a lift to some Yanks last week,' said the driver. 'Drunk as lords and miles from camp but I was going that way anyway. They was too plastered to pay. And this morning, would you believe it, there was two of those jerrycans at my gate, full. Four gallons of what they call gas.'

The taxi crept through the bleak shadows. 'Still don't like these masks on they headlights,' said Wilks. 'My eyes don't get any better and how am I expected to see the road? Good job I knows it like my hand. Time they did away with the blackout, anyway. Jerry won't bomb us now.'

Paget felt the vehicle going up a familiar slope to where he knew there was a break in the hedgerow and he could look towards the cricket ground. It was glowing faintly luminous with frost, the pavilion hunched by the road. Wilks said: 'I 'member when you played for the men's team and you were only a boy, Mr Paget. You did all right, too. They have the odd match in the season now, fire brigade versus the police and that, but the pavilion's full of air-raid stuff, pumps and ladders. Not that we 'ad much need of them around these parts, thank God. One land-mine in the lake, hundreds of dead fish, and that was about it.'

Paget laughed in the dark. 'My mother wrote to me about the fish. She said you could smell the frying for miles.'

'That was all the war we've really 'ad down 'ere,' said Wilks. 'Except the boys going away to join up and never coming back. And there's been a few of them.' The church tower rose at the crossroads, black even against the darkness. 'I spent a few cold hours up .there,' said Wilks. 'Fire-watching. One night I'm up there sitting on my deck-chair, wrapped up, with a tot of whisky, and I could see them bombing Bristol. It were burning like 'ell. Grandstand view.'

They were almost there now. He was home again. The taxi pulled up, shuddering at the gate. 'Do they know you're coming, Mr Paget?' asked Wilks as he took the one-and-sixpence fare and refused a tip. 'Tip me when the war's over,' he said.

'They'll hear the gate squeak,' said Paget. 'My father will probably come down with his sword.'

Wilks laughed. 'I heard tell about 'is sword. God, if they Jerries *had* landed 'ere they would have 'ad some trouble with your dad.'

They shook hands, neither taking off his gloves, and wished each other a Happy Christmas. Carrying Skinner's rabbit, Paget opened the gate and nodded to the familiar squeak. A curtain twitched above as he watched for it. Then there came a candle glow in the fanlight, the latch sounded and the chain rattled throatily, like a memory. The door was pulled open. His father stood there in his bulky dressing-gown, his grin below his grey moustache deepened by the candlelight. His mother was behind him. 'Martin,' she whispered. 'You're home for Christmas.'

'Didn't I say he would be,' said his father. Paget embraced his mother and handed her the rabbit.

Chapter Two

He slept until the early afternoon, woken by the arid branch of a dog rose tapping at the glass, as it had done when he was a boy. He used to imagine it was someone, perhaps a beautiful woman, wanting to come in. Now he lay deeply enjoying the room around him, the feel of the remembered bed, how he fitted into it, the shadowed walls and the beams crossing the ceiling; the safeness. The blackleaded fireplace was empty but the room was warm for it shared a chimney with the living-room below where there was a log fire all the winter. Twenty-five years of nights he had lain there familiar with the beams above him, their twists, cracks, shadows and generations of spiders who had eluded his mother's duster. Nothing had changed. He was grateful to be back.

By instinct, his mother Emma knew he was awake. She appeared at the sloping door, her happiness apparent even in the low light. 'It's two o'clock,' she said. 'I've brought you a cup of tea. And I'm making a stew for tonight.' She hesitated. 'Rabbit.'

As she put the tea on the side of the bed she kissed him. 'Perhaps before long you'll be home for good,' she said. 'Do you think it will all be over next year?'

He laughed and patted her face gently. 'If I knew that, Mother, I'd be up there with the big chiefs, with Eisenhower, Montgomery. And they probably don't know either.' He tried to sound reassuring: 'But we're going to win now, that's certain.'

'Tanner's boy was lost at sea,' she said, 'and Tommy Andrews was killed in Italy.'

He grimaced sadly. In a village the casualties were personal.

'You've got something on your hand,' she said. He was wearing a pair of pyjamas she had given him from a drawer smelling of mothballs.

Turning his wrist, he pretended. 'Oh, that. That's nothing. A bit of a scorch.'

'It goes up, right up to your elbow.'

'It's better now. That's what you get for being careless, putting your arm on the block of a Ford.'

She regarded him accusingly. 'There's a mark, a scar, on your neck also.'

'Same thing.'

She went to the door and hesitated. 'Did you bring your ration coupons, Martin?' she asked. 'I'm going to the shop. Adamson promised me a tin of apricots.'

'I've got them,' he said, reaching for his wallet. He took out the coloured, small-squared, pieces of paper. 'And my subsistence allowance.' He gave her a white five-pound note with the coupons.

'Five pounds,' said Emma Paget. 'That seems a lot.'

'I might be here for months,' he joked. 'At least five days, unless they dream up some reason to drag me back.'

She kissed him again but repeated: 'It seems a lot,' as she went from the room and down the stairs.

He got up and put on his familiar dressing-gown which hung behind the door. He looked out of the tight window, over the paved garden with its skeletal apple tree, to the diminishing fields. He remembered the window framing a scene of high summer, the borders brimming with flowers, busy with birds, the apple tree loaded, the meadow beyond lush and green. Everywhere was white now, even the afternoon sky.

His father called up the stairs. 'There's hot water for a bath, Martin. We're just walking to the shop.'

He went to the bathroom on the wooden landing. In there was a small oil heater which he remembered being in the greenhouse. The water was heated from the living-room fire. He ran the bath and lay in it, wishing deeply that he could be there, home in that house, the war finished and done. He thought of the people he knew in France and of Antoinette.

His uniform, already pressed by his mother, was in the wardrobe. Hanging beside it was a rough, familiar shirt, a pair of corduroys and a brown pullover. There was underwear and socks and his shoes, new in 1940, on the low chest by the window. He got dressed and went down the creaking staircase into the living-room, enclosed and silent but for the ticking of the mantelpiece clock. It was surrounded by Christmas cards and there were others on the dresser. On a plant stand was a low Christmas tree, hung with a few baubles but no lights and a silver star sagging slightly to one side.

He walked into his mother's kitchen; everything was as she would always have it, shining, ordered. The rabbit stew was simmering on the stove, its good smell growing.

Back in the living-room he picked up that morning's copy of *The Times*, four pages of it, and sat in comfort in the armchair before the fire. The war was stalled. Russian winter had frozen the invading Germans in their tracks, in Italy battles had sunk into the December mud. In Burma, so far away it was almost forgotten, the Japanese were still trying to reach for India. Americans, landing on Pacific islands defended by manically brave Japanese soldiers, were in heavy combat. The extra Christmas issue of chocolate had gone swiftly from British shops.

His mother and father came into the hall, pink from the cold.

'Ah, that's more like you,' said his mother.

'Do the civvies still fit?' asked his father. 'They look a bit big.'

'They are,' said his mother, giving a gentle tug at the pullover sleeve. 'He'll have to grow into them again. Once he's not so busy.'

They went into the kitchen. His father filled the brass kettle and put it on the stove while his mother began unloading her shopping basket.

'Two ounces of butter each,' she recited. 'And four of margarine. A pound of sugar between us . . .'

'And a bit of cheese that would scarcely fill a mousetrap,' added his father. 'Thank God bread's not rationed.'

'When you can get it,' said his wife.

'I promise not to eat more than my ration,' smiled their son.

'Your coupons were useful,' said his mother. 'He had our apricots.' She held up an oblong tin. 'We even got some sardines.'

At nine o'clock in the evening they always listened to the news. Most of the population did so; it had become the meeting place of the nation. Schoolchildren did not go to bed until it was finished. They grew up with a geography lesson of battles: Dunkirk, Leningrad, El Alamein, the Irrawaddy River in Burma. The voices of the newsreaders were as recognisable as those of a family: Alvar Lidell, Bruce Belfrage, John Snagge. Some people christened their children Alvar.

The wooden wireless set was like a pointed hat standing on a wicker table in the corner. His mother polished its case once a week and dusted its dials daily. Every fortnight the wet battery had to be changed; the dry battery lasted longer.

'This is London.' The voice, modulated, important, filtered through the patterned fabric of the loudspeaker.

Paget saw his mother glance at her husband who gave a formal cough, as though chairing a meeting, and said awkwardly: 'We've . . . Well, we've formed the habit, like a lot of people, of giving some thought to those close to us who are away . . .'

'In the war,' put in his mother, attempting to get to the point. Big Ben began resoundingly to strike nine o'clock.

'We do it every evening while Big Ben is striking,' hurried Geoffrey Paget.

His mother said: 'We say a prayer for you, Martin.'

They were silent. After the successive shivering sounds had faded the BBC voice said: 'Here is the nine o'clock news and this is Alvar Lidell reading it.'

They had eaten the stew that evening. 'The rabbits are suffering heavy casualties,' his father had said.

'We have a duck for Christmas dinner,' Emma Paget said in a proud way. 'Hemmings promised.'

'And the very last of the Christmas puddings,' said his father. 'Vintage 1939.'

'Remember the puddings I made the week the war began in September,' his mother added. 'We've had one each Christmas.'

'She calculated the war would last five years.'

'That's as close as the experts,' said Martin.

'Do you ever see General Eisenhower?' enquired Emma genuinely.

Martin laughed. 'Not to speak to,' he said. 'On the newsreels.'

The reader of the nine o'clock news was saying: 'General Dwight Eisenhower has been appointed Supreme Commander Allied Expeditionary Force. General Montgomery is to be Commander of Allied Ground Forces . . .'

Geoffrey Paget took a bottle of whisky from the cupboard and they toasted Eisenhower, Montgomery and victory. When the news was over his mother went into the kitchen to wash up. 'This Scotch has just about lasted, like the puddings,' said his father, peering through the glass. 'How long before we get some more, I wonder?'

'Well, we've got Eisenhower and Monty in command, so all we have to do is go and win.' Martin raised his glass and added grimly: 'Nothing to it. Easy.'

Christmas morning was rosy. The sun came up over the rigid countryside, and children were out early sliding on trays down the slope behind the school and on the pond where the ice had been inches deep for a week. Bare trees stood like iron. Bascombe, the postman, made his Christmas morning delivery, collecting a doorstep gift of a couple of shillings or a tot of whisky at each house and riding his bicycle with increasing unsteadiness.

It was almost as it had always been in Crockbourne; except for the faces that would never return, and the fact that there were no bells. The ban on ringing bells had been lifted – nobody expected an invasion by German paratroops now – but it was feared the ropes were unsafe. Next year, the villagers promised themselves, the ringers would be able to continue their happy business. Next year, when the war would be over.

In uniform Paget walked to the church, talking with people he had not seen for a long time, his mother on one side of him, proudly, and his upright-walking father on the other. There were twenty others in uniform: soldiers, two army nurses, airmen who had once been his schoolmates.

As the scarved-and-coated congregation sang the opening carol, their breath clouding the cold church, he saw Margaret across the aisle, two rows in front. It had been over four years. She turned purposely, and their glances connected as they sang. At the end of the service, coming out beneath the crackling churchyard trees, he saw her, smiling, leaning against a tilting gravestone.

'You're not supposed to do that,' he grinned. She wore a long, warm, grey coat and a fur hat. He kissed her on the cheek and she returned the kiss on his. 'Propping yourself up on tombstones.'

'I'm allowed.' There was that slightly careless smile, the well-formed face, the touch of dark hair below the fur of the hat. But her eyes were deeper. 'It's my grandfather.' She patted the tombstone. 'And how are you, Martin?'

'Getting through,' he said. 'Like everybody else.'

'You look splendid in your uniform. Have you been doing brave things?'

'Not outstandingly brave,' he smiled. 'Although I could lie.' They began to walk familiarly among the other villagers, speaking briefly to people as they passed. His parents were still conversing at the church door.

Oddly she said: 'What do you suppose the Germans are up to today?'

'More or less what we're doing, I suppose.'

'Going to church, praying, singing carols.'

'"Silent Night" is a German carol.'

'Seems a bit mad,' Margaret said.

He said: 'You don't still live down here, do you?'

'No, in London. It's just for Christmas.' Two small boys came to her and she held their hands. 'I've brought my twins,' she said.

For Christmas dinner they had half the duck with boiled and roast potatoes, long parsnips, carrots and sprouts. There had never been a vegetable shortage; the nation had been told to 'Dig for Victory' to save shipping space, and gardens, lawns, parks and sports grounds had been dug over.

Following the last of the 1939 pudding the family sat, replete and solemn, around the wireless and listened to the traditional speech of King George VI spoken in his stumbling way. When the national anthem was played they stood, unselfconsciously, at attention. Outside it was bitterly dark. At five o'clock there was a knock at the door. Geoffrey and Emma Paget put down their wineglasses. Martin stood but his father said: 'I'll answer it,' and went into the hallway. Emma regarded her son. It might be a policeman with an instruction for him to report back. The department avoided using the telephone. It might be an order; another landing, another mission, another risk, another death. Perhaps his. He drained his wineglass.

His mother said: 'Not long ago your father would have taken his sword, in case it was a Hun paratrooper.' They heard Geoffrey removing the chains from the door. 'He very nearly sliced me in half once when I came back early from the Mothers' Union.'

The door opened and there were voices. 'It's an American,' whispered Emma Paget. 'A Yank. How exciting.'

The man who came politely into the room could almost have been Martin's older brother. He wore a smooth, olive uniform. He looked around smiling a little, and said: 'Just like home.'

'I'm afraid I didn't hear your name,' said Geoffrey Paget, following him in.

'Miller,' said the man. 'Harry.' Then: 'Lieutenant.'

'You must have a drink,' said Geoffrey as they shook hands.

'We have sherry or whisky or a glass of wine. Red, white, but not all that good.'

'I'll take the sherry. It's not a drink I'm familiar with.'

'An amontillado. We've still got some. We're hoping it will last out the war.'

He went to the cupboard in the next room. 'Please sit down,' said Emma Paget to the American soldier. 'I'm sorry our weather is so lousy.'

Her son laughed and Miller accepted a chair and grinned. 'Lousy, Mother?' said Martin. 'Wherever did you get that?'

'Doesn't it sound right?' asked Emma. Carefully she repeated: 'Lousy.'

'Not coming from you.'

'Oh, dear. Well, I thought I'd make the attempt. I saw a picture, a film in Bridgwater. I went with Mrs Timms. It had a gangster chap . . . Edward Gee . . .'

'Robinson,' filled in Miller. 'Edward G. Robinson. He says "lousy" a lot in his movies.'

Geoffrey appeared with four neat glasses on an engraved silver tray that they only used at special times. His wife eyed it, glad that she had polished it that week. Miller sat with them in front of the burning logs. They raised their sherry glasses and toasted: 'Happy Christmas.'

The American said: 'I only got here six days ago. This is wonderful.'

Geoffrey Paget peered into his glass. 'Thank God we had some left. There's a British sherry but it's appalling.'

The American shook his head: 'This is fine. But I was meaning this house, the fire . . .'

'Was there someone with you?' asked Geoffrey. 'I thought there might be somebody in the jeep.'

Miller said: 'Oh, sure . . . It's the driver. We have some other calls to make . . .'

Emma Paget rose. 'We can't leave him out there.'

Her husband stood. 'Of course not.'

'I'll call him,' said Miller.

He went towards the door. Martin followed him and opened it, waiting in the hall listening to the voices, until the American returned with a tall black soldier whose eyes showed brightly in the outside dark. He let them in, closed the door and turned in time to see his mother's astonished expression.

'This is Harcourt,' introduced Miller. 'Private Benjamin Harcourt.'

'Junior, sir,' added the black man and the officer said: 'Oh, sure, Junior.'

Geoffrey pulled a chair out from below the table and the young man sat, lofty and awkward, holding his army cap on his knees. 'I'm sure you'd like a drink,' said Emma eagerly. 'A sherry?'

'No, ma'am, thank you, ma'am.' He glanced at the glasses. 'I've never tried alcohol.' He smiled honestly. 'My ma wouldn't let me.'

'Then some coffee. You must have some coffee.'

The driver glanced briefly at his officer before accepting. Emma went into the kitchen. 'Where are you from, lieutenant?' asked Martin.

'I hail from Bismarck,' said Miller. 'North Dakota.'

Martin knew his father would say it: 'Bismarck? It sounds German.'

'It is. The folks who settled that region, a lot came from Germany. My grandfather and grandmother were German. They changed their name from Müller.'

'And you're American,' said Geoffrey, as if to be sure.

'I'm American, sir. That's why I'm in this army.'

Geoffrey turned in his chair. 'And you, young man?' he asked Harcourt.

'Charleston, South Carolina, sir.' He grinned expansively. 'And my folks came from Africa.'

They joined his laugh uncertainly. Emma brought a cup of coffee from the kitchen. 'I'm afraid it's not *exactly* like American coffee,' she apologised.

'Wartime coffee, made from burnt acorns,' said Geoffrey.

Harcourt believed him. He took a sip and closed his eyes briefly. They waited. 'Pretty good,' he lied. 'Pretty, pretty good for acorn coffee.' He sipped his way painfully down the cup.

Miller said: 'We'll need to be going. We came to ask if you would care to visit with us at the big house, the Grange, where we are billeted. It's tomorrow night. None of our men have had a bundle of laughs this Christmas. We're an advance party. We have to establish a headquarters. There'll be a lot more personnel arriving soon. Most of us have only just got here from the States.'

'Poor fellows,' said Emma sincerely. 'We should have entertained *you*. We should have enquired but we don't like to ask in case it's all secret.'

'We'll be there,' decided her husband. 'Boxing Day. In America do you celebrate Boxing Day?'

Miller grinned. 'We will tomorrow. We'll send transportation, about six. I'm trying to visit as many people as I can.'

Bravely, Harcourt drained his cup. 'Thank you,' he said gravely, examining the bottom of it. 'I'll always remember that.'

They went out into the dark. The Pagets heard Harcourt say as they reached their jeep: 'Sure was unusual coffee, sir. Acorns.'

Before Martin closed the door the black soldier hurriedly returned down the short path carrying a container. 'Ice-cream,' he said. 'Does anybody here like ice-cream?'

Geoffrey's hands went out swiftly. They tried not to make their thanks too profuse but the moment the jeep had driven away they bore the canister into the house as eagerly as a prize.

'My God, ice-cream,' muttered Geoffrey. 'It's been bloody years.'

He levered open the top of the container and they all stared at the thick, beautiful, yellow contents.

'Nineteen-forty,' said Emma, making for the kitchen. 'August.'

'And this is American,' said Martin. He had eaten ice-cream in a café in Paris only a month before, a special brand from Holland reserved for German officers.

His mother returned, hurrying, with three dishes and spoons

rattling as if in anticipation. Eagerly, like children, they sat around the table while she served it. The remembered creamy smell rose to their noses. They dug in their spoons and hummed and rolled their eyes at the first rich taste. Then they delved avidly, eventually looking up shamefaced and laughing. Geoffrey had a vanilla layer across his moustache.

'Second helpings?' asked Emma unnecessarily. 'It won't keep long even in the cold pantry. They ate again, eventually sitting back and smiling. 'Glorious,' said Geoffrey, wiping his upper lip. 'God bless the Yanks.'

Thoughtfully his wife picked up the empty bowls. 'I've never spoken to a black person before,' she said.

Chapter Three

Since the early nineteenth century the Crockbourne Hunt had met in the stable yard of the Red Rover at noon on Boxing Day. Country people came from miles to see it: the steaming horses, the jostling hounds, the huntsmen with their pink coats and faces. The coats were fading now – the master had one elbow patched – the horses had been labouring on the farms, and the pack was diminished. 'Not killed a fox since afore the war,' said one of the village men.

''Bout the time of Munich,' agreed another. 'When Chamberlain met old 'Itler, for all the good that did.'

'Give us time, di'n't it, time to get a bit ready.'

Spectators came in carts and traps and on quivering bicycles to stand in their thick, shabby coats and their winding scarves and winter hats, their breath clouding the air. It was a day of heavy hoar-frost, hanging pink from trees glowing in the low, muffled sun. No hunting horn was sounded because, like the ringing of church bells, the blowing of trumpets had been prohibited under the Defence of the Realm regulations and, even though the law had now been altered, the horn itself had since been lost.

'I wonder if we'd be doing this if the Germans had come,' said Margaret. Her small sons were with other children giggling at the horses discharging their cloudy droppings. A bent man appeared and with difficulty scraped the rounded pieces with a coal shovel into a bucket. 'For my rhubarb,' he told the children, displaying the steaming contents. 'We 'ave custard on ours,' said a village man. It was a familiar joke but the people laughed, even some of the children.

Familiarly Margaret's hands went out to Martin and his to her. 'I think the Germans would rather shoot things than hunt,' he said.

'Jews,' she replied. She looked guilty and said: 'I didn't mean it to sound so glib.' She added quickly: 'Are you going up to the Americans' party at the Grange tonight?'

'We certainly are,' said Martin. 'It'll be a change from pontoon.'

'We play whist,' she sighed. 'Every Boxing Day since I was five.'

He said: 'Where is your husband?'

'In Italy, with the Eighth Army.' She halted. 'That's what I tell people, anyway. But I'm lying. He's a conscientious objector. He doesn't approve of fighting.'

'Nor do I.'

'But you're *prepared* to fight. Not him. Anyway, he's in a reserved occupation, he's a schoolteacher.'

'There have to be schoolteachers,' he said. 'Nine out of ten people in this country are civilians.'

'Counting the women and children,' she said. 'Clifford is quite open. He could say he's in a reserved occupation, but he owns up to being a conscientious objector.'

'It takes a sort of courage to do that,' he said.

Her eyelids lowered. 'Men go to prison for it,' she said. 'He was quite prepared for that. The tribunal asked him ridiculous questions like: "If a Hun were about to bayonet your sister, would you stop him?" But he said he didn't have a sister. They asked him about his religious convictions and he said he didn't have any of those either, he was simply against war and killing. In the end they gave up on him. As he was in a reserved occupation anyway they probably thought that was a good way out.'

The hunt began to stir; the master raised his hand, gave a call and they trotted out of the yard in a lazy cloud of steam. 'Don't look as if they could even frighten a fox, do they?' said Martin.

'Worn out, weary,' she nodded. 'Like the rest of us, the whole country.'

'It's been long enough,' he said. 'Four years and the rest.'

'I'm looking forward to tonight. It's ages since I've been to a party. I may get horribly drunk. I may go off with a Yank.'

'So where is your husband now?'

'He's got elderly parents. He's with them. It's better that way for both of us. My father, with his stories of the First World War, can't stand Clifford anyway. He'd prefer me married to a gallant guards officer.' She smiled wearily. 'He believes the only good German is a dead one.'

'A lot of people do – especially fathers,' he said.

At a quarter to six they were ready, sitting by the low fire with their coats on their laps. Martin had changed into uniform. His mother had washed and ironed his air force shirt. Geoffrey Paget leaned across and fingered the edge of the greatcoat. 'They do give you a good coat these days,' he said. 'And shoes.'

The knock on the door came briskly. A round-faced American soldier with a pinkish complexion stood beneath the porch. 'You folks all ready for the party?' He saw they were. 'That's fine. We'll all have such a good time. Forget the war.'

They followed him into the darkness. 'Good heavens,' Emma said mildly. 'They've sent a whole lorry.'

There was a semblance of a moon over the truck's tarpaulin. 'Sorry, people,' said the GI. 'It's all we could use. Unless maybe a Sherman tank.'

There was a short ladder and they climbed, the older pair with difficulty, into the dark back of the vehicle. There were laughing shadows along benches and as they felt for seats there were greetings and jokes. A torch shone around. Humphrey Timms, the chairman of the parish council, was wearing evening dress with a stiff wing collar. The doctor, Ralph Macaulay, wore his kilt. Emma, as she climbed in, had put her hand on his naked knee. 'Oh, so sorry, doctor,' she said.

'It's a fine knee,' he laughed.

The American soldier came to the rear. 'Everybody aboard okay?'

He startled them with a springing leap like an acrobat from the ground and over the metal tailboard. He tumbled inside and sat on the floor in the dark. 'Berlin, here I come,' he said.

They joined in the joke and, encouraged, he produced a torch and shone it on his own face, round and young, surmounted by a cropped fringe of ginger hair. 'I'm Wal,' he said. 'Private First Class Walter Barrows, US Army. Pleased to meet y'all.'

Hands reached out and shook his. His torch caught the starched shirt front of Humphrey Timms and after a surprised jolt moved on to the thin, defiant knees beneath the tartan of Dr Macaulay.

The American breathed audibly. 'That's cute,' he said. 'That's real cute.'

Betty Forsyth, who had lived in the village for eighty years, began to ask him something and he shone his torch towards her. She covered her eyes and he took the beam hurriedly away. 'Were you able to see the meet of our hunt today?' she said.

'Sure,' said Wal. 'We hunt where I come from, ma'am. Georgia. We go coon hunting. With dogs.'

There was an uncertain silence. Then Betty asked carefully: 'What exactly does coon hunting entail?'

Wal said: 'It's not easy. That racoon is a mean critter.'

Everyone laughed.

Standing half a mile from the village in its two hundred acres, Crockbourne Grange was one of the stately houses requisitioned by the British government on the first working morning of the war. On that Monday, 4 September 1939, as soon as the civil servants, with their uniform bowler hats and umbrellas, had marched with new resolve into their Whitehall offices, orders, plans and contingencies which had been in readiness for months, even years, were energetically, and without a second thought, put into operation. Mansions with expansive grounds, schools, hotels, sports clubs and some golf courses were appropriated under the emergency regulations, many standing empty for months before a use was found for them, if it ever was. Seaside hotels were evacuated of their guests, some elderly and with no other home.

'When they came back, just for a day, and when her saw the state of the place,' Wilks the taxi-driver related, 'Lady Marion were lost for words. And she weren't often that, sir.'

Lieutenant Miller listened to him in the high-ceilinged hall. A piled wood fire was crackling in the marble fireplace. Those villagers who lived close enough to come on foot were just beginning to arrive. The American peered up into the recesses and shadows. 'Must have been some place to live.'

'Got very dusty,' said Mrs Wilks. Her husband added: 'Four 'undred years the family been 'ere.'

'By the end of next year maybe they'll be able to come back,' said Miller.

Wilks was tight in his best pre-war suit. 'Never come back now, sir,' he said. 'Sir George died in Plymouth in the raids. Bomb dropped while they were at their tea, and he choked on a sausage. They got 'im to 'ospital but there was a lot of casualties from the bombing and by the time they could deal with him he was a goner. All bread these wartime sausages.'

'And 'im a peer of the realm,' said Mrs Wilks sadly.

'His family can come back here, can't they?' said Miller. 'The place will be put right.'

'Flats,' sniffed Wilks. 'Turned into flats this will be. You just see.' He looked a touch discomfited. 'Well, you won't see, will you, sir, because you'll be back 'ome in your own country. But that's what will 'appen. Flats. The eldest boy Rupert, he died in France, beginning of 'ostilities, and there's a girl, Rosemary, I 'member her when she went to school. I used to pick 'er up from the station when she came back for 'olidays. She's far away, safe in New Zealand, nice and quiet. Whether she'll ever come back, I doubt. This country won't be the same again. Never.'

The walls of the hallway were stark; the paintings had been

removed, the big chandelier was gone. The Americans had lit a Christmas tree with a few lights in a corner. Three young soldiers began to assemble a drum-kit. From outside came the sound of heavy wheels on gravel.

'The trucks,' said Miller, making to go out. He shook hands with Wilks and his wife. 'Thanks for the history.'

'We've got plenty of that,' said the taxi-driver. ''Istory.' He frowned at the bare walls. 'But we may 'ave come to the end of it.'

Four US Army trucks were on the weedy gravel of the drive. Some pre-war peacocks in the park still remained, and they began wailing.

Martin helped his mother from the steps set against the tailboard of the lorry. His father descended and stood on the grave, trying to survey the front of the house. There were splits and slits in the blackout blinds. 'Jerry would see this easy from twenty thousand feet,' said fat Bertie Cook.

'You tell 'em, Bert,' said Mrs Cook. 'You're an air-raid warden.'

'Rescue Section,' he said, as if she did not know. 'The Yanks don't know about war, nothing, not yet.'

'If they don't know, 'ow do they reckon to win it?'

'Cos there's more of 'em,' he said.

The villagers, in their ancient coats and heavy hats, entered the Grange with anticipation. After Dunkirk, when the Germans were expected to land next morning, it had been a hurried assembly base for the shreds of the British Army escaped from France. Their tents had filled the grounds that summer. It had been hot and the Germans never came. As the weeks went on towards a bronze autumn, the sunburnt soldiers helped with the harvest, played football and cricket, and swam in the river like scouts or schoolboys in camp. Later, part of a fresh division, new from Canada and eager to fight, had been quartered there; they had played baseball and had filled the Red Rover pub and the church. Many had left their bodies on the French shore after the blundering amphibious raid on Dieppe in 1942. The Crockbourne people never knew who had died or who had lived but they remembered them.

People were crowding the cavernous hall now, admiring the soaring wood fire. The three young soldiers who made up the band began to play, not very well, on drums, maracas and saxophone. A boy who looked too frail to be a soldier, shook the maracas, and began to sing mournfully about buying a paper doll instead of having a real girl.

Some avid young girls gathered around the dais and swayed to the lament, their eyes on the scanty singer as he swirled the maracas. The other players, a plump pink youth, pinker as he blew into the saxophone, and the drummer, eyes ringed with melancholy, cast glances at the girls.

'They forgot to invite the village lads,' pointed out Dr Macaulay.

'Busy tonight, doctor, I 'spect. Telling their jokes down the pub,' said Bert Cook.

The doctor smoothed his sporran and took in the youths on the platform, wondering how they could be expected to fight real German soldiers. Geoffrey Paget caught his gaze and muttered: 'Don't look very threatening, do they, doctor?'

Margaret came through the door, escorted by a fleshy American sergeant who had contrived a special journey in his jeep to pick her up. He entered behind her with proprietorial pride. Four soldiers, two of them black, all wearing white jackets, took trays of drinks around the village people, chanting: 'Chow coming up.' Trays of food appeared, American food.

'They does theirselves well, these Yanks,' said Mrs Cook, biting swiftly around a doughnut.

Margaret led her fussy escort to the group where Martin and his parents were standing with Miller and the doctor. 'Sergeant . . .' She paused, then remembered in time. '. . . Smith kindly offered to bring me. Dad's not well. He's got flu. I had to get my children to bed.'

Martin noted the cloud briefly crossing Sergeant Smith's face. The American said: 'Kids come first.'

Lieutenant Miller asked: 'How long has this house been occup — used by the military? We found some traces, things written on walls.'

'In the latrines,' put in Sergeant Smith.

'In Polish,' said Miller. There was an equality between the American officer and the sergeant. Geoffrey Paget noted it, so did the doctor.

'We have some guys who come from Polish families but nobody has translated it for me,' said the lieutenant. 'Maybe they don't think I'll understand.'

'The Poles were billeted here about two years ago,' said Dr Macaulay. 'It was rumoured that they wore hairnets in bed.' He pursed his lips professionally. 'Although who made that discovery I don't know.'

'They certainly *did* wear hairnets,' put in Emma Paget. 'Their commanding officer told me. Colonel Walinski, an impressive chap.' She turned to Miller. 'They were a choir, you see, lieutenant. A Polish Army choir. Wonderful singers. We went to one of their concerts in Bridgwater.'

'Not that you needed to go to a concert because you could hear them marching about the grounds here, singing,' said Geoffrey. 'In the middle of the night sometimes.'

'"Loch Lomond",' said Emma.

'Fine song,' said the Scots doctor. 'Even for Poles.'

'They were very . . . aristocratic . . . if that's the word,' remembered Emma. 'Rather . . . well . . . haughty. And so smart. Their buttons so bright.'

'*And* they wore hairnets in bed,' reiterated Geoffrey carefully, looking into his glass.

'They hated only one race more than the Germans,' observed the doctor. 'And that was the Russians.'

One of the polite, white-coated black waiters offered the doctor another drink, handing the glass to him with a shy smile before moving away. A tray appeared with thick chocolate biscuits. Macaulay took one. 'Just like India,' he mused. 'Pre-war.'

The musicians had struggled and eventually stopped. 'We guys just don't know each other,' the plump saxophonist shrugged at the clustered village girls. 'It's only a scratch band.' The maracas player was fumbling with some sheet music but it slid to the floor. The girls giggled and gathered it, handing it back with blushes. The drummer said: 'We gotta find some songs we *all* know.'

As though they had been lurking outside, a double line of twenty young soldiers appeared abruptly, marched into the room, and in a moment had formed a cordon around the girls. Sergeant Smith said: 'Okay, you guys. Spread out. Talk to some of these other nice people.'

The girls simpered at them. 'Go talk,' the sergeant ordered sternly and the soldiers reluctantly broke the circle, some shifting to other parts of the room but others lingering. 'And no drinking, men. Coffee and lemonade only. Or there's sarsaparilla.'

'We'll need more than sarsaparilla when we go into battle with those Nazis,' said one young man, tall and olive-skinned, directly to a village girl. 'Maybe to die.' He thrust out his hand determinedly. 'Benedict J. Soroyan,' he said.

No boy had ever introduced himself like that to her. She bit her lip, almost made to curtsy, and said: 'Kate Scratchpole.'

'I'd be honoured if you called me Ben,' he said.

The band had found some music they could play and Benedict held both hands out, bowed in a courtly way and invited her to dance. 'I'm not very good at the quickstep,' she hesitated.

'This,' said the GI dramatically, 'is called a jitterbug.'

'But . . . I can't . . . I've never . . .'

'Let's try,' said Ben. He took her hands from her sides, his eyes widened and his feet flew sideways, his knees buckled and his hips swivelled.

'I can't,' repeated Kate faintly. She backed away.

A thin girl in a lace blouse, who had experience of Americans in Bristol, held out her hands. Soroyan took her, whirled her and hoisted her in the air. The others formed a circle and clapped and shouted. Kate Scratchpole thought she was going to cry.

The villagers watched with amazement. As the youth flung the girl over his shoulder her dress flew up to her suspenders. 'Okay, okay, big star,' bellowed the sergeant. 'That's plenty. Quit.'

The GI slowly let the girl to the floor and looked away from the glowering sergeant. The girl staggered, stood, and straightened her hair moodily.

Margaret approached Martin and asked quietly: 'Would you like to walk in the cold?'

Chapter Four

Thick in their coats they went from the main door. In the stony outer hall as they left, the GI Ben Soroyan was sitting shyly with Kate Scratchpole on an oak coffer. The door rasped rudely in the cold as it opened and the village girl giggled and said: 'Got rheumatics.'

Martin and Margaret half turned and smiled at the sitting pair, young and awkward. The white wintry moon was framed by the doorway. Martin closed the door behind them and they crunched along the stiff gravel at the front of the house. Only a triangle of Margaret's face was visible between her collar and her warm hat. She took his coated arm.

They idled through the eerie moonbeams caught among a framework of branches over the worn road that led from the house. Encumbered as they were in their coats, Margaret half encircled his waist and he put his arm about her. 'You're like a polar bear,' she laughed. 'How do they expect anybody to fight a war in those coats?'

'Plod,' he said. 'That's what they have to do in Russia. Fighting in slow motion.'

'I bet you do something really dangerous, dramatic,' she said, eyeing him sideways. The path there was so layered with weeds that their footsteps scarcely sounded on the gravel.

Martin shook his head. 'I almost fell off my chair at the Air Ministry once. Oh . . . and one day I spilled my afternoon tea.'

She said: 'You're lying. Am I asking top-secret information?'

'I don't think the enemy would be helped by knowing what I

do. I'm at the ministry most of the time. I sit at my desk and admire the changing seasons out of the window. In my lunch-hour I walk in St James's Park, what's not occupied by Nissen huts and tanks and suchlike.'

'They drained the lake,' she said. 'I wonder what happened to the pelicans?'

'Eaten, probably.'

'Stop it, Martin. Do you remember where this path goes?'

'Down to the stables,' he said.

'We used to creep down there, didn't we, after school. Remember?'

'Among the horses.'

'And their droppings. My mother always knew where I'd been.'

For a moment it was as though there had been no years in between. She put her head against his shoulder and said: 'Just think what might have happened.'

They stopped on the path, turned to each other and kissed. She undid the buttons on the front of her coat and then undid his. Again they kissed and this time held each other close. 'You were there inside that coat all the time,' she said.

She pulled away suddenly. 'But it's a bit hopeless, all this, isn't it, Martin? Trying to recapture the past times.'

He concluded the thought for her. 'And knowing they'll never come back? That it's all gone?' He looked at her kindly.

They walked on in silence until she said: 'It doesn't have to be the same.' There was a note of desperation underneath the sadness. 'I've missed you, Martin. We could still meet, couldn't we, maybe if you're ever in London? I could easily make some excuse.' She looked down and sighed heavily. 'Not that Clifford would mind, anyway,' she said. 'He really doesn't care. And I have someone who could look after the boys.'

'You really want to?'

'I'm sure. I don't know how I got into this bloody mess. I can't even blame the war, like everyone does. I just blundered into it. So did he.'

They had reached the stables, where there was a farm gate across the path. 'We used to jump over this,' he said.

'In shorts.'

There was a rusted chain on the gate and an immovable padlock. 'They've locked up our memories,' she said.

He said: 'Shall we give it a go?'

She unbuttoned his coat again and said: 'You go first.' He took the coat off and climbed the gate, holding up his hands to her from the other side. She opened her buttons before clambering over and dropped softly against him. He could feel her breasts and he kissed her face. 'Let's take a peep inside,' she said. Their eyes held for a moment. He pulled the bolt.

It was smelly and dim and warm. Something was stirring. 'There are still horses here,' she said. 'Two.'

She turned and put her flushed face against his. 'They won't mind,' she said. Both horses fidgeted and snorted quietly. They were in stalls next to each other. She patted their rumps. One of them let off a puff of wind and she said: 'Thank you.'

'They were always doing that, making us laugh, remember?' said Martin.

'Perhaps they recognise us,' she said.

Almost politely she pushed him against the wooden side of a vacant stall, the deep, warm, rotten, animal smell all around. She opened her coat and pressed her breasts against him. 'I need some comfort,' she said quietly. 'I want to forget everything, wipe it out.'

'We're here together,' he said. 'Like we were once before.'

He felt her giggle. 'In that corner on the straw,' she said. 'But we never did anything, did we? Not properly.'

'We weren't sure how.'

He began kissing her deeply, his hands stroking her face, her neck and her covered breasts, the odour of the stable close around them. One of the horses whinnied. 'This time,' Martin said. 'We can make up for the time that's gone missing.'

*

In the hall the youthful GI and the village girl both glanced back into the main room, then at each other, before he lifted the great iron latch and opened the door like a hint. Kate gave a short smile and nodded. 'I'll get my fur.'

He waited until she reappeared from the cloakroom overwhelmed by a scraggy fur coat, her hands lost up its sleeves, her round and tentative face peering over it. 'You look a million dollars, Kate Scratchpole,' he said.

She was pleased. 'What about you?' she said. 'Don't they give you a coat?'

'I'll get one.' He came back with an outsized US Army padded jacket. She saw on the sleeve a coloured shield and the words: 'Hell on Wheels'.

'This is okay,' he said. 'It's not mine.'

'It looks lovely and warm.' They walked into the moonlight, tiptoeing through the crackling gravel. 'What's "Hell on Wheels" mean?' she asked.

'Tank man,' he told her. 'It's just a spare coat.'

'Where are we going?'

'Let's take a ride,' he said with a swagger, placing a protective hand about her furry waist while straightening his cap with the other.

'What on?' she asked nervously. 'A bike?'

'My jeep,' he shrugged. 'Okay, Uncle Sam's jeep.'

'You can *drive*?' She turned to him in genuine astonishment.

'That's what I do. I drive the jeep.'

Kate was deeply impressed. 'I don't know any boys who can drive,' she said in a low voice. 'Not one. Dopey Daniel has a funny cart for grocery deliveries but it's not like a proper car.' She gave him an anxious glance. 'You won't get into trouble, will you?'

'Not a chance. I drive it all the time. All we need to do is to get by the guy at the gate. Keep your head down low.'

'Oh, I will.' She began enjoying the excitement. She squeezed his arm.

'It's just over in the vehicle park,' he said.

With no hesitation now she slid her arm about his uniformed waist. The padding of the thick, silky jacket felt luxurious. Her eyes were becoming accustomed to the night and the moon. 'What are those?' she said, pointing. The ground that fell away was lined with low buildings.

'Quonset huts,' he said. 'Quarters. There's going to be two thousand GIs here soon. Remember – I saw you first.'

'I will,' she promised. 'I really will, Ben.'

'This fur feels good,' he said, rubbing her ribs. 'Is it bear?'

'Bear!' she laughed. 'It's fox. Imitation, not even a real fox. It was my gran's. She was bigger than me but she's shrunk now. She bought it years ago, with some insurance money after my first granddad got killed in the war. She said it always reminded her of him, mouldy though it is. She's still got the receipt.'

'Your grandfather was killed in the . . .'

'The first one, nineteen whatever to nineteen whatever it was. What they always call the Great War, I don't know why.'

'There's nothing great about war,' he said sombrely, hugging her waist.

'Careful,' she giggled. 'You're squashing granddad.'

They reached an open area where outlined vehicles were parked, jeeps, trucks and the single shape of a Sherman tank. Kate stared at it. 'You don't have to drive that, do you?'

'Not yet, but you never know in this man's army.' He led her to a jeep and opened the door for her. 'This thing ain't cosy,' he said.

When she was in the metal seat he climbed in beside her. She still felt unsure. 'We've got our love to keep us warm,' she said throatily, adapting the words of a song.

She surveyed him from inside her collar and tapped his glowing nose. Awkwardly they kissed.

'Are you frightened, Ben?' she asked in a whisper. 'Scared?'

In the dark he nodded. 'Scared? Hell, *am* I scared? Excuse my language . . . but I'm *scared*, Kate. I'm only twenty and I have to go and fight those Nazis, invade France, and I don't even know where France is, and be gunned down and maybe get . . .'

'No, I didn't mean that, Ben. Really I meant, like, *nervous*. Being in this jeep with me. I am – scared, nervous, Ben, I really am.'

He kissed her reassuringly. They had difficulty in embracing because of their volume of clothing and the shortness of her arms. He disengaged himself and started the jeep's engine. 'Are you sure you can just drive it away like that?' she said. 'Won't they notice? What about the petrol?'

Ben's laugh emerged as a nervy gurgle. He had never driven the jeep on the open road; he had only been in the country four days. 'I'll get it back in one piece,' he said. 'We'll require it for the invasion.'

'Oh, Ben.' She put her furry arm around the back of his neck. It gave him confidence and he drove the vehicle with its hooded lights out of the parking area and down the path to the main gate.

'It's this dim-out, blackout, you call it,' he said. 'How does anybody see where they are, where they're going?'

'You get used to it. But we'd better not go far.'

Nearing the gate he said: 'Now's the time to lie low.' She shrank down in the seat but there was no need. The sentry was in his box, only the red tip of his cigarette showing in the dark. They drove past. The red dot waved.

Kate uncurled and pushed herself close to the young soldier, enjoying the feel of him. 'You're on the wrong side of the road,' she pointed out.

They had driven only for a few minutes, in a circle around the village when he pulled the jeep in to the side of the road and they sat, side by side, awkwardly in the dark.

Eventually Kate said thoughtfully: 'You know, here we are, in a US Army jeep, and we don't know anything about each other really.'

'We don't,' agreed Ben. 'Just fate brought us together, Kate Scratchpole.'

'How did you get over here?' she asked. 'To England?'

'On a ship,' he said. 'The *Queen Mary*.'

She was astonished. 'The *Queen* . . . oh, now you're telling me fibs.'

'It's true,' he said. He began to fumble with the ancient buttons of the fur coat. 'The ocean liner.'

'The *Queen Mary* is very posh for just soldiers.'

He took no offence. 'Sixteen to a cabin,' he said. 'Doubling up. One squad slept at night and one squad stayed on the deck, then switched. And when you were on deck all you did was watch out for Nazi submarines. I was scared. I didn't like the look of that ocean, no, sir.'

'Oh, you poor love.'

'Is there anywhere . . . anywhere we can go around here? It's kinda tight in this jeep.'

'You have to sit side by side,' agreed Kate. 'Nowhere to stretch out.' She thought, then smiled in the dark. 'I know somewhere, Ben.'

'Show me,' he said, kissing her and starting the jeep in one movement.

In the dark and aromatic stable Margaret leaned close to Martin as he stood against the partition of the horse stall. They were warm in their opened coats and their embrace. He could feel her breasts harden.

'I'm wearing my winter woollies, I'm afraid,' she confided. 'My mother still makes me.'

'You must keep warm,' he said.

'She used to make me wear a wool liberty bodice to school. *And* a vest.'

They kissed deeply. 'You were beautiful,' he said. 'Just as you are now.'

'I used to get the tingles about you. But all you were really interested in was cricket and rugby.'

Martin whispered: 'That's what you call a wasted youth.'

Her hand went to his groin and she began to stroke him.

Then the door opened and the moon beamed in. 'Fuck it,' muttered Margaret.

Martin held her against him, her hand caressing him a little. Two young voices sounded at the door, one American, one Somerset. 'Here 'tis,' said the girl. 'Bit niffy.'

'Horses,' said the American soldier. 'In the States we have hundreds of horses.'

'There are 'undreds in England, too,' she argued. 'These are only two of the horses we got in England.'

'I mean on *our* ranch. My dad has a ranch.'

'There's some cows in the field at the back of our house,' said Kate defensively. There was a soft impact as he eased her against the wooden stall at the side of the two horses. Martin and Margaret remained close together at the other side. She began laughing silently against his chest.

'Now, Ben,' warned the girl after a silence. 'Not like that. It's dark in here.'

'But baby, I want to hold you. I've *got* to. I'm not getting fresh. I . . . I could be leaving this earth next week.'

'Where are you goin'?'

'I could die. Invading that France place with those damned Nazi machine-guns shooting at me. Tonight could be my goodbye to life.'

'Oh, it won't be so bad as that,' Kate responded confidently. 'My dad works in the Food Office in Taunton, one of the 'eads, so 'e knows a thing or two. He reckons all this invasion talk is mazed. It won't be for a year, if ever.'

'He says that?'

''E *knows* it, Ben. Secrets. And 'e reckons that they'll just keep on bombing the Jerries, bombing them and bombing them until they pack it in, give up. Then you won't have to go and do the invasion at all.'

Benedict breathed deeply. Martin was holding Margaret's mouth against his chest. Her body was gently trembling.

'You mean that?' breathed Ben. 'So we could be together, Kate. Get married and . . .'

'Married, Ben? But I only just met you.'

She became silent. Ben began to caress her. 'You've got such a beautiful body,' he breathed. 'And see what I have . . .'

There was a short gasp from the girl. 'Ben! . . . You put that gurt thing away this minute.'

'But baby, hold it for a while . . . Just touch it . . .'

Martin and Margaret eased away from each other. Her finger went to her lips.

The horses shifted restlessly. Then came Kate's voice. 'All right, just once I'll touch it. Just one tap. Only one. I be a Sunday school teacher.'

The young soldier began to groan. Kate's voice became softer. 'There, there,' she comforted. 'You're a poor boy.' The two older people, fifteen feet away, stood transfixed.

'That's it,' said Kate decidedly, her voice firm. 'There's no further I be goin'. I bet you got a girl in America.'

'Kate Scratchpole, I'll never be able to love anybody but you.'

She was impressed. 'Nobody's *ever* told me they loved me before. No boys, 'specially. Not around this hole of a place. Somerset boys don't talk like that.'

She made up her mind. 'All right. Let's go to the pictures in Bridgwater where I works, next week. What about Wednesday? I could meet you off the six o'clock bus from the village.'

One of the horses began to urinate, followed by the other.

'Poor fellow,' said Margaret as they walked back towards the big, darkened house. The music was still drifting from it but one of the trucks had its engine running and they could see figures climbing into the back. 'He really expected she would do it, just like that, first time.'

'Who knows what he was told,' said Martin. ' "The natives are willing and you are a hero." Some of these boys had no idea where this country even *was* before they were sent over. They'd never moved outside their own state, hardly outside their own town, and they thought England was full of beautiful and willing girls.'

'And the girls think the GIs all live on ranches or in skyscrapers,' she said. 'Just like in the films.'

They were walking a little apart but now she slid her arm around him and he enclosed her waist. He said, 'It was just the same with our farm boys who rushed to join up in the 1914 war. Suddenly they were going to France and Mademoiselle from Armentières, *ooh, la, la*. Then they were slaughtered wholesale.'

'You think about things rather deeply, don't you, Martin,' she said. 'Even when we were at school you were a bit like that.'

'I must have been dull,' he said. 'Perhaps I still am.'

They stopped and kissed again. She said: 'You really *will* meet me in London, won't you?' He said he would. She paused and he saw her smile in the moonlight. 'That girl's father in the Food Office in Taunton – "one of the 'eads" – seems pretty well informed. No need for an invasion.'

'There are people at the top who think that. They believe our bombers could make Germany surrender just by dropping more and more high explosives.'

'And no invasion?'

'Absolutely so,' he said. 'But they forget the Russians coming from the east. We don't want them across the Channel instead of the Germans.'

'It seems never-ending,' she sighed. 'What would I give to be back in the old days.'

'You might find they weren't there,' he said. 'Perhaps they never were.'

They had almost reached the house.

Paget said: 'You're not going back just yet, are you? How about coming for a run in my car tomorrow? I want to go and see the sea. If that's still there.'

Chapter Five

Paget walked along the village street, so empty and hushed that mid-morning that he could hear his own footsteps echoing sharply against the walls of the cottages. Then there came the distant sound of a vehicle and a US Army jeep, followed by a bouncing dispatch-rider motorcyclist, came rushing along the confined road. They were racing as they entered the village and the motor-cycle rider overtook the jeep on the blind corner by the church, waving a taunt as he passed. Then they were gone and the scene again fell into silence.

Hannaford's Garage was between Hemmings, the butcher's, and the vicarage, set back from the road up an overgrown path that led to its open double doors, sagging on their hinges. There was a dingy light showing from inside. 'No regulations to stop you having a bulb on in the day,' said Bert Hannaford. 'And letting it shine out into the world. And, my goodness, this world needs a bit of commonplace light, sir.'

He wore a brown overall, like a grocer's but grubbier. He would have retired two years before but both his sons had been called into the services and somebody had to look after the business, such as it was. The single petrol pump went unused now. It stood rustily where the path met the street, its pumping handle hanging limply.

'I been lookin' after your pretty little car,' Hannaford said to Paget. 'And I've enjoyed it. In a way it's kept me going, doing the bits and pieces, trying all over the place to get the parts. Gave me something to do, something to get me out of bed in the morning. There's not a lot else going on.'

He was small and bald and bent as a clerk. 'The military won't bring their tanks in 'ere,' he joked. 'Everybody's so busy with this invasion business 'cept for me.' His eyes were deeply incised; it was as if years of oil had got into his crevices. 'I expect that's keeping you occupied, Mr Paget.' He put a grimy finger to his lips. 'But then I shouldn't be asking you that. Come and look at your car.'

He led the way, shuffling towards the inner workshop, past dusty benches and oily parts. There was a wooden wireless set, big as an orange box, on the bench. The signature tune for 'Music While You Work', broadcast to factories, was playing. Hannaford turned it off.

'Powerful set this. It's got "Melbourne" on the dial,' he said, pointing proudly. 'Be able to hear the cricket after the war. Don Bradman.' On the walls old tyres hung like pictures in a gallery. 'I never did work on a motor like yours,' said Hannaford. 'Never 'ad the chance. But I've 'ad all this time and, like I say, it's kept me going through hostilities.'

He rattled open a sliding inner door and turned on a fly-encrusted light bulb. Below it the car stood, jauntily red-bonneted, her metalwork gleaming softly. 'She looks terrific, Bert,' breathed Paget. 'Terrific.'

'And what's more she *goes* now, she *works*.' A small frown appeared on the garage man's face. 'Well, she ought to. I haven't taken 'er out, of course, although my boys both wanted to when they came on leave, but I wouldn't 'ear of it. One drives a ten tonner.'

'I'm going to drive her,' said Paget. 'Today.'

'You can, sir. I hope. The tank's still full, fifteen gallons, except for the sparse drop when I've been turning the engine over, once I'd got all the parts. I think she ought to drive fine. You want to take her now then?'

'Yes, I certainly do.'

'Drive her up the street and back?'

'No,' said Martin. 'I'm going to drive her to the sea.'

It was a 1937 MG TA Midget, a beautiful, low car with swept-back mudguards and running-board, and a drop-head top, capable of speeds up to seventy-six miles an hour.

'They didn't build many,' the man who had sold it to him had told him three years before. 'I'm selling it reasonably because there's a few things wrong with it. It was my son's. He died in France – pneumonia. He'd only been out there three weeks. I'll take one hundred and seventy-five pounds.'

Paget had not hesitated. He would have to borrow some of the money from his father.

'You'll have to get it taken,' the man had said. 'It won't move like it is. The parts might be hard to come by but somebody, somewhere's got them.'

'I'll have it,' Paget had repeated touching the paintwork.

'Anything else you want?' the man had asked, half seriously. 'I'm getting rid of everything. House, beds, lawnmower, everything. There's not a lot of future in England. This country's finished.'

Paget wondered what had happened to him.

Hannaford now opened the low door of the car. It swung easily, silently. 'I thought I'd drive her over the Quantock to Watchet and get a sniff of the Bristol Channel,' said Paget.

'Good idea. That ought to be far enough. You can't get on the beaches because they're still mined. We used to go to Watchet and Ilfracombe a lot before the outbreak. Every summer. I'd like to go again sometime.'

Paget said: 'You had better give me a bill.'

Hannaford croaked a short laugh. 'It won't cost you the earth, sir. She's been good company. The spares and the work on the engine will be a bit. I'll write it all down and pass it to your mother when I see her going to the butcher's.'

Paget closed the car door and opened it again with one silent twist of the shining handle. Hannaford nodded in a pleased way. 'It's cold but the roads are dry,' he said. 'Who knows what it'll be like this afternoon. We have to do our own weather forecasts these days, don't we.'

A little embarrassed, Paget dropped two leather flying helmets in the passenger seat.

'Ah,' said Hannaford. 'There's more uses for they than bein' a pilot in a Spitfire.'

Paget grinned and climbed into the confined space. His eyes were close to the windscreen and his chest almost on the steering-wheel.

He found the adjusting ratchet and moved the seat back. Each time he had been home on leave he had gone to the garage just to sit in the car, feeling it around him, touching his head on the canvas roof. 'Now,' he said quietly. 'This is the real thing.'

He eased out the choke. The key was in the dashboard. He ensured the gear lever was in neutral and turned the key, touching the accelerator at the same time. The roar filled the garage, rattling the corrugated-iron walls, making even Hannaford step back. One of the old tyres fell from its hook and bounced until the old man stopped it with his boot. Paget lightly pressed the accelerator again and the exhaust smoke shot from the back. 'What I call a healthy row!' shouted Hannaford amid the fumes. 'Take it steady as you drive out, sir. One of those Yankees might be coming along the street.'

Paget released the handbrake, put the car into first gear and moved forward cautiously from the garage. Hannaford saw him out into the close lane and followed him through the wafts of yellow smoke. 'Hold her there, sir.'

Paget braked and the old man ambled ahead down the short path to the village street. He waved both arms like a windmill, calling the car on, and in a moment, with a half-turn of the wheel and a brief salute to Hannaford, Paget was in the main street, in second gear and then into third. He called out with the excitement of a boy as the low red car moved forward. Gently he pushed in the choke. Outside his parents' house he sounded the horn and they both came to the door. 'She goes!' he shouted. 'Started first time!'

The street remained empty, the wintry sun streaking it. Cottage curtains moved as he drove. Margaret was waiting by the church. 'Oh, my God,' she said, putting her hands to her face. 'It's so gay . . . And red . . . It's just lovely. How my boys would love it. They've never even been in a car.'

Paget climbed out and opened the door for her. 'This is for you,' he said once they were in the car. He handed her one of the flying helmets and put the other on himself. 'Bags being Biggles,' he said.

'Who can I be?' She was trying to look in the mirror to see her face enclosed by the flying helmet. 'I'll be Amy Johnson that was. Except I won't crash. I've brought a Thermos and some sandwiches. Where are we going?'

'Watchet. Over the hills to the sea.'

She lowered herself in the seat and nestled against him. 'I bet this can do a speed,' she said.

'In excess of seventy. This is the first time I've driven it. It's been in Hannaford's garage. I bought it one day and I went into the Air Force the next.'

Leaving the village they moved across Somerset, low, long hills rising before them. They passed a line of parked American trucks, one after the other for half a mile. The soldiers stared and half waved as they drove by. 'Hi, where you goin'?' 'Where d'you get that auto?' 'Baby, come and drive with me!'

'Shall we put the hood down?' said Margaret.

He pulled the car into the farm gateway. 'It's cold,' he said.

'We've got our helmets.'

With difficulty he eased back the creaking roof. Some dust fell. A farm labourer with two dogs observed them from the gate, the dogs with their heads between the bars. 'Joyriders,' said the man, shaking his head and talking to himself. 'War must be over. And no bugger told oi.'

Paget was back in the car by then. He drove easily in the sharp air, the engine splitting the silence. They went into the modest hills, down into the still green coombs and villages locked into the landscape. There was no wind and the cold air only brushed their faces as they crouched behind the windscreen, encased in the leather flying helmets. The car had no heater.

They did not speak nor even try to shout. But as they increased speed and dipped into a valley where there were a few cottages and a grey church, and up again on the rise the other side, Margaret called out like a girl.

They rounded a bend and were confronted by a camouflaged truck lying half sideways in a ditch, surrounded by shapeless British soldiers standing with their hands in their pockets. A red-capped military policeman bounded into the road and waved a white glove towards Paget.

'Daft sod couldn't take the bend,' he announced. He abruptly realised that one of the car's passengers, under the helmet, was a woman. 'Silly billy,' he said.

He was joined by a military police sergeant who scowled. 'Where are you going in this?'

'We're heading for the Bristol Channel,' said Paget.

'Why's that?'

'To make sure it's still there.'

The hard face below the red cap became a touch pink. 'There's a war on,' he sniffed as if they might not know. 'I'd like to see your papers. Identity card, please, miss.'

'I haven't got it,' said Margaret flatly. 'I do have my ration book.' She handed it over.

'Mrs Margaret Hallstead,' the sergeant recited slowly. 'From London.' He glanced at Paget. 'And you, sir?' He handed the ration book back. Paget produced his RAF identity papers and the man perused them even more pedantically. 'Right, sir,' he said. 'Didn't realise, you being in civvies and in a car like this.' He decided to become helpful. 'If you go back half a mile there's a road to the left. This mess won't be cleared up for hours.'

He threw up a stiff salute and Paget thanked him for his help. The man guided his reversing of the car. 'Nice motor this, sir,' he commented. 'Take much petrol?'

'She's had a full tank since the beginning of the war,' said Paget. 'It's the first time I've taken her out.'

Paget revved the engine and the sergeant, with a sharp drill movement, took his toes away. The soldiers were smirking. 'Bloody snobs,' muttered the sergeant when the car had gone. 'Them and their posh voices. This war makes no difference to some.'

Half a mile back Paget took the side turning and drove through the tight lanes until he was able to join the climbing road again. Briefly the sun came out and touched the washed-out fields. The tops of the Quantock Hills were dabbed with white. They skirted a village pond with hunched ducks on the ice. Eventually they surmounted a hill, stopped the car, got out, and looked across the Bristol Channel. The enclosed harbour of Watchet lay beneath them. There were landing barges outlined against its walls and on the end of the jetty was a Bofors anti-aircraft gun. Out in the flat sea were two fishing boats. They could just see a shadow that was the coast of Wales.

'Shall we eat the sandwiches?' she said. 'Leftover chicken. And there's coffee in the Thermos.' They leaned against the low, gleaming car and ate and drank, watching the dull, scarcely moving sea.

Up there, by themselves, they each stretched an arm around the other's waist. Still looking out to the Bristol Channel Margaret said: 'Martin, after the war is over I think we ought to marry each other.'

Paget said: 'We could give it a try.'

Chapter Six

By that winter of 1943 it had already been a long and comfortless war for Cook Sergeant Frederick Weber of the German Army. He was grateful for the respite he was enjoying in the occupied English Channel Islands, although he could not help but wonder how long it would last.

That January day he had been fishing; it had been a fine winter's morning with the sun hazy and the water like paper. With him in the small boat was Gino, the Italian chief steward of the German officers' mess in Jersey, who before he came to the island had been a waiter in the Hotel Bristol, Berlin, and then at the Savoy, London.

They often fished together, the squat German and the elongated Italian, saying little out among the eddies, but enjoying the peace of the water and the weather. The catch would appear on the German *Kommandant*'s table that night, prepared as only Cook Sergeant Weber knew how, as his superior often boasted. It would be sole and bacon, *Sohle und Speck*. One good fish was kept privately aside for Fred and Gino to eat in the kitchen, after everyone had gone except the local Jersey women who did the washing-up.

About them, as they pottered that day, the islands lay languidly, as though without a care in the world at war. They could see calm beaches and tall cliffs and the placid roofs of houses, but they were aware that they were floating between two armies: north and west of the German defences on the French coast and south of the Allied troops massing to cross the Channel from England. But that morning nowhere seemed further from the front line. The islands had been abandoned, written off, by the British after their evacuation from Dunkirk in the summer of 1940, and claimed by a solitary *Luftwaffe* officer who landed unopposed and telephoned the governor to obtain the surrender. It was legend that the pilot had borrowed two pennies from a local man and made the call from a telephone box.

There was no resistance. An attempt to cut telephone wires inconvenienced only the island tradesmen. The people had no choice but to settle down alongside their occupiers. There grew friendships and liaisons. Children were born. As the years of war drifted on, it began to dawn on the inhabitants and their conquerors that they had been overlooked. The war had bypassed them. 'Let them starve,' Churchill had said, referring, as he later made clear, to the Germans. It was not until the final day, 5 May 1945, that they were liberated by which time civilians and German soldiers had become a community, united in starvation.

'I don't know what Hitler thinks he is doing,' said Cook Sergeant Weber that fine January morning. Out there with the gulls and seals, they could talk. He surveyed the catch.

'Not bad,' said Gino. 'Which one will we keep for us, Fred?'

'Him,' said the cook, pointing. 'He has a smile on his face. Who is this big shot coming for dinner anyway? Only *Luftwaffe*, isn't he? First sign of the *Luftwaffe* we've seen around here for a long time.'

As though someone might have heard him there came the lofty sound of an aeroplane. Weber stared guiltily. 'The enemy, I expect,' said Gino, trying to spot it in the pale blue sky.

'Better get the flag out,' said Weber.

Gino fumbled in the locker and emerged with a flag, a red cross. Between them they draped it flat across the front of the boat. The whine of the plane faded.

Gino continued: 'He's famous, this *Luftwaffe* officer, Fred. He was the one who occupied this place single-handed in 1940.'

'So?' shrugged Weber. 'Nobody stopped him. Nobody shot at him. What sort of hero is that?'

Gino began to row for the harbour of St Aubin. 'I don't know what Hitler thinks he is doing,' repeated Weber. 'He has no military mind.'

'Once a corporal always a corporal,' said Gino.

Out of habit Weber glanced about him, but there were only three seals, their inquisitive heads poking from the water. 'I was a corporal when I was in Russia,' he said. 'God, that's a cold place, Russia.'

'You've mentioned it,' said Gino. 'A lot. Good job your boss had to be transferred here. I see he is still limping.'

'He's very brave for a general,' said Weber who had also suffered frostbite and had only the middle finger on his right hand. Sometimes he used it to dip into a sauce for testing purposes. Now he raised his arm and with the solitary digit gave the Nazi salute: '*Heil Hitler*,' he said.

The Cherbourg peninsula lay shadowed on the eastern horizon. Weber turned towards England. 'Over there,' he said, 'all their ships are waiting.' He grimaced towards his companion. 'It's fine for you,' he said. 'You are from Italy, from Germany, *and* from England. All three. Who knows where. You only have to make sure you are on the right side on the last day.'

'You're a wise man Fred. I cannot believe that you're only a cook.'

Weber tapped his ample nose and said: 'Cooks die last.'

They eased the boat into St Aubin's harbour entrance. The plop of the oars resounded in the grey stillness, gulls set up a frayed chorus. Weber threw a handful of fish pieces into the water.

'Everybody is hungry,' said Gino as the birds dived and screamed.

His friend surveyed the stone town. 'When this war is finished,' he said, 'if we're still alive, I think we ought to come here and open a restaurant.'

'A good one,' nodded the Italian. The boat bumped against the quay. Half a dozen women wrapped in hapless coats, their heads buried in scarves, two with pallid children crying against their skirts, waited with cooking pots. Weber put in a few fish. 'Frederick the cook and Gino the head waiter, Fred and Gino's Restaurant,' went on Gino. 'It is something to look forward to.'

A bottle of schnapps between them, they sat by the scrubbed wooden table in the kitchen after the German officers had gone from their mess at the Royal Hotel that night. Immediately before the war Gino had been the head waiter there and it was he who knew of the little alcove where they kept the schnapps and anything else that they considered private, perhaps a spare cheese.

'The *Luftwaffe* hero had some bad news,' Gino had said when he came in from the dining-room. The local women who washed up, and took away concealed parcels of scraps, had gone back to their homes with an escort of German soldiers that night. Two slave workers from the prison island of Alderney had escaped. Two Poles, it had been reported; said to be desperate.

'He had bad news?' said Weber. 'What other kind is there?'

'The *Luftwaffe* colonel, the conqueror of Jersey,' said Gino. 'He liked the fish and bacon. He ate it all, every bone. He said there was no fish in Germany, even for a hero.'

Weber had filled both glasses from the schnapps bottle and Gino had drained his at one gulp and put it expectantly in place for a refill. The German obliged. 'So what's the bad news?'

'The British have sunk your battleship, the *Scharnhorst*.'

Frederick's glass was halfway to his mouth but he replaced it on the table. 'It's probably the last battleship. I don't think we've got any more.'

'The colonel was telling them at the table. They were down in the mouth. And he said that when she sank all her crew, two thousand men, stood on the deck singing.'

'That's a hell of a time to sing.'

'Most of them drowned. They were singing a song called something like: "On a Sailor's Grave, No Roses Bloom". Some of the officers in the mess began to sing it. They were crying.'

'It's a very tearful song,' shrugged Weber. 'Especially when the ship is sinking under you.' He began to sing thoughtfully.

> *'Auf einem Seemannsgrab,*
> *da blühen keine Rosen.'*

They drank the schnapps dismally until Weber said: 'It's good they gave an escort to the washing-up women. Those men from Alderney, Poles or whatever they are, Spaniards even, are all mad. Not enough food, no booze, no women, stuck behind barbed wire. Going for a shit must be a nice change.' He glanced at his friend. 'That blonde washer-up likes you, Gino,' he said. 'I've noticed. She's a bit thin, but who isn't.'

Gino grunted. 'She worked in this hotel before the war. Cocktail waitress. I liked her then but she went off and married someone, a Frenchman, I think. Now all she wants me for is a bowl of pasta.'

'My superior may be posted soon,' mentioned Weber. He poured two more glasses from the bottle and put his single finger to his lips. 'So I understand.'

Gino became desolate. 'He'll take you with him, Fred.'

The German said: 'He likes the way I cook. As long as it's not back to freezing, fucking Russia.'

'They won't post him there again. He's still wounded.'

'No, I don't think it will be so far. Just across the water. Northern France. To wait for the day, for the invasion.'

'No more fishing,' said Gino sorrowfully.

Weber picked up the bottle and turned it upside down, just in case, before tossing it the length of the room accurately into a metal bin. Unsteadily the two men made their way out of the kitchen, tiptoeing through the officers' empty mess and, first collecting overcoats, went out into the starry night. They staggered a little, close together for support. Gino had acquired a *Wehrmacht* coat. 'Everything is so peaceful,' he muttered. 'Maybe they have finished the war.'

A patrol of soldiers appeared through the dark of the sloping town, their rifles and their boots noisy, their faces only shadows. The helmet of one of them fell forward over his eyes and his sergeant cursed him before turning on Gino and Weber. 'Hands up!' he ordered.

Prudently they obeyed. 'Where are you going? Who are you?' demanded the sergeant. He was old for a soldier and so were the others.

'You must be new,' said Weber. 'I am the *Kommandant*'s cook.'

'Oh, for certain. And I'm Hitler's mother.'

'That is possible, but I am still the *Kommandant*'s cook.'

The sergeant took in Gino. 'And this one?' he said, still addressing Weber. 'This one in an army coat and underneath no uniform.' Decisively he stepped forward. 'You will come with us. Two prisoners have escaped.'

Gino said: 'We have our papers.'

Both he and Weber made for their pockets but the sergeant pointed his pistol in alarm first at one, then the other. 'Put your hands on your heads,' he said. 'And walk.'

They began to walk. Weber started singing gently:

> *'Auf einem Seemannsgrab,*
> *da blühen keine Rosen . . .'*

The sergeant emitted a squeak. 'No singing! You are drunk! You will be shot!'

'Don't upset him, Fred,' warned Gino.

'Bollocks,' said Weber. 'This old dolt couldn't shoot straight even from there.'

'Not so much of the old,' snapped the sergeant.

'You're all old,' said Weber surveying his countrymen. 'They only send old soldiers here.'

The sergeant was beginning to have doubts. 'Even if you are not escaped I am taking you in. You're both drunk.'

'Schnapps,' confirmed Weber.

There was a trudging step from the shadows and a British policeman, his helmet like a dome, trod towards them. 'Trouble?' he asked the sergeant.

'This pair are drunk, and they may be escaped Todt men.'

'Oh, those.' He seemed unimpressed. But then he drew himself up importantly to deliver his own news. 'Well, I thought I heard a cat meowing.'

The Germans all looked at each other. 'Are you going to report this cat?' asked Weber in an interested way.

'It's very unusual,' said the British constable. 'All dogs and cats were destroyed years ago.'

'This conversation is stupid. Come on, get moving,' said the sergeant. He attempted to look threatening with his pistol and the other soldiers lifted the muzzles of their rifles. First Weber, then Gino, replaced their hands on their heads and the group headed towards the police station, with the constable carefully leading the way.

A British police sergeant was slouched at the desk. In the background were two cells, each occupied by a drunk snarling at the man in the next cell. 'One from Guernsey and the other from Jersey,' said the policeman at the desk with a yawn.

'*Ach, so.*'

'They don't get on,' the police sergeant said as the men began to spit at each other. 'The Guernsey man calls the Jersey man a *crapaud*, a toad.'

The German sergeant said: 'That's a terrible thing.'

'Can we go home?' interjected Weber. 'I have to be up to get the general's breakfast.' He beamed at the British man behind the desk. 'I am his cook.'

'Well, you're not the blokes who escaped. They've been cornered at Trinity. Stealing apples.' He sighed. 'I'll still have to file a report, though, since you've been brought in.' Wearily he took up a pen. 'Name and rank?'

'I am a member of the occupying forces,' sniffed Weber.

'It's the occupying forces who make us do the report.

55

Everything at night has to be entered in the book, no matter what.'

The German patrol, with a collective scowl at Weber and Gino, filed out after their sergeant into the chilly night. The British policeman lingered.

Gino said: 'He has something to report.'

'Yes, that's right,' said Weber. 'He heard a cat.'

Chapter Seven

Once, years ago, on Salisbury Plain the grass could be heard blowing. Before the soldiers came the chalky hills were wandered by sheep; a handful of hamlets concealed themselves in its folds. It was a strange land known mostly to shepherds. The air then was bright and bursting with birdsong but there are no larks at Larkhill now, for it is the main artillery range; tanks trundle over the bald uplands, and infantry train for battle. Regimental badges carved shallowly in the chalk are souvenirs, and memorials, of troops long gone into action. For more than a century it has been the domain of the fighting soldier; villages have vanished except for the ghostly Imber, and another place built oddly like a German hamlet, both used for perfecting house-to-house fighting. Few of the soldiers who have manoeuvred there in peace or wartime have come to love it.

'This fucking hole!' said Gunner Blackie as he entered the billet for the first time. The twenty members of the squad filed in and shuffled around dismally. They were mainly young men, with a couple of older soldiers; Blackie, Treadwell, Lance-bombardier Jock Gordon, Gannick who at twenty sucked on a pipe (generally empty), Peters, Brown, Hinchcliffe, Chaffey, Cloony the Paddy, and the others. May and Foster were the older men. They had seen it all.

'Indian troops was in here,' said Treadwell peering through his rimless army glasses. 'You can niff the curry.' He had put in for a transfer to the Pay Corps on account of poor eyesight, a disadvantage in an artillery man.

'It's freezing,' said Gannick.

Sergeant Harris, the section NCO, was framed by the door. 'There's one bucket of coke per night, per hut, he said.'

'That's no' going to warm us for long,' said Gordon.

'Rub your hands together and sleep in your greatcoats,' said the sergeant. 'In the meantime you could sit around that contraption . . .' He indicated the iron stove in the middle of the billet. '. . . and pretend it's hot.'

Three other men came into the hut, Warren, Rayley and Bond, nondescript as ordinary soldiers become, their kitbags pulled behind them like heavy dogs on leads. 'Find a bed,' said Harris. 'And get yourselves down to the cookhouse before it's dark. You can see what you're eating then.'

A small, exhausted-looking officer appeared in the doorway. 'Attention!' snapped the sergeant and the men obeyed in their various ways. Blackie hardly shuffled his feet together. 'Just getting them settled down, sir,' said Harris. 'We're short of coke for the stove. The supplies haven't turned up.'

Lieutenant Wilson said: 'Oh, dear. You'll have to stamp your feet.'

'Yes, sir.'

Wilson said: 'All right. Carry on. Now I've got to find where I sleep. Being pushed around like this is a damned nuisance. We've only come three miles. I suppose there may be some major plan behind it.' He went out into the dimming afternoon. 'But I doubt it.'

Blackie remembered one of the three men who had come in after the sergeant. Harris looked about as though he might somehow improve the billet but then shrugged and, pushing the blackout curtain, went out. Blackie pointed to the man he recognised. 'You're that bloke Warren,' he said. 'We was on the train back at Christmas.'

'That's right. Bunny Warren.' He was twice the bulk of Blackie.

'There's a bed next to mine, mucker,' said Blackie.

'No taking the mickey about they did to Oi in school with my trucks.'

Blackie shook his head and opened his kitbag on the stiff mattress. 'There's some empty old 'uts,' he said thoughtfully. 'Wood walls.'

'Chop them up,' said Gordon.

'Soon as it gets dark.'

They took three of the twenty-five-pounder guns up to the firing range at Larkhill the next morning, trucks hauling them over the long, austere hills and making trails into the frosty valleys. Blackie enjoyed the guns, it was the best part of the army; the echoing orders, the shattering discharge, the swift recoil, the sharp stench, the earth exploding a mile away. Once, after firing for an hour, they discovered they had killed a rabbit. 'Died of fright,' said Sergeant Harris.

When they had gained the higher ground of the plain, where the landscape seemed to press against the sulky sky, they could see other troops moving across the scene: a whole battalion of American infantry in lines, as though pushing forward to confront an enemy. There were Canadians skidding about with light armoured cars. A squadron of tanks, big Shermans, sidled down the longest incline towards the main road south to Salisbury. The sound of small-arms fire drifted from the ruined village of Imber. All training for the day, the day of the invasion.

On the return from Larkhill Harris called a halt on the humped side of the chalky path. As soon as they had secured the guns and taken out their mess tins to drink what was left of the day's tea, a group of American soldiers appeared over the rise at the opposite side of the track and sat down, studying them in silence as a pack of animals might survey another unknown pack.

The British troops returned the scrutiny. Not a word came from either side; the firing had died away, the whine of the upland wind was sharp. The American troops were all white men and on their legs they wore the long puttees that gave them the look of infantrymen from the First War. 'Hey,' one eventually called. 'What you guys figuring on doing with that peashooter?' He pointed his rifle at one of the twenty-five-pounders.

'It's to cover your arses when you run away,' Blackie called back at once.

Sergeant Harris stood quickly. 'He's joking,' he called across the divide. 'He's the regimental comic.' Blackie scowled but prudently and politely waved.

A flock of sheep appeared, following their daily path, well worn by successive years, and ambled along the narrow track between the two slopes and the two sets of soldiers. The Americans and the British watched the scraggy animals pushing forward between them, complaining and jostling. An elderly shepherd came behind, stumbling with a stave, his dog worrying around the flanks of the flock.

The shepherd did nothing to acknowledge the soldiers on either bank but, eyes down, moved on. On the timeless track his sheep knew where to change direction. When they had reached the place, the shepherd lifted his old head and shouted like an ancient drill sergeant. The flock turned.

'God-dam, did you see that?' exclaimed the American at the front.

'Bloody clever, our sheep,' Blackie called back.

A single-track railway used by miniature engines crossed the military miles of the plain, connecting the fixed garrisons to the main line of the Great Western Railway. There were stations at the military bases, Tidworth, Bulford, Larkhill and others. The British garrison towns were spotless: white painted stones bordering gravelled roads between the barrack blocks, the clean outlines of churches, the tended graves, the marked sports fields and the parade-grounds where generations of home and Empire troops had drilled, ceremonial volleys had been fired, flags had flown and bands had played.

There were three cinemas in the scattered barracks showing

Hollywood musicals with beautiful actresses in technicolour, and less luxurious black-and-white patriotic films like *Mrs Miniver* with Greer Garson and *In Which We Serve*, starring the stiff-lipped Noel Coward.

'Now, I'd like to be takin' that Greer Garson into my bed on a cold Highland night,' said Jock Gordon. 'If only to keep the lass warm.'

'You'd've more chance with that Coward bloke,' said Treadwell. 'They reckons he's one of them nancy boys.'

'And there's him in these heroic fillums,' muttered Gannick, taking his pipe from his mouth. 'Where's the justice?'

'B'aint justice for the likes of you and me,' said Warren. 'We're just good for war or the Labour Exchange.'

Blackie, bent double with an armful of planks, crashed through the door and its blackout curtain followed by Brown and Hinchcliffe, similarly loaded.

'It's going out,' said Warren. He took a plank from Blackie and began to break it up with his thick hands. The others stamped on the wood, dropped it into the iron stove and stood back, grinning, as it started to crackle. The door opened with its customary bleak blast and Harris came in around the curtain. 'Now I wonder where you came across that,' he said.

'Lying around, sarge,' said Blackie.

'The remains of Noah's Ark,' said Gordon.

The sergeant sat on the iron end of Blackie's bed near the fire, putting his hands out to warm.

'It had better be a big ark,' he said. 'The coke's been delayed again. The railways are too busy with the war.'

'I'm going to write to the War Office about it,' said Treadwell. 'Complain.'

'There'll be no one to fight their war if we die of pneumonia,' said Blackie. He glanced at the sergeant. 'There's not much wood left.'

From outside in the night came a noise. 'Ghosts,' said Gannick. 'Dead soldiers.'

'Bollocks,' said Blackie.

He pulled on his greatcoat and went to the door. Harris got up and unhurriedly followed him, then some of the others. From there they could see the dark outline of the nearest hut they had been cannibalising for wood. There were loose sheets of corrugated iron, held up only by a few flimsy metal supports, rattling and groaning in the dark wind. 'You've made your own ghosts,' said Harris.

As though it were another spectre, a clanking figure advanced towards the hut door. Warren said: 'Gunfire. Good old Cloony.'

The soldier was humping a heavy bucket, banging its side with a metal mug. 'That bog Irish bugger was in the cookhouse,' said Cloony. 'I told him us Paddies have got to stick together, for a Free Ireland, so I got the tea.' He saw Harris. 'Want a cup, sarge?'

He put the bucket on the billet floor and handed the sergeant the mug. 'Why do they call it gunfire, sarge?' asked Peters who was eighteen.

'Because when the Tommies were in the trenches in France that's what woke them up in the morning, tea and gunfire.'

The stove was heating up now and with odd domesticity they sat on the beds around it. 'Ever been in the trenches, sarge?' asked Blackie.

Harris shook his head. 'This is my only posting, Salisbury Plain. In three years I've never shifted.'

Warren said: 'Will you be along with us when we . . . go to France?'

'I hope so. I'm fed up with pretending war.' He surveyed their army faces, softly lit by the dim lamps. 'You've been in action, haven't you, Gordon?'

'Norway, sarge, 1940,' replied the Scot. 'It was no' so much action as inaction. They landed us on this wee island, hardly room to stand up. Then they left us there for a week, then shoved us aboard another ship and off we went home. Niver even saw the nose of a German. But some of the others had a terriba' time. The equipment didna' work, the guns froze.'

'Same as Dunkirk,' said Blackie. 'Oi must have walked forty miles in the blazing 'eat, and the French closed their doors in your bloody face. Wouldn't give you a cup of water.' He glanced about. 'Now we got to go and rescue 'em.'

Harris said: 'The only time I've seen action, real action, was right here on the plain.'

It had been a spring morning, three years before, green and lucid, the curved back of the plain in its colours of the early year like a pale rainbow against a pale sky. A squad of twenty-five recruits, fresh from the training depot at Woolwich Arsenal had been taken for their introduction to the gunnery range, and were climbing aboard the truck to go back. It was the middle of a normal day. The landscape was patterned with soldiers. Some pre-war Bren gun carriers went like beetles along a track and smoke grenades were exploding with puffs of white. Harris was observing a well-spaced line of infantry strung along the skyline, slowly moving and clearly outlined. Abruptly the figures vanished and a moment later he saw the Messerschmitt 110 fighter-bomber, low and daring, dive into the bower of the valley. The unaware squad in the truck and the others grouped around it pointed at the moving shape with excitement but no alarm. 'Oh, Christ!' Harris had time to say to himself. He was two hundred yards from the truck, rigid, rooted, as the German plane streaked towards the squad, picking them out, its machine-guns sparking, the bullets throwing up the earth. Then as it began to roll away, its black crosses revealed, it released a lone lucky bomb.

It hit the truck. Harris was knocked backwards, down a slope, his mouth full of dirt. Gasping, he got to his knees and clawed his way up the bank. The truck had disintegrated and was burning in a strangely sedate way. The bodies lay where they had been flung. One man was trying to crawl away on his hands and knees.

Two others, clear of the truck, were sitting on the bank below him, holding on to each other like terrified children. Shouting to them to take cover, he stumbled down. There was no need for his warning; the solitary plane had gone. The two soldiers seemed welded together, weeping and trembling. He pulled them apart and, one at a time, to their feet. All around was uproar. Men were running towards the flaming remains of the truck and there were shouts for the medics. A stretcher was being dragged up a slope. A lot of good that would do. 'I'm deaf,' shouted one of the two recruits at Harris. 'I can't hear anything.'

The other sank down again, weakly shaking, on to the grass. 'We thought it was part of the practice,' he sobbed. Harris saw that he was bleeding from a shoulder wound. He tore the boy's shirt away and clumsily tried to apply his field dressing. 'Keep still!' he ordered. 'Keep still.' The recruit's eyes were wild, uncomprehending. 'Nobody told us,' he babbled. 'They didn't say.'

Nineteen young men died.

Harris walked through mud and darkness towards the sergeants' mess. The place was almost deserted; it was NCOs' night at the garrison cinema. A solitary sergeant crouched like a shadow in a corner listening to the wireless, Tommy Handley in *ITMA*, shaking his head and laughing soundlessly.

The duty steward got Harris an egg sandwich and a cup of tea. There was a *Sunday Express* on one of the worn armchairs. Allied forces were still bogged down by winter mud and German resistance as they tried to advance up the limb of Italy. There had been more bomber raids on the industrial Ruhr and there was a picture of the handful of survivors from the sunken battleship *Scharnhorst*. There was also a quarter column advertisement for Bisto. He turned to the final page of four. There had been racing at Doncaster and there was a half-page of football reports and results.

He called: 'Good-night,' to the sergeant still silently guffawing in the corner and the man waved an arm and replied: 'Ta-ta for now.' In the lobby there was a letter-board. Harris did not get many letters but today there were two. One was from

Southampton library warning him that a book was overdue by six months and the fines were mounting. He had asked Enid to take it back. The second letter was from a spiteful neighbour who wrote that Enid was sleeping with another man.

Grimly he went to his billet and thought it over in his comfortless bunk. He slept fitfully, the wind still moaning as though bereft through the bones of the neighbouring hut which his squad had stripped of wood.

In the bleak morning he went through his soldier's routine, going to the latrines where there was ice in the lavatory pans, to the wash-house where the water was also frigid. He shaved in a mug of tea; then to breakfast and the early parade. The men went to the gunnery range, joining others who were marching that way. Harris sharply turned from the barrack square and slowly, uncertainly walked towards the adjutant's office.

He had always thought of Captain Moon as a bit of a fool. Now he found him feeding his spaniel behind his desk. 'Oh, oh, sergeant,' he said, straightening. He had gingery hair and pale eyes. He was hoping to be replaced, transferred somewhere remote but safe, before the invasion.

Harris saluted. 'I would like twenty-four hours' compassionate leave, sir, if it can be managed.'

'What is it, sergeant? Missus trouble?'

'Might be, sir.'

'They're absolute swines, aren't they, wives. Is it a Yank?'

'No, sir. A merchant seaman, I'm told.'

'Ho, a sailor. Be a job to catch up with him, won't it? I know – mine was having the best of three falls with a commercial traveller once, sold boot polish. First wife, that is. Took a long time to catch up with him, I can tell you. He was here, there and everywhere. Cardiff, Bolton. Not that I cared that much in the end.'

He seemed to be talking to himself and appeared surprised when he looked up and saw Harris still there.

'Right you are, sergeant,' he said. He reached for a pad and scribbled on it. 'The orderly room will see to it. You know the drill.' He handed the note to Harris. 'Hope you catch the jolly sailor,' he said. 'Good luck.'

Harris went out into the ashen morning and skirted the wet parade-ground. Even the lowest hills were opaque, misty. 'I can't see that prat leading us up the beach,' he muttered.

He intended to get the narrow garrison train to Salisbury where the main line travelled down to Southampton, but a fifteen-hundredweight stopped and he threw his greatcoat, pack and steel helmet in the back and climbed in beside the driver of the truck.

'Bleedin' Yanks,' complained the lance-corporal. 'They're like dirt-track riders, you know, showin' off.' He was a small, rat-like soldier and he peered close to the rim of the steering-wheel as though fearing an ambush at every bend.

'Round the corners,' nodded Harris. 'I've seen them.'

'That's just them jeeps. The motor bikes don't even *know* about corners. They just goes over the top, over the banks. I wonder if they'll be so keen when they get to France?'

They were coming down from the plain, down to the main Salisbury-to-Bath road. Under the low sky the land looked baleful, closed in, clumps of cloud gathered in its crevices. There were soldiers gathered on an incline, sitting listening to an instructor, hunched together, reluctantly accepting their fate.

'Have you seen Bulford, sarge?'

'Haven't been down there since the Americans took it over,' said Harris. 'They probably wouldn't let me in.'

'You'd 'ave been shocked. Mud everywhere, churned up. When you think how all reggie it used to be, everything just so, shining, neat. It's a cryin' bloody shame.'

'Maybe they're training for a muddy war,' suggested Harris. He was thinking about Enid and the man, whoever he was. What would he find when he got home? What would she say? She was ten years younger than him and he had known what she was like when they married. Enid was not a woman who could be left on her own.

66

''Ow long do you reckon it'll be, sarge?' asked the lance-corporal. 'Before we go in.' They were joining the main road. Harris was sure the driver had suspect eyesight because he leaned both ways as far as he could and squeezed his eyes together. A convoy of a dozen military ambulances went by. In the other direction, going west, two wedge-shaped landing-craft were being transported, on long low-loaders, white American stars on their hulls.

'How long?' said Harris. 'Nobody tells me anything.'

'Not yet, I don't reckon,' said the driver. 'Wait for the nice weather. When the water's not so chilly.'

They drove into grey, grave Salisbury, its cathedral spire encased in mist. There was little civilian traffic. Three tanks were parked in the market square, their crews talking to some girls. A horse-drawn dray delivered barrels outside a public house and an old man washed down the pavement. 'Got a twenty-four-hour pass?' asked the driver. It was Monday. Not many passes were issued on a Monday.

'Right,' said Harris.

'Trouble?' said the man.

'Something like that.' He wanted to tell the man to shut up but instead he joked: 'I'm going to see Montgomery. I've got a few ideas for him. But keep it under your hat.' The driver laughed and said: 'I should cocoa, sarge.' They were at the station now and Harris was relieved.

Calling out his thanks, he put his overcoat over one shoulder and the small pack and steel helmet over the other, and went towards the station entrance.

The driver sniffed: 'Monty, be buggered.'

Harris showed his rail warrant. There was a wait of ten minutes for the train which was running forty minutes late. On the platform were some mothers and children, going to Southampton to see the pantomime, revived this year. There was a notice-board. Pinned to it were leaflets, almost rubbed out by time and weather, warnings about Air Raids, Careless Talk and Venereal Disease.

There was to be a concert by the pipe band of a Canadian regiment, a Red Cross bring-and-buy sale and an All-Services Dance at the Corn Exchange with a Royal Army Dental Corps swing quartet called the Gnashers.

A woman wearing a headscarf came on to the platform with two children. The boy said to Harris: 'We're off to see *Jack and the Beanstalk.*'

'I've seen it,' said Harris. 'Very good.'

'You must be a good father,' said the woman. 'Do you miss your kids?'

'Yes,' he said with a sort of truth, although he did not have any.

The train arrived, its steam spouting up among the rusting iron and grimy glass of the station roof. Children jumped with excitement. He wondered if the little boy would ever have to be a soldier, one with a wandering wife.

Although the train was crushed with passengers the mothers somehow pushed their families aboard and climbed in after them. It had come from South Wales and Harris found himself wedged in a group of Royal Navy men going to Portsmouth. 'You have to have submarine training for this lark,' said one. 'Roll on, butty, don't let anybody else get aboard. We'll all suffocate.'

The young sailor's face was almost next to his. He was Welsh. 'Got engaged this leave,' he said. 'Known her since school. Now I've gone and put her up the spout.' He needed to tell somebody. 'Only done it twice, we 'ave. I'm putting in for leave to marry her when I get to Pompey. What's it like in the army for getting compassionate leave?'

Harris smiled grimly and said: 'Nothing to it.'

Chapter Eight

The countryside levelled as they went towards the coast. Harris had a narrow view over the sailor's shoulder. The cold had not been so severe down here and he caught a glimpse of a river with a muffled man fishing from a small boat. 'Did you see him, fishing?' said the Welsh youth. 'All right for some.'

Harris suggested the man might be a night worker or a wounded commando on leave. The sailor said: 'I wouldn't want to be doing that anyway. On that water, I 'ate water, man. My old chap got hisself drowned. Merchant Navy, 1942, sunk by a U-boat. And there's 'undreds down in Davy Jones's with him. I didn't want to go in the navy because I'm scared bloody rigid of the sea. I wish I could swap places with you, man. You can't be scared of the land, can you? You can always run on land. But the sea is nasty. They might never find you.'

It was not a long journey – even at the wartime pace of the train it took less than an hour – but long enough to see how the invasion army was taking shape. For all the manoeuvres of battalions and guns and tanks, Salisbury Plain, in its lofty isolation, was a place apart, away and above the massing of men and the materials of war, which had been given a code-name: 'Bolero', after the insistent ever-growing music of Ravel.

From the train he could see tanks beneath trees and crouching under camouflage nets, armoured vehicles lining villages and blocking suburban streets. Children played around the wheels and tracks, the crews teasing and laughing and engaging their older sisters and mothers in earnest conversations.

The widespread winter-brown acres of the New Forest were thick with tents and huts, armoured vehicles lurking below fir trees. On the narrow forest roads were creeping lines of trucks and there was a squadron of American Sherman tanks hugging a copse, camouflage netting slung between the tree-trunks. Somehow all that had to be taken across the English Channel.

They passed the grounds of a stately house, ranks of ambulances lining its drive, a red cross painted above its portico. There was a public park where only the playground remained uncommandeered by the military. Amid parked armoured cars, troop carriers and squads of drilling soldiers, small girls swung on swings and two boys bounced on a see-saw.

As they neared Southampton docks Harris saw that the familiar sidings and marshalling yards were lined for miles with railway trucks loaded with ammunition crates. The Welsh sailor watched also. 'If you dropped a Swan Vesta on that lot, just one match, I bet all of Southampton would blow up, Pompey too.'

When the train stopped he had to fight his way out and across the platform. Soldiers, airmen, sailors, blocked the route to the exit, sitting on their kit, drawing at cigarettes, some talking but not many. Nobody was laughing. Some looked exhausted. A uniformed crowd jostled around a mobile canteen marked 'Church Army', where three sweaty-faced women served in a sheet of steam. 'I'll be glad when this bleedin' war is over!' shouted one. In the centre of the platform, grouped tightly together as if for safety, were a dozen grey-uniformed and bonneted nurses.

At last Harris gained the exit and went out into the damp city air. But now he could smell the sea on the breeze coming off the docks, and he sniffed at it gratefully. This was his home town.

There was a bus with only a number on its destination board among the others outside the station. The youthfully spotted conductor stood on the platform reading the *Dandy*. He looked up and said: 'Korky the Cat's good this week.'

Harris said he was pleased. 'You go down Gosport Street, don't you?' he asked.

'All the way down,' said the conductor, folding the *Dandy*. 'Then to the dock gates. That'll be tuppence.'

Harris paid while he stood on the platform. The conductor gave him a ticket and offered him the folded comic, as if it were part of his war effort, saying: 'I've read it.'

Harris took the comic anyway and went to the upper deck. There were only some headscarfed women with their shopping and their fags on the top deck and they were at the back. He put his greatcoat on a seat at the front and his pack and steel helmet on top of it, lit a cigarette and looked out of the forward window on to the wet station yard.

He did not know what he was going to say to Enid.

The bus trembled and started. It was not far to Gosport Street. His council house was two-thirds of the way down the terrace. When they were almost there he saw a car, a taxi by the look of it, standing outside. Christ, perhaps she was running away.

The bus-stop was a hundred and fifty yards short of the taxi. He peered close to the window and then, picking up his coat and his kit, clattered down the stairs. The housewives were enveloped in a cloud of cigarette smoke. One of them called: 'Hurry up, mate, you'll miss the invasion!'

As he was getting off the bus Harris saw a man leaving his front door. He felt his eyebrows rise. The man was carrying a canvas kitbag which he tossed into the back of the taxi and then climbed in after. 'Wait, wait a minute,' said Harris, turning to the bus conductor. 'I'll stay on to the dock gates.' He pulled his equipment back on to the platform. 'That's another tuppence,' said the conductor, looking at him quaintly. 'Thruppence if you're going to the eastern docks.'

'I don't know yet,' said Harris. He handed the man a threepenny piece. 'I'm chasing somebody.'

The conductor regarded him with concern and moved quickly out of the way when Harris began to remount the stairs. 'Roll on,' he sighed to himself. 'What a job.'

Harris reached the upper deck and one of the women said: 'He *did* miss it.' He went again to the front seats without looking at them. He sat watching the taxi.

They approached the first of the dock gates but the taxi did not stop until the second. Harris picked up his equipment and overcoat, and made a dash for the stairs at the rear. 'Here he comes again!' hooted one of the women.

There was no bus-stop. Urgently he pressed the bell. They passed the stationary taxi. The man was getting out. 'Hang on, wait for the stop!' called the conductor.

Harris could not wait. Clutching his load, he dropped backwards off the platform and hit the road at a run, landing on his backside. The steel helmet bounced with a clang. People on the pavement shouted and a tut-tutting woman tried to help him to his feet. A schoolboy picked up the *Dandy*, glanced at the front and gave it back to him.

People gathered as they did in wartime at any sign of an incident, no matter how minor, some laughing outright, some smirking, some indifferent, a few looking concerned and sorry for him. He regained his feet, gathered his belongings, and marched from the scene.

His quarry was just entering the iron gates of the dock; as Harris hurried his pace, they began to close again.

'Wait!' He was still two hundred yards away. He shouted to the sailor who was inside the compound now, changing shoulders with his bag, waving cheerily to another man who was going in the same direction, and then to the gatekeeper and a police sergeant standing beside him. A soldier with a fixed bayonet occupied a sentry-box next to the gate. A merchant ship, patterned whorled grey, camouflage along its bow, was standing at the quayside. A skein of steam oozed from its funnel. Other cargo ships were unloading and a fleet of invasion barges and landing-craft huddled in the open water beyond. Harris lumbered towards the gate. 'That man,' he pointed breathlessly. 'Stop him, will you. I want to punch his lights out.'

Both the gatekeeper and the police sergeant frowned. 'Can't let you in through here unless you've got a dock-gate pass,' said the gatekeeper.

'Have you got a pass, sergeant?' demanded the policeman.

'No, I haven't, *sergeant*,' Harris replied.

'Well, sergeant, you can't go through, and that's that.'

The gateman said: 'Why do you want to bash him?'

'The bastard's just got out of bed with my wife.'

'I'd say he was Greek,' said the gateman, as if it might have some bearing on the matter. Harris could see the man was going away quickly. He called hopelessly through the railings: 'You, you!' The sailor vanished unknowingly around the corner of a warehouse.

Harris felt himself sag. 'Bollocks,' he said. 'I'll get him when the swine comes back.'

'*That's* the time,' agreed the gatekeeper. 'Wait for him.'

'*If* he gets back,' sniffed the policeman. 'A lot of 'em don't.' He turned to Harris and said kindly: 'Go and have a cup of tea. There's a forces' canteen just over the road.'

Harris stood hopelessly. He found he was still holding the *Dandy* and he absently offered it to the police sergeant who shook his head: 'I'm a *Beano* man, myself.'

'Oh, sod it,' said Harris dismally. The bus from which he had fallen had turned and now waited at the stop prepared for its return journey. He trudged towards it and was greeted by the same conductor. 'Back again,' said the youth cheerfully. 'Gosport Street, wasn't it? Thruppence like before.'

'With my luck,' said Harris miserably, 'I thought the fares might have gone up.'

'They will do, I expect,' said the conductor. 'After our strike.'

Harris sat wearily on the bench seat next to the platform. 'Strike?' he said. 'You're going on strike? I wish I could go on strike.'

'Ah, but you're a soldier. That would be mutiny, wouldn't it? This is a strike. It's against the summer schedules. We're out from midnight Friday.'

Harris felt crushed, defeated; the conductor, the Greek, the gatekeeper, the policeman, the whole lunacy. 'That's what we're fighting for, isn't it?' the conductor said with surprising passion. 'Freedom. That includes the right to strike.'

The bus went along Gosport Street and Harris left at the stop nearest his house. He walked slowly towards it. He wondered how he would confront her; what to say, how to accuse her.

Knowing neighbours eyed him around their curtains. He tried to walk casually. He waved to the peeping woman next door. He took in a heavy breath and put his key in the lock of the front door. Then he took it out again. He rang the bell.

Enid appeared like a sleepy vision, her pink silk dressing-gown open, her breasts lolling half out of her crumpled nightdress. 'Oh, Harris,' she said. 'What a really nice surprise.' She took him in with a widening smile. 'I didn't know you read the *Dandy*.'

Chapter Nine

She had always called him Harris because she refused to use his Christian name which was Neville. Enid was twenty-four and he was ten years older. They had been married for two years.

'He only came to pick up his sea bag,' she said. 'He was so drunk last night he couldn't carry it and he had to join his ship.'

They were facing each other across the kitchen table. The ashes of a small coal fire in the cooking range warmed the room. She poured him a cup of tea from the teapot his mother had won at Brighton before the war, then nodded to a clutch of empty bottles on the draining-board. 'They all were.'

'How many?' he asked, relieved that she had not been alone with the sailor. It was some sort of excuse to himself because he did not want to lose her. This morning, in her creased nightclothes and with her stringy hair she was desirable to him and she knew it. Her eyes were grinning at him.

'God knows,' she answered. 'People are always coming in and out. You know I can't stand it on my own. I'm glad you're here, Harris, darling. I miss you a terrible lot.'

They leaned across the wooden table, her brimming breasts resting on it, and kissed. Careful not to capsize his cup he got up and went round the table to her, his boots sounding on the linoleum, putting his arms about her from the rear. 'You've been away a long time,' she murmured.

'Two weeks,' he said, close against her hair. He eased Enid to her feet and turned her to him, sensing the glow of her body.

'Uniforms always feel so scratchy,' she said. 'Even those three stripes dig into me. It's not meant for lovers, is it?' Her mouth went to his face. 'It's meant for fighting war. Get it off and let's go to our bed.'

Now he did knock his teacup over. 'Leave it, leave it,' she said. 'It won't flood the place.' The spilt tea ran across the table and was dripping thinly on the floor. 'I was going to give it a mop some time this week anyway.'

She led him like a new acquaintance up the council-house stairs. Harris followed dumbly. He would never know enough about her, how to keep her, how to leave her. They went into the bedroom where the bedclothes were spread like an avalanche on the floor. 'I was thinking of staying in bed,' she said by way of an excuse. 'The last few nights have been a bit hairy.'

'Where have they been hairy?' he asked inadequately. They were standing a little apart, facing each other.

She shrugged. 'Down at the pub, at Maggie Phillips's house, and here. It's the war's to blame. It's been a bit of a travelling party, believe me.'

'I do believe you.'

She pouted, making the dark seams below her eyes contract. 'Harris, you wouldn't want me to stay at home knitting. I can't knit anyway. I can't do hardly anything. But you knew that when we got married. Your mother told you.'

He nodded. 'I knew.'

Encouragingly she smiled, and with offhand titillation let her robe slip away. Her creamy breasts curved the straps of her night-dress, swelling and swelling more when she breathed deeply which she did now. He took a pace to her and eased away the silk straps; the nightdress dropped in slow motion, the left-hand strap hooking on her roused nipple. Laughing, she gave it a modest tug and stood with her upper body fine and naked, the nightdress held around her waist. 'Don't tread on my toes with those army boots,' she said.

She pushed him backwards on to the bed and climbed on top of his rough uniform, propping herself on her forearms and rubbing herself into him. 'Actually, in a way, it's quite exciting this khaki stuff,' she mumbled. 'Rough as a pig's bum.'

Harris encircled her and she wriggled and kissed him. 'Better undress,' she said, 'or you'll be untidy on parade.'

'I might not have time to iron it,' he said.

'When is it?' She eased herself up. 'How long have you got?'

'Twenty-four hours,' he said.

'Christ, is that all? Let's get your togs off then.'

Eagerly she began to help him, undoing the buttons of his battledress. He had taken off his belt in the kitchen. 'You unbutton the shirt,' she said. 'I'll do your flies. I'm better at doing flies.'

'Boots,' he said breathlessly. 'We'll never get anything off with them still on my feet.'

'It's taking so long,' she complained. 'I *want* you, Harris.'

'You really do?' He peered down at her near his bootlaces.

'I don't do this for fun,' she said.

He began to laugh, something he had not done for weeks. One boot hit the wood floor in the corner, followed by another. Earnestly she tugged at his socks. 'These are thicker than the boots,' she panted. 'There. Now let's see what present you've got for me.' He closed his eyes and enjoyed the sensation of her manoeuvring his trousers down his legs. She eased herself from the bed to complete the removal and flung them as though in disgust into a corner after the boots. She turned to inspect him. 'Oh, God,' she said in a sad way. 'I'd forgotten.'

'Combinations,' he said solidly. 'Army issue. You need them on Salisbury Plain.'

'I suppose you do,' Enid said. She undid the front buttons and inserted her fingers. 'Come on out,' she said. It did. 'There,' she said.

She leaned to put her lips to him, her hair falling across his groin. She eased herself away, still crouching at his hip level but looking up along his white-flannelled stomach and chest as if considering a new plan. She began to crawl inch over inch like a slow animal up his covered body. 'Oh, Harris,' she said dreamily. 'I quite like these combination things. Keep them on.'

He did, and then turned her firmly on to her back and pulled up the rim of her nightdress. He stared at the pale cleft of her thighs. His hands parted them and with a deep sigh from wife and from husband he entered her. 'It feels really different,' she eventually whispered. 'And not a bit itchy.'

'Everything's grey outside the window,' she said. 'All the world's grey except in here with you.'

Harris, luxurious in the bed, said: 'Get me a cup of tea, will you, love.'

'Let's have it once more,' she said. 'Just another one. Then I'll get you tea. A whole pot if you like, although I think we're a bit short on milk.' She smirked. 'Only condensed. Plenty of condensed.'

'Tea, then after tea more of the same,' he insisted. 'It will give me strength.'

'In that case, I *will* get it.' She looked at the bedside clock. 'It's half eleven,' she said. 'I've got to go somewhere this afternoon.'

Now naked, he sat up in the bed. 'Where? Can't you not go?'

She laughed at his dismay. 'I won't be gone long. It's a little job I do.' She pulled on her robe and went downstairs. Harris, mystified by her as ever, sat up in bed and said: 'Christ.'

She brought him the tea in the pot and, like a mother, poured it for him at the side of the bed. 'So this Greek sailor just left his kitbag here, did he?' he asked.

'He wasn't Greek,' she said, adept at diverting the question. 'He was something else, somewhere near there, Greece.' She laughed. 'He couldn't say a word of English and he got drunk double quick.' Looking at Harris squarely over the top of his raised cup, she said: 'But you don't have to worry. I don't care what the old chin-waggers around here say.' She took the cup from him. 'You can't have a refill,' she said. 'I'm getting back in with you.'

She mounted him naked, pink with effort and enjoyment, her

hair spreading wildly across her face and neck, her eyes glistening through it. As she was reaching her climax she threw her head one way and then the other, her hair like a mad brush, before giving a childlike cry and collapsing against his chest. 'Now you've done it,' he breathed, linking his arms across her back. 'I'm knackered.'

'You can sleep,' she said. 'All the afternoon. A lot of people would like to do that on a nasty day like this. After the war we'll stay in bed all day.'

She slid off him and lay against his side, her hair still veiling her face. Carefully he touched it aside. 'What's this job?' he asked.

'Oh, it's just a couple of hours every day,' she said, her eyes closed. 'It's not hard and the money's good, two quid for one afternoon. But it's illegal.'

Harris groaned. 'It sounds like you're on the game?'

'It's a bit like that,' she admitted, smiling close to his face. 'I have to be on the streets and get about.'

'All right. What is it?'

Enid giggled. 'I'm a bookie's runner.'

Harris snorted with disbelief. 'You're crazy. You could land in court.'

'I have,' she said, trying to shrug as she lay against him. 'But they let me off.'

'Bloody hell. I can't believe this.' Solemnly he studied her face. 'But then there's not a lot I can believe, one way and another.'

'Harris,' she admonished. 'You must *always* believe me, believe me. Always. The job is dead easy. I go to a few pubs about one o'clock and pick up the bets, a shilling on this, two bob each way on that, sometimes more. Then I collect from some regulars, shopkeepers and so on. One's the undertaker, Mr Thackeray, and sometimes he writes out his betting slips on people's coffins. He'll put a quid each way on something he fancies.'

'And you get commission.'

'Five per cent. I take the money and the slips back to Charlie Parks, the bookie in Swathling Street, and that's all. He's got some bloke who takes around the winnings. He thinks I might get knocked on the head.' She sat up in the bed, smoothing her warm, bare breasts with her hands. 'It's sort of war work.'

'How is it sort of war work?'

'Entertainment,' she said. 'Giving people a bit of excitement, making them feel happy for a while. There's not much makes anybody happy these days.'

She began surveying her own skin, her shoulders, her arms, her body. 'When the war's over I want to go somewhere hot, where there's sun. I met this couple who went to Spain once and they said it was sunny and hot. I wouldn't mind trying that.'

She slipped from the bed and padded towards the bathroom on the landing. Her legs were glistening. She saw him look and with a smile wiped her thighs with her hands. 'You like the idea of Spain?' she said.

'Love it.'

She closed the bathroom door but after she had flushed the lavatory she opened it again and called: 'That sailor chap came from Albania, I remember now. Are they on our side?' There was no reply and when she looked around the door she saw he was deeply asleep. She went to the bed and quietly pulled the covers over him. 'You poor bloke,' she said.

Harris awoke when she came back into the house. He heard the front door open and she called: 'I'm home. I got some cake.'

He sat up in the bed. It was five o'clock. He noticed that she had piled his army equipment, his pack and helmet and web belt, in the corner of the bedroom. He could hear her in the kitchen. Then she came up with the teapot once more and on the tray also a modest wedding cake.

'Look at that,' she said proudly. 'Bailey's the baker's. He's a regular and he had a long-odds win last week so he gave me it. Somebody's wedding didn't happen.'

'Changed their minds?'

'No choice. The bridegroom got shot down over Germany.'

'That's bad luck.'

'Life's full of it these days,' she said. 'That's why you've got to make the most of it. When you go out of this house in the morning, Harris, it could be the last we see of each other. For ever.'

She offered him a slice of the cake and he bit into it. 'Nice,' he said.

'It's not real icing,' she said. 'Bloody shame. They're hoping he might be a prisoner.'

'I've thought about that myself,' he said. 'You know, not coming back.'

'You're the thoughtful type.'

'I remember those boys who got bombed on Salisbury Plain three years ago. In front of my eyes. A lad goes off to the army, waves bye-bye to Mum and the next thing she knows is a telegram telling her he's dead.'

Enid sniffed. 'Don't. You'll make me cry, and I'm determined not to cry whatever happens. Jesus, there's some women in this street who cry for anything, just reading the papers. They'd cry if the tea ration was cut.'

'I don't blame you,' he said, laughing at her expression. 'There's enough tears. But one thing . . .'

'What's that, Harris?' She was sitting beside him on the bed. They took another slice of cake each. He said: 'When we go to France, whenever that is, we'll probably march right down this street, Gosport Street, to the docks. We've done it three times already in rehearsals. I've looked up at the window but I've never seen you.'

'Busy, I expect,' she said throatily.

'When we go for the real thing I'll wave. Try and wave back.'

'I will,' she said, beginning to cry. 'I'll wave my hankie.'

Somehow wartime rain seemed thicker, more persistent and colder, than rain had been before.

Enid said: 'I didn't mind it pouring before they brought in this blackout, when you could see the street lights and the shop windows shining on the pavements. Coming out of the pictures and seeing it.'

They were walking, heads down against the dark drizzle, eating Spam fritters and chips out of newspaper. She wiped the vinegar from her chin. 'Shame there was no fish,' she said. 'They do get some now and again.'

'Fishing's dangerous,' said Harris. 'And these fritters are all right.'

'We had to have a war to discover Spam,' she said.

They reached the Sailor's Blessing and opened the door into a different world, confined and comforting. Enid said: 'Sorry, Billy, I forgot my coal.'

The rotund barman eyed Harris and said: 'Slipped your mind, I 'spect. Bring it in next time you come.'

A woman came in after them, pushing aside the blackout curtain; she took from her sackcloth shopping bag four lumps of coke, wrapped like presents in silver paper, and undoing each one carefully put them in a scuttle next to the smoky fire at the end of the bar. She folded the silver paper, putting it piece by piece back into her bag.

It was early but the public bar was already crowded. Enid pushed two elderly women along the window-seat and indicated to Harris to sit down. 'It's my husband,' she said as though forestalling questions. He found himself sitting next to a man bent like a gargoyle, his head protruding from the collar of his greasy coat. 'Been off fightin' that bastard 'Itler, 'ave you?' he said.

'Haven't got close to him yet,' said Harris.

'There'll be time,' said the man. 'I hope it goes all right. That Channel can be cold.'

'We'll wait until it's warmed up,' said Harris.

Enid said: 'His name's Wordsworth. He more or less lives in here.'

'A pint, thanks,' said Wordsworth although no one had asked. 'If you're going in that direction.'

Harris got two pints of ale and a gin and orange for Enid. 'There's some rum on the way,' said the barman. 'Be here soon.'

'Good job,' said Wordsworth, peering at the liquid through the side of the glass. 'This stuff is like horse's –'

'Rum?' said Harris. 'What's he mean?'

'It'll come in the back way,' said Enid. She raised her drink to her husband and said: 'Darling.'

'Just 'ark at her,' grumbled one of the elderly women. 'Darlin'.' Her mouth worked round as if she were mixing something.

Wordsworth said: 'It's come from the docks, see. Over the wall when nobody's lookin'. There's a big American cargo boat, one of them Liberty ships, come in today. It's got official cargo, if you get me, and unofficial cargo. The second comes off on the quiet and gets out over the dock wall. The gatekeepers turn a blind eye.' He winked. 'I was one myself once.'

'What comes off?' asked Harris.

'Rum for a start,' answered Enid. 'This time. Might be something else next time.'

'And Spam,' said the old man. 'Like you just came in eating them fritters. A few crates of Spam today. They reckon they nearly brained some poor bloke when they chucked it over the wall.'

'Killed by Spam,' muttered one of the old women.

'It tasted all right,' said Harris. 'As good as ham.'

One of the crones said: ''Cos it's Yankee.'

''Ardly saw 'am before the war,' said her companion.

'Not down 'ere. Sunday tea, now and again. Like a tin of salmon.'

'And pineapple chunks,' her friend reminded them.

'Some people eat better now than pre-war,' said Enid.

'You 'ave to 'ave your rations,' said the woman. 'Even if you can't *afford* them. People would talk behind your back.'

'Bananas,' said Enid. 'That's what the Yanks should bring in. For the kiddies. They've never seen a banana.'

'If one solitary banana came over that wall,' said Wordsworth profoundly, 'there'd be a riot, ructions. Fights, civil disturbance. Police. And that would be the end of stuff findin' its way from the docks.'

The unseen back door opened, the long curtain was ruffled, and the barman quickly went around and took a milk crate from someone still behind the curtain. 'The milk's come,' he laughed as he emerged. He made for the bar. 'Straight from Jamaica.'

The customers moved forward expectantly. 'Half price, first drinks,' announced the barman. 'After that, double.'

They laughed, passed remarks and carried their tots away. Some had orange juice with the rum and some Tizer, and some tried it straight. Harris could not recall drinking rum before. 'I always liked Tizer,' said Wordsworth. 'Used to bring it around the streets. Fizzy stuff. As kids we used to make out it was beer.'

To Harris's surprise Enid had thrown her drink down in one movement and was now sitting with the empty glass in front of her like an open invitation. He picked it up and went to the bar. 'Mine's with Tizer,' called Wordsworth. The two crones said nothing but stared challengingly. He bought rum for them all and Enid said loudly: 'Somebody else's round next.'

Harris remembered only a few of the continuing rounds. The thick, sickly smell of the rum filled the closed room. He sat like a lump, wondering vaguely how he was going to get out of the place. No one else seemed to be affected. A young man in a blue jersey came in and began to play a concertina. There was singing and Harris recalled attempting to join in. Then the young man's tall, gaunt friend danced a tango with Enid, customers pushing back to make a space on the floor. Dimly Harris was aware of his wife swirling by to the sway of the music.

'Jealousy,' said Wordsworth wisely. 'That's what they're dancing. The song's called "Jealousy".' He glanced at Harris: 'But you're past that.'

The evening did not seem long to Harris, only confused. The concertina played and they all sang about hanging out the washing on the Siegfried Line and other inaccurate wartime songs. He was conscious of Enid being at the centre of a laughing group at the other side of the room while he closed his eyes, lying against one of the old ladies. She placed her arms protectively around him and said: 'There, there.'

Then they were in the wet street, going home, not alone but in the jolly company of three young sailors, one the concertina player, who were French. Harris did not care any longer. Let her distribute herself, let her laugh, sing, do whatever she liked. He only wanted to sleep.

He crawled up the stairs and somehow set the alarm for six. She followed him, kissed him as if he were a small son and helped him into bed. The last thing he heard was them chorusing about Dover's white cliffs accompanied wheezily by the concertina.

The alarm jerked him awake. He sat up on the edge of the bed, rubbing his eyes and face, and became aware that Enid was out of bed also. He could hear her urinating. He turned on the light. She was squatting close to the floor.

'Christ!' he groaned. 'Enid, you're peeing into my steel helmet.'

'Oh, Harris,' she groaned back. 'I'm so drunk. And it was just handy.'

Chapter Ten

In the middle days of February the West of England spring made a pale and brief appearance. 'You can see as far as Bristol on a day like this,' pointed Miller from his office window. It sounded like a sort of local pride. His replacement, Captain Brand, said: 'How long did you say you'd been in these parts?'

Miller realised what he meant. 'Eight weeks,' he said. 'Eight cold, wet weeks. For someone from the States, that is, even Dakota. The British take it as normal.'

Brand, tough faced with a combat medal, said: 'Well, it's sure nice today. This time of year Seattle is no Honolulu.'

'See the barrage balloons over Bristol,' said Miller. All at once he realised he would be strangely sorry to go. The balloons in the blue spring sky floated like small fish in a clear pool. 'The British have a joke, I heard a guy tell it at a show. They put it on in Taunton for everybody, the GIs, the British services, air-raid people, hospital staff, everybody. The comedian said that there's so much US war material over here now, it's only the balloons that stop the country sinking.'

Brand said: 'I heard on the radio, some funny guy said that the elastic women here have in their panties is too weak – one yank and they're down.'

Brand had been in Manchester. 'Two days. Waiting for my orders. So I listened to the British radio.'

They turned back into the room. Miller sat behind the desk and Brand in the battered and solitary armchair. The arm moved as he leaned on it. 'Is it old?' he asked with concern.

'So old,' said the other American, 'it's almost dead.'

'I came by plane,' continued Brand. 'God, I would have given a year's service just to be on the ocean. Forget the submarines.'

'You're lying.'

Brand grinned. 'Sure. But it's not a nice trip, take it from me. Ten days to get here. And what a God-dam plane. The seats wore out my ass. We had two days in Greenland, delayed by the weather. Iceland was no improvement. After that Manchester was like dreamland.' He studied Miller. 'Where are they posting you?'

'London,' said Miller. 'Training directorate. I did my paratroop training Stateside, Fort Bragg, but I don't think I'm going to be doing any jumping out of planes. It don't look that way.'

'Manchester,' said Brand, shaking his head. 'Full of holes made by bombs. But the British don't seem to notice. They just go about their business like nothing happened.'

Miller nodded at the clasp on Brand's tunic. 'Where did you get the combat medal?'

'North African landings last year. I don't think anybody here realises how God-dam hard and hairy amphibious operations are.'

Miller nodded. 'Some of our troops think it's going to be a breeze. Get over there and straight down the road to Paris. No problems.'

Brand asked: 'How many personnel do we have here right now?'

'I came with the advance party, headquarters, a handful of guys, but right now, today, in transit, about two thousand soldiers and a hundred vehicles. Every couple of weeks it changes. They'll move on and another bunch will move in. God knows where they're all going. It's a small country.'

Brand looked at a photograph on the desk. 'Your wife,' he nodded. 'And your dog.'

'Both called Adele,' said Miller.

'You called the dog after your wife?'

'No. My wife's family breed Dalmatians, and when Adele was

born they'd just won Best in America or something so they named the baby after the winning dog.'

Brand glanced at him quizzically and said: 'How about that.'

Miller opened the door and led the way into the bare corridor. 'This is some old house,' said Brand.

'It's aged more in four years than in four hundred.' Miller tapped the frame of the window and a wedge of wood and ancient paint came away. He nodded at the muddy field outside, sloping away into the green spring countryside. It was patterned with huts, wooden duckboards between them, and in the foreground was a clutter of parked military trucks and jeeps.

'Did our Corps of Engineers construct those quarters?' asked Brand. A few fatigue-clad men were in the vehicle park.

'Some Southern Irishmen built them.'

Brand said: 'The neutral Irish?'

'Right. They go around building things.'

'But they have Germans right there, don't they? In Ireland. An embassy and so forth.'

Miller nodded. 'They sure do. I met a guy who played baseball in Dublin and he said that after the game he found there were two Nazis on the other side.'

'It gets crazier,' said Brand. 'So what do you do with the boys when they get here?'

'Keep them occupied. Send them on long marches, mostly. I march with them myself to keep in shape.'

They went back into the room. There was a coal fire in the small grate. 'That's nice,' observed Brand. 'Nice and homely.' Miller suspected he wanted to ask something. Brand made to pull up the armchair, intending to sit on the arm, but prudently changed his mind and took a small wooden chair instead.

'It's these I can't figure,' he said. From his pocket he took an assortment of small change. 'All these cute little coins, for Christsake.' He put them on the desk. 'Now I can get along with the pound note and the five pounds. But, God help me, what is thirteen and a tanner?'

'I know, I know,' laughed Miller. 'After dollars and cents it's crazy. A tanner is sixpence, so thirteen and a tanner is thirteen full shillings and half a shilling.'

'You don't say.'

Miller spread the coins out and told Brand each one's value. 'There's half a penny like this,' he said, pointing to the small brown coin. 'Called the ha'penny.'

'That's the smallest.'

'Unfortunately, no. There's a farthing which is half a ha'penny. There are nine hundred and sixty farthings to a pound.'

'This is fun,' said Brand unhappily.

'And this is a shilling, also known as a bob.' Miller felt in his own pocket. 'And this is half a crown, known as half a dollar, and a threepenny bit . . . not "piece" but "bit".'

'Which is called . . .?'

'A joey, but not so often. I've had to learn this the hard way, being Administration Officer. I have to deal with the English milk sellers. There's a two-shilling piece called a two bob.'

'Ah! That's easy.'

Miller showed him the coin. 'It says "one florin" on it. And a ten-shilling note which is called ten bob. That's half a pound since there are twenty shillings to a pound.'

'It's so exciting.' Brand picked up the half-crown.

'Half a crown,' recited Miller. 'It's the biggest in size.'

'So two of these make a crown?'

Miller shook his head and said: 'There's no crown. Two make five shillings.'

'Oh, exactly.'

He paused, then said: 'Why do they use the letter "d" instead of "p" for a penny?'

'I don't know,' admitted Miller.

'And they teach all this to English kids in school?'

'Sure thing. Kids soon learn about money.'

Brand looked hopefully at his fellow American. 'And that's all? There's no more? Tell me there's no more.'

'There's a guinea,' said Miller. 'But it's used by lawyers mostly, or if you want to buy a civilian suit of clothes which, believe me, you won't. That's a pound and a shilling. When they buy racehorses, they deal in guineas.'

'No racehorses, I promise. Anything more?'

'No, that's it. Sometimes you hear the British talk about a sovereign, but it's mostly just talk now. It went out of use. The sovereign.'

'It's redundant. Good.'

'It was known as a Jimmy O'Goblin.'

'Jesus.'

It was Sunday morning. When Miller went through the low front door into the Pagets' house there was the sound of a man and a woman singing about a nightingale in Berkeley Square. He sniffed the pleasing, homely smell of a roast lunch cooking in the kitchen.

'Ann Zeigler and Webster Booth,' Geoffrey Paget told him, nodding at the wooden wireless. 'It's *Forces Favourites* on the BBC. Do you listen to that?' He poured a sherry for the American.

'Most of our fellows listen to AFN, the American Forces Network,' said Miller. He had absorbed himself into the village through the pub and the church; he had even been to the annual social of the cricket club. The Pagets had become his friends.

'We usually listen to the Home Service,' said Paget. 'Jazz and crooners aren't for us.'

Emma Paget came from the kitchen, a grey lock of hair adhering to her forehead with steam. 'This is such a nice song,' she sighed. 'Berkeley Square.' To his surprise she sang a pleasing snatch with the wireless duet. 'So romantic, pre-war. Will you stay for lunch? If you don't mind having just one slice of beef.'

The American sat in the now familiar chair by the fire. 'I won't stay,' he said. 'I just dropped in to say goodbye.'

The English couple looked distressed. 'That's awful,' said Emma. She moved forward involuntarily and touched his shoulder with affection. 'We thought, we hoped, you'd be here for a long time.'

'It's a pity,' said Geoffrey. He filled each of the glasses.

Miller smiled. 'The run on your sherry supply is finished.' He lifted the slender glass. 'I've enjoyed it but not as much as your company. I'm leaving tomorrow.'

Emma began wiping her eyes and blaming the kitchen steam. 'Nowhere dangerous, I hope.'

'Highly dangerous,' he grinned. 'London.'

'We'll miss you,' said Geoffrey slowly. 'Perhaps you will be able to have a drink with Martin. If he's still up there.'

'We don't know where he is,' said Emma like a complaint. 'He wrote when he went back after Christmas and we had a postcard from Bournemouth, of all places.' She nodded at the mantelpiece over the low fire. 'It's up there. Goodness knows what he was doing in Bournemouth.'

Geoffrey sniffed. 'He wasn't sunbathing.'

Emma almost blurted: 'He had a long burn on his hand and arm. He said it was from a motor car.'

'Cars get hot,' said Miller.

The woman announcer on *Forces Favourites* ended the programme and asked God to bless all who listened. Swirling strings played the signature tune. Geoffrey turned the knob then and as an afterthought said: 'Perhaps you want to hear the news?'

Miller held up his hand. 'I heard it at breakfast.'

'It's better,' said Geoffrey. 'But only a little.'

It seemed as if they wanted to tell him something. 'It's so sad and so long,' said Emma. 'Is it ever going to end?'

'I sure wish I knew,' said Miller.

'You'd be able to go home,' said Geoffrey, seeming suddenly very old. 'This village, this small place,' he said, 'has twelve sons who will never come back. And two daughters. There'll be a village war memorial with their names carved on it. There's one from the last war, twenty names. Five for each year.'

'I've read them,' said Miller. 'Outside the church.'

There was the sound of a vehicle drawing up outside. 'Harcourt,' said Miller. 'I have to go.' There came a tentative knock from the front door.

They called, the latch sounded and Harcourt bent to get under the transom. 'He's been promoted,' said Miller. 'Private First Class.'

They congratulated him and he grinned his big white grin and said: 'Sure thing. More bucks.' He pointed to the inverted stripe on his arm, then hesitated. 'And Lieutenant Miller . . .' He looked towards Miller '. . . is now Captain Miller.'

They all shook hands. Miller said: 'They had to give us something to make up for leaving here.'

'Would you like some acorn coffee, Benji?' asked Geoffrey. 'We know how you like it.'

The tall black man glanced at Miller. 'I don't think so today,' he said carefully. 'But it was good. Really good.'

They shook hands again and Emma embraced Harcourt and then Miller. 'God be with you,' she sniffed. 'And keep you safe.'

'Safe from all the temptations of London,' said Geoffrey, trying to smile. 'Especially you, young man.' He poked Harcourt on the middle button of his tunic. 'Be careful of the wicked women up there.'

'Sir,' said Harcourt seriously, 'the first thing I aim to do is to find a Southern Baptist Church. If I can't, then any Baptist church will be okay.'

General Dwight Eisenhower, the newly appointed Supreme Commander of the Allied Expeditionary Forces, had arrived in London and by mid-February 1944 was established in one of the tall Georgian houses in Grosvenor Square as his home and headquarters. At once, as if they had been told, the Germans began in earnest to bomb the capital again, after an interval of three years, much of the attack falling on the Mayfair and Belgravia districts surrounding the Supreme Commander. Art Galleries and fine-art businesses were destroyed overnight; there were books, some rare, two feet deep in the next London square to the Invasion Headquarters, the result of a direct hit on the London Library. A damaged barrage balloon settled like a silver roof over Wandsworth prison, causing fear among the convicts, and a stuffed crocodile from a famous antique shop lay in an apt pool caused by a burst water main in St James's. General Eisenhower said he preferred to be in the country and, at night, he moved to quieter quarters outside London.

In Russia the Red Army encircled five German divisions who refused to surrender and were slaughtered in the snow. In the Pacific the island of Kwajalein was taken by American Marines with one hundred and forty-two dead against a Japanese loss of five thousand soldiers; the British Fourteenth Army stemmed the final attempt by Japan to invade India and the RAF dropped 2,500 tons of bombs in under forty minutes on Berlin. The war was turning a circle. Fighting in the mud and mountains of Italy was suspended by a temporary cease-fire so that both sides could bury their dead, and Allied soldiers and Germans were photographed sharing cigarettes among the bodies of their comrades. A foggy, freezing winter in Britain meant that the shops had few fresh vegetables apart from baleful swedes and turnips. The *Kitchen Front* programme on the BBC broadcast a recipe for swede-and-turnip casserole.

Captain Miller and Private First Class Harcourt drove towards London on a Monday morning that again was tinged with spring, the low hills and fields a promising green but the trees still naked. Rivers reflected the placid sky. Smoke wriggled from cottage chimneys for there was still enough wood, though little coal except at Swindon, which was on their route and where railway loco-motives were replenished and the inhabitants found ways of diverting small quantities of steam coal to their own hearths.

The road went through the town and on to Marlborough, Newbury, Reading and eventually into London, but it was a protracted journey. Military vehicles were on the road, American with their white star signs, British troops flying pennants from armoured cars, Polish, Canadian, and an Indian battalion, dark eyes embedded below turbans.

'I guess those oddball hats keep the guys warm,' said Harcourt. Miller had told him to pull up in front of a thatched inn. They went in below the wooden sign showing St George and the Dragon. The wet-moustached landlord smiled as he saw Miller but his face dropped when Harcourt ducked under the door. Harcourt knew the look. 'Maybe I'll go and stay with the car,' he suggested.

'You need a break,' said Miller. He caught the publican's expression. 'Anything wrong?'

'We can't have blacks in here,' said the man bluntly. He was wiping a glass and he began to do so defiantly.

'What exactly does that mean?' said Miller.

'I'll leave,' repeated Harcourt.

'You stay,' said Miller.

'No blacks,' repeated the landlord. He was polishing the beer glass so fiercely that it cracked loudly in his hands. He said something under his breath and threw it in a bin. 'US Provost Marshal's orders. It's not my rule, it's yours. Blacks and whites don't mix. There's been too much trouble, too many fights.'

Miller kept his dismay, his anger, in check. Once again Harcourt said: 'I'll leave.'

'You'll have to,' said the publican. 'Because I won't serve you. There's enough battles going on in the world without having one on my premises. There's one of your truck depots down the street and if those whites have seen you come in, they'll be in after you.'

'I'll leave,' repeated Harcourt yet again. 'I don't want no trouble.'

'We'll both leave,' said Miller. 'Sometimes I can't figure who's fighting who in this war.'

The landlord picked up another glass and leaned on the bar. 'Not my rules, like I say, but your Military Police – snowdrops you call them, isn't it? And I got a consignment of whisky delivered this morning, two whole bottles, and I mean to keep them, not smashed over somebody's head like the last time.'

When they returned to the car Harcourt said: 'Sir, I'm used to this. It's worse than Stateside. In America we know where everybody stands, we just keep with our own kind.'

Miller scowled. 'It's a God-dam scandal nothing's been done about it.'

'They *do* things about it,' said Harcourt, starting the engine. 'Like hit you between the eyes with a knuckleduster. Some guys got into a brawl in Bridgwater last week and six whites, six coloured ended in hospital. But the British put them in the same medical ward and they started fighting again. Smashed the hospital.'

For ten miles they drove in silence. Then Miller said quietly: 'Stop along here, Benji. There's a place. We've got to eat something.'

'Where the pot is hanging, sir?' said Harcourt.

'Right.'

It was called the Copper Kettle and a bulbous and shining kettle was suspended outside. The bay window was screened with lace curtains and steam. Cautiously they went inside. A feathery woman in a flowered pinafore smiled genuinely. 'Welcome, gentlemen. You're just in time. We're running out of food.'

Five of the dozen tables were occupied. Harcourt made a quick check but all the customers were civilian. 'It's okay then, ma'am? You take blacks?' he asked loudly before Miller could speak.

The woman was nonplussed. 'Black what?'

Miller laughed and said: 'We just had a little trouble back there. The pub wouldn't allow coloured people.'

A shocked and haughty expression climbed on her face. 'Oh, we wouldn't allow any nonsense like that,' she said. 'Here's a table. Let me tell you what we have.'

Other people in the restaurant were grinning. 'Everybody but Germans and Japs served in here,' said a crimson-faced man struggling into his overcoat. 'And conscientious objectors.'

'What about farmers?' suggested another man, still seated. 'And auctioneers,' retorted the one who was leaving. Some of the other customers laughed.

The woman warbled: 'We don't have any disturbances of that nature in here. The Copper Kettle is democratic. If there were any nonsense, our Margaret Rose would deal with it.' She simpered a little. 'The same name, of course, as one of our little princesses . . . Ah, she heard me mention her. Here she is.'

The Americans looked up and saw a fat, aproned woman filling the doorway to the kitchen. She had hairs sprouting on her face and a belligerent eye, and she was holding a steaming saucepan.

'We get the picture,' smiled Miller.

'Beans on toast,' mused Miller, attempting a genteel English accent once they were in the car again. 'Egg on toast, sardines on toast.' They laughed at the memory of the feathery woman holding aloft a thin tin of sardines like some trophy.

'The egg was good, sir,' said Harcourt. 'Best single egg I ever did eat. And, sir, that toast . . . wow, that toast.'

'The sardine was fine,' said Miller. 'And I agree about the toast.'

Through the closing afternoon they continued towards London in the military traffic. A squadron of British tanks was being transported on long, flat-bed trailers, the pulling trucks snorting fumes, just negotiating the two-lane road. A shop had been demolished to facilitate their turning of a tight village corner. 'They pulled somebody's store down,' observed Miller. Harcourt said: 'Tomorrow they call in the engineers and build it up again. Then maybe knock it down the next time.'

As they tentatively overtook each of the trailers and tanks they saw, tucked in the middle of the convoy like a brightly painted toy, an electrically propelled milk float, jolting to keep pace with the gigantic vehicles.

It was almost dark by the time they reached the suburbs. Harcourt had spent a day studying the route maps but suddenly, faced with the darkening horizon, he became unsure. 'There's a snowdrop at the crossway here, captain,' he called back to Miller. 'Maybe he'll know?'

Harcourt wound down the window as they approached the military policeman in his white helmet, belt, gaiters, and white gloves directing the army traffic, but he had no time to ask the question. The snowdrop thrust out a finger grunting: 'London that way.'

'We need this street called Bayswater Road,' complained Harcourt as the white glove waved them on. 'I can see London.'

They reached Hammersmith, where grimy double-decker buses circled the bombed ruins. 'They got buses like houses,' mused Harcourt. 'People upstairs.' There were crowds moving thickly along the pavements, heads down in the chilly blackout. 'Everybody's heading the same way,' said Miller.

'Going home,' said a British policeman, also wearing white gloves. 'Rush hour.' He had a service revolver, massive and antique, in a holster at his hip. Harcourt had stopped and asked directions and then enquired, a little nervously, about the hurrying people. 'I thought maybe there was a Nazi air raid going on,' he said to the policeman. 'People getting to shelter.'

'All quiet at the moment,' said the constable. 'Tonight Jerry will be back, I expect. He's turned up every night for a week.' He gave them directions to Bayswater Road.

'After that I have to find Wormwood Scrubs, sir,' said Harcourt to his officer. 'That's where my quarters are. On the map it looks like they have some prison there.'

'Maybe you'll get parole,' said Miller.

Harcourt laughed and said: 'Don't tell my mom, sir.' He stopped the car again and this time asked an airman on the pavement for directions. The man was Czechoslovak but he knew the way. 'One hour later and you could follow the lines of women,' he said mysteriously. The car crawled forward, its narrowed headlights barely pointing the way. 'No lights and wrong side of the street,' grumbled Harcourt. There were buildings on the left but beyond the other pavement there were trees and the lighter grey of the sky. 'That's a park, sir,' said Harcourt, proud to have got the map right. 'They call it Hyde Park. Looks like it's hiding right now.'

They turned into a dark square, the car crawling around the corner from the main road. A man in American uniform flagged them down. Another uniformed man took Miller's bag as he turned, shook hands with Harcourt and thanked him. The doormen glanced at each other as the black man saluted.

'They'll tell you when I need you, Benji,' said Miller. 'I think we may be doing a little travelling, you and me.'

He turned to the two doormen. 'Would you direct my driver to . . . where was it, son?'

'Place called Wormwood Scrubs,' said Harcourt.

'Transit camp or the prison?' smirked the man with Miller's bag.

Harcourt fixed him with a steady eye. 'The camp — at this moment,' he said. 'I ain't done nothing yet.'

Chapter Eleven

There was a reception area in the American Officers' Club, warm, well lit and comfortable, like a hotel. Bright lights were reflected in mirrors from a cocktail bar in one corner and in the lobby was the sound of a subdued Tommy Dorsey dance tune. At the desk was a message that Miller was to report to Colonel Henry Jeffries at eight o'clock that evening. An escort would pick him up. It was now six thirty.

He hesitated, then went straight to the bar and gratefully drank the first Manhattan he had tasted since leaving the United States. He felt like having another, but thought maybe he'd better not. Colonel Henry Jeffries might not like it. He found his room, narrow but neat, tested the bed and had a shower. At seven he was back in the lobby.

An army chaplain was also standing waiting. 'Just got here?' he enquired.

'A couple of hours ago. I've been in Western England. What's it like?'

'London? Speaking as a man of God I could tell you it is like Sodom and Gomorrah,' said the padre. 'Sin everywhere. But in these times quite a lot of folks believe in sin. Deeply.'

He was from Maine. 'I've been getting around some of the churches here,' he said. 'What's left of them. They've been rocked about and whole pieces have been blown away, masonry and so forth, bell ropes gone missing. So until the war's over they mostly don't want to risk using them. They've got this great, darn bell at St Paul's Cathedral and the first time they tolled it, they say everybody – clergy, choir, congregation – dived for cover.'

Cautiously Miller said: 'I heard the Germans have started bombing again.'

'And how. Are you feeling nervous?'

'Nobody else seems to be. It's one way of getting to know what it's like to be under fire, I guess.'

The chaplain pointed a long clerical finger. 'See that door marked with a letter "S". That's the air-raid shelter. If it gets too hot, get your ass down there quick. I'll be right ahead of you. Even God has His limits.'

'How is it? The bombing.'

'Noisy. But to see it, kinda beautiful. Two nights ago I got brave and, with some English people who were visiting, I went outside on the veranda on the upper floor and took it in. The bombers, four Nazi bombers, were clear like crosses in the moonlight over the park across the street. The searchlights had fixed them, shining up from all over London, and you could see the puffs of anti-aircraft shells exploding. It was almost heavenly, if it hadn't been such a helluva racket.'

'How about the British?'

'Now and then they duck. Nothing more. When the air-raid warning sounded, and that's enough to scare the pants off you, most folks in this building scuttled for the shelter. But not the British barman or the cocktail waitresses. They just carried on. It gave them a laugh, I guess, but once you've been hunched in the shelter about an hour and nothing's happened, no direct hits, no bombs nearby, then you come out kinda embarrassed, and in the end you don't go down at all unless the racket gets really close.'

'Do you know where there's a Southern Baptist Church?' asked Miller.

The chaplain blinked but then reached for his pocket. 'My driver,' said Miller, 'is anxious to locate one.'

'There's a Baptist chaplain, Billy Longo, who's a good preacher. Not Southern Baptist, but as near as dammit. They have a church, somewhere . . .' He had produced a list. 'Right, Wandsworth, not too far from the centre of town. The building was damaged in the big raids of 1940, but the GIs have patched it up. It's been turned into an American church. I went to a service there. Great choir, great singing.'

'And everybody gets along, no colour barriers?'

The padre glanced at him. 'The white singers in the choir sit on one side of the church and the black singers on the other.' He looked downcast. 'They say they like it that way.'

Lieutenant Danny Gonzales drove Miller into darkened London. 'These women on the sidewalks,' said Miller unbelievingly, 'are they all . . . all . . .'

'Prostitooots!' exclaimed Danny. 'That's what they are, captain. They ain't waiting for a bus.'

He laughed a touch sourly. 'End-to-end sex, this town,' he said. 'If it's not whores, it's young good-time girls on the make. Try going to the movies, full houses and in the dark it's like a rolling sea. And there's bars and dives and dancehalls, all crowded with GI Joes and what the English call tarts.'

They drove into quieter streets, gaps between the buildings outlining them like huge tombstones against the night sky. 'That's old damage,' said Danny, as if he were a long-time resident. 'From the 1940 Blitz. But here, at the corner, is a place where a high explosive came down only last week. Nobody's going to live there any more.'

'Anybody killed?' asked Miller.

'Maybe. I didn't hear. The British never admit to casualties anyhow. They'll come up with some figure sometime. They generally only detail the planes they've shot down and nobody believes that. There wouldn't be any *Luftwaffe* left.'

He swung the car into a square, blocked off and with a sentry post at the entrance. He showed his papers and said: 'For Colonel Jeffries.'

'He just got back,' said the sergeant. The man with the fixed bayonet stayed motionless; only his eyes moved and they were on the sky.

'Expecting bombers?' asked Danny.

'You tell me, lieutenant. They called around last night and the night before that. We had guys out helping to pull civilians from a hotel around the corner. Some dead.' The barrier was lifted and they drove in.

Gonzales remained on the ground floor while Miller went up in an old and narrow elevator escorted by an American army girl with a big bust. There was scarcely an inch between them.

'Where do you hail from?' he asked.

'Buffalo,' she said. 'New York.'

There were only five floors. On the landing waited a sergeant who saluted and showed him into a fine, large room, with a heavy desk in front of thick velvet curtains over the bay windows. 'Colonel Jeffries will be right with you, captain,' said the sergeant. 'He asks that you take a seat.'

The furniture seemed to be from the original house, before it was requisitioned; gilt chairs with red cushions were lined along a wall with a panoramic painting of a battle above them. He had to lean close to see the title: 'The Field at Waterloo'.

The full lights went up in the room. 'Famous victory for the British, Waterloo,' said Colonel Jeffries as he entered. He had a slight stoop, was greying and had dark hoods around his eyes. 'With the help of the Austrians who arrived late but in time. They often need a little help in battle, the British.'

He indicated that Miller should sit down.

'I'm going to have a drink,' said the colonel. 'I need a drink by this time of the day. Will you join me? I'm taking a rye on the rocks.'

Miller thanked him. The colonel cocked an eye at the sergeant and said: 'Large ones.'

Jeffries sat uncomfortably behind the desk. 'I hope to God there'll be someplace to put my feet up at the end of D-Day,' he yawned. 'We've got to capture just one house, one house, with an easy chair. I'm getting too weary for war.'

Miller smiled seriously and said: 'Maybe everybody will be able to put their feet up, sir.'

'I hope so, but I doubt it, captain. If the invasion is anything like the planning meetings we'll be on our feet a good deal longer than that. Eisenhower seems to be running on electricity. From seven thirty this morning until now . . .' He looked at his military watch. 'Eight ten. The guy doesn't stop.'

The sergeant brought a tray with the drinks. They raised a glass to each other. 'And today,' said the colonel, 'we had the added attraction of Montgomery, the British big hero. Christ, he's got a voice like my sister's little dog. You feel like throwing him a bone.'

'He's a popular commander,' said Miller cautiously.

'Oh, sure. He's had a major victory. El Alamein. And they haven't had too many of those. But the guy *barks*.'

He took a deep drink of the rye whiskey and closed his eyes in appreciation.

'How long you been in this country?'

'Eight weeks.'

'I've been here eight months. I don't like it. France, even Germany, can only be better.' Jeffries shrugged. 'Well, captain, you're going to be seeing some more of it. The Training Inspectorate is being expanded, and how. There'll now be fifty inspectors of different kinds and you'll be one.' He rose from the desk, went to the window and stared at the folds of the velvet curtains with the same intensity as if he were examining a distant view. He kept his back turned. 'This is because the training standards are falling way below what is acceptable in the US Military. If we send these men into action in their present state of readiness they are going to finish up dead in the ocean. Floating.'

He turned from the curtains with dismay in his face. 'Something's got to be done and we're running out of time. Everybody from Eisenhower down, including the barking dog, knows this. Montgomery has even sold Ike on a scheme in the West of England where he conducted some pre-war manoeuvres, an amphibious landing in . . .' He glanced at a document he ruffled on his desk. '... Yeah, Devon.' He sniffed. 'And that showed some foresight for the British, a landing from the sea prior to the war, all of six years ago. Maybe he's cuter than we think.'

Jeffries looked into his empty glass as if he could do with another rye but desisted. Miller asked: 'Why are the training schedules so bad, sir? I did parachuting training Stateside and everybody was pretty gung-ho. I think the rest of the military felt the same. Some guys seemed to think they could sail straight to invade France without even any build-up in this country. Right in there to the nearest beach.'

'Tell that to Snow White,' said Jeffries. 'It was okay in America, the training, but this is not America. There's no *room*, captain. Not enough space. It's small this country, and rained on, and difficult, and you can't train an army – not one this big, eventually two million men or more, not correctly, satisfactorily. There are only two areas that are any use for training. One is Salisbury Plain which the British have used for years. But they don't have a big army. The other is somewhere in north England. In Wales and Scotland it's mountains, or what they call mountains locally, but they're big enough to get in the way. Christ, we've had paratroops practising by jumping out of God-dam trees! There's not sufficient airspace to give them enough drops for proper training.' He shook his head and muttered: 'Trees,' again and then to himself: 'Trees.'

'As for amphibious landings,' he continued, 'well, have you seen the sea around this itty-bitty island? It's so rough that we haven't been able to get men in the boats, let alone out of them and on to beaches.' Now he appeared a touch embarrassed. 'And some of the people in charge of training have not been people Uncle Sam would have wanted. There seems to be an attitude that somebody else, the next guy, will win the battle, anybody but us. Well, that's not going to happen, captain. There *is* nobody else. Some, who are seriously screwy, believe that the Germans will turn tail and run like fuck. Well, that's not going to happen either.'

He sat behind the desk, his shoulders slumped like a failed

managing director. 'You won't believe this, Captain Miller, but two weeks ago we got a nice day and simulated a landing on a beach, walking the men to the tide line because the boats would have been sunk in the swell – and just while we mention it, there's not enough landing-craft either, not so many as you can afford to have them wrecked. In Washington there are politicians who want them all sent to the Pacific. They think this situation, the big invasion of Europe, is nothing more than some sideshow.'

'That's incredible,' said Miller.

'It is, but keep it quiet. Morale is a factor too.' He made a motion with his clasped hands and the sergeant appeared. Jeffries pushed his glass towards him. 'Another one, Frank. And one for Captain Miller.' The drinks came and Jeffries waited until the sergeant had left the room. 'This landing we fixed, this simulated beach landing,' he continued. 'With the assault troops just kidding they had come ashore good and dry, and with no opposing fire, and advancing up the beach. Great, but then there was a breakdown in orders, some communications screw-up or somebody had gone for coffee or some damn story, and once they were on the beach nobody told the invaders what to do. So, d'you know what they did?'

'Went home,' guessed Miller.

'Worse. They hung about for a while, then they dug cute little holes in the beach, in the dunes, and they climbed into them and hugged each other and . . . and they went to fucking *sleep*.'

Miller choked on his whiskey. 'Exactly,' said the colonel. 'That was my reaction. Asleep, for God's sake. Taking a nap in action.'

He stood and went to the window again. 'That's got to stop. The breakdowns have got to stop. We've brought in a further twenty inspectors and you're the most senior. There's not a lot of time. Four months, maybe less.' He stood up and held out his hand, still scowling. 'Go to work, captain.'

As Miller reached his door he said: 'As from tomorrow a number of exercises will be using live ammunition. That should stop them snoozing.'

*

The same busty army girl took him down again in the lift. 'Ever been to Buffalo, captain?' she asked on the five-floor journey. Again he was conscious of the tight space between her tunic buttons and his. He said he had never been to Buffalo.

'I used to hate that place,' she said sadly. 'But now I love it. Oh, boy, I wish I was back.'

As they reached the ground floor and he stepped out, the air-raid sirens sounded. He said to Gonzales, who was waiting: 'I've never heard them before, not for real.'

'This will be for real,' said the lift girl. 'Every night they come back. Keep your heads down, sirs.'

He caught the lieutenant's eye. 'You want to stay?' asked Gonzales.

The lift girl warned hurriedly: 'You'd better get going. This building could get a direct hit. We're closing up anyway.'

They went out into the dark square and found their eyes rising apprehensively to the sky. The sergeant at the gate was eyeing it too, as was the sentry. Guns began to sound very close. 'In the park,' said the sergeant.

'What should we do?' Miller asked Gonzales.

Hurriedly they got into the car. 'I've not been out in a raid,' said Gonzales, his face taut. 'I've always got into a shelter. This is a time you don't need fresh air.'

He started the car and they skidded noisily out of the gates. The sergeant gave them half a salute, half a wave, glad to see them go. The streets were deserted. 'They've been targeting this area,' muttered Gonzales, 'because they know Eisenhower has his headquarters around here.'

Immediately there was loud gunfire overhead and a flash of explosive light that reflected against the buildings and was quickly followed by two more detonations. Shrapnel from the bursting shells showered the street. The car seemed to leap. Gonzales shouted: 'They're bombing us!' but hung on to the wheel. He braked.

'Don't stop!' exclaimed Miller. 'It's the AA guns.'

Searchlights were swinging in the sky.

'We might be driving right into a bomb,' said Gonzales.

'The bomb may drop here,' said Miller.

To his consternation, Gonzales stopped the car and opened the door. 'Let's go, captain,' he said, breathing hard. 'They tell you to get out of your car and take cover.' Miller felt sweat on his hands.

Another burst of vivid gunfire detonated overhead. Miller shouted and followed the lieutenant who was reinforcing his cap with his hands and running for a stone arch. Shielding his head in the same way, Miller ran after him. They crouched against the masonry of the arch and peered up fearfully. 'Never had any training for air raids,' said Gonzales. 'Me neither,' said Miller. 'Somehow they forgot.'

'We should have brought our helmets.'

As the shrapnel continued clinking like heavy rain, a slight woman in a fur coat and a hat with a feather appeared and sedately took shelter alongside them. 'Fuckin' guns,' she said plaintively.

Miller and Gonzales stared at her. ''Scuse my bloody French,' said the woman. 'But those buggers blastin' off like that. They're a lot more dangerous than the soddin' bombs.' There was a further sharp clink of shrapnel. 'If one of those lumps 'it you on the napper,' she said, 'it would go straight through you and out of your bum.'

'Is that so,' said Miller.

'Is that so,' said Gonzales.

'I been workin' down 'ere for years,' she sniffed. 'In the proper Blitz. I used to wear a tin hat on my 'ead. Only sensible. I took it off indoors, of course.'

'You . . . work here?' said Gonzales stupidly.

'It's my beat,' she said in a proprietorial way. 'I live in the East End but I come up every night on the bus.' She turned an angry look on the sky. Her profile was abruptly illuminated. 'Them with their searchlights and their guns. All that row and chucking down any old iron. I'd like to know 'ow many bloody bombers they shoot down.'

She turned to them fully for the first time and they saw she had a sharp pointed face that might once have been pretty. 'That shrapnel stuff kills people,' she told them. 'A lot of poor geezers died because of ovver things apart from the bombs. Beffnal Green tube, nearly four 'undred 'ad their lot when some bloke tripped and they all fell down the bloomin' stairs. Suvvercated, smovvered. Just panic, not a Jerry bomber in sight.'

'You just . . . walk around in an air raid?' said Miller.

'Got to earn a few bob, mate,' she said airily. 'If you pick your time careful when it's not too busy up there,' she nodded at the sky, 'you can carry on like usual. Lots of the girls do.' She looked at them prospectively. 'I'll give you a short time in 'ere,' she suggested. 'It will pass, 'arf an 'our till the all-clear.'

'Both of us?' said Gonzales, bemused.

'Both,' she confirmed. 'Different times, o' course. I'm not having any of that clever stuff. One can 'ave a short time, and one can look away. Then the ovver.'

Miller grinned. The gunfire had passed over like a fading storm. Gonzales was fascinated. 'How much do you charge?' he enquired.

'Short time? Five dollars. But I've got a room 'round the corner. That's ten.'

Gonzales said: 'Ten dollars. Is that for all night?'

Her nose went up sarcastically. 'No, all bleedin' week,' she said.

Chapter Twelve

Miller's three-year marriage had been one of disappointment but no great surprise. He considered his wife with some sadness now as he read her latest, flimsy letter, his shoulders slightly hunched as he sat on his military bed. Outside the window the London traffic hissed softly in the rain. In Dakota it had been snowing again, normal for February, and one of the dogs, not the favourite Adele who was kept in the house and groomed for special events, had won a best rosette at a show in Helena. There were up to eighteen dogs in the heated kennels outside, too many to fix their names. But he could remember Adele because she was the one snug indoors and, of course, had the same name as his wife.

His wife wrote to him regularly, he thought automatically, every two weeks. There was never anything new in her letters; she might as well have told him she was still five feet, four inches tall and weighed a trifle over a hundred and ten pounds. Dutifully, he always replied within a couple of days but there was not much he could say within the censor's allowance and he realised that his news might sound as if he were on some sabbatical in a country where very little ever happened. Stretching on the bed, he wondered what was now expected of him by the US Army; what it had in mind for him. Was the plan for him to go diligently about his inspection duties, and then to bow out, withdraw unneeded like a bit-part player leaving the stage, when D-Day was finally launched? He did not consider himself a brave man but he had no intention of doing that. He did not plan to observe the greatest military operation in history from the wrong side of the Channel.

The first briefing of the newly reinforced Training Inspectorate had been in a metal hut in the middle of a hundred others, like a pig farm set among the exposed acres of Bushy Park, on the south-west fringe of London. The men, intent as he was, were all military specialists – weapons, logistics, assault techniques, tactics, feeding, care for the wounded and dying, transport, and morale. Some were specialists in a single area but he and nine others were charged with an overall view of the preparation and training for the assault on Continental Europe, whenever, wherever, it might be in the months ahead.

Following the briefing, the officers, strangers to each other, went out into the chill and downcast day and towards the commissary hut for lunch, conversing about everything but what they had just been told: their home states, their families, their baseball and football teams and when the war might be over. Miller asked the waiting Harcourt to drive him to Hampton Court which was next to Bushy Park. The broad red-brick palace of Henry VIII rose like a serene and sturdy backcloth against the scrubby sky, aloof from the war. The Thames outside its walls flowed with grey sluggishness. It was a landscape containing few figures. It was not a time for tourists. The gatekeeper, his old soldier medals on his tunic, said: 'Some of the rooms are closed, sir,' adding: 'open after the war.'

Miller walked into the palace while Harcourt stayed with the car. 'I don't know nothin' about history, sir,' he said. 'All I know about is now.' He had found a friendly church. 'But that Wormwood Scrubs camp ain't no resort, sir. The prison looks nice.'

Alone, Miller went between the tall walls of the palace, his head tilted as he attempted to study the lofty decorations, paintings and ornaments. There was an armoury of ancient weapons fixed to the walls, pikes and axes and early firearms, relics of old wars now forgotten except in books, and he wondered if there had been a Training Inspectorate in those days.

At first he saw no one else. He could have been the only visitor to that echoing, empty, raw place. Walking casually and looking about him, he passed a small brick room, hardly more than a cupboard; it was lit within and looked cosy and enclosed; coming from its sanctuary he heard the faint echo of a radio programme.

Miller's footsteps clipped the stone floor. It was like exploring a tomb. He walked into another chamber and he heard his footsteps joined by others, light, slow, meditative.

He was in a large, dim room with a vaulted ceiling. In one corner of the flagstoned floor was a pile of sandbags and some fire-fighting equipment. Around them came a woman, stepping carefully to avoid a coiled hose. Like the last two people on earth they looked up and smiled towards each other. She was in her early thirties with a slim and tired face, her hair hidden beneath a colourless scarf.

'Not much here that Henry VIII would recognise,' she said.

He laughed quietly. 'He would have wondered about the fire pumps.'

They were standing only two yards apart. 'Some incendiary bombs did fall here,' she said. 'But they managed to deal with them.'

As though they were acquainted and had walked into the building together, they continued on the same path. 'Are you stationed in Bushy Park?' she said. 'Or shouldn't I ask?'

'For today only,' he said. 'I figured I'd take the chance to come over here. I don't know when I'll be able to do it again.' He sensed there was a special reason she was there and she volunteered it, together with her name. 'I'm Kathleen Burgess,' she said. He introduced himself and they walked on through the shadowy passages. 'I haven't been here for ages,' she continued. 'Not since before the war. But I have a friend who lives nearby and she's just lost her husband so I came to see her. I feel very sad about it. He was a prisoner in a Japanese camp and he died at Christmas, aged twenty-eight, but they have only just informed her. For weeks she had been writing to him and he was already dead.'

Miller said: 'That's certainly sad. It's sometimes easy to forget that there's another war the other side of the world, we get so busy with this one.'

'So I came in here for some solace,' she went on, as though she had not heard him. 'It seemed the right thing, the correct sort of place. Better than some church.' She smiled reflectively. 'Perhaps there should be a Society for Solace.'

'They'd be busy right now.'

They were walking in a paved corridor, their footsteps still sounding. An old man, prodding a lawn with a garden fork, looked up at them with brief curiosity. 'Have you been in the chapel?' she asked.

'No. I've only been here a few minutes.'

'It's just along here, if it's open.' She led him down a few dank steps, tried a heavy handle on an ancient wooden door and smiled as it swung open easily, allowing them into a carved chapel, small and sombre, with dark choir-stalls and a heavy bible on a lectern.

'Henry was married here,' she said. 'I don't know how many times.'

Miller grimaced. 'He made some habit of it.'

She laughed quietly. 'I'm an actress,' she said. 'And I was once in a play about the six wives of Henry VIII. It was a very hard-up company and I had to play three of the wives.' She paused.

'I imagine they weren't around at the same time.'

'Certainly not on the stage. It helped with the budget of the play.'

They walked pensively, almost intimately, in step, until they went out to the approach of the palace. The light was fading early. Miller could see Harcourt standing by the car in the distance. 'I'd like to offer you a lift,' he said, 'but Uncle Sam won't let me.'

She smiled with a touch of warmth and said: 'I shouldn't think he would. Don't worry. The station is very close.' They paused and shook hands. 'I'm in a play at the moment,' she said. 'It's in London but for how long I don't know. It's Chekov. *The Seagull.* If you have a moment, why don't you come.'

'I'd like that very much. I'm in London most of the time.'

'Come around to the stage door and ask for me, Kathleen Burgess,' she said. 'You might tell me if you think the play is as gloomy as I think it is.'

They shook hands and slowly went their separate paths. He glanced towards her as she walked and she turned and looked back at almost the same moment. She sent him a slightly embarrassed wave and he waved back. It began to rain quietly and she adjusted her headscarf and walked on.

At ten o'clock in the drab morning they drove through London, on their way to Suffolk. 'The trouble is, sir,' said Harcourt, 'the streets don't look like the map no more.'

'They've been rearranged,' agreed Miller.

Both men were reduced to silence by the gutting of London. It was history now but the signs were still there. Solid buildings had become single walls, caverns, deep holes, the outlines of what had been rooms where patterns of wallpaper could still be discerned. 'All this was three years ago,' said Miller.

Harcourt nodded. 'They cleaned the place since then. Tidied up.' The bombed acres had long been cleared, buildings buttressed, the skeletal walls that remained now weathered into the landscape. Weeds and even bushes were growing from hollowed chimneys, sky looked through holes. A painted slogan on a brick wall demanded: 'Second Front Now!' The words were faded and flaking.

They went through the City, the business streets, where the damaged buildings showed an affronted dignity. Roofless churches stood with the wind rustling through them; perhaps a single remaining wall with the stone tracery of what had once been a stained-glass window. Some office buildings had been lopped to a single floor but people were still working within. Two men were stoically painting a door red. A street sweeper pushed his brush.

Before them the dome of St Paul's rose against the sky like the head of a bald giant. 'Take a look at that, sir,' said Harcourt. 'Still got the roof. I'm going to write home about this.' He took it in again. 'If it's okay with the censor man. That guy cuts out everything except what I get to eat.'

'One day,' said Miller, 'they'll build it all again. Maybe even better. When we beat the Germans.'

To Americans the enemy were Nazis but Miller called them Germans, as the British did. Hun, a First World War word, was scarcely used now, and Boche even less. Now they were Jerry or the Jerries, it was said because the *Wehrmacht* soldiers wore a helmet shaped like a jerry – a chamber-pot. Then, at other times, the whole enemy race was labelled by the name of its dictator – Hitler or, familiarly, Adolf.

'Adolf was over last night again,' said a newspaper seller when they reached London's East End. 'That's every soddin' night this week he's been over.' The grainy-faced man was selling the three London evening newspapers at a penny each. He was sitting on a stool behind an orange box. 'And last night,' he jerked his head up the street, 'the bugger got Clarence Road again. 'E must aim straight for it.'

Miller left the car and his gaze travelled along the shattered houses. Harcourt watched white-eyed from his driver's seat. Firemen, with a red engine, were damping down the wreckage. Another fire engine was preparing to leave. Some houses had been entirely demolished, the walls, ceilings and floors left like an open-fronted cupboard. There was a bed hanging as if it were sliding from a shelf, shabby furniture was piled on the pavement. Roofs had caved in, the guts of the people's homes were hanging out, but a brick chimney stayed staunchly upright. The street was paved with glass, slates and broken bricks, a fountain from a fractured water main spouted almost formally. The air smelt of burning. A postman trudged through the scene, handing a letter and making a comment to an overcoated man sitting round-shouldered on a chair in front of a wrecked house. A woman with a shawl and a shopping basket urged along a toddling child who wanted to splash in the growing puddles; a group of neighbours stood dumbstruck and a frail old man tried to clear the pavement in front of his gate using a dustpan and a hearth brush.

'Six dead,' sniffed the paper seller. 'That makes twenty-three in this street altogether in this war. Two brothers, little nippers, five and six, caught it last night, but the old gran, eighty-odd, not a scratch on her when they lugged her out. All she wanted was her teeth.'

Miller handed him three pennies and the man recited: '*Star, News, Standard*,' as he handed them over. 'Racing papers,' he said. 'All today's runners.' He nodded towards the bomb damage. 'You won't find no news of this mess,' he said. 'They reports that the bombers was over but they won't let on any more. All the news is about Russia or Italy or some place what you've never 'eard of.' A fire engine backed out of the street, the crew's faces black, their eyes seeming sightless.

On a wall was written the same slogan as he'd seen before, in rough, faded paint 'Second Front Now!'

Miller asked the newspaper vendor: 'Who did that?'

The man half turned. 'Oh, that,' he said dismissively. 'Painted by bleedin' lefties, wanting to help out their mates in Russia. Wanted us to invade years ago. 'Cept, of course, them buggers didn't 'ave to do the invading.'

Miller got back into the car and as they drove he looked at the headlines. 'Red Army Traps Germans' . . . 'RAF Pounds Berlin' . . . 'Dockers Threaten Strike'.

They travelled unspeaking, looking at the wide spaces like football pitches in the East End streets, bombed in the Blitz of three years before; ruins that by now had been absorbed into the London landscape, scarcely noticed by the inhabitants.

'My home-town people would never have any idea about this,' ruminated Miller. He thought of Adele and the Dalmatians.

'No, siree,' agreed Harcourt. 'Only pictures in the newspapers or at the movies. It ain't like being here, seeing it real. In Charleston nobody's getting killed, getting their houses blown apart.'

They drove through the bomb-rent suburbs, houses with blanked bay windows, shops with boarded fronts. The inhabitants, wrapped in shabby garments, plodded about their wartime lives. There was a man singing and squeezing an accordion at a corner, only a small dog listening. In a school playground boys with outstretched arms were pretending to be fighter planes.

They reached the first fields, still solid from winter, wind streaming from the East across frozen mud. It looked like Russia. In the distance rose the masts and funnels of ships in the docks, barrage balloons overlooking them. They passed a convoy of lorries carrying what at first seemed to be tanks. When the vehicles had dropped behind, Harcourt said thoughtfully: 'We goin' to fight with wooden tanks, sir?'

'Mock-ups, dummies,' said Miller. 'From the air they look the same.'

'Gee, what they goin' to think of next,' hummed the driver.

'Don't you write that to your mom, or the censor will cross it right out.'

'Dummies,' confirmed Major Al Pitt. He indicated the plywood aircraft shapes spread around the rim of the Suffolk airfield. 'Just like Pinocchio, all made of wood.'

He and Miller sat in his Quonset hut office. There was a rusty electric fire glowering on the floor and a photograph of his wife on the green metal desk. 'Gliders,' he added, '. . . that will never fly. Take a look at the harbours around here – they're full of boats, landing-craft, cardboard and wood. They'd sink before they floated.'

'And German reconnaissance?' asked Miller.

'We let 'em come. We're happy to pose for their pictures. We show them all we've got – trick tanks, vehicles, boats. One of the English carpenters even made a nice kennel for his dog. Maybe Goering's air force will think it's hiding some kind of secret weapon. It's a big kennel.'

'And you think they're fooled?'

'Who can tell? We can only hope to get them in two minds, or more if we can. If they look at this show and think it's a build-up for a landing in the obvious part of the French coast, in the region of Calais, then that's okay with us. But maybe it's a double bluff. Maybe Calais *is* where the landing will really be. I don't know. Nobody tells me.'

He poured Miller a second cup of coffee from a chipped enamel jug. He was ten years older than Miller and weary with the war. 'But tomorrow it's for real,' he said. 'A real parachute drop.'

Miller said: 'The training's been frustrating?'

'Frustrating? That's putting it nicely. We've got the men and we've got the 'chutes but we can't get them working together. The airspace and the ground space available just ain't enough, captain. Then we've got what the English call weather. If it's lousy then the bombers from the bases about here can't fly, but neither can we. When the sun comes out we can't operate either because they want the airspace.'

'I heard that your men had to drop out of trees.'

'Don't kill me. Out of fucking trees, out of windows, anything for a jump, or at least playing at it. We've had to take them in trucks and push them off the tailgate. That's an airborne landing! Why couldn't we have had to invade *England* from *France*. Then we'd have more room.'

'But tomorrow is going to be okay?' asked Miller.

'We've got clearance. After breakfast.'

That morning the East Anglian sky seemed to go beyond even the level horizon. The early March sun was washed out and the wind edgy. 'You can work out why the painters came from here,' said Pitt. 'Constable got famous because of these skies.'

He raised the palm of his hand. 'Straight from Russia, this wind, from the Ural Mountains. Not a thing in between to stop it.'

'How d'you like this place?' asked Miller. They were walking across to a formation of parked aircraft, nine Dakotas, blunt noses held high like sniffing dogs.

'I like it okay. I'm a career soldier and I figure that you *need* to like places, get to know them, or you're just wishing time away, wishing your life gone. On the other hand, it's not such fun as the Philippines pre-war.'

He led the way into one of a series of stark steel huts below pine trees. It was over-warm in there. Men in unzipped flying kit were sitting in cane chairs drinking coffee. On the wall was a Hollywood poster of Shirley Temple and another of Rita Hayworth. Someone had crayoned a black eye on Shirley Temple.

The men did not stand as the officers entered. They were young and languid. Pitt said: 'Okay, you fellows. This is Captain Miller from the Training Inspectorate, US Army, and he's here to check how good or how bad you are. That's his job. He'll be flying with you and he trained with 82nd Airborne at Fort Bragg so he knows the business.'

'I'll just be sitting in.' Miller felt the need to assure them. The young faces surveyed him without enthusiasm. 'I've completed my Airborne training but I don't know about flying a plane, only jumping out of one.'

He looked around. 'Is there a volunteer to take me?'

A round-faced, pudgy-looking youth with tight blond hair saluted casually and said: 'Sure, I'll fly you, sir.'

'With him up front you'll *want* to jump,' said another of the pilots. There was a guarded laugh.

Miller strode forward and shook the young pilot's hand as he rose. 'Remember, sir,' the youth said, 'up front where we sit there's no room for a 'chute.'

Miller said: 'What's your name?'

'Butterfield.'

Someone called: 'Butterball.' There was another brief laugh.

Some of them had another cup of coffee and Miller talked with them about their home towns, their families, their service life. Same routine. 'We flew these planes across,' said Butterfield as they were walking towards them.

'How were they? Did they behave?'

'They're okay. Slow and heavy. But they won't let you down, sir. It just took one long time.'

'You flew up through Nova Scotia, Greenland, Iceland?'

'Certainly did. Over the top of the world. For ever and a day. But we got here.'

'You always fly the same aircraft?'

'The very one,' said the young man. 'I wouldn't know how to handle one of the others.' At the bottom of the steps leading to the Dakota he stopped and pushed out his hand again to shake with Miller. There were two ground crew sizing up the twin propellers.

They boarded the Dakota. Fifteen paratroops were already crammed in sideways along the hull, piled beneath their equipment. Miller wished them good morning and there were grunts and some nods but none of them spoke.

A small man, seemingly swamped in his flying suit, was waiting in the seat next to the one into which Butterfield now manoeuvred himself. Miller sat behind them. The airman was already wearing earphones and stared intently ahead as though he was not hearing or seeing well. 'That's Rushton,' said Butterfield, talking to Miller over his shoulder. 'He don't talk to no one, except me in exceptional circumstances. Like the plane's on fire.'

Rushton said: 'Good morning, sir,' to Miller as he kept listening and looking fixedly ahead.

'He's from Wyoming,' said Butterfield. 'They all stare like that, way into the distance. They got so much distance in Wyoming.'

He remembered that Miller had said that he was from Dakota. 'You got some good space in your home state, sir. Nice they named this aircraft after it.'

He started first one engine, then the other, stopping all conversation. He began muttering into his mouthpiece and Rushton muttered into his. Theirs was to be the leading aircraft of three. Half turning, Miller watched the engines of the other Dakotas start in clouds of pale smoke.

It took ten minutes to warm the engines, then they were waved on by the ground-control man, his orange overalls vivid in the wan daylight. The plane coughed and began to turn, then straightened, trundling towards the concrete runway. Rabbits ran away. The sky remained flat. He watched Butterfield and saw how comfortable he was with the clumsy plane, almost ushering, persuading, it on to the runway. 'Here we go,' the young man said as though to himself. The door behind them opened and a para-troop sergeant appeared. 'Okay, loadmaster,' said Butterfield. 'Tell your guys to be ready to leave the earth.'

Miller glanced at him from the tight seat behind Rushton. He felt the glance and half turned. 'They don't mind. They enjoy a joke.'

The loadmaster said: 'We love 'em.' He returned to the back and closed the door.

Butterfield gave the engines more power. The plane seemed glad to be moving and bounded along the runway, taking off with surprising grace and swiftly gaining height across the pale green Suffolk countryside. 'Like an elevator with a view,' laughed the young pilot. He spoke into his mouthpiece, then half turned. 'You married, sir?'

'Who's been asking?' smiled Miller.

'Only me, sir,' said the pilot. 'I got married just before I left the States.'

Miller saw the worry suddenly touch Butterfield's face. 'Is this going to be so dangerous?' he asked. He patted Butterfield's shoulder.

'This will be okay,' said Butterfield. 'But the real thing it ain't. Nobody's shooting to get you.'

Miller sensed his fear. 'It will be straight in to the dropping zone, out go the passengers and then straight out,' he said reassuringly. 'There'll be nothing to it.'

'I hope that's right, sir,' said the young man. 'I've never flown into anti-aircraft fire and this is a farmhorse, not a racehorse.'

It took only minutes to reach the dropping area. Suffolk, sunlit, spread green below them, the blue-grey band of the sea beyond the port engine. 'No wind,' said Rushton suddenly. 'It's quit.' He turned to smile at Miller. 'Today nobody's going to float down into the ocean.'

'It's cold, that ocean,' said Butterfield.

Miller watched and admired them executing a concise manoeuvre, the plane turning, then flattening. Butterfield spoke into his mouthpiece. 'Okay, sergeant. Abandon ship!'

They watched the parachutes open below them like sudden flowers, floating away as the Dakota turned. 'Perfect,' said Miller. 'Great.'

'Best we've done so far,' nodded Butterfield. 'So good, maybe we ought to go and get 'em back and do it again.'

'Real nice day for jumping,' said Major Pitt. He looked from the hut window of his bare office into the drifting afternoon. 'Couldn't have been better.'

Miller nodded. 'Perfect conditions. But the real thing won't be so easy. It'll be a night drop, dawn at latest.'

Pitt clasped his hands and gently pummelled the desk. 'It's got to be. They need to secure targets before the beach landings,' he said. 'These guys have had some night drops but not many.'

'How did they make out?'

'Somebody landed on a roof and woke the people out of bed, and a bunch dropped in the middle of a herd of cows.'

'At least at night the enemy have difficulty locating you.'

'But you don't know where the hell you are,' shrugged Pitt.

He could see Miller was worried.

'It's the pilots,' Miller said carefully.

Pitt looked surprised. 'They're good,' he said. 'First-rate guys. They flew those boxes all the way from the States in all kinds of conditions.'

'Sure, sure. But they've never flown over enemy territory yet.'

'Ninety-five per cent of our ground troops have never set foot on enemy territory. Never had a sniff of action.'

'Nearly all of us,' admitted Miller. 'But these men have only to go in once. In, drop the 'chutes, and out. They may never have to fly into anti-aircraft fire again. But they will this time. This once.'

'You think they'll blow it?'

'They're concerned. There's got to be no going back – not on the big night. We can't have anyone losing their nerve. Anti-aircraft fire can look pretty in the distance, but in front of your face it's not nice. It's frightening. We can't allow them to turn away.'

Pitt said: 'You mean run away.'

'If you are a bomber pilot, okay, you can get away with it,' persisted Miller. 'There's always a next time. But there'll be no next time, this time. They need to get to their target zone and drop their paratroops. Every man they drop is needed. Once they've done it, and only then, they can head for home.'

'As fast as their asses will take them,' nodded Pitt. He looked cornered. 'What's in your mind? Practice drops over Nazi lines, just to get the experience?'

Miller held up his hand. 'It's my job to think about angles, foul-ups that could happen, and we don't want those Dakotas coming back with the paratroops still in the back. There'll be no second try.'

'Okay, what?'

'I'll need to think it through. But I believe that, somehow, some way, those pilots will need to have flown over enemy territory before the big day, even if it's some place of no significance, if there is such a place, where the opposition will be light. Just to make them feel that they've done it – and there's nothing to it.'

'So they fly over, cruise around, see it's all safe and harmless, and come back?'

'That's the idea,' said Miller. 'I'll expand it in my report. And next time I come here I'd like to make a jump myself.' He grinned. 'I got the taste up there today.'

Pitt said: 'You're fit?'

'I believe so. I've kept in shape and I'll get up early and do some track work. Hyde Park is just across the street.' He could see Pitt was still doubtful. 'I've been right through Fort Bragg, in one way, out the other,' he said. 'And I'd like to keep my hand in. Major, I don't intend to sit on my ass and watch all the other guys go off to a war. I didn't come here to do that.'

Pitt understood. 'Next time,' he said, 'I'll see if we can fit you in for a practice drop. But I can't make any promises.'

Miller stood and they shook hands. 'And if I can sell the idea of the pilots getting a taste of enemy airspace,' he said, 'I'll be going with them.'

Chapter Thirteen

By that spring of 1944 the traffic in agents and prospective saboteurs across the English Channel had reached its most active. Although the occupying Germans had built a concrete shield along the French upper coast, north-eastwards into the low countries, extending to Norway, and south to the Spanish border, there were still isolated inlets in Brittany, and landing grounds concealed in the interior of France, where the useful Lysander high-winged monoplane might alight; and there were hidden meadows that could easily accommodate a secret parachute drop.

As far back as 1938, a year before hostilities, the War Office in London had established the roots – a solitary officer and a secret shorthand typist – of a bureau to conduct covert operations in enemy territory and from this, two years later, had grown the initial organisation of the Special Operations Executive.

An eccentric entity, hardly an organisation, it was staffed by unusual people. Its critics have scorned it, alleging that it cost more money and lives than it was ever worth. There was a dashing unorthodoxy to it that at times bordered on the amateur, and it went about even its serious business with a touch of comic opera. The comedy ceased abruptly when agents, some of them brave women, were arrested, tortured by the Gestapo, and executed.

Almost thirteen hundred agents had been shipped and smuggled into occupied France by the springtime before the Normandy invasion of June 1944. Some sections of the French resistance actively shunned them; to others they were just a British oddity, a sideshow. There were some notably failed exploits. One parachutist famously landed on the tiles of a police station; codes were cracked routinely by the Germans who were sometimes aware of secret landings but did not interrupt them, preferring to follow the interlopers back to what the agents believed were safe houses; and it was an astonished and grateful French peasant (or possibly a German soldier) who found a bag containing half a million francs dropped by parachute to finance a guerilla cell that no longer existed.

For all its detractors, however, the Special Operations Executive, one of a number of covert agencies working in France – organisations which at times got dramatically in each other's way – helped, by wireless contact and operatives, to point the often disparate sections of the French resistance in the triumphantly right direction following the Allied landings of June 1944, in sabotaging rail communications and delaying reinforcements.

In London the bureaucracy had proliferated, military fashion, to occupy blocks of Baker Street, a tangle of backstairs offices.

Paget invariably reported at the bureau with a sense of both excitement and foreboding. He did not count himself a brave man nor a particularly resourceful one; nor was he filled particularly with either zeal or hatred. Why they had picked his name he did not know; unless it was out of a hat. This office was a threadbare upper floor only reached once you had shown your pass and spelt out your appointment to the short-sighted man behind the desk by the street door. There were quaintly silly code-names for the people he had to see. Friar was one, Fairy was another. No one liked playing spies more than the spies. They believed it was only faintly daring to take a captured Nazi officer out to lunch at a decent restaurant in the hope that he might become talkative with drink. At senior level the bureau was nothing if not civilised.

At the reception desk on the top floor there was invariably an upper-crust girl with a pearly voice. Whatever her name, she was known as Fanny, the letters FANY displayed on the shoulder flash of her uniform. It stood for First Aid Nursing Yeomanry, a title provoking even more confusion in that den of disguises and subterfuge. Many women agents who parachuted into occupied territories, some never to be recovered alive, were in the ranks of FANY.

Today's Fanny was a pink, plumpish young woman with strong teeth which she concealed for much of the time by not smiling. 'Please wait, squadron leader,' she instructed Paget. 'Fairy will be with you shortly.'

Fairy was. He puffed up the carpetless stairs, cheeks expanded, waving a worn briefcase that appeared to be empty. He tried to regain his breath. 'Would it be beyond the war effort to get somebody to mend the lift?' he demanded. He offered Paget a damp, resigned palm.

'Next week earliest, sir,' Fanny told him.

'What a way to run a war,' said Fairy.

'When I became insistent they asked me if I realised there *is* a war on,' pouted the girl. 'We're in the queue.'

'Behind the War Office canteen, I'll wager.'

'Aliens Archives,' she said.

'Come on in,' the man said in a deflated way to Paget. He was Colonel Peter MacConnel and he preferred his everyday name to be used rather than Fairy, except under operational conditions. He called back through the door: 'Coffee please, Fanny.' Paget could hear her already making it.

MacConnel sat in an oriental armchair with dragons for arms. The room appeared to have been furnished with properties from the stage show *Chu Chin Chow*, including an exotic screen and a bamboo desk.

Fanny brought in the coffee tray. The coffee pot and cups were bluntly stamped with the initials of the War Department. The plump girl poured the coffee and added the cream in a motherly way. 'Saccharin only,' she said sadly. 'Balkans have appropriated the sugar bowl.'

'Damn them,' said MacConnel absently. He thanked the young woman and took a long and longing look at her thickly stockinged legs as she left. 'Sorry to pull you in again so soon, Paget,' he said.

'But you've done so well in the past despite your lack of a convincing French accent.'

Paget said: 'I say I'm from Alsace. Even the Germans think that's amusing.'

'Good, excellent.' He stood up from behind the desk and wandered in a circle. There was a worn, almost ceremonial, ring on the carpet which he had trodden since 1941. 'Agents are always fallible,' he ruminated. 'Not far short of stupid at times. You can only hope that Jerry is even more so. There was a useful chap down at Poitiers, I think, yes, Poitiers, stopped at a barrier, produced his forged identity card, and then absent-mindedly produced *another* with the same photograph and a *different* name.'

He went on: 'Then other dimwits were in a school at night outlining a railway sabotage operation on a blackboard. When they had done they went off home and left the bloody plan chalked *on the board*. You wouldn't believe that, would you?'

'And the Germans found it?' said Paget.

'The school caretaker spotted it first and rubbed it off.' He returned to the desk. 'Anyway. Here you are.' He leaned closer as if to prevent anyone in the empty room overhearing. 'Operation Hole.'

'Hole?' said Paget. 'Who dreamed that up?'

'Me, actually.'

There was no point in apologising. 'It's not bad, as it happens,' said MacConnel, taking no umbrage. 'Reasonably appropriate. There are seventy resistance members, from northern and mid-France, the usual mixture, in prison, awaiting execution. The Germans are just getting the paperwork done. The RAF claim they can drop a bomb accurately enough to breach the wall of the jail and allow the prisoners to make a dash for it.' He studied Paget. 'I know it sounds implausible. I sometimes thought that these blue jobs could hardly hit Hamburg, but they claim they can do it.' He took in Paget's air force uniform as if it were the first time he had noticed it. 'No offence, mind.'

Paget did not take any. He said: 'We're improving.'

'But to hit a single wall strikes me as being a touch difficult.' MacConnel leaned close and studied a sheet of paper. He saw Paget was waiting. 'I expect you want to know what your part in this will be.'

Paget said: 'Yes.'

'It will be in your patch, the area where you have worked before, Bookbinder Circuit, so you'll know the locals. It will be our aim . . . well, your aim . . . to coordinate these resistance bods once they've done their bunk from prison. Try and keep them from fighting among themselves. You know what they're usually like, Gaullists, Communists, general bandits. The local people will hopefully have arranged where to hide them. You're there to sort them into some form of organisation and to make sure that Jerry doesn't recapture them.'

'Seventy of them.'

'Give or take a few. You'll be going in through the sea route.'

'When is it?'

'Soon. It has to be. The Germans will start shooting them.'

Paget knew he would get no more information there. The conversation drifted on to how cricket might recover after the war, how restrictions in restaurants permitting two courses only at five shillings each was ruining decent dining out, how fishing in Scotland had improved now that so many former participants were away fighting.

Just before Paget left, the telephone on the desk jangled and MacConnel picked up the earpiece. 'Right you are. One o'clock at the Ritz.' He held out his hand to Paget. 'The Ritz seems to manage,' he said.

'I'll remember that,' said Paget, who had never been inside the Ritz. MacConnel walked with him towards the door. 'Know anything about Verlaine?' he asked casually.

'Verlaine? It's not somewhere I'm familiar with.'

'It's not a place, it's a chap,' said MacConnel. 'Never heard of him myself. Paul Verlaine. He's a poet, a Frog, or was. Been dead a while.'

'I don't know his work,' said Paget.

'Limericks are more to my taste. Ha! What was that one we used to have fun with in the desert? . . . "There once was a chap of Benghazi, whose arse got stuck in the kazi" . . . or something. Anyway, mug up on Verlaine, will you. We may be needing him.'

Lyon's Corner House was some distance from the Ritz in a number of ways, but it served a wartime tea accompanied by the afternoon melodies of a string quartet. Black-dressed, white-lace-pinafored waitresses, traditionally called nippies, clipped about, busy and balanced with trays, pots of tea, dainty milk jugs and two lumps of sugar per customer. It was a large place, but with a warm and comforting ambience, a low ceiling, peachy lighting, melodic 'Tales from the Vienna Woods' (the rural idyll of Hitler's home land), and the pleasant chink of china.

'It's only Joe Lyon's, but it bucks me up just to sit here,' said Margaret. She wore a neat hat and a fur collar on her dark costume. She unbuttoned it. 'It's warm,' she said. 'And romantic.'

Smiling, Paget held her fingers across the table. 'You must have a good posting to be able to get away for tea,' she said.

'The war doesn't need me this afternoon,' he replied.

The waitress appeared brightly and said her feet were killing her. 'The first thing I'll do when shoes come off the ration,' she told them, 'is to buy a nice soft pair.' They sympathised. 'Mind you,' she added darkly, 'as soon as the war's over they'll throw us old biddies out and get young girls in.'

She brought them tea, the tray held high above the heads in the big room. 'No cream cakes,' she said. 'Though we do get them.'

But there were small buns with a few currants visible and shrimp paste sandwiches. The room was busy with conversation.

Margaret poured the tea and her extravagant eyes came up over the pot. She laughed slightly. 'When I tell the boys about Lyon's they'll think I've been to the zoo.'

He took his teacup from her. She added the milk and they took one piece of sugar each with the silver-plate tongs. 'Will they tell their father about it?' he asked.

'I doubt it. He's as remote from them as he is from me. He says all he wants is peace.'

'Don't we all.'

'He means personal peace. Inward.' She needed to change the subject. 'We've never had a real date, you and I, Martin.'

'Under the conker trees,' he smiled.

'In summer. Now it's like a bit of a dream. These days there doesn't seem to be any room, any time, for anyone to be in love.' The string quartet was playing 'Red Sails in the Sunset'. Quietly she said: 'I want to have a real love affair with you. A longish one.'

His hand went back to hers. 'We could start soon,' he smiled.

'Tomorrow,' she said. 'I have to be back by nine thirty tonight. The children are with somebody.'

'Tomorrow I'll be on duty.'

'In the evening?'

'Yes.' He said it firmly.

Her eyes became mischievous. 'All right, Martin. Tonight.' She held her teacup as though proposing a toast. He lifted his as she said: 'But I still have to be back at nine thirty. We'd better get a move on.'

The house in Warwick Avenue loomed high, neglected, dark. A full-grown sycamore in the front garden rattled irritably, some ornamental masonry was lying flat where it had fallen and the path to the door was padded with last autumn's leaves.

'You're not a burglar in your spare time, are you?' he asked.

'There's not much worth burgling in here,' replied Margaret. 'Some old bits of furniture. The rest is in storage. It belongs to my sister and brother-in-law.' She produced a heavy key and they went up the half-dozen stone steps to the forbidding door. 'I've never been here in the dark,' she said. She took a small torch from her handbag, passed the handbag to him and found the keyhole. There was a rattle, a heavy click and then a creak and a sigh as she turned a tarnished handle and the door swung. Their feet sounded in the abandoned entrance hall. 'Poor house,' she said.

She played the torch across the empty walls and halted its beam on a panelled inner door. 'I wouldn't come in here alone,' she said. 'Not at night.'

'Nor would I,' said Paget. He smiled at the pale, indistinct oval of her face and kissed her. 'In here,' she said, pushing the inner door she had picked out with her torch. 'There are curtains and some of the bulbs work.'

She clicked a switch and two grimy lights in a chandelier flickered and lit making deep shadows. There was a thick round table and some chairs, covered with dust, an almost empty bookcase, damp patches on the walls and outlined spaces where large pictures had hung, a four-seater settee and two bulbous armchairs. 'It's very homely,' said Paget.

'It has hidden secrets,' she whispered, going to a cupboard below the bookcase. 'Champagne,' she said, holding up the bottle. 'Well chilled. Let's go upstairs.'

The puny beam of the torch led their way. The staircase had once been grand, the curving banisters heavy and carved. 'They'll never be back until after the war,' she said. 'Ben's in the Middle East and Mollie won't come to London any more. She's in Scotland. I come every now and again to see the roof hasn't fallen in.' She paused. 'It's the first time I've used the place socially.'

'Wonderful place for a party,' he said on the landing. He heard her giggle and she led him through another wide doorway. The narrow torchlight ran over a cold bed and bulky furniture; open curtains let in a pale suggestion of night sky. She went to the bed and touched a pile of blankets folded at its bottom. 'Not at all damp,' she said in a housewifely way. She turned her eyes on him. 'Now what do you suggest?'

'Open the champagne,' he said.

She said: 'Let's sit in the bed.'

'Glasses?'

'Bathroom,' said Margaret.

She went quickly and he heard the squealing of the tap followed by the sound of water. 'Cobwebs,' she grimaced as she came back. He could just see her face in the thin light seeping through the window.

Martin eased the wire cage from the champagne cork and she went again briskly into the bathroom and returned with a small towel. 'It's cleanish,' she said.

Putting the towel over his forearm, he approached her closely, performed a brief bow and said: 'Champagne for Modom?' He used the towel to extract the cork. It came out with a sharp discharge and at that moment the London air-raid sirens began to howl.

'My God,' she laughed. 'That bang started them off.'

'You don't want to run for shelter, do you?'

'No fear. I feel quite safe here. With you.'

There was only a little froth from the bottle.

'Let's get in the bed,' she said. 'It's a bit exposed out here.'

It seemed so strange; fifteen years after they had first met they were close together in this deserted, cold, old house in London in an air raid, and they were about to make love. 'You go your side and I'll stay this,' Margaret said.

He went to the far side of the wide bed. 'Can you see me?' she asked. She was sitting on the bed.

'Just about.'

'Then I'll start.'

Her shape began to move as she took off the jacket with the little fur collar, then the skirt, and opened out one of the folded blankets. 'I'm getting in the warm,' she said.

He took his clothes off down to his underwear and they climbed into the bed, quaintly still sitting, sipping from their glasses. 'Margaret,' he said quietly. 'You are still wearing your hat.'

She let out a squeal and attempted to pull it away but it got snared by the pins. He helped her disentangle her hair. They fell against each other and kissed and laughed again. He kissed her down her shoulders and her neck. Then she pulled his RAF vest over his head, threw it aside, and bit his chest playfully.

She let him take the brassière away from her breasts and they eased each other gently down into the rough and immediate warmth of the blankets. 'I've waited for this,' she whispered, clutching him, 'for years.'

'I'll try not to lose you again.' As he said it he knew that, in only a matter of hours, they would have no choice.

'God almighty,' she said. 'What wasted time. You're never going anywhere without me again, Martin. We are going to be together always. After the war. Things being what they are, who knows what's going to happen to us. But when it's over we'll be together – and faithful.'

The scratchy blankets oddly comforted their skins. She caressed him and he put his tongue to her breasts. 'Let's start now,' she muttered. 'Don't let's wait.'

He rolled above her and her legs spread at his touch. Then a diffuse silver light moved across the window. Margaret said: 'Searchlights. Don't stop.' Outside, the beams were probing the night sky. For a moment the room became lighter.

'Now I can see you,' said Margaret. 'By searchlight.'

'And I can see you.'

It seemed that from just outside the window sounded the massive crack of an anti-aircraft gun firing from Regents Park, followed by another and a third. Margaret squealed. He covered her with his body and they clutched each other at the long whistling scream of a falling bomb. The explosion shook the room, the glass of the window fell in and the ceiling came down as they lay petrified together in the bed.

Margaret cried out again and he held her as they heard the screeching descent of another bomb. 'Under the bed!' he shouted, jumping over her and pulling her to the carpet. He tried to push her naked body below the bed. The bomb exploded a street away. Choking dust erupted from floorboards and carpet. A standard lamp fell on its face. Glass was flung around the room. Again the guns sounded and the house trembled.

They lay shivering and naked, holding each other on the floor by the bed. The gun fired another salvo and as a pathetic encore, a single picture clattered from the wall.

They sensed the action above them move away.

'Oh, Martin,' she sobbed, half laugh, half cry. 'When will we ever do it?'

'At this rate after the war,' he said.

Cold air came through the shattered window. Covered with plaster from the ceiling, coated with grit from the upheaval of the room, they crawled out. There was a smell of smoke. 'Don't say the sodding house is on fire,' she complained. He staggered to the window. 'It's down the street,' he reported. 'Something is blazing down there.'

'Oh, Martin,' she said, sitting naked among the debris. 'I'll have to go home.' He sat beside her and they hugged each other hopelessly. The champagne bottle was still upright and he picked it up and offered it to her with a wry smile. She drank it from the neck, then handed it to him. 'Bastard Hitler,' she said. 'Spoilsport.'

Paget was picked up by a civilian car, a cumbersome Humber driven by a uniformed woman, at eight the next morning. The driver was young and neat with a face like a coin below her cap and straw-blonde hair pulled back behind her neck. The tone of her voice was upper class and she had the flash of FANY on her shoulder.

'Do you know where we are going, sir?' she asked within a few minutes of beginning the journey. Men were clearing the streets after the previous night's air raid; firemen were still playing hoses on the smoking wreckage of a line of shops, their stocks piled outside. A man in a grey suit, probably the proprietor, stood arms stretched sideways in a shattered shop window like an actor on a small stage.

'No. I hoped you might know,' said Paget.

'Bournemouth,' she replied, regarding him in the driving mirror. 'About four hours if we're lucky. Five if we're not. Everything is ready there.'

He knew what she meant. 'I got as far as Bournemouth last time,' he said. 'But then I was recalled.'

'As happens,' she said. 'Unless that occurs again we will continue to the embarkation point tomorrow.'

Her tone was official, almost prim, as if she had learned her instructions by rote. His mood was not for conversation anyway and he eased himself back in the deep rear seat of the Humber, closed his eyes and wondered about Margaret.

As they had attempted to clean themselves of the dust and the rubble in the house they had discovered there was no water. They tried to brush the debris from them in the eerie half-light coming through the gaping window. There was ceiling plaster in their hair and sticking to their naked bodies.

'The bomb must have fractured a main,' he said.

Sneezing with the dust, she began to laugh softly but with an edge of hysteria. 'Oh, Jesus, Martin. What can I do? I can't pick up my children like this.'

She followed him into the bathroom. The floor was white with lumps of ceiling. He looked down the grim dim hole of the toilet pan, then closed the lid, stood on it and lifted the top of the high cistern. 'Water,' he said, inserting his hand.

'Oh, thank God. Good job we didn't use it. I'll get something.' She went out and reappeared with the champagne glasses. He ladled the stale water from the cistern and she plugged the sink and poured it in. She began to wash her face with it. 'Horrible,' she said.

Thinking of it now as the car travelled through the London suburbs, downcast and worn, he began slowly to smile. He wondered if he loved Margaret, if she loved him. He leaned deeper into the seat and slept for an hour. When he woke the girl was driving through Surrey, heading for Hampshire along the

A30, heavy with military traffic. Several times they were stopped at barriers by British and American military policemen and she had to produce a pass. Each of them threw up a brisk salute as she drove on.

She said to Paget: 'I'm Penelope, by the way. Penelope Bryant-Cross.'

'Is this what you do all the time?' he asked. 'Drive?'

'This is the job FANY have given me. Not very glamorous. I've volunteered for parachute training but they've turned me down. Supposedly I'm too small and light. They say I'd be blown off course. It's a pity. I've got good French, I went to school in Arles. But the chances seem to be diminishing anyway. We're running out of war.'

'What happens when we get to Bournemouth?' he asked. 'The last time I came, when I was recalled, I had supper and went back.'

'This time you'll be billeted in a nice apartment,' she said, still primly. 'It's my job to look after you. It's a pity it's not summer, sir, we could go on the sands.'

Outside the window they could see the coils of rusty barbed wire curled along the dark-yellow beach. There were brick and concrete pillboxes decaying on the rainy esplanade, apertures for machine-guns gaping like empty eye sockets; protective sandbags had turned green and split, their contents fallen out and hardened to cement. Invaders were no longer expected.

'What a view,' said Penelope, pulling back the curtains. The apartment was across the wet road from the sand and the grubby waves that reached the shore from the metallic sea. At the extreme ends of the view were outcrops of land, smudgy shadows. A few disconsolate-sounding gulls struggled with the early afternoon wind.

She remained peering at the desolate scene and said: 'A chaperone can be arranged if necessary.'

'A chaperone? Oh, I see. Well, if you would like . . .'

'Not for me,' she said turning in to the room. 'For you. Some people might consider this a compromising situation.'

Paget laughed and said: 'I don't think . . .'

'You wouldn't like him anyway,' she said. 'He's a retired lighthouse man with a fearful pipe and a nasty cough. But he is available.'

Dismissing the subject she said: 'You'd like a cup of tea, I imagine.' Paget said he would. He was surveying the flat. It had a bereft air, the furniture was 1920s, there was an amateur painting of Boscombe over the fireplace and a disfunctional calendar still fixed on October 1943. An almost denuded bookcase in grim, dark wood occupied part of one wall and there was a moquette armchair in front of it. A second armchair was opposite and a settee at right angles, all in a faint mauve. 'A holiday flat before the war,' summed up Penelope. 'Requisitioned. There's quite a number along here. I don't imagine anyone uses them now, apart from people like us.'

She took her tunic off and became busy in a housewifely way, going into the kitchen and putting the kettle on the gas stove. When she returned she had a box of matches and, brushing aside Martin's offer of assistance, she knelt and lit the gas fire. 'It works. That will cheer the place up,' she said. She looked compact, neat, in her linen blouse and fitted khaki skirt.

Paget looked along the sparse bookshelves. '*Round the World in Eighty Days*,' he said. 'I've read that. About twenty years ago. And *A Thousand Happy Hobbies*. That might be worthwhile.'

She laughed. 'Nobody is resident long enough to get into *War and Peace*,' she said. She returned to the kitchen and called back: 'Strong, with milk and one sugar, isn't it?' He said it was. 'It's on your file,' she said. 'I know all sorts of things about you. Now we're here, can I call you Martin? In these circumstances we're permitted to drop the formalities.'

'I wish you would,' he said. 'Do you like Penelope or Penny?'

'Penelope,' she said. 'My mother always says that Penny has the sound of a shopgirl about it. Incidentally, I have to go shopping. I have some decent sandwiches, smoked salmon, would you believe, from Harrods, especially packed for the War Office, which we can have now with the tea. I'll do some shopping for dinner.'

'It's extremely domesticated,' he observed. She put the tea tray on a low table, took it away again and returned with a duster which she rubbed over the table's surface. 'It gets a little disused, I'm afraid.'

They sat, oddly comfortable, by the spluttering fire, with the sandwiches and tea. The day before he had been eating shrimp paste in Lyon's Corner House. 'Secret agents seem to do themselves well,' he said.

'And why not? Heaven knows what you'll manage to eat in France.'

Paget said: 'In the country it's not too bad, or by the sea, although you have to really like fish. The French will always manage.'

'To look after number one?' she finished. 'My father says that. Even in war.'

'They haven't any choice at the moment. When they sur-rendered, the old man Pétain told them country, family, work. Many French people just keep their heads down and wait for better times. On the farms and in the vineyards they eat and drink enough and they enjoy selling wine to the Germans at exorbitant prices.'

'What about the resistance?' she asked.

'Many people in France curse it. Some boy, seventeen, tried foolishly to do something brave and the Germans caught him and executed him. His mother committed suicide and when his father came back from her funeral he did the same.'

She finished her tea and said in a matter-of-fact way: 'Imagine what it would be like.' She took the cups, saucers and plates to the kitchen. 'I'll wash up later,' she said. 'I'll have to go.'

'Before the shops shut.'

'This is a special shop,' she said. She put on her tunic. 'You may be surprised.'

There was a double bedroom and a single in the flat. When she had left he opened the wardrobe in the double room and saw the civilian clothes hanging there: a worn jacket and trousers, a collarless shirt and a rough blue jersey. On the floor was a pair of thick black shoes and on a shelf socks and underwear. He checked the labels on each garment. You could buy them anywhere in France.

The seaside wind buffeting at the window woke him. There was a wartime alarm clock, marked 'Utility' on the bedside table. He had been asleep for two hours. Penelope had come back without waking him and he could hear her in the kitchen.

She brought him a cup of tea. 'You're like my mother,' he grinned.

'That is what I'm supposed to be. I have to look after you.' She went from the room and returned quickly with two newspapers. 'One *Daily Mail*, one *Bournemouth Echo*,' she said.

'Let the war wait,' said Paget, selecting the local paper. 'Let's see what the council is up to.'

She laughed pleasingly. 'I prefer to read about a wedding than some faraway battle.'

'You did your shopping?'

'Yes. I hope you like Fortnum and Mason's chicken pie. Winston Churchill doesn't get any better. Cold with boiled potatoes and vegetables. Smoked trout to start.'

'There's a Fortnum's in Bournemouth?'

'Only by special arrangement,' she said, putting a finger to her lips. 'They send groceries down for us. I also managed some wine, French, one red, one white. Rare stuff these days, so they inform me. And some gin and proper tonic water.' She regarded him quizzically. 'I should have asked you if you drink gin. I do.'

'So do I,' he said. While he was stirring the tea she said: 'If we had dinner early we could go to the cinema. There's an Abbott and Costello funny.'

'I don't think so,' he said. 'Not tonight.'

'It's not always the best idea. One chap I looked after here wanted to go and the film was *Before I Die*.'

Momentarily she looked shamefaced and left the room. 'On the other hand,' she said, putting her head around the door, 'they're broadcasting a jolly good play. *The Good Companions*, J. B. Priestley.'

'That sounds more like it,' he said. 'An evening by the wireless.'

He drank the tea and scanned the newspaper. 'Would you like me to run a bath for you?' she asked from the door. He said he would and heard her turning the taps. She began to sing. A light, sweet voice.

'I don't know that song,' he called.

'"Shining Hour",' she responded. 'It's always on American Forces Network. They have all the latest songs. It's from a Broadway show, I think.' She paused. 'Wouldn't it be blissful to see a show on Broadway?'

When she said it was ready, he went into the bathroom. There was a fresh towelling dressing-gown behind the door. He lay in the soapy water and wondered how long it would be before he would get another bath. Afterwards he put on the French civilian clothes. 'Might as well wear them in,' he said when he went into the sitting-room. The gas fire sizzled amiably, the curtains were tightly drawn and the commonplace lights mellowed the room.

'One of the fellows going to France had to wear sabots,' said Penelope. 'He had trouble walking in them.'

'To be a saboteur you have to wear sabots,' he said. 'It wouldn't do to let the Germans spot you hobbling.'

They sat domestically in front of the fire. 'Houses are very expensive down here,' she said, paging through the local newspaper. 'Eight hundred pounds. Here's another almost a thousand.'

'This used to be one of the so-called "safe areas" estate agents once advertised,' he recalled. 'Very few turned out to be safe. Dover was one, Croydon another.'

'The Germans will probably stop bombing soon,' she said.

'They'll run out of planes. Or bombs. No more nights like last night.'

Paget laughed reflectively. 'I was caught bang in the middle of it. A ceiling fell on my head.'

She looked shocked. 'But you should have said. You ought to have a medical before you go.'

'Too late now,' he said. 'And it was quite a small ceiling.'

They each had a gin and tonic. 'This taste always makes me think of pre-war days,' she said. 'I remember my very first gin. What was your life like then?'

'Ordinary,' he said. 'Grammar school, lived in a village in the West Country. Started in a land agent's office. Along came the war. Put in for an exciting job, rather recklessly. And here I am. What about you?'

'Posh, I'm afraid,' she said. 'My father's in the House of Lords. Mummy was bringing me up nicely. As far as she knew, anyway. I was going to be a debutante, presented at court and off to polo, Henley Regatta and weeks of balls.' Wryly she glanced up. 'Dancing, that is.'

'Of course.'

'The war saved me. God, I dreaded the deb part. Photographed with all those lumpish girls.'

She knew where everything was in the apartment. She laid a white cloth and set the table for two with quality cutlery and glasses. 'We have an hour before the play,' she said. 'That's providing the wireless is working.' She turned a knob on the mahogany cabinet and after a moment while it warmed up, jaunty organ music came out. 'Sandy MacPherson,' said Paget. 'The man who played for hours and hours the day they declared war. Between the official forecasts of doom, and the warning of immediate air raids which never happened.'

'I know,' she sighed. 'Unfortunately you can't *stop* him playing the thing now. I'll try the Forces Programme if you like. It's a bit more lively. I don't think I'll be able to get AFN on here.'

'Don't bother. I'll just sit with this gin and stare into the fire, thanks.'

She switched it off and went into the kitchen. 'In France, people listen to American programmes,' she called. 'While they're waiting for the BBC news and those everlasting secret messages. Glenn Miller and his Orchestra are very popular. Even the Germans listen.'

'We pinched the Germans' best song, "Lili Marlene",' pointed out Paget. 'Everyone sings it now, no matter which side they're on.'

'How odd that you can capture a song,' she said. She walked into the second bedroom and reappeared wearing a blue jumper and a pair of dark trousers. 'I'm off duty now,' she explained. 'I had to be in uniform when I went for the shopping. They like you to be dressed the part.' She put a bowl of small, bright spring flowers on the table. 'Martin, will you open the wine?' she said, as if it had been his task for years. 'It will give the red time to see if it feels like being poured, as my father says every evening.'

A corkscrew was on the kitchen table and the white wine in a refrigerator. He could not remember opening a domestic refrigerator before. He opened and shut the door twice, watching the light go on and off. He felt how cold the wine was. 'How do you feel about women wearing slacks?' she asked from the other room. 'You don't mind, do you?'

'Not at all.'

'Some men object. Something to do with being threatened, women taking over. There was that picture in the papers of Princess Elizabeth in the ATS, wearing khaki trousers.'

When the potatoes were boiled she suggested he sat at the table. A bemused, comfortable sensation had come over him; the warmth of the room, the odd homeliness of the situation. She brought in the smoked trout and they followed it with the chicken pie. They drank the red wine with the pie. He raised his glass. 'Thank you for all you've done for me,' he said. 'It's almost worth going.'

She regarded him seriously. 'You could be taken ill,' she suggested. 'Right now, Martin.'

He laughed and then realised she meant it. 'If everybody cried off sick,' he said, 'we'd never get the war finished.'

'Of course not,' she agreed over the top of her glass. 'Cheers.' She seemed embarrassed. 'God look after you.'

They ate the meal and then listened to the play, one each side of the wireless set. They leaned attentively towards it, hardly exchanging a word in an hour and a half, while the gas fire stuttered and sometimes a vehicle sounded as it passed beyond the windows. They finished the white wine while they listened. When the play was finished Penelope went to the curtains, putting her head between them and wrapping them around her neck so that only a little light escaped.

'There's a large moon now,' she said from the other side of the drapes. 'It's shining on the sea.'

'Would you like to go for a walk?' Martin asked.

'I was thinking that. I'll get our coats.'

They went down the single run of stairs and out of the door on to the beach-side road. They crossed it with scarcely the need to look either way. It was as empty as a canyon. Then they walked, the easy wind coming through the night and brushing against their faces. Bright moonlight made the scene silvery. 'They can't black out the moon,' she said, singing a line of a popular song.

'They've tried,' he laughed. 'Smokescreens, those Heath Robinson boilers on lorries belching out smoke, enough to choke anybody within ten miles, then the breeze comes up and blows it all away and there's the moon. Just loitering up there.'

She put her coated arm in his and they walked familiarly. 'You're quite a romantic, Martin.'

'For a land agent,' he laughed. 'I can make up a good yarn, which is probably why I was dragooned into this business.'

He wondered what Margaret might say if she could see him now. They strolled silently for twenty minutes until from the shadow of one of the decayed machine-gun posts a policeman materialised. He might have been having a secret smoke. They wished him good evening and he asked to see Martin's papers. 'Not many suspects around to ask tonight, constable,' said Penelope.

The policeman looked puzzled and said: 'Have to do my job, miss. Can I see your identity card too, please?'

She shrugged and handed it to him. He returned Paget's papers and checked hers. He was impressed. 'Sorry to have troubled you both,' he said. 'In civvies like you are, it's hard to tell.' He pointed to himself. 'I'm glad to get out of this get-up, I can tell you, especially the boots. It's them that kill you. We just got a new issue and we was forced to take them because nobody knows when there'll be another. But they're tight as rissoles.'

They walked on, keeping their laughter subdued. 'Tight as rissoles,' repeated Penelope. 'Wherever did he get that?'

'Heard it somewhere and repeated it without thinking. Maybe he didn't see the joke.'

She pushed her arm into his more firmly and dropped her voice. 'It would have been very strange if you had been arrested as a spy in this country.' Abruptly she turned her small, neat face to him. 'Shall we go back?'

'Yes, of course,' he said. 'I enjoyed the walk.'

They let themselves in and felt the warmth of the apartment as they went up the stairs. They had left the fire burning low. She took their coats and poured the last of the red wine. 'There'll be some music on now,' she said. 'It's late.' She switched on the wireless. A dance band was playing.

Martin said: 'May I have this waltz?' They smiled at each other and he held out his arms. They danced formally in front of the fire until the end of the tune when a BBC voice announced: 'The Forces Programme is now going off the air until tomorrow at six o'clock.' The National Anthem began to play. Penelope giggled, leaning her head against him. 'I simply can't stand to attention at this time of night. Not straight from a waltz,' she said. 'I'm getting ready for bed.'

With sudden sadness Martin sat in front of the fire. Where would he be this time tomorrow? What would his fate be? When would this strange life end? The gas fire was reflecting on his face, the orange and blue gas jets hummed. He heard her come from the bedroom. 'Me, too,' he said. 'I'd better get some sleep when I can.'

He only turned as he rose from the chair. She was wearing a woolly dressing-gown with pyjama legs protruding from the bottom. Her feet were bare and her face was touched with the same sadness. She undid the belt of the dressing-gown and let it open. He said: 'Khaki pyjamas.'

'Army issue,' she said.

They set out on an overcast morning at eight, heading west, hardly conversing, driving along the grey coast and to the ferry at Poole harbour. As they waited, a military policeman noted the number of the car and strode towards them. 'Sorry about this, sir. Aircraft about to land. We have to stop the traffic.'

They were both now in uniform. 'Where is there for a plane to land?' asked Penelope looking at the English Channel on one side of the car and the ample but hemmed-in reaches of the harbour on the other.

'It's a Sunderland,' Paget said.

As though he had given it an introduction the rotund but graceful flying boat appeared noisily from seawards, coming to the narrow entrance of the anchorage, its floats just above the roof levels of the waiting traffic, and ploughed confidently through the enclosed water, tossing up waves of white spray. The clamour of its four engines filled the morning. Penelope put her fingers in her ears. It had almost disappeared from view before the roar ceased and then they saw it returning passively to the landing place.

'Where does that come from?' she asked. 'Or is that careless talk?'

'It probably was once but everybody for miles around knows by now. It's the comfortable way from the US, across the Atlantic to the Azores, up to Madeira or Lisbon and then here. It's for top brass and people like Bob Hope and Joe Louis, the boxer, when they come over to entertain the Americans. It's a lot more cosy than the northern route.'

The ungainly chain ferry across the narrow channel began busily loading now. Confidently Penelope drove the car aboard. Some smirking GIs squatted on a truck and with pretended coyness crooked their fingers at her but she ignored them. When she drove up the ramp on the other bank the Americans, all together, stood and saluted extravagantly. 'You wouldn't think they were soldiers,' she smiled. 'They're like boys.'

'They will be until they land on the beach.'

Now they were travelling through slight hills which fell serenely towards the sea, their flanks touched with the green of spring. 'Thomas Hardy country,' said Paget.

'We read him at school. Tess was my first heroine.'

Mostly they were quiet. They reached Honiton and were held up for half an hour by a Sherman tank blocking the main street, the Devon country people taking only mild notice from the pavements. A heavy crane was clumsily shifting it. A man in a muffler and a cap tapped on the window of the car and Penelope wound it down. 'They tanks won't never be as good as 'orses,' said the man.

''Orses don't break down,' said his wife, from the depths of a voluminous old coat. As though encouraged she went on: 'Throwed us out of our cottage, they Yanks did.'

'Blowed it up,' said the man. 'Just for practice.'

Penelope said lamely: 'I'm so sorry,' before driving on and winding up the window.

The sun shone as they went across the south of Devon, diverted by barbed wire and skull-and-crossbone signs warning: 'Training Area. Beware Live Ammunition.'

They reached the main road, moving with military traffic, and more than an hour later they were entering Plymouth. Much of the naval city had been levelled by bombing. From a mile inland there was an uninterrupted view of the sea and the masts of warships. Daffodils were growing yellow about the ordered ruins and two battle cruisers were lying off Plymouth Hoe. All was peaceful and sunlit there now, the upper structures of other vessels could be seen across the scarred land. Some boys were kicking a football on a cleared bomb-site, goalposts painted on what had once been a cellar wall.

Penelope knew her way. They were admitted through three successive barriers guarded by sailor sentries with fixed bayonets and pulled up outside a building hidden behind a pyramid of sandbags.

Before Paget got out of the car she said quietly: 'I may not be taking you any further. Sometimes I'm required to carry on to the embarkation point in Cornwall, but sometimes not. They will tell me here.'

'I see. Are you driving back to London?'

'By tomorrow,' she said. 'I'll stop in Exeter tonight. I . . . I have a dinner date.'

He got out of the car at an entrance like a cave buried in the sandbags. 'The sooner they get rid of these old things the better,' said the naval lieutenant who greeted him. 'They really whiff when it's raining.'

He was shown into a waiting-room with a tall, buttercup-yellow pile of American *National Geographic* magazines on a central table. There was no one else there. He picked up the top magazine and was surveying photographs of a village in the Andes when a sharp young woman in the uniform of the Women's Royal Naval Service appeared, treated him to an official smile and invited him through the door. 'Interesting, those *National Geographics*,' she said as he followed her along the corridor. 'The naval types enjoy them because it shows them the places they'd like to go to but probably won't.'

She indicated for him to enter a long panelled room, too elaborate for an office despite the single desk at the extreme end. A naval commander rose and came almost the length of the room, hand extended. 'Squadron Leader Paget,' he said. 'Glad you could come.'

'They said I had to,' said Paget. They walked back and he took the offered chair. The man's name was Hawksworth. He sighed. 'I wouldn't care to do what you do,' he confessed. 'It's bloody dull here but it's safe and roomy. I was in submarines before. Hopefully before long none of us will have to play these games.' He took out a file after unlocking a steel drawer in the desk. 'Anyway, briefly you'll be embarking at about eight this evening with another chap, who is on a different mission, from Helford Passage in Cornwall.' He looked up. 'But you've been before.'

'Not this way,' Paget said. 'Last time I was supposed to go in by sea but it was aborted. The time before I went by air.'

'Lysander pranged, didn't it? According to this.' He patted the file. 'Unpleasant.'

'Yes, caught fire. The pilot died but two of us got out.'

Hawksworth said: 'Well, good. You got off. The sea passage is generally less risky. You'll be going on what's called the VAD route, although I can't for the life of me remember why. There are a number of places on the Brest peninsula used for landings. The Hun hasn't got eyes everywhere. You have your civvy clothes and we have your dummy papers here. Don't, for Christ's sake, forget *who* you're supposed to be. One bright spark did. With great difficulty we managed to get him out. He's up in Scotland now, at that place they stick the failures.'

'With the people who don't get through the training,' nodded Paget.

Hawksworth said: 'The misfits. Inver . . . somewhere. One of the Invers. Miles from anywhere.'

'I've wondered what they do,' said Paget.

'There's a workshop. They sit at benches and make things. God knows what. Fluffy toys perhaps.'

He shuffled the papers. 'Your contact from the Bookbinder Circuit – where do they get these names? – will be on the beach.

You'll get a decent hot meal at Helford. We've got a mess down there. Dry, I'm afraid, no booze. We can't have anybody singing and shouting as they approach a secret landing.'

'I imagine not,' said Paget.

They were only occupied for fifteen minutes. As they reached the door Hawksworth said: 'We have a driver to take you on. Your Fanny can go back to wherever she came from.'

Paget went out. Penelope was waiting in the central area, small in her uniform. 'They are sending me on with another driver,' he said.

'Yes, so I understand. I've handed over your civvies and your overnight bag. Somebody is taking care of that.'

They stood without speaking for a moment. Then her face tautened and she came to attention and saluted him. His face reddened. He returned the salute.

'Goodbye, sir.'

'Goodbye. And thank you.'

She turned and clipped briskly towards the door. It swung and she was gone. They never saw each other again.

Chapter Fourteen

There was an easy rolling of the sea which, even though the night was dark, gave it a visible sheen. They were five miles off the coast of Brittany. The man who was on a separate mission but was to be landed with Paget, and whose name was Clegg, came on to the deck and stood alongside him. They were both drinking coffee. There were no lights on the boat.

'In half an hour there'll be no talking,' said Clegg. 'It's a bit like being at boarding-school, really. Have you been in this way before?'

'No. I've only been in once. By plane.'

'That used to be a bugger, but it's easier now. When they moved into the Unoccupied Zone the Germans gave themselves a bigger chunk of France to watch. The last air drop I did there were two hundred people waiting on the ground. Flares, everything. Like a fairground. Not a Jerry in sight.'

'Let's hope they're absent tonight.'

'This bit of the coast isn't too bad. As long as you remember to scrape your footprints from the sand. Jerry has become half-hearted. He'll fight like he always did, like hell, once we invade but he knows he's done for. The last time I landed I went by submarine.'

'That's a bit extravagant, isn't it?' said Paget.

'In the Med. Sometimes it's one of those felucca things, fishing boats from Gib, bloody uncomfortable, but they've also got this French submarine which is otherwise useless. It's got some fault in the torpedo tubes and its torpedoes tend to go around in circles.'

Paget laughed quietly. 'Another part of the pantomime.'

'It is a pantomime,' agreed Clegg. 'But you tend to stop laughing if the Gestapo get hold of you. They are not funny people.'

They drank their coffee. A naval lieutenant came from the wheel-house and said: 'Nice night for a landing. I'll have to ask you to come below now, gents. We're getting closer. And you'd better say your good-lucks because from here on we must keep dead silence.'

'Good luck,' said Clegg.

'And you,' said Paget. 'Good luck.'

The strangers shook hands.

The clumsy boat moved towards the shore. Everyone on board, the two passengers and the four crew, eyed the darkness, the lieutenant through night binoculars. They had slowed to three knots. Eventually a black line rose ahead even darker than the sky. Then there was a single pinprick of light followed by another a minute later. They were there.

The boat moved close in and Clegg and Paget, first hanging their shoes around their necks by the knotted laces and rolling up their trousers like schoolboys going shrimping, climbed into a rubber dinghy with a rating who paddled easily and silently to the shore. From the beach came another blip of light.

At a nod from the sailor they eased themselves over the side. Paget found himself in a foot of cold water. Four dark cut-outs on the shore made towards them. He heard a soft precautionary click as the sailor in the dinghy cocked a gun. Paget and Clegg had no weapons. No words were spoken but they were led in from the beach to where the black cliffs stood above it. A man with a rake appeared and began to erase their footprints from the sand.

There was a hooded person leading the group who, without speaking but with an odd formality, shook hands with the two arrivals. They realised it was a woman by the size of her hands. She pointed ahead and they made their way up a firm cliff path to a road where a Renault van was parked. It was blatantly white, smudgy in the darkness. The driver was waiting and without noise he opened the rear doors. Clegg and Paget clambered in and the woman climbed in after them. It smelt of fish. She pushed back her hood. She was dark and middle-aged. She smiled. 'Welcome to France,' she said quietly.

The train for Rennes left at seven in the morning. Paget stood with a group of early workers as they waited with everyday indifference, most of them smoking, one drinking from a bottle, while the train steamed in. There was a dozy German sentry at the end of the platform.

Paget felt his heart tighten but the bleak normality of the scene reassured him. He got into a compartment and sat on a wooden seat with a line of unspeaking men carrying their lunch-boxes and their newspapers. It was getting light and two men, one each side of the compartment, released the blackout blinds to let in the drab daylight. One man smoked a pipe, two sucked at cigarette stubs. They opened their newspapers. Paget wished he had bought one.

For twenty minutes the train chuffed without speed through the flat landscape. He began to look out of the window, but then realised it might mark him as a stranger and instead pretended to read the back of the newspaper of the man sitting opposite. It was the sports page and there was a report of a boxing match with a picture. Then, at a minor station, the engine hissed and stopped.

The occupants of the compartment looked up with annoyance. One checked his watch. '*Des Boches*,' said another and the rest grunted or nodded and went back to their reading. Paget felt fear running through him. It was too late to do anything but sit, wait, and try to look like the others. The Germans were moving through the train; he could hear them opening the doors of each compartment and demanding identity documents. He hoped his forgeries were good forgeries. Men were being taken from the train on to the platform and he could see them standing unconcerned, apparently unguarded; a random check.

The door of the next compartment opened loudly and he heard

a subdued commotion there. Without a word the Frenchman opposite took the outside pages from his newspaper and handed them to Paget. They heard the next door close and a thin and bespectacled young German officer appeared outside their compartment, opened their door and took a step inside. He seemed bored, as indifferent as the Frenchmen who scarcely looked up at him. Wordlessly, each produced an identity document and held it up. Paget was the last to produce his. The German barely glanced at it but retreated to the door and crooked a finger, calling him to follow.

He made himself cease trembling. As he tried to get to his feet from between the other men he almost handed the man opposite the page of his newspaper but stopped himself. He went between the pairs of rough trousered knees and into the corridor. With a little relief he saw that other passengers were being ordered to leave the train. There were twenty, all men, on the platform when he joined them.

The passengers all seemed indifferent to the interruption of their journey. The short-sighted German officer and two soldiers with rifles shuffled them around two corners and into the wooden station building. Mentally, Paget began rehearsing his French accent.

In single file they were shepherded into the waiting-room of the station. Some sat on the benches and the Germans told them to stub out their brown cigarettes. There was a corridor which led through the station building with a closed door at the platform end; off this was another room where there was evidently a senior officer. He called something from the inner room and the two soldiers organised the men into a single file. Five of them were moved along the corridor and turned left into the room where the officer was waiting. One German soldier went into the room with them and the other, with little enthusiasm or alertness, chivvied them from behind. Paget sat down on a bench, eyeing the door at the platform end of the corridor. The five who had been taken into the inner room emerged after a few minutes and with Gallic shrugs turned left and went down the corridor, through the far door and, Paget could see, out on to the platform. Another five were moved into the inner room and Paget positioned himself to be part of the next section. In a few minutes the second batch of men came out and turned left along the passage and out through the door.

He steeled himself. The soldier indicated that the next five, with Paget one from the end, should go in for examination. His comrade had remained in the inner room and the lieutenant was also in there. Only the one dull German soldier ushered the men forward. He went to the front of the line as they shuffled in and for a few moments he was out of sight. Paget firmly but quietly walked straight along the passage, opened the door, and let himself out on to the platform.

Standing there was a grubby local train of three carriages. It was just moving away. He looked over his shoulder, then went at a stiff-legged hurry along the platform and, opening the final door, jumped aboard.

He looked back a second time at the platform but there was no commotion. His group of men had been released from the interrogation and they were slouching through the door. Amazed that it should have been so easy, he turned into the compartment and sat on the wooden seat opposite the only other occupants. There was a gross-faced fat man, enfolded in jerseys and grasping a heavy white stick; he had one blank eye and the nondescript dog that took up the seat beside him was also missing an eye.

Paget muttered something under his breath and his fellow passenger responded by banging his stick on the floor twice. Paget wondered where they were going.

They passed a station whose name meant nothing to him. The sun had come from behind the miserly morning clouds and they were travelling roughly west. Then the train slowed and hesitatingly halted. Voices came from the corridor. The blind man pointed with his stick to the outside carriage door and muttered a single word: '*Partez.*'

Paget went. He slipped open the door and jumped down on to the embankment, toppling with the force of his descent and rolling through soaked bushes and rough grass until he came to rest against a wall. He lay still, moving only his eyes to see if he could fix what was happening in the train. Nothing was apparent and after a few minutes it began to move again.

He lay against the wall, trying to calm the sound of his breathing. He was cut and wet. Carefully he got to his knees and then to his feet. His head came inch by inch over the wall and he found he was looking into a churchyard, full of old and cockeyed graves with a grim church and some meagre trees. He could see there was a road beyond, a red bus making its slow way to some unknown destination. He needed to avoid the railway now.

Apart from the bus there was no discernible movement anywhere. He climbed over the wall, feeling the old bricks shudder, and landed on the other side directly on top of an abandoned angel, its wings broken, leaning against the wall among other cemetery detritus.

Dodging sharply between the tombs and vaults he made his way towards the church. He was only yards short, one gravestone away, when a priest came from the porch accompanied by two unpleasant-looking men who were in civilian clothes but one of whom was carrying a gun. The other saw him immediately, shouted and pointed. He ran, zigzagging between the masonry, expecting a shot and a fragment of flying angel. Abruptly he was confronted with a vault like a small house, stained, dark and dripping. The door was hanging open and he almost fell down the ragged steps and into the deathly and smelly gloom. He could hear the men searching, calling in French to each other. At least they weren't the Gestapo. From where he crouched he could see the edges of two mouldy coffins lying on shelves. He wanted to go home.

They found him quite easily. There was nowhere he could run. The two men, with the priest hovering like a crow behind them, appeared at the top of the broken steps and the one with the gun pointed it directly at him. He came out with his hands above his head.

It was a close, wooden-panelled room containing nothing but the upright chair on which he sat. The men had left him and locked him in although he suspected that one remained outside the door. During the journey in a clanking Citroën, which once broke down and had to be coaxed into restarting, the man holding the gun had kept nudging his ribs with the muzzle, but there was an amateurish air about them that gave him hope; they did not tie his wrists and although they had discussed blindfolding him they had no blindfold and instead, rather shamefacedly, they instructed him to keep his eyes closed.

Through his eyelashes he perceived that they leaned forward to check him at intervals; he barely saw that the car was entering a heavy stone gate and going up a long drive with regular trees at its sides. They took him out with clumsy roughness and, with further warnings about shutting his eyes, pushed him up a flight of stone steps. A rusty but resounding bell was rung and a creaking door opened. The man who responded greeted them civilly and asked no questions. Paget was then led into the panelled room and the door closed behind him.

After half an hour it opened and he quickly closed his eyes. But a grave voice told him that the precaution was unnecessary and he opened them to see a seedy-looking man wearing a servant's coat, old-fashioned and dusty, who said: 'Madame Dupard will receive you in a few moments.'

By now nothing surprised Paget and, at the man's invitation, he went into a baronial hall where every floorboard sighed as he trod towards an ornate door. The servant followed him and, once he was in an old, dim and overfurnished room, suggested that he took a chair and waited for Madame Dupard.

He was not kept waiting long. She came through a draped entrance at the extreme end of the room. She was elderly and wore ancient clothes but her eyes were bright and she approached him in a sprightly manner as though genuinely pleased to see him.

'Monsieur,' she said in a chesty voice. 'How nice of you to come. I am sure you would like a glass of champagne.'

Paget said he would. The dusty servant, almost at once, brought a tray with two flutes and a bottle of Bollinger with a touch of froth at the neck. Nothing was said while he poured the glasses with a shaky hand. Then he went from the room, backing across the frayed carpet, and Madame Dupard, speaking in English, said: 'I'm afraid I do not know your name. But perhaps it is better that I don't.'

'I am afraid so,' said Paget. It was difficult to believe he was standing there lifting a champagne glass when an hour before he had been a fugitive hiding for his life in a smelly tomb. He grinned at her. 'We are trained never to give our names.'

She cackled drily. 'Hah, that is always the first rule to go under interrogation, you know. But I will call you Eric. I like the English actor Eric Portman.'

Paget bowed briefly. 'I'm Eric,' he acknowledged and said: 'I know you are Madame Dupard.'

'Celestine Dupard,' she said. 'A sad widow. My husband Clovis was well known in the former Unoccupied Zone, in Vichy itself. He knew everything and everybody from Marshal Pétain down to the most confused resistance fighter. The Gestapo, everyone. He died from strain.'

'I'm sorry,' said Paget inadequately.

'He had a young, active and demanding mistress,' she shrugged, waving her glass slightly. 'A mere enemy occupation does not stop such liaisons. But the pace was too much for poor Clovis.'

The servant paddled into the room and refilled their glasses. 'Please, Eric,' she said, 'sit comfortably and tell me your adventures, as much as you can allow. Nothing surprises me in this war and I am very trustworthy. Bruno will bring us some food. I expect you are hungry.'

It was as though he were telling her a tall story, something he made up as he went along. He could scarcely believe it himself. Only forty-eight hours before he had been in Bournemouth with Penelope listening to a J. B. Priestley play. 'You must rest too before you continue your journey,' Madame Dupard said. 'There is no difficulty. The Germans call here only by appointment.'

'You seem to have everything arranged very nicely,' he commented.

'We have had some practice. The occupation has been for almost four years. We know the Hun and he knows us. It is a temporary but almost workable arrangement. Now tell me.'

Cautiously Paget said: 'I was sent to contact a circuit, a resistance group, in Rennes.'

'Bookbinder, I think,' she said.

'Yes. Bookbinder. You know.'

'Very well.'

'The Germans stopped the train and took me with a group, a random check I imagine, into a station. It was all very loose, very haphazard.'

'No one is more haphazard than the ordinary occupation soldier,' said Madame Dupard. 'Their minds are elsewhere.'

'This was amazingly easy. I managed to slip out while they were checking papers and I jumped on a train that was just leaving. They came after me. Someone might even have told them.'

'One learns quickly,' she shrugged. 'There is a lot of treachery. All it needs sometimes is the reward of extra rations.'

'Anyway, I jumped from the train and ended up in a churchyard where the priest and two men, one with a gun, caught me. I thought I was done for. But now I am here.'

'The Diderot brothers,' she sighed. 'They play games like little boys. Spies and agents, Gestapo and resistance. They are fools. They shot a man dead once and he was only an innocent employee of the bus company.'

'They go around playing these games? Guns and all?'

She laughed. 'Monsieur, you should have seen people like them before, in the Unoccupied Zone, in Vichy, when there was more opportunity for these sorts of activities. There were agents and double agents and others who were not anything but believed they were. Old scores to be settled, you know, private crimes to be committed, bribery and fraud, businesses to be obtained at bargain prices once the local Jews had been sent off to Germany. It was a confused scene. People indulged in their fantasies. Once two of these fools arrested, well kidnapped, a man . . . What do you call it . . .? Shanghaied? And the man turned out to be a *Nazi* agent. There was some trouble over that.'

'Do they always bring wanted men to your door?' asked Paget.

She smiled reflectively. 'Ah, now that is something I cannot tell you. We must both keep our secrets. Sometimes the most unsuitable people have arrived, vagabonds, burglars, all manner. One man went off with a set of my towels.'

The silent servant Bruno reappeared and pulled two chairs out from a graceful table which had been laid for two with shining cutlery, shapely glasses and white napkins. 'We should eat,' said Madame Dupard. 'I'm sure you are hungry. Then you must rest and while you do so I will discover where to send you.'

Le Coq Noir was in the centre of Rennes. 'It is a good place,' Paget was told by the taxi-driver who had brought him from the station. The taxi was fuelled by gas from a balloon on its roof. 'Nice clean women and the wine's not too bad. The Boche like it.'

It was eleven at night. He paid two francs at the door and went through the nightclub dimness towards a diffuse light over the bar. There was a band playing 'Moonlight Serenade', trying and failing to sound like the Glenn Miller Orchestra. A dozen people were dancing, others were at tables, and there was conversation and some laughter. He saw the girl at the bar. Black hair, short as a bathing cap, red home-made dress, large eyes and crucifix. Just as Madame Dupard had described her. As instructed, he asked her if she would like a Hermann Goering frappé and she said yes.

'You would like to meet Gilbert,' she said, answering him in English.

'You knew?'

'Anyone who buys me that stupid cocktail needs to see Gilbert,' she said. 'Somebody told you. Come with me.'

She made for the dance floor and held out her pale arms. Once more he wondered what was happening to him. He began to dance with her, a foxtrot, and she eased him closer to her body. 'It is better to go to see Gilbert by dancing,' she said in a not particularly confidential voice. 'Walking straight to the office could create suspicion.'

'Are there Germans in?' he whispered.

'Not yet. They come later. It is the French I worry about, monsieur. We have a black-market war at the moment and there has been enough trouble.'

They reached the far side of the room. The band hiding behind garish lights played indomitably. She guided him off the floor and led him without hurry to a padded door in the shadows. She knocked and went in immediately. 'For you,' she said to a perspiring fat man in a sagging dinner jacket. He was standing to one side of the desk upon which was an anti-tank rocket launcher.

'A beauty, eh?' he said as he glanced up at Paget. 'Made in Czechoslovakia. They always make the best.'

He was unsurprised to see Paget. 'I thought you would have been here before this,' he said.

'I had trouble,' replied Paget. He nodded to the menacing weapon on the desk. 'Should you be displaying that?'

Gilbert laughed. He had a moustache which he seemed to be trying to sniff up his nose. 'It is okay, monsieur,' he assured. 'The Germans will not be in yet. Last night, after business, we had an expert who came in and gave a dozen of us a lecture on how to use the weapon.' He tapped a box with his foot. 'We have twelve rocket shells also. Each one would pierce a tank. And we hope for another launcher. Please, monsieur, take a seat.'

Staring at the lean launcher at eye-level, Paget felt his way to a chair by the desk. Gilbert leaned over, picked up the weapon with heavy forearms and eased it on to the floor. 'I must not leave it there,' he said. 'You will think I'm showing off.'

Without asking, he poured two glasses of brandy from a bottle on a side-table. 'You seem to have the Germans all worked out,' said Paget. 'Everybody does.'

'We think so. Then sometimes they turn nasty and execute someone, often the wrong person. But they are weary, monsieur, they want to go home. If they have a home when they get there. They have no spirit. They will fight,' he patted his heart, 'but not with this.'

Paget said: 'The way things go on here, as far as I can see, the German intelligence service must be pretty thick.'

'Services,' corrected Gilbert. 'Intelligence *services*. There's the Abwehr, the GFP, the SD and three more at least. They all work against each other. Piggledy-higgledy. They do more damage to each other than we could ever do to them. Each one knows something but will not tell the others. Jealousies, betrayals, impotence . . . I mean, of course, incompetence. It is worse even than the French resistance.'

'Don't you want to check my identity?' suggested Paget.

Gilbert flapped a hand. 'If you like. It makes no difference. Many people come through here without papers. I know who is who. *Why* did you come?'

Paget was dismayed. 'You don't know?'

'I knew you were due, but I forgot why. I am very busy. Apart from the espionage, I have this nightclub to run.'

'The RAF are to bomb the prison,' Paget said, looking for astonishment in Gilbert's face but finding none. 'They believe they can hit the outer wall and facilitate the escape of the French resistance members who are under sentence of death there. Seventy, I believe.'

'Sixty-eight,' sniffed Gilbert. 'The odd two were in the sickbay when it happened. Imagine being in the sickbay when you are under a death sentence.'

Paget was stunned. 'It's already happened?'

Gilbert nodded. 'Excellent bombing, too. Everyone escaped through the hole in the wall.'

'But . . . but . . . I was supposed to come here to coordinate the escapees.' Gilbert pulled his moustache from his nostrils and smiled wryly. Paget went on: 'To . . . well, sort them out. To make sure they were dispersed and not recaptured.'

Gilbert laughed as though he had been told a genuine joke. His shoulders continued to shake as he poured two more brandies. 'Well, it was all done without your help, monsieur. Everyone is now tuckered away, as you say. I'm afraid your people in London are sometimes out of touch with what is happening. Maybe even with real life. It's like one of the games they play at your noble schools . . . public schools, is it?'

'So I came for nothing.' Paget's voice was a whisper.

Gilbert appeared sorry for him. 'Monsieur,' he said, leaning on the table. 'Everything in this war is one grand fuck-up. Well, most things. Both sides. The side that has the fewest fuck-ups will win, with the help of superior forces, of course.'

He sighed. 'This whole resistance business is raddled with it. Many French people want nothing to do with the resistance. They want a quiet life. Then someone who likes to make a name assassinates some Nazi and what happens? Twenty-five perfectly good Frenchmen are taken and shot. You have to weigh up the consequences.'

He finished his brandy with a gulp. 'Sometimes the resistance fights itself,' he continued, spreading his large hands. 'Communists, who didn't even join in until Hitler invaded Russia, Republicans, Gaullists, Corsicans, Spaniards, Fascists even. Believe me, monsieur, the liberation of France may only be the beginning of a civil war.'

He took in Paget's downcast expression. 'All the sabotage we have been able to arrange, sometimes at great risk, has been little beyond an annoyance to the Boche.' His voice became suddenly encouraging: 'The real action will be when the invasion happens.

Then the resistance will come into its glory. Every rail track, every junction, every signal-box on the French railways will be disabled. The Germans will be attacked from the backside at every opportunity.' He leaned over and patted the rocket launcher.

'I think I'll have to come back later,' said Paget caustically.

'Once the signal is given,' agreed Gilbert. 'When we hear on your BBC that terrible poetry from Verlaine.'

Slowly Paget said: 'You know about Verlaine?'

'The sobbing of violins in the autumn,' recited Gilbert. 'Everybody knows it. The Germans also, I expect. It is difficult to keep any secret in France these days.'

The Englishman, still taking it in, said: 'I wasn't aware of the exact words. It could be a trick. Maybe it will be replaced by something else nearer the invasion.'

Gilbert smiled thinly. '*Sur le pont d'Avignon*,' he suggested.

'Ding dong dell, pussy down the well,' sighed Paget.

'Anything will do,' said Gilbert. 'Three blonde mice is a good one.' He stood up and patted Paget on the shoulder. 'I am sorry it has been such a disappointment. We must make arrangements to get you back to England.'

Paget's eye was caught by a wall calendar. It said: '*Avril 1.*'

'I came here once before,' he said.

'Oh, sure. You were in the Lysander that hit the sheep and caught fire. We pulled you out.'

'No, I got out myself. You pulled out the pilot and he was dead.'

'That's correct, now I remember. The sheep suffered too. Everyone in the area had mutton that night.'

'Is Antoinette still in this region?'

Gilbert appeared puzzled but then said: 'Antoinette Barre. Beautiful, eh? She was the one who sheltered you afterwards.'

'Yes.'

'She has gone to Bordeaux, I think. Yes, Bordeaux. She is doing good work for us. She is very well informed.'

'Good contacts?'

'The best. She has married a German officer.'

Chapter Fifteen

'I 'ate these bleedin' guns,' sniffed Blackie as they were cleaning the twenty-five-pounders.

'Bloody things,' grunted Hinchcliffe. 'Lugging them around.' Chaffey and Rayley nodded.

'Wiping their noses,' said Warren. He polished the already shining muzzle and, bending, looked at the contorted reflection of his already unlovely face.

'Wipin' their arses,' said Blackie, flicking the breach. He gave it some spit.

'I hope they ackle when they're supposed to,' said Treadwell, standing back to survey the gun which he was buffing. 'We going to be right in the shit if they don't.'

'Fuckin' things,' added Blackie. He polished off the spit.

Sergeant Harris, who had been standing at the door, walked with his measured pace into the shed. The men's profanity had echoed against the corrugated-iron roof. He stopped and revolved on his heel at a right angle. 'You won't have to do it much longer,' he announced. 'Take that pipe out of your mouth, Gannick.'

'It's empty, sarge,' said Gannick.

Every man had stopped his cleaning. 'Why not, sarge?' asked Warren cautiously. 'Why won't we have to do it?' Changes in the army were rarely for the better.

'Ceremonial duties,' guessed Gordon unconvincingly. 'Firing the salute for the King's birthday.'

'You won't be firing them at all,' said Harris. His face creased grimly. 'You're all being transferred. Me as well. So the rumour has it.'

'Not the commandos is it?' said the scrawny Blackie. 'Oi bloody 'ope not.'

'They're not that hard up,' sniffed Harris. 'It's the infantry. The foot sloggers. Hampshire Regiment.'

Their rough faces became blank. Nobody spoke until Treadwell said: 'I wrote in for the pay corps.'

'Well, you didn't get in,' said Harris. 'You can't count, for a start.' He surveyed them standing wretchedly beside the guns they had served for three years: Gannick, May and Forster, the older men, Rayley, Bond and the others. 'The adjutant will come and comfort you when he's got a minute.'

'You've been posted as well, sarge?'

'Me, too. You'd be lost without me. We're going to be charging up those beaches, fixed bayonets, in the face of the enemy, instead of getting the guns ashore in good order and firing from a respectable distance. Personally, I'm very pissed off, but don't mention that to General Montgomery.' He surveyed their miffed faces. 'All right, get fell in. And try and march smartly. You're infantry now.'

As they marched away Blackie and some of the others looked back at the twenty-five-pounders. 'I was fond of that gun,' muttered Blackie.

They waited in the hut, squatting disconsolately on the iron ends of their beds or gathered around the dead stove. 'I don't ken this "over the top" mentality,' said Gordon sternly. 'Charging the Jerry trenches and getting buggered.'

'And *early* in the morning,' ventured the young Peters. 'Getting you up at four on a cold morning to go and get killed.'

'You'd reckon they ought to let you have a lie-in,' said Warren. ''Ave the attack later.'

'It's not too much to ask. If it's the last morning you're alive.'

Blackie said: 'Anyhow, now we don't have the guns to worry about. No more bullshit.'

Harris came in. He had pressed his uniform, and burnished his brasses and his Royal Artillery badge with its cannon. Blackie said: 'What about the guns, sarge? Where're they going?'

'Scrap,' suggested May. Only Forster laughed.

'God knows, I don't. Maybe they'll give them to a museum or the army cadets, for something to play with. The adjutant is coming in to have a word.'

They waited a further ten minutes before Captain Moon appeared. They came to attention. It was not often they saw him and he seemed to have trouble in remembering them. 'Pulled the damned rug from under our feet, I'm afraid, soldiers,' he said in his pompous way. 'No warning, not an inkling. One day gunners and the next cannon fodder.' He paused with something like embarrassment. 'As for me, I'm being transferred to the depot at Woolwich.'

Bond at the rear of the group breathed: 'You're glad to say.'

Moon looked up slowly, but said sharply: 'Did someone make a comment?'

'Me sir,' said Bond. 'I just said, could we come with you?'

'Ha! Good joke! Afraid not, fellows. You're young and fit. They'll need every chap of you on the assault beaches. My soldiering days are drawing to a close. But I'll be there with you in spirit.' He surveyed them as if asking for a smile. Nothing appeared. 'But cheer up, you'll be swapping big guns for little guns, that's all. And the rifle's a jolly sight easier to move.'

The faces remained unbroken. 'That's all, sergeant,' he said to Harris in a disappointed way. 'Carry on.'

Sergeant Harris called them to attention and saluted Moon. The captain returned the salute. 'Good luck,' he called airily over his shoulder as he headed out of the door.

'Bollocks,' said Blackie when he was sure the adjutant had gone.

'Say one for me,' muttered Harris.

'Bollocks,' said Blackie again.

'Are we the only ones?' asked Treadwell. 'What about the other batteries?'

'Nobody tells me,' said Harris. 'Only what I hear in the sergeants' mess, but what I gather is there'll be others transferred as well. They've suddenly realised they're short of infantry. So much for planning.'

'So much for espirit de corps,' sighed Treadwell.

'You have to give your espirit to the Hampshires,' said Harris.

'We'll get new cap badges,' said Warren, as if trying to show interest.

'And shoulder flashes,' added Rayley. He described a half-moon on his upper arm.

'No extra pay, I s'pose?' chipped in Blackie.

'There might be extra if you get a bullet.'

'That'll please the wife.'

Gordon asked: 'How do we transform ourselves into these gallant foot sloggers? March up and down?'

'Learn to run,' suggested Warren dolefully.

'We start today,' Harris told him. 'We won't have to move from this billet just yet. They'll cart the guns away first. We're going over to Tidworth to begin retraining as infantry. Right on time, they've got a tactical exercise starting.' He appeared to brighten. 'You're going to fight the Yanks.'

They lay against the face of a ditch. The rain was unrelenting, spilling down the bare, banked earth in front of them, running from the brims of their steel helmets, and trickling down the crevices of their camouflage oilskins. ''Ave a dekko over the top, Bunny,' suggested Blackie. 'You're 'igher than Oi.'

Warren handed his wet rifle to Blackie and, getting a hold in the mud of the bank with the heavy toes of his boots, lifted himself clear of the ditch. 'Bugger all,' he summed up. 'Miles of it.'

Harris arrived with a cursing lieutenant crushed under oilskins. 'See that building down below, lad?' said the officer.

Warren looked. 'Yes, sir.'

'That's the enemy,' the officer sniffed. 'Christ, I'm cold.' He surveyed the crouching squad, then said to Harris: 'Are you all gunners? Where's the guns?'

'We've transferred to the Hampshires, sir,' said Harris. 'Haven't got our new flashes yet.'

'That's bad luck. The artillery has got to be better than this.'

'Drier generally, sir.'

'Right. Well, here we are. Down there in that barn, or whatever the place is, are the enemy who for the sake of this exercise are the Yanks. We . . . well, *you* that is, are going to wipe the buggers out, figuratively speaking of course, although you'll have to watch how you do it because they might wipe you out first – and with those mad bastards they'll probably be using live ammo.'

He shook the water from his helmet and then his cape, sending it over May who looked offended and attempted to wipe it off. 'Right, sergeant,' said the officer to Harris. 'Deploy your men to the right. There's a good slope there and it should make it easier to jump the door in.' He looked momentarily pleased with his strategy and added: 'Then rush them.'

'Yes, sir,' said Harris. 'Rush them.'

'It's the only way,' the lieutenant said. 'There's only one aperture apart from the door and they'll have that covered. If you get the door down and get at them you might take them by surprise and you won't suffer too many casualties.'

'They've probably got the door covered too, sir.'

The officer ill-temperedly shook more water from his helmet. 'Come on, sergeant,' he grunted. 'It's only a bloody practice.' He crawled between the men to the end of the ditch. 'I'll be back after lunch to see how you've managed,' he said. He splashed away.

'Don't be 'urryin' your lunch,' groaned Warren quietly.

'Right,' sighed Harris. 'Let's do what the superior officer said. Treadwell, you go to the other side of the building and when I discharge the Very pistol,' he held up the flare gun to show them, then returned it to beneath his cape, 'you begin firing at the window or whatever it is. Then we'll attack the door from the other side. Let's hope they have blanks as well.'

He said to Treadwell: 'Get going, lad.'

The soldier looked anxious. 'Can't somebody come with me, sarge?' He looked around. 'Even Peters.'

'Sod off,' said Peters.

Harris said: 'Get going.'

Holding the long, heavy 303 rifle before him, Treadwell climbed from the ditch and, after glancing back timidly, went towards the slope flanking the building. Tentatively he waved from there like somebody greeting a possible friend. Harris muttered: 'Christ. Afraid to be on his own.'

'He's always been with us before,' pointed out Gannick solemnly. 'With the guns.'

'Well, now he's on his own. In the infantry you often are.' Harris took in their wet faces. 'Now, let's believe this is the real thing. Before long it might be.'

They slithered to the bank opposite the wooden door to the barn. It was an old door, the planks wet and weathered with splits and gaps. From the rain and mist cloaking the plain they continued to hear the crackle of a simulated battle. Smoke was trapped beneath the low clouds.

'Have a look,' said Harris to Warren, 'through the cracks in the door.'

Warren looked shocked. 'Me, sarge?'

'Yes,' said Harris. 'You, Warren.'

Warren gave him another look, then slid in the mud to the door and tentatively looked through. He scrambled back. 'Couldn't see 'em but Oi could hear them talkin',' he reported.

They took up the crouch position. Harris was not sure it was correct although he had looked up a manual the previous night – it was more than three years since he had done his basic infantry training. 'Right,' he said. 'Let's go.' Then he remembered he had to fire the Very pistol to signal Treadwell's diversion. 'No, hang on.' Blackie was already going down the bank. 'Obey the last order, lad,' Harris told him. Blackie climbed back up the mud. Harris took the pistol from its holster concealed in his cape and stared at it. He had never fired one before. As he raised it the squad, as a man, shifted to one side. He pressed the trigger and the crack made them duck. But up soared the yellow rocket. Harris looked surprised and pleased. He replaced the signal pistol with a touch of a swagger and heard Treadwell obediently open fire from the other side of the barn. Grimly he ordered: 'Let's get them. Charge!'

The ten men rose from the slippery bank and trotted after Harris down the slope. Two fell over on the mud and he stopped, turned, and cursed them. The sergeant reached the door with the squad just behind him, and fell against the woodwork. It collapsed spectacularly. It flattened like a drawbridge and the soldiers toppled into the dim barn.

A dozen Americans were sitting against the stone wall, most of them smoking, their weapons stacked carelessly.

'On your feet! Hands up!' shouted Harris. He felt he was acting in a film. 'Come on. You're prisoners.'

'Okay, okay, we surrender,' drawled a thick man in the middle. He was chewing gum. He and his companions made no attempt to get to their feet and only two casually raised their hands.

The British soldiers looked towards Harris. 'Ain't you going to put up a fight?' Blackie demanded. Harris scowled at him and he said: 'Sorry, sarge.'

'No, we're not fighting,' said the heavy-faced American. 'We give up unconditionally. We're waiting for chow.'

Harris did not know what to do next. The Americans continued lounging, chewing and smoking. Those who had half raised their arms put them down again. He motioned to Peters who carried the field telephone. He took the bulky phone from its container and instructed Peters to turn the handle. With an embarrassed look at the Americans the British soldier did so. The GIs watched as though fascinated. 'What's it going to play?' asked one. 'Glenn Miller?' Some of them laughed but not roughly. Harris pressed the button and nothing happened. Violently he shook the instrument and pressed the button again. Again there was no response.

'Nobody home?' suggested the American in the middle.

Abruptly Treadwell's helmeted head appeared at the glassless window at which he had been firing his blanks. 'Everything all right?' he enquired squeakily.

'Oh, fuck!' said Harris.

They all laughed uproariously, the Americans and the British. The leading GI, wiping his eyes, put his arm on Harris's shoulder. 'I'm Albie,' he said. 'Jeez, you guys really *scared* us.' He looked around. 'Didn't they, fellas?'

'Yeah,' they said. 'Like hell,' added one.

'We didn't expect you to surrender,' said Harris in a hurt way. 'We thought you'd put up a fight. I'm Harris, by the way.' He shook Albie's hand and all the other men joined in the greeting.

'Why fight?' said an American called Danny. 'There's already too much fighting in the world, and especially now the chow's arriving.'

He had heard the sound of a vehicle. It stopped outside. Even from there they could smell the drifting fragrance of food. American food.

All the soldiers, British and American, turned expectantly towards the gaping barn door. Four ebullient and bulky GIs in fatigues appeared in its frame, carrying steaming steel canisters, and clattered in their combat boots across the felled door. They were swathed in smells, hot, tasty smells. 'Okay, soldiers, here it is,' proclaimed the man at the front. He suddenly spotted the British troops. 'Oh, 'scuse us. Are we interrupting sumphin'?'

'We've been captured, taken POW,' said Albie.

'Don't let that stop your lunch,' said Harris decisively.

The food party put the canisters on the barn floor and then went back for more, including a volcanic urn of coffee. 'Don't expect service like this on the beach,' said the leader.

The jolly group went out and their vehicle drove away. The Americans studied the containers. So did the British. Noses were twitching. 'Is it okay if the prisoners eat?' asked Albie. 'They've had zero since breakfast.'

'Go ahead,' said Harris. He and his men sat on the ground and watched intensely. The containers were opened and extra smells gushed out. A man was pouring hot coffee. Enamel plates appeared, and metal cutlery and drinking mugs. The eyes of the British troops went up as steaks and sausages and beans and fried potatoes were piled on to plates. The Americans attacked the food. The British watched enviously.

Albie suddenly stopped, a forkful of beef halfway to his mouth. 'Would you guys like some of this stuff?' he asked. 'There's plenty. Gee, enough for an army. Two armies.'

Harris put out restraining arms as his men rose from the ground like runners out of starting blocks. 'Wait. Get in single file,' he ordered. 'I'll lead the way.'

Great grins spread across the rough faces of his squad. Gordon briefly hesitated. 'It could be a trap, sergeant,' he said.

'Shut your trap, Jock,' warned Blackie.

'Single file,' repeated Harris. They obeyed, eager as small boys. Gordon was pushed to the back. Albie stood behind the food. 'Millions of plates,' he assured them. 'Come and get it.'

The British had never eaten food like that. Rich, hot, fatty food. Each went away from the serving plate holding a precious, smouldering plate under his nose and found somewhere, any-where, to dig into it. Some had never even seen a steak and cut into it with amazement, filled their mouths and groaned with pleasure. They ate and ate. Wholesale pork sausages, piles of fried potatoes, ladles of beans and candied carrots, with apple pie and ice-cream afterwards.

Harris said eventually: 'Tomorrow night you've got to come over to us, to the billet – we'll tell you where – and we'll return the compliment. Somehow.'

'Rabbit stew,' said Treadwell, stirring it with doubt. 'What's better than a rabbit stew? They've probably never even tried it.'

'And spuds and carrots . . . *and* turnips,' said Gordon sadly. 'Imagine, turnips.'

'They'll go bloody crazy about them,' muttered Blackie.

'Bollocks,' sighed Warren. 'After their sort of grub, this stuff will make them sick.'

Downcast, they stood around the big iron cauldron, the pot-bellied stove glowing red beneath it.

'Smells all right,' said Harris, coming through the door. He saw their faces. 'What's the matter?'

Gordon said: 'It's na' what they're used to.'

'We could go down to Salisbury and get a few quids' worth of fish and chips,' suggested Treadwell. 'If they've got any fish.'

'If we had a few quid,' said Peters.

'We'll have a singsong,' suggested Harris hopefully. 'Everybody likes a singsong.'

'No bugger likes turnips,' said Blackie.

They stood around the bubbling pot for another hour and then heard, with dropping hearts, a vehicle pull up. 'Here they are,' said Harris. 'For Christ's sake, try to look cheerful.'

He went to the door and opened it. Ten Americans, led by the striding Albie, came in. 'Nice,' said Albie, looking around the basic billet. 'Real cosy.'

One of the Americans had a guitar hanging over his shoulder, two others carried a big crate of bottled beer and two more a tin bath full of coal.

'Where did you get that?' asked Harris. 'We have to scrounge every shovelful.'

The Americans were making themselves comfortable, sitting on the beds, sniffing the stew, opening bottles of beer. 'From the locomotive,' said Albie. 'That little toy one they run from place to place. We have a key to the yard.'

Plates had been lifted from the cookhouse, and cutlery by Harris from the sergeants' mess. Cups came from the NAAFI canteen. Gordon dished out the hot stew. He had skinned and dismembered the three rabbits, shot by the unerring Warren with a 303 and a clip of stolen bullets, and they had all peeled the vegetables.

It was warm in the hut and everybody had a good time. Towards the end, the man with the guitar began to strum it. The Americans sang 'Deep in the Heart of Texas' and the British 'On Ilkley Moor'. Then they joined:

> *'And in the park she wheeled a perambulator,*
> *She wheeled a perambulator in the merry month of May.*
> *And if you ask her where the hell she got it,*
> *She got it from a Yankee who is far far away . . .'*

They sang until they were hoarse. All the beer went and the stew pot was emptied. The GIs swore they had enjoyed it. At the end they sang the ballad their comrades had captured from the Germans, the song both enemies now claimed:

> *'Underneath the lantern by the barrack gate,*
> *Darling, I remember the way you used to wait . . .*
> *. . . my Lili of the lamplight,*
> *My own Lili Marlene.'*

The hut on the wide plain glowed within and the voices came through the corrugated-iron roof and the shuttered windows and drifted over the starry, springtime night.

April advanced, with its pale green touch spread across the plain. Daylight hours were longer now that British Double Summertime had begun. By government decree there was one-hour summertime throughout the year, even in darkest, deepest winter, for it provided longer working hours. Now that spring had really arrived the weather was often sunny, the smoke of the practising guns rising blue instead of grey, tanks and armoured cars almost jaunty as they advanced through the rising flowers, and some birds whistled as did the soldiers on the march. There was a sense that the day of the great invasion was not far away.

In full battle order – with steel helmets, packs and ammunition pouches, capes for rain and gas, water bottles, first-aid kits, and each with the soldier's 'housewife' for sewing on buttons and darning socks, and armed with rifles and bayonets – the squad stoically marched three miles across the curved countryside to where a mock Bavarian village had been constructed. Harris halted them and looked down on the prettily carved roofs and the wooden verandas incongruous in the Wiltshire dell. 'Can't you almost hear the cowbells?' he said.

'How be it that there's no 'oles in the 'ouses, sarge?' enquired Blackie.

'Because it's all blanks,' said Harris patiently. 'And blanks don't make holes.'

'Thank ee kindly, sergeant,' said Blackie, reverting to West Country sarcasm. 'Oi'd never 'o thought o' that, would you, Bunny?'

'Oi might 'ave,' said Warren. 'But it would 'ave took a long time.'

'Bloody turnips,' muttered Gannick.

They rounded the shoulder of sprouting hillside and saw that there were already a hundred or more infantrymen assembled in front of the dummy village and more were arriving. Harris led his men down the slope. They wore their new Hampshire Regiment flashes on their sleeves. The other soldiers were from the Hampshires, the Dorsets, the Wiltshires and the Somerset Light Infantry, country boys mostly, now almost trained, nearly ready for battle.

At the edge of the bizarre clump of houses were three stiffly upright men, one a regimental sergeant-major with a face like a bruise. The trio studied the soldiers with noses high as if trying to smell them. The sergeant-major marched two paces, stamped to attention and roared: 'Parade! Parade att–en–shun!'

The men in the dell came to attention but not all at once and he made them do it again. Then he strode straight-backed and mounted a platform of ammunition cases. The two other men, sergeants with dread faces, stamped across the open ground and snapped to attention alongside.

'Parade, a–t ease! Stand easy!'

The infantrymen relaxed, spreading their feet, each one linking his hands behind his back. Their steel helmets seemed too big, and they gazed at the bullshit figure on the ammunition boxes from below the rims.

Every word from him was a shout, some louder than others. 'Any of you know Mrs Rumbleton?' he blared. 'Anybody?' There was a wide silence. 'No? Well, I am her only son – Sergeant-Major Cecil Rumbleton. I am a Warrant-officer Class One and you will call me SIR! Understood?'

There was a hesitant and mumbled: 'Yes, sir.'

'*Again! Understood?*'

Everyone shouted: 'YES, SIR.'

'And I repeat, it is *Rumbleton*. If I hear any soldier calling me *Rumblebum* he will be on a charge, a fizzer. That man's feet will not touch the ground. For, believe me, although I am a *nice* man – I like animals and women, and I have both at home – I can be NASTY. What can I be?'

'NASTY!' they all shouted.

'Right. You are going to be in battle soon . . .' He paused and screwed his eyes at a list on a clipboard in his hand. 'Where are the artillery men, the gunners, who've been transferred?'

'Here, sir,' called Harris.

Rumbleton surveyed them icily. 'Well, now you'll be proper soldiers. Not sitting all comfy behind a gun sending high explosives on to some poor Jerry three miles away who you can't even see. Now you'll be eyeball to ruddy eyeball with him!'

His stony face turned the width of the parade. 'The two sergeants present on parade,' he nodded each side at the men standing with him,' Sergeant Burkitt and Sergeant Hare, have been thrown out of the commandos for being too rough. Sergeant Burkitt will now tell you what's what.'

Harris thought he had never seen an uglier human being. Although young, Burkitt was short and hard, his eyes like a squinting pig, his jaw like a bucket. 'Today we are going to do 'ouse-to-'ouse fightin',' he barked. 'Unarmed combat, close-quarter combat, and silent killing.' His jaw swung in a half circle.

'Anybody 'ere done silent killing?'

Nobody had. 'Right. You'll learn. But first we are goin' to fight our way through these Kraut 'ouses. You might wonder why they are Kraut 'ouses because we're on Salisbury Plain and you'll be fighting in France, but it don't matter. After they first built these, years ago now, we had some men goin' off to kill them Japs in Burma where the 'ouses are made of bamboo and paper. But an 'ouse is an 'ouse except some burn quicker than others.'

Suddenly he seemed less assured, like an actor unsure of his lines. He said: 'Sergeant Hare will carry on from here.'

Hare was a cherubic-looking man with fair curls, but his blue eyes were vindictive. Despite his round face he stood stiff as iron and spoke in a nasal cockney voice. 'You got to remember that in the real fing these houses might have proper Krauts in them, and Krautesses. You are not allowed to *shoot* them! It's against the Geneva Convention, bein' as they are civilians. You must get them into a cellar or somewhere a bit safe. But don't lock 'em in.'

He surveyed the expressions in front of him, then said: 'During today's bit of fun you will be divided into two armies. Red army will be advancing from the north, like the left, and blue army from the south, the right. You've got to clear the 'ouses as you go and then try and clear each other out of 'em. Got it? Section leaders will make sure that their men only have *blank* ammunition. Real ammo has been known to sneak in by mistake and men get 'urt. Or dead.'

He sniffed around. 'Sergeant Burkitt and me will be in charge, geeing you up a bit, making a noise. We will chuck the odd thunderflash in the winders. If a thunderflash lands near you *do not attempt to pick it up*. Cover your ears and scarper, cos it can blow your arse off. Any questions?'

To Harris's astonishment, Gordon raised his hand. Hare stared at him as if he were mad and said: 'What?'

'Sergeant, how will we know who's the enemy?' asked Gordon. 'We all look the same.'

Hare drew in a breath. 'A Jock,' he muttered. 'Trust a Jock.' Sergeant Burkitt moved forward. 'We was coming to THAT!' he bawled. 'In a minute, wasn't we, Reggie?' Hare gave a nodding grunt. Burkitt continued: 'The red army will wear their tin 'ats, the blue army will not.'

'Thank you, sergeant,' said Gordon politely. 'I just thought I'd ask.'

'I haven't had so much fun since I was a kid!' Treadwell was gripped by the excitement. He fired another three random blanks from the window, then rolled over to reload the rifle. He was out of breath, his face was gritty, his eyes raw.

'Beats lugging those field guns around,' shouted Gordon busily reloading.

Across the dust-covered room of the Bavarian house, among tables and chairs, Blackie was enjoying a single-handed battle with soldiers in the next house and hoping they were the enemy. Warren was sitting in an armchair tugging the bolt from his jammed rifle. All day they had advanced and retreated. Chaffey, the mildest of men, had a black eye from a stand-up fist fight, and Gannick had bitten through his pipe. Noise and smoke erupted around them. Breathing hard, Harris charged up the stairs. 'They're coming from the right flank,' he panted. They could see he was enjoying himself too. 'Cover those windows. Come on, move!'

Almost playfully, an object came through the glassless window and bounced like a toy on the bare boards. They all knew what it was but nobody reacted until Harris shouted: 'Thunderflash! Move! Take cover!'

In a single rush they made for the head of the stairs, falling on top of each other. Harris was physically pushing them down the steps when the thunderflash went off with a shattering explosion and a streak of light. As Harris tried to cover his ears he tipped forward, over the top of Warren, and tumbled to the foot of the stairs. As he fell he heard and felt his ankle crack.

They were in a heap, legs, arms and rifles entangled. Harris was in pain. They realised he was not pretending. 'Stretcher-bearers!' shouted Gordon, putting his head out of the door. 'Stretcher-bearers here!'

Sergeant-Major Rumbleton was pacing through the smoke and the din of the street outside. He strode to the door. 'Who's hurt?' he demanded.

'Ankle, sir,' said Harris, propping himself against the banister. 'Feels like it's broken.'

Rumbleton turned to the door and over the noise in the street his huge voice bellowed: 'Stretcher party here!'

Four panting soldiers ran between the littered houses bearing a stretcher, one flying a Red Cross flag above his head. 'Christ,' muttered Rumbleton. 'It's the Swiss Army.'

The stretcher party were pleased and eager. With excited shouts they almost pushed Rumbleton aside and then burrowed through the other soldiers until they had space to lift Harris on to the stretcher. They did so clumsily, dropped him once, and finally rolled him on to it.

'Move! Come on!' shouted Rumbleton. 'He'll be dead before you know it.'

A man at each corner, the stretcher was charged like a battering-ram through the smoke and the bedlam. The mock battle was at its pitch. 'Sod 'im,' snorted one of the stretcher-bearers. 'That sodding sergeant-major.'

'He's got a poker up his bum,' panted the other.

They reached the edge of the imitation village. Two ambulances were parked, cigarette smoke rising from behind them. One orderly doused his Woodbine when he saw the stretcher party. 'Casualty!' shouted one of the advancing bearers. Both drivers opened the doors of one ambulance and Harris was heaved in.

A medical corps officer appeared. 'Oh good, a real casualty,' he enthused. 'Not dead, is he?'

They cut the boot from the injured ankle and the officer gave a disappointed sniff. 'Broken,' he diagnosed loftily. 'Or badly sprained. Get him to hospital.'

One of the orderlies stayed in the back of the ambulance with Harris as it bumped across the plain towards the main Salisbury road.

'You're lucky, sarge. That ought to keep you out of the invasion,' he told Harris. He had youthful spots all over his face.

Harris said: 'So they've told you the date, have they?'

He arrived outside his Southampton door at eleven in the morning, placed one of his crutches against the jamb and rang the bell. Enid answered, wearing an alluring and short pink silk nightdress and negligée. She said: 'Harris! What a lovely surprise!'

'What a lovely outfit.'

'It's American,' she said. 'I got it from . . . Oh, Harris, you've got a poorly leg! Let me get you a chair.'

'I'm standing on the doorstep.'

'Silly, stupid me,' she said, opening the door further to allow him into the narrow hall. He stumped forward into the kitchen, put his crutches, his backpack, his belt and his forage cap in one corner and opened his battledress tunic. 'Now I'll have a chair,' he said.

She made a performance of getting one from the other side of the kitchen table and then found a cushion which she punched into shape before putting it on the chair and gently sitting him down.

'Whatever have you done?' She surveyed the foot in its lump of plaster of Paris. 'It looks enormous.'

'Broken ankle,' he said. 'In training.'

Suddenly she realised. 'Oh, Harris – does it mean you won't have to go . . .?'

'Where?' he said bluntly.

'Oh, you know. To the thingy . . . Dunkirk.'

'Dunkirk was four years ago,' he said. 'The invasion, you mean.'

'Yes. The invasion. I get all mixed up with these war things. But you won't need to go?'

Harris put his arms out to her and pulled her towards him, wallowing in the luxury of her body and the soft silk.

'Watch it,' she warned. 'We'll have this chair arse over tit.'

He kissed her common, pretty face. 'Well, tell me,' she said. 'Will you be excused duty or whatever it is? Excused the invasion.'

'I hope the ankle will be mended,' he said simply. 'Depends when the invasion day is. They say this will take about six weeks.'

Enid eased herself away from him and stood with her hands accusingly on her hips. 'You sound like you actually *want* to go,' she said.

He shrugged. 'I've got to do it, love. That's why I joined. That's why I'm a soldier. Besides which, the rest of them would be lost without me. They'd probably run away.' He regarded her carefully. 'Is there a cup of tea?'

She almost jumped. 'Of course there is, darling. I should have asked, but what with your poorly foot and everything . . .' She made for the kettle. He thought how sexual she looked, even when she was so unkempt. There was a voluptuous slovenliness about her, her eyes still smudged with make-up, her hair falling about.

'Tell me about the nightdress,' he said.

'American, like I said. You know Maggie Phillips. It was a present from a Yank. But she couldn't tell Brian that, could she? And he's home from the air force almost every weekend. She wanted to keep it and she was going to spin some story about winning it in a competition in War Weapons Week, you know, that War Savings thing they have. But Brian has a suspicious mind, a touch on the sharp side, and he would have smelt a rat.'

'A Yank,' corrected Harris. 'It wouldn't have fitted her anyway, would it? She's twice your size. A lot taller for a start.' He took in the short nightdress. 'That thing would have ended up around her waist.'

Enid seemed to blush, then she giggled. 'Perhaps that was the idea. Anyway, I got it for two pounds ten.'

She brought him the tea. The saucer was cracked. 'Just like your ankle,' she said. 'Is it ever so painful?'

'Not now. Can't feel anything.'

His wife prodded the solid plaster of Paris. 'It's ever so hard.'

He took a sip of the tea but he had no time for another. As if she had suddenly spotted something she liked, Enid took the cup and saucer from him and placed them on the table, then knelt in front of him and, with a single warm glance at the swift expectancy of his face, began to open the metal buttons at the front of his army trousers.

'I'll never get these off now,' she whispered, opening them. 'Not with that lump on your foot. And you're still wearing those horrible underpants.

Harris said nothing while she unloaded his penis and tenderly put it between her lips and then into her mouth. He did not care whatever she got up to when he was away. As long as she did this when he was here.

She turned her lascivious sleepy eyes up to him and then levered herself up and spread her bare thighs across him. With a practised movement she reached down and guided his penis into her, squatting astride him until his climax and, he was pleased to know, hers. 'There's knickers that go with this outfit,' she mentioned. 'I'm glad I didn't wear them.'

Her slight arms embraced his waist and then lightly pounded his body. 'You're hard, Harris,' she said. 'Every part of you. Hard as iron.'

'It's the infantry training,' he told her, stroking her tangled hair. 'They've transferred us to the Hampshires.'

It meant little to her. She punched his ribs more firmly and then his stomach. 'Hard,' she repeated. 'Even a German bullet wouldn't get through that.'

'Kippers,' he muttered as he woke up. It was three in the afternoon. The window was full of a windy sky.

'Kippers!' Enid called up the stairs. 'Can you smell them?'

She appeared at the bedroom door. She was wearing a housewifely pinafore, her young face bright above it; her hair was carefully done and she was carrying a cup of tea.

'You could smell 'em in Portsmouth,' he said.

'That's the trouble.' She put the tea on the bedside table, kissed him on the forehead, leaning her breasts on his chest, went to his plastered ankle and patted it as if it were a pet. 'They came from the pub; from the docks. You know what I mean. But I had to have a whole ruddy box of them, twelve pairs, so I had to sell some of them, didn't I? They'd have gone off. I kept two pairs and got shot of the rest. Half the houses in this street will be wiffing of kippers today. I hope the coppers don't sniff 'em.'

Harris sipped the strong tea. 'What's happened to your betting round?' he asked.

'Don't do it any more,' she told him a little sulkily. 'That Charlie Parker, that bookie, he started to get personal, and he's not my type, all whisky and whiskery. So I'm out of a job.' As if suddenly remembering, she took an opened brown envelope from her pinafore pocket. 'The taxman is after you again,' she said. 'He wants twenty-one quid. You'd think the bugger would leave you alone since you're fighting for your country and he's safe behind a comfy bloody desk.'

Harris took the envelope with disdain. 'It's not even *me*. I've written to them. The army's been paying me for four years almost, and the army deducts the tax. Anyway, this bloke Harris has got the same name but a different middle initial than me. See.' He showed her the front of the buff envelope. 'His middle name begins with W.'

A touch shamefacedly she asked: 'What's yours?'

He had ceased to be astonished by her. 'Adrian,' he said. 'Didn't you know?'

'I forgot,' she said, sitting on the side of the bed. She began to smooth the bedclothes over him. 'It's never been mentioned since the wedding and it's not much better than Neville, so I think I'll still call you Harris.' Absent-mindedly she was caressing his groin through the counterpane. 'Do you want a kipper or a nice time?' she asked.

'Don't burn the kipper,' he said, kissing her cheek.

'The kipper's not quite ready but I am,' she said and with a sort of decorum, she lifted her pinafore and her skirt. She was naked underneath. 'Watch the ankle,' he warned, strongly but gently easing her on top of him. He felt her soft underneath and her thighs willingly opened. Her face moved next to his and her hair tumbled over his neck.

'I'm worried about those kippers,' she said when she next raised her head and looked at him. 'I'll have to go.'

She tugged her skirt down and trotted from the room, returning with a warm flannel and a towel. She gently worked first one, then the other, over him. He lay against the pillow, savouring the feel of what she was doing, then he kissed her warmly.

Primly she replaced the bedclothes over him. 'Do you want your kipper up here?' she asked.

Harris laughed. 'A bit niffy, won't it be?'

'Bedrooms do get niffy, what with one thing or another. We'll open the window a bit. It's not a bad day. I'll bring them up.'

He sat, satisfied as he would ever be, drained and yet complete. He was away from the army and the war, if only for a time, in bed in the middle of a weekday afternoon, and waiting for a beautiful woman to bring him a kipper. She came up the stairs with two on a single plate on a tray with bread and margarine and two bottles of Watney's ale. 'It's what they called room service,' she said, pulling up a chair and balancing the tray between them. She began to dismember the smoked fish. 'There's a dance tonight. Will you be able to come? How long will you be home, by the way? I did mean to ask.'

'Seven days,' he told her. 'I have to report to the hospital again next Friday. They may send me back for another seven days' sick leave.'

'That will be nice,' she said, not altogether convincingly. 'What about the dance?'

'Enid, I've got a broken ankle.'

'You could still come.'

'You'll be going anyway?' He knew she would.

'It's only at Eastleigh.' She hesitated. 'I was getting a lift.' She looked at the swelling of the plaster of Paris on his ankle beneath the bedclothes. 'On a motor bike.' She regarded the mound again and added: 'He's got a side-car.'

She had put on a slim red dress and red shoes. Swirling in front of the full-length mirror in the bedroom, she laughed at Harris's gaze. 'Do you like me in the looking-glass, darling?' she said. She suddenly stopped and put her hand to her mouth. 'Oh, I forgot my stockings. Will you put them on for me?'

He had done it before. 'Get the seams straight,' she said. 'They were a bit wobbly last time.' She pulled the dress over her head and shook off the shoes, then lay in her underwear on her front, crossways on the bed. 'The pencil's on the dressing-table,' she told him.

Her face and her dangling hands were over the edge of the counterpane. He kissed her hair. 'Other end, Harris,' she said.

Harris surveyed the naked backs of her legs. Then, taking the eyebrow pencil and starting at her left ankle, he began to trace a slim, black seam up the back of her calf. 'It's not wobbly, is it?' she asked anxiously.

'Straight up the back and no blodges,' he promised. He took the line carefully to the back of her knee and then up her firm thigh. 'It looks all right but it won't keep your legs warm,' he said. 'How high do you want it to go?'

'Up to my bum, please. Not that anyone will see. Except you.'

He straightened up and looked at his work. Then he etched a seam on the other leg. 'Done,' he said, patting her pants. 'Take a look.'

'In a minute,' she said. 'Let it set.'

He went around to her head again, pushed her hair back and kissed her pleased face. She waited a moment, then carefully left the bed and, first putting on her shoes, went to the mirror. 'Perfect,' she approved. 'As good as nylons.'

She put on her dress again and looked at him in his solid uniform. 'You look beautiful, too,' she said.

'When I'm not here, who puts your seams on?' he asked, smiling.

'I try myself, but it's difficult,' Enid answered. 'Sometimes Maggie and I do each other's. We do have a laugh.'

They went to the Sailors' Blessing and sat in the saloon bar. It was seven in the evening.

She had conscientiously brought him a pint of beer, returning to him across the pub like a tightrope artiste so she did not spill any.

He grimaced. 'I'm not going in any side-car,' he said again. 'What do you think I am? A roll of lino?'

Her concern dissolved in a giggle. 'All right,' she said, sipping her port and lemon daintily. 'We'll go on the bus. Johnny Fallon will be disappointed, but he'll have to lump it.'

Harris said: 'What am I going to a dance for, anyway?' He nodded at his foot. 'I can't drag this lump around the floor.'

'You can manage a waltz,' she argued. 'You only have to pull it after you.'

A tall, skinny young man, wearing a flashy tie and a blazer, came through the door.

'Sorry I'm late, Enid.' He took in Harris. 'Who's this? A wounded soldier?'

Blushing, Enid said: 'He's my husband . . .' She searched for it, then said: 'Adrian.'

Harris glanced at her. He held out his hard soldier's hand and shook the equally hard, thin fingers of Johnny. 'Didn't she tell you she had a husband called Adrian – or Neville?'

Johnny looked confused. 'No . . . well, she might have done. But I forgot.'

'We can't accept your kind offer of a lift,' sniffed Enid. 'He won't go in the side-car.'

'Probably wouldn't fit,' said Johnny. 'You're still going to the dance?'

'We'll go on the bus,' said Harris. 'I'm no good in side-cars.' Grimly he smiled at the other man. 'See you there.'

'Please yourselves,' grunted Johnny, turning towards the bar.

Enid said: 'You didn't have to be so snotty, Harris.'

'Why isn't he in the army?'

'He's a docker, that's why. Work of National Importance, in case you don't know. Not everybody is dashing around playing soldiers, playing bang-bangs. And he's good as gold, too. Ask a lot of people in this pub. You, for a start, had one of his kippers today.'

'And you think I go around playing bang-bangs.'

'That's all that's happened for three or four years,' she retorted. 'Not like Sue Billings's George. Out in Burma. You've even got yourself wounded *pretending* to fight. Look at the state you're in.'

He regarded her sulky expression. 'Sorry I haven't been awarded the Victoria Cross,' he said. 'I'll try harder. I'll probably get the chance soon.'

Enid seemed ashamed. 'Let's get the bus,' she sighed. 'It'll be along in a mo'.' He drank his beer and she put her port glass down before realising there was still some in the bottom and taking a final swallow. She waved to Johnny at the bar and then helped Harris to his foot. Slotting his crutches in his armpits, he swung clumsily and moodily towards the door.

It had begun to rain thinly. It was as dark as nights had been for four years. The bus came along the road like a heavy ghost. Enid waved a white handkerchief to stop it.

There was a small, chirpy conductress on the platform, her shabby uniform hanging in folds. 'Oh, let's get you up,' she said when she saw Harris. She looked at Enid. 'You get one side and I'll get the other. But don't let the poor sod slip.'

'I won't,' promised Enid. 'He's my husband.'

Between them they pulled him up on to the platform. The few passengers on the bottom deck turned half-heartedly to look and a drunk at the front began pumping his arm and calling: 'Left, right, left, right . . .'

'Bollocks,' said Harris under his breath.

'That bloke ought to be in the army,' said Enid.

'Too old,' said the conductress. 'And too sozzled.'

'I was on the Somme!' shouted the drunk. 'That was a real war, mate, lots getting killed, not like this nancying about.'

Harris and Enid sat on the bench seats next to the platform. Enid took some coins from her handbag. 'Two to Eastleigh,' she said.

'Going to the hop, are you?' asked the conductress. 'There's a few upstairs that's going. They're all smoking up there. I feel like I'm going up into the clouds. I'm sure it don't do you no good.' She still had the pennies in her hand and she returned them to Enid. 'I'm not charging a wounded soldier and his missus,' she said. 'That's the least I can do.'

'You took my soddin' fare quick enough,' bellowed the man in the front. He began to cough spectacularly, bent with the effort of it. 'Listen to that phlegm,' he challenged. 'Poison gas, that is.'

The conductress sniffed and smiled at them, revealing broken teeth. 'Hope you enjoy the dance.' Her wrinkles deepened. 'He can't dance like that, can he?' she said, nodding down at Harris's ankle and up at his crutches. 'Not with that lump.'

Harris said: 'I'll watch. I'm good at watching.'

It was a US Air Force band in slinky blue uniforms. The leader was peering through rimless spectacles, trying to look like Benny Goodman. The band were popular locally, bringing a touch of transatlantic glamour to provincial people who had never been to America and believed they were unlikely ever to go. Some had never even visited London, a hundred miles distant. Their visions of the USA came from Hollywood films which packed the cinemas every night, and from the incursion of these smooth-talking strangers in their smooth uniforms.

'Yanks,' sneered Johnny Fallon who, because of his motorcycle and side-car, had reached the dance before Harris and Enid. 'Useless.'

Sportingly he bought Harris a beer and Enid a port and lemon. He stood close to Enid. 'Why do you reckon they're useless?'

Harris asked. Enid turned to a group of young, anticipatory women.

Johnny said: 'They done bugger all, 'ave they? Except talk and shag.'

'They've not had much chance yet,' pointed out Harris. 'That'll come soon enough. Like it will for the rest of us.'

Johnny blew a raspberry. ''Ave you seen the way the Yanks march? They did a parade through Southampton and, even though I'm no soldier, they was a bloody shambles. They slouch, not march. And they had some bloke like a clown at the front jangling bells. *Bells*, I ask you.'

The big place was full by now. A mirrored glass ball spun from the ceiling. There were plenty of local girls, done up in their amateur best, buffed and brassièred, thick with make-up, heavy with scent and hope. The men were mostly Americans with blue and khaki tailored uniforms, glistening shoes, shiny hair and roving eyes. Some local men, civilians, eyed the US servicemen with a mixture of envy and scorn. There were British soldiers, sailors and airmen, some loutish, others sheepish, keeping to the region of the bar.

The band, which had been playing 'American Patrol', now switched to 'Twelfth Street Rag' and at once the floor was flying with jitterbugging couples, the men whirling and flinging girls whose skirts flew to their waists. The local watchers edged forward. 'Can you do that?' Harris asked Johnny.

'What? That bollocks? That ain't dancing. It's so the girls can flash their knicks.'

Enid came from the cloakroom and purred: 'Oh, what a nice lot of Yanks.'

'Crawling with them,' sniffed Johnny. Harris grinned and accepted a whisky at the same time as Enid had a ginger-beer shandy. Johnny had a wallet thick with notes.

After the jitterbug, the rimless-spectacled band leader announced a waltz and, with hardly a glance at Harris, Johnny held out inviting arms to Enid. She was just about to enter them when Harris interpolated himself. 'My dance with my wife, I think.'

Enid said: 'Ooooh.' She helped Harris to stumble towards the music.

'It's no good getting upset with Johnny,' she said when they were dancing on the spot, Harris merely pumping his plastered leg up and down. 'He don't mean any harm.'

'I do,' muttered Harris.

She giggled. 'My hero. Go on, kick him with your poorly foot.'

He eased her to him and they snuggled into each other on the floor. The air was warm, stuffy, redolent with Southampton Woolworth's perfume, and the music dreamy. Then a raw, arrogant American voice halted them: 'No niggers. Get those niggers out o' here.'

The music faded, the dancers faltered, the band leader blinked, his baton dropped. A thick, uncouth-looking American jumped on to the dais, pushing him aside. The reflected light from the mirrored ball shone on the soldier's cropped head. The band leader said: 'Okay, okay,' and hurriedly got down from the platform.

A clutch of about twenty black soldiers was coming through the doors at the distant end of the room. They kept walking.

'Let's get out of the way,' said Harris, pushing Enid to the side of the floor.

She looked excited. 'Is there going to be a fight?'

'They haven't come to play hopscotch.'

They reached the bar, where the locals had gathered. Some who had been dancing were prudently making their way back, others were already heading for the exit.

'I want to see!' Enid was bouncing like a child. She swallowed a gin which wasn't hers. 'I've never seen a really big fight.'

She wriggled between the watchers to the end of the bar, with Harris hobbling after her. Johnny, grinning, helped her on to the stool and she climbed, awkward in her tight red dress, on to the bar itself. There were already girls and men up there for a good view.

The black soldiers had forced their way on to the vacated dance floor. The band were packing their instruments in panic. From the dais the raw-faced American was still bawling: 'Here come the crows!' and, as the black men advanced towards him, there was an instinctive rush of other white soldiers from the flanks. In a moment the floor was a mêlée of shouting, cursing men, black versus white, slugging it out. Above them the mirror ball revolved serenely.

The drum-kit of the band was resoundingly overturned and the small, frightened drummer tipped on to his head as he attempted to save it. From just below the ceiling of the bar the excited English girls screamed even above the din, the local men waved their beer glasses and urged anybody on. Harris was still trying to get Enid back down to the floor. She was not listening. 'Bugger it,' he muttered and with a shrug picked up his drink.

As though at a known signal, the mass fight on the dance floor suddenly ceased. The heavy white American, the one who had first shouted, moved to the centre of the polished boards, and a giant black soldier detached himself from the mob, and moved towards him. 'Nigger,' grunted the white man. He spat on the ground in front of the black man's feet. 'Nigger.'

Silence held the room and the black soldier's answer, although only in little more than conversational tone, was clear: 'Come and get me, honky.'

'They're calling each other names!' Enid squeaked.

'Are you coming down from there?' demanded Harris.

'Not for five quid! I want to see this.'

He leaned on the bar, peering through the legs of the people standing on it, and said: 'A pint, please,' to the barman who was going imperturbably about his business. He pulled it and handed it across saying: 'Ninepence, please.'

Pushing the money to him, Harris took a first sip and then turned the way the crowd were looking. Everything was suspense now, taut, no catcalls, no screams from the girls. The air was hung with smoke, beer, scent and sweat. He could see the heads of the black man and the white man as they moved around each other, the silvery light of the innocently circling ball on their hardened faces.

Enid could take no more and suddenly shouted: "It 'im, blackie!' As if it were enough the two American soldiers began hitting out viciously, big men, unafraid, strong and well trained. They traded full punches. With each one the shuddering force seemed to jolt the room. The white man abruptly fell sideways, demolishing the drums again. The black man waited until he had regained his feet and then closed in again but was met by a ferocious head-butt that sent him staggering into the onlookers, breaking the human perimeter and the silence. Everyone was shouting, beer was spilt and fists were raised, but the central fight was not disturbed.

'Not fair! Not fair!' screeched Enid. "Itting with 'eads. Not fair!'

The animated spectators were swaying with the fight, moving like a formation dance. The two men were streaming blood – it was easier to see on the white man – but nevertheless they lunged into each other again, slugging it out unrelentingly.

'Where's the police?' Harris quietly asked the barman.

'Be a while yet.' The man gave a sniff of experience.

'Oooh,' shouted Enid. "E's got a knife! Whitey's got a knife.' The other girls began to screech. The combatants were locked close with each other now. Blood was smeared across the polished floor. As they parted the black soldier fell like a ton on to his back, the knife thrust into his chest, its blade blinking in the light of the mirrored ball.

There was a swift, shocked silence. It seemed to last for minutes. Eventually one of the civilian men said: 'He's stabbed him.' It was almost a mutter. Then they realised. There came a huge collective shout and, as the appalled crowd fell back so the American soldiers rushed each other, fighting savagely.

There was a gust of shouting and screaming from the spectators. Enid, still standing on the bar, was shrieking and pointing. Some of the women were trying to get down from the bar but Enid remained above the mayhem. Determinedly, Harris reached up and attempted to pull her from her place over the crowd.

Then from the struggling pile of soldiers on the dance floor came a gunshot. It stunned the room to silence again. Then came another and two more. An oddly gentle cloud of blue smoke rose. There were more sudden cries and screams and the tumult restarted. Another shot sounded. Enid was screeching. Harris reached for her and caught hold of her leg. She fell off, almost head first, and he managed to catch her, her dress around her waist. Other girls were jumping and sliding off like a crew abandoning ship. Johnny appeared through the chaos and said: 'Time to go home.'

'Good idea,' grunted Harris gratefully. They each took one of the weeping Enid's arms, and then legs, and hauled her out like a battering-ram. As they reached the door, so the US military police were pouring in, truncheons drawn, white helmets above glistening eyes.

People were streaming out around them. From within the hall there were two more gunshots. 'Some dance,' said Harris.

It was tipping with rain but nobody noticed. Johnny found his motorcycle and with the sobbing and coatless Enid bundled into the side-car and Harris, his leg stretched out before him, riding pillion and clutching Johnny's waist, they skidded through the unlit soaking streets until they arrived at the front gate. They unrolled Enid from the side-car. She was whimpering. Harris and Johnny between them got her to the door. Harris said: 'Thanks,' and extended a conclusive hand to Johnny.

The docker shook it. 'That's all right, mate. Good night out, don't you reckon? If them Yanks fight the Jerries like they fight each other, there'll be bugger all to worry about.'

Chapter Sixteen

Every evening now the light stayed a few minutes longer. London, despite its sorrows and its wounds, took on a springtime air. Bars and cinemas and dancehalls of the West End did their best business since the start of the war; the pavements were crowded early with uniformed men of many nationalities heading for what they wanted most – a good time. They were looking for drink and women and there was plenty of both. The official blackout time was not until nine thirty and there was a while for some lights to remain lit, those that had not fallen into utter disuse. Even though the final battle was still to come, there was a lightness of feeling, an uplift, brought about by the balm of the weather and the conviction that soon, perhaps in only a matter of weeks, peace would be back where it belonged.

Miller walked through Hyde Park, passing the disused air-raid shelters, the clutter of military vehicles and materials, and the daffodils. Ducks quacked on the big circular water tanks built for the fire brigade in strategic places and sometimes young, sometimes pretty girls casually solicited for sex under the newly sprouting trees.

He answered them politely as he strolled towards Marble Arch. 'Not tonight, thanks. Maybe tomorrow.' He did not like to upset them. He had seen them loitering, not only like owls at their natural time, dusk, or folded in later darkness, but also in the pale mornings when he took his training run around the park. He felt sorry for the early girls. One of them had halted him in mid-run and offered him what she called a cheap thrill.

She had said she was on her way to her normal job in an Oxford Street store.

This evening was fine enough to walk to the West End. Piccadilly Circus was thronged. Foreign soldiers were taking laughing photographs of each other under the plinth of Eros which was banked up with patriotic posters about war savings and avoiding coughs and sneezes and venereal diseases, but was lacking the famous winged statue who had long been taken, with his bow and arrow, to some safe accommodation. Other London memorials had not been so lucky. King Richard the Lionheart still held his bronze sword aloft outside Parliament, but bent by a bomb at the middle of its blade.

The pre-war illuminated advertising signs for Guinness, Johnny Walker whisky and Carter's Little Liver Pills ('Wake up your liver bile') remained tacked to the buildings around the circus but now they were only metal shapes, dusty and lightless.

Few people bothered to look at them anyway, or at the sky, a darkening jigsaw piece fixed among the Piccadilly roofs; all attention and noisy activity were on the pavements. Buses, taxis and a few furtive cars whirled slowly around the circus and a group of exuberant French sailors, their hats enlivened by red pom-poms, linked arms with a chorus of singing shopgirls.

Miller found the theatre behind Shaftesbury Avenue. The adjoining building had been demolished by a bomb and there were fortifications of rotting sandbags around a police telephone box on the pavement. Like an ever-present extra, an old, mufflered man shouted as he touted the London evening newspapers: 'RAF Clobbers Germany. Ruskies Advance.'

Above the theatre's doors was a plain poster: 'Chekov's *The Seagull.*' Only a few people were going in. He paid at the cubbyhole of the box office and sat in the middle stalls. By the time the lights dimmed, the theatre was only half full; some were men in uniform but mostly they were civilians.

Kathleen, as Arkadina, came on to the stage and he watched her carefully. She was slim, almost thin, intense and careful, her voice notable. After the performance he went around to the stage door and asked for her.

She had not changed from her stage clothes when she came down the dim, curving steps. The stage-door keeper in a faded, striped deck-chair, nodded dozily over his newspaper. 'Oh, how very good of you to come,' Kathleen said, surprised and a touch mystified.

'I enjoyed it,' he said as they shook hands. 'I don't get a lot of culture, I'm afraid.'

'Not much of an audience,' she smiled. 'It's the first time I can honestly say anyone has come especially to see me. My goodness – me, pulling in the crowds.'

She looked embarrassed. 'I can't invite you to my dressing-room for a drink,' she said. 'It's shared and it's like a cupboard. There's not enough room for three.'

'I'll wait,' he said. 'Perhaps we could go somewhere for dinner.'

She gave a small laugh. 'We'd be lucky,' she said. 'But we could try. I'll be down in ten minutes. Don't go away.'

'I won't,' he promised. The stage-door keeper, who could scarcely keep awake, lifted his head and, heavy lidded, tapped his *Evening News*. 'Them Reds will be in Berlin afore you lot, if you're not sharp,' he mentioned.

Five minutes' walk through the moving shadows of the West End crowd brought them to a mews with a small restaurant among the low houses which years before had been stables. She took Miller's arm and they threaded their way carefully. There were drunken soldiers and airmen pushing along the pavements and he knew the fact that he was an officer meant nothing. London was thronged. Boisterous songs and impromptu dances filled the streets as if the war were already over. There was an unbridled fist fight going on at one corner. Policemen, in their pointed helmets and with truncheons drawn, were heading ponderously towards the fracas.

It was necessary to knock. 'Luigi, are you still open?' asked Kathleen as the door of the restaurant widened cautiously.

Through the dim aperture a young man's face beamed. 'For you, madam, we are always open.' The door swung wide. 'But we only have a little food left.'

Kathleen laughed. 'But you have some wine.'

'Wine we have. Not as good wine as we would like, but some there is. Before long maybe we will get some new supplies from Italy.'

It was like a cave with candles and empty tables. An elderly guitar player was just packing away his instrument. He looked up. Kathleen said: 'You were just going.'

'For you,' said the man, retrieving the guitar from his case, 'I will play through the night.'

'Until the last train,' corrected Luigi as he showed them to a corner table. He walked with difficulty. 'We have no tonic water although we have a whole bottle of gin. Tomorrow we get the tonic maybe.'

Kathleen glanced at Miller. 'Wine, Luigi,' she said. 'This is my friend Captain Miller.'

Luigi bowed and they shook hands. 'His mother was British,' said Kathleen when he had gone for the wine. 'His father Italian. His father was in Italy when they came into the war. He was put in the Italian Army and I think he's a prisoner now.'

The young man returned. He had heard. 'Prisoner of the Teds, the Germans,' he said. 'But I hear he is okay. The *Tedeschi* are finished. How did we get mixed up with them?'

He opened a bottle of Chianti and gave it to Miller, who handed it to Kathleen, who took a token sniff and then returned it to Luigi to pour. 'There is a big fight in the street, isn't there?' he said as he did so. Miller shrugged: 'These soldiers are boys. They can't wait to fight.'

They each ordered a mushroom omelette with sautéed potatoes and mashed turnips and carrots. 'Very often it's the blacks versus the whites,' said Kathleen.

Miller nodded. 'Three men were killed – one knifed, two shot – and five injured in a fight, blacks and whites, in Southampton only the other night. At a dance.'

'And yet they are expected to go into battle together,' she said. 'Side by side.'

Miller shook his head. 'The United States has no black combat troops. They do the other jobs but not fighting. I have a black driver who's the best man I know.'

Kathleen said: 'Why don't they allow them to fight?'

'Maybe Uncle Sam doesn't trust their resolve, shall we say. Personally, I think that's crazy. They'll be good in battle. In that way maybe they'll get some due respect. In the not-too-distant future they'll have to use black troops in the front line. It depends on the casualties.'

Kathleen sighed. 'It's so terrible that you, that we, have to think like that. Will you . . . when the invasion happens will you . . .?'

'I hope so,' he smiled. 'I didn't come all this way to watch.'

'Are you married?'

She said it as though it were not important. She did not look up from her food. 'Sure,' he said. 'She's back in Bismarck, North Dakota, looking after the dogs.'

'No children?'

'No, just dogs. They win prizes, cups and ribbons and rosettes. It's the big thing in her life. And you?'

'I'm on my second husband,' she said. 'The first was a disaster. This one's worse.'

They both laughed. 'Full marks for being frank,' he said. 'For both of us.'

She had grey eyes slightly melancholy. 'That's all there's time for these days, frankness.'

'Is your husband in the services?'

'Entertaining them,' she said. 'He's an actor and he's some-where in the Middle East, or Italy, being Hamlet for soldiers. Sadly he's a drunk. He once dropped off to sleep in the middle of the famous soliloquy.'

He asked her about the play he had seen that evening. 'On its last legs, I think,' she said. 'You saw the audience. In wartime most of them want lots of flesh and jokes. There's a show called *Soldiers in Skirts*. It's a sell-out every night.'

She smiled reflectively. 'And our audiences, they complain. There's always something. During that recent bombing someone moaned to the manager that the scenery was wobbling. It was, too. So was I, for that matter.'

'You didn't quit the stage during an air raid?'

'It's routine by now. The manager comes on and announces that an air raid is in progress and we carry on through it. Some people leave but not many. Londoners have become very tough. During the big Blitz, in 1940, there were queues outside the cinema in Leicester Square for *Gone With the Wind* and the firemen still hadn't put the previous night's fires out.'

They were there for an hour. The guitarist played dreamily but then had to leave to get the last underground train.

Luigi saw them to the door, locking it behind them. The streets seemed more crowded in the dark. They searched for a taxi. Eventually one stopped.

'I'd like to see you home,' said Miller.

'I wish you would.'

The shuddering taxi took them into Belgravia, where there were fine, upstanding houses, dark against the sky; beyond the clamour of the crowds, they were surrounded by a refined silence.

'It's very posh,' said Kathleen, almost like a warning. 'You can rent these houses and apartments for very little just now. One of the few good things about this war is the bargains. Soon, I imagine, the prices will be going up again. When those people who ran off begin creeping back.'

Miller paid the driver in his box-like cab. The London taxis amused him for they appeared hardly removed from pictures of the nineteenth-century hansom cabs. 'Good luck over there, sir,' said the driver knowingly. He was wrapped in a muffler, despite the spring weather. 'I wish I could come with you. The Huns in the First War was all right. Just soldiers. But I 'aven't got time for this lot. Them and their 'Itler. Too big for their boots, if you ask me. Give 'em what for.'

'I'll do my best,' promised Miller.

Kathleen opened the high black front door and touched her finger to her lips. 'There's a Lord and Lady Somebody in the flat on this floor,' she whispered. 'They complain if you come in late and the door bangs.'

With caution they went up the curved staircase. The building felt warm and cared for. She took a key from her handbag, opened a door on the first landing and switched on the lights as they went in.

Miller whistled briefly: 'This is some place.'

The apartment was tall and finely furnished. They went from a marble-floored vestibule into a grand reception room. 'Not bad at the rent,' she said. 'I'll get you a drink. I have some champagne. It's been waiting for somebody to drink it.'

There was an ornate electric fire which she turned on. He sat on a large sofa and wondered how many yards of material had gone into the ceiling-to-floor drapes at the windows, how much the oversized paintings were worth. He began to feel pleased and comfortable.

'That taxi-driver was keen to fight,' she called from the next room. She brought in a tray with two champagne glasses and the bottle. 'There's even a refrigerator with ice,' she said.

'He couldn't wait,' said Miller. 'But I guess he'll stay with his taxi.' He stood to open the bottle but she insisted on doing it. 'It's my bottle,' she said.

She opened it without fuss and poured two glasses. It was good champagne; it did not fizz or overflow but sat obediently shimmering in the glasses. 'I liked his muffler,' she said. 'A London muffler is the trademark of elderly taxi-drivers and the newspaper sellers.'

'We call a silencer on an automobile a muffler,' he said.

They raised their glasses to each other and she said: 'Enough of the small talk, captain.' Confidently she moved against him; he could smell her deft perfume. 'I have to confess that I want you desperately,' she said, putting her forehead against his neck.

Miller put down his glass but she kept hers. His arms moved about her slender body and he said: 'I guess I'm out of practice.'

'You'll soon pick it up again,' she smiled.

Now she put her glass beside his on the table and her arms slid up his back. For a slight woman she kissed voluptuously. 'Good,' she said frankly. 'I knew this would happen, from the moment we met.'

He smiled, surprised at her intensity. They eased apart and studied each other's faces. With a sly look she took his left hand and guided it around her slim back, closing it on her wrist so that he held her like a prisoner. 'There are a lot of things you'll have to find out about me,' she whispered.

'I'm prepared to learn,' he said.

'Will you undress me? I want you to undress me here in front of the fire.' Her voice was steady, almost matter-of-fact, but hardly above a whisper.

Miller kissed her cheek-bone. After a few moments her eyes half opened as if to make sure he was still there. 'Start now,' she said.

'Take me through it,' he said.

She eased his hands to buttons and catches. The pale blouse came away and then she helped him with her brassière and she stood, head bowed, displaying her breasts to him, pointing the nipples at him. 'Don't crease your uniform, darling,' she murmured. 'Let me take it.'

She undid the buttons of his tunic and then slipped it away from him. She took off his officer's tie and undid his shirt. 'Hmm. Bare chest,' she observed, suddenly practical. 'Don't you get cold?'

'Not right now.'

Stage by stage, garment by garment, they took turns until they were standing naked against each other, the electric fire glowing pink on their bodies. She kept her eyes on his face but moved a little away, as if for a dare, picked up his champagne glass, refilled it and handed it to him. Then she replenished her own. They were only inches apart as she, and then he, raised a glass. 'Cheers,' she said. 'Darling.'

'Cheers to you,' he said.

They moved against each other. 'Don't you think I'm skinny?' she asked.

'Slender,' he said.

'This is beautiful,' she observed. She poured a trickle of champagne on his penis and then guided his glass to let a dribble fall between her breasts.

Miller had never had an experience like this. Such things did not happen in North Dakota, not outside dreams. It was like being in a play with her.

'Come down here now,' she said. 'This soft carpet is wasted on people's feet.'

She tenderly pulled him towards her and then sank to the carpet, easing him down to her. 'I have to tell you something,' she said. 'But it must wait.'

'This is no time for conversation,' he agreed.

At five in the morning he awoke in her four-poster bed. She stirred with him. 'Do you have to go now?'

'Unless I want a court martial,' he said.

Kathleen slid down beside him and he folded her into his body. They made love again, sleepily, and she said: 'Before you go I must tell you what I wanted to tell you last night. But I was afraid it would spoil it.'

'Try me,' he said.

'I am the most terrible liar.'

'I haven't caught you out yet.'

'But I am. I make things up as I go along. That day we met, I told you that I had gone into Hampton Court for some solitude. Because my friend's husband had died in a Japanese prison camp. I'm sorry to say that was so much balls. I don't have a friend with a dead prisoner-of-war husband.'

He turned on the bedside light and studied her face. She looked almost gaunt. 'Why would you want to say that?'

'I wanted to pick you up, that's why. I saw you going in there and I wanted you.'

He laughed calmly. 'Well, you sure enough succeeded. And I'm glad. It's a great line.'

'I was down there to take something I wanted to sell to an antique shop. He's bought things from me before, jewellery and suchlike. Sometimes I find myself behind with the rent. I felt very lonely that day, very melancholy. And then I saw you by yourself and I made up the story.'

Naked, he eased himself from the bed. 'It was a good, sad story,' he said. 'And it didn't do anybody any harm. We're here together.'

'And another thing. Last night when I said my husband was a drunken actor entertaining the troops in the Middle East. That wasn't true either.' Her eyes fell. '. . . Only it's a bit true.'

'Which bit?'

She looked miserable. 'Well, he's an actor of sorts but he's not a drunk. You remember I mentioned that revue *Soldiers in Skirts*? Well, he's one of them. And I mean *one of them.*'

Miller began to laugh and leaned over to kiss her. 'Anything else? Anything you want to get off your mind?'

'Not at the moment. I'll try to make up some more before we see each other again.' Her face was drawn, anxious, in the light from the single lamp. 'That's if we do.'

Her eyes were bright, even sharp. Her slim hand went to his face.

'I'm not going to let you vanish just yet,' he said. 'Not until Uncle Sam sends me somewhere. Then I'll be back as soon as I can.' He grinned encouragingly. 'How about tonight?'

She eased herself from the bed, her small buttocks tight, and reached for her robe. 'Tonight would be wonderful,' she said. 'I won't ask you to come to the play again.' She went into the bathroom. 'I'll get some coffee,' she called. 'The number is on the telephone by the bed, Belgravia 8592. Will you ring me early evening anyway? Today I have a matinée.'

At five forty-five he left, carrying his shoes; he crept down the main stairs and stealthily opened the street door. As he did he turned and she was standing on the landing, like a wraith, slightly waving. He waved back, put on his shoes as he stood on the doorstep, closed the door, and went out.

It was getting light. The only movement was a cat walking in the middle of the street. It saw Miller and walked to him, unafraid, and rubbed itself against his legs. A taxi drove lazily around the corner.

'I been on duty all night,' said the driver. 'I 'spect you have too, sir.'

Miller mumbled. The driver said: 'You don't have to tell me nothing. I know it's all top secret these days.'

They went unhurriedly through Belgravia and out on to Park Lane. 'It's quieter now,' persisted the driver. 'For a bit. Blimey, London's a disgrace at night. Prossies and pimps and pickpockets, and deserters and black men and black-market gangs, not to mention the drunks. Sometimes I think it might have been better if 'Itler 'ad taken over.'

They reached Bayswater Road and turned into the US Army building. At the door one of the uniformed porters grinned knowingly as he let Miller in. 'Busy night, sir?'

'Very,' said Miller. He went to his room and took off his outer clothes. He had been lying on the bed for only ten minutes when the telephone rang. It was a woman: 'Captain Miller, Colonel Jeffries for you.' A distressed and weary voice came on the line. 'Captain, we've had a disaster. We've lost six, maybe seven *hundred* men on a seaborne training exercise, maybe even more. Just *practising* for Christ-sake. A simulated beach landing. Off the coast of Devon county. You get to Exeter, US headquarters. I'm just leaving. Get your ass down there, fast as you can.'

He was the last to enter the room. A military policeman opened the door and determinedly closed it after him. Outside the Devon drizzle drifted through the evening. Colonel Jeffries was on a low platform, the harsh neon lights cutting deep grooves in his face. In the two months since Miller had gone to his office in Mayfair he seemed to have aged ten years. In the room were four rows of eight chairs, all occupied by American officers.

On the platform behind Jeffries were seated three more officers. No one talked. No one looked at each other.

Jeffries came forward at a shuffle but his voice was firm. 'You know who I am. Colonel John H. Jeffries of the Training Executive. You also know something of why you've been brought here in a hurry today. At the very outset I want to warn you that what you hear at this briefing is *top secret*. You are not to divulge any part of it to anyone, you must not discuss it with any other person. Keep it to a minimum even between yourselves. You can bet the word will get around smartly enough as it is. Bad news travels fast. So it's between these walls. Any officer giving information outside them will face the worst consequences. Understood?'

An almost embarrassed mumble came from the assembled men. Jeffries raised his tone. He looked like a man on the edge. 'That's understood?' he repeated fiercely.

This time the agreement was loud and clear. 'Okay,' said Jeffries. 'Will the military police leave us. Stay outside the door.'

There was a clatter as the white-helmeted men left. The room was left in grim silence. Jeffries was handed a single sheet of paper by one of the officers behind him on the platform. 'Okay,' he said. 'Okay.' He took a breath. 'We have suffered a major reverse. We have lost seven hundred plus American soldiers and sailors in a single night, in a single action, in which hardly a shot was fired from our side.'

His puffy eyes circled the room. His reading glasses slipped down his nose and he put them back irritably. 'Exercise Tiger,' he said. 'An amphibious training scheme was mounted forty-eight hours ago. Eight landing ships were scheduled to perform a mock invasion on the beaches at Slapton, South Devon.' One of the officers behind him rose and pressed a switch revealing a map on the rear wall. He then handed a military cane to Jeffries who used it as a pointer.

'The exercise involved these landing ships taking an easterly course into Lyme Bay, then turning back to land their consignment of troops here on the beach at Slapton.

'During the night this convoy was attacked by a number of German motor torpedo-boats, E-boats as they're called, apparently from Cherbourg, how many we're not sure. As a result, one transport was sunk and two others damaged, one so severely that it had to be scuttled today by the British Royal Navy. At this time we do not have anything like a complete roll of casualties but, as I told you, we believe we lost over seven hundred of our boys.'

He adjusted his spectacles again. Miller thought how sad, how low, how defeated, he seemed. 'The training aspects of this Exercise Tiger, which are my responsibility, don't make for a happy story. Quite apart from set emergency procedures, which not many soldiers even tried to follow, there were several other failures. Some of the bodies which have been washed up on the shore in this area yesterday and today were found wearing their life-jackets *the wrong way around. They drowned themselves.* So much for what we have been trying to drum into these guys. When they hit the water they were turned face down.' He paused briefly.

'Aboard the landing vessels there was panic. Some soldiers thought that the whole thing was just part of the war games. When the first tank-landing ship caught fire everything went crazy. No one knew what to do. All drills, all orders, were forgotten, the ship was burning, the sea was burning, our young men were burning.'

Miller closed his eyes. He kept them closed while Jeffries continued for another ten minutes. Then there was silence.

After a moment Jeffries said: 'I can take some questions but I may not know the answers, nobody does yet. There'll be an official inquiry, naturally, but until then we are going to be a whole lot in the dark. The major point, at this moment, is that nothing must be revealed about this tragedy. We cannot give any further comfort to our enemy.'

An hour later the officers trooped despondently from the building and went to a rough mess hall. Hardly a word was spoken and not much food was eaten. Colonel Jeffries arrived and called for attention. 'Tomorrow some of you will be assigned to talk to survivors. Go easy with them. Some may be okay physically, but mentally they are in a bad way for sure. What we need to know is how the training let us down. This kind of screw-up must not happen again. It's too expensive.'

Miller slept in a tent with three other officers, all strangers. All night the Devon rain sounded on the canvas. At midnight he thought of Kathleen. Kathleen would have to wait.

The next morning he and other officers went to a guarded, barbed-wire compound. Colonel Jeffries arrived. 'I want you to talk to these soldiers and hear what they have to tell you. But this is *not* an interrogation, in no way is it a debriefing; some of them are in no fit state for that as yet. It's bad enough putting them behind wire like they are prisoners but it's a matter of security considerations. Even the wounded are under armed guard in hospitals. I'd like your reports by tomorrow morning.'

It was like visiting a psychiatric ward. The young men were stunned, some of them rendered almost dumb, by the horror of their experience. Miller trod carefully. 'It was a real nice night,' said one soldier, his mouth trembling. 'Like a cruise across Chesapeake Bay. There was a guy playing a mandolin, other guys were playing cards. It was warm enough to sit on the deck. Those life-jackets made good warmers, even if they're no good as life-jackets.'

Miller said gently: 'So I hear.'

The soldier said: 'When it happened it was fire everywhere. At first we thought it was just part of the game. We didn't even see them in the dark. I don't mind fighting the Nazis, sir, that's what

I came for. But this was just *practising*, for Christ-sake.' His face shook. 'I don't know where my buddies are.'

As Miller was about to leave, he said: 'I remember you, sir. At Christmas in that big house when we first came to England. Somerset county.'

Miller looked again at the youth's name. Soroyan. Benedict Soroyan. 'Sure,' he said. 'That's a name I remember. I'm sorry for what you've been through, son.'

'Yes, sir. I am too.' Now he began to weep openly. 'I just want to go home. That's all I want, to go home to my folks.'

Miller was leaving that night. Harcourt had driven him as far as the guard post at the entrance to the military base when a sergeant there halted the car. 'Message from Colonel Jeffries, sir. He's about to leave and he'd like you to wait for him here.'

The colonel arrived in his car after a few minutes. He said: 'Captain Miller, just get in here with me. We'll ride together. Tell your driver to tag along behind. You are going back to London, I take it?'

Miller got into the back seat with the colonel. He glanced backwards to make sure Harcourt was following. 'I'm going to London on the way to Suffolk, sir,' he said.

'Ah, yes. That was something I meant to bring up with you. All this terrible business put it out of my mind.' The older man's head sagged. Then he pulled the partition between them and the driver tight. There were blinds at the window and a reading light in the roof.

'As far as the Suffolk matter is concerned, Miller, your suggestion about the Dakota pilots being sent over enemy territory, blooded as it were – and I hope that's not a bad choice of phrase . . . My God, we've had enough losses. Anyway, it's been okayed.'

He opened his briefcase on the seat beside him and after some sorting extracted a single sheet of paper. 'That's it. I remembered to bring it in the thick of all this. I can't be going completely crazy.'

Miller looked at the order. 'Right, sir, I think I can handle that. I'm going with them.'

'Great. These young guys, they're just . . . well, young guys, kids. We can't expect too much of them. See what's just happened down here.' He rubbed his face with both hands. 'Gee, what a nightmare.'

He looked sideways at Miller. 'Even I need somebody to talk to,' he said. 'The whole thing was such a fuck-up. We can discuss it now. Nobody else is listening.'

'Did this convoy of landing ships have an escort?' asked Miller.

'Oh, sure. Of a kind. The British navy had two small warships as escorts. One had to turn back to Plymouth, would you believe, because she had a hole in her hull. A collision they had patched up but apparently she started leaking.' He shook his head in silent disbelief.

He went on: 'It seems they couldn't plug their fucking leak so they turned around and headed back home.'

'What about the other escort?'

'She sailed all night and didn't see a God-dam thing. She must have been miles away. The sky was on fire. She picked up some radio distress signals but it was too late. The British will have one of their jolly inquiries and everybody will go away, patting each other on the back and saying: "Not to worry, old chap." Like they do. All that warship did was to get there after the action was finished, after the Germans were back home in bed, the next morning, and sink our disabled landing ship. A danger to navigation, they said. That was the only thing the British opened fire on.' He repeated almost in a whisper: 'A danger to navigation.'

He took out a huge red handkerchief and wiped his face. Miller thought he would have been better back in the States somewhere, sitting in an armchair, far from the war.

'Of course, the British warship would have been as helpless as the US transports anyway,' Jeffries went on. 'Those German E-boats have a speed of thirty knots, plus some. The warship could manage twelve, maybe fourteen, and the landing ships four knots. None of them had a chance. It was only a miracle that the E-boats didn't stick around and sink the rest of the convoy like sitting ducks. Those seven hundred guys we lost could have been thousands. The invasion would have been completely screwed.'

Miller said: 'Wasn't there any intelligence about the E-boats? No warning?'

'Intelligence!' Jeffries almost spat it out. 'Intelligence is shit, captain. There was some general information about *possible* U-boat or E-boat activity but who's going to take any heed of that. Nobody did anyway. Those boats came out of Cherbourg. Now it's too late, I bet, for the air force to bomb them.'

The car stopped at a junction. Jeffries put the light out and lifted the blind. There was a military convoy going across. Miller was startled. 'Those trucks,' he said. 'They've got full headlights on.'

'I know, I know,' sighed Jeffries. 'Another cute idea. I told you how I feel about so-called intelligence. They figure that if the Nazis pick up those lights from a reconnaissance aircraft they'll think it's some sort of trick to make them believe that the invasion is coming from this direction and not from the Dover region.' He paused and pulled down the blind. 'And it *is* coming from this direction. It's a double bluff. Somebody thought it up in a dream. Who knows what the Nazis think? If their intelligence is anything like ours they'll probably file the information and forget about it.'

They drove on through the night. Jeffries was thoughtful for a few minutes, then he said: 'And guess what Washington says about us losing seven hundred young guys?'

'What does Washington say?'

'Washington don't give a pile of horse shit. Washington is more worried about the fucking landing ships. Soldiers are expendable. They die, so they die. That's what they're for. Dying. That's their job. But the ships, that's different. There's a major shortage, even after all this build-up, because too many have been sent to the Pacific where, according to some Washington politicians, the *real* war is. Even two, like we lost just now, is a major setback. Like I say, if those E-boats had done a complete job and sunk the rest of the convoy, and they had six more ships at their mercy, we could forget the invasion.'

He closed his eyes and Miller thought he had gone into an exhausted sleep. But he stirred after a few minutes and said: 'You'd better get out soon, captain. Be on your way.'

He opened the screen and told the driver to pull in where he could. Two minutes later, by the side of the black and empty road, he did so. Miller left the car and saluted at the door. 'Sure, sure,' murmured Jeffries, flapping his hand. 'Take it easy, son.'

Harcourt had been following closely and now pulled in behind the colonel's car as it drove away. As Miller was about to climb into the back of his own vehicle, he saw a public telephone box at the side of the lay-by.

'Hold it, Benji. I'll just be a couple of minutes.'

By his watch it was eleven thirty. He got the operator. 'A London number, please,' he said. 'Belgravia 8592.'

Kathleen was very drunk. 'Now you ring,' she said nastily. 'Now, for Christ's sake. Where were you last night?'

'Something important came up,' he said.

She did not want to hear it. Her tone was petulant. 'Something more important than me?'

'Yes,' he said evenly. 'More than you.'

'Then you can fuck off,' she suddenly screeched. 'You're like every fucking man who ever was. Get out of my life, Yank!'

She put the phone down. He did the same, very slowly. Then he walked back to the car, his head down. Seven hundred men had died and *she* was annoyed.

They sat in their flying gear in a suspicious half circle, not so much looking at him as watching him. 'The reason for this exercise, okay, this operation, is to give you the experience of flying above enemy territory,' said Miller.

When he had gone into the hut he had found them crowding

around the wall map. As soon as he and Major Pitt had come through the door they scattered guiltily and went back to their seats like boys caught cheating before a lesson. Butterfield was in the middle and he and Miller exchanged nods, but the others were stone faced. A shaft of East Anglian sunlight fell through the window and across the map. Pitt sat behind the pilots.

Miller tapped the map with his index finger. 'The English Channel Islands were overcome by the Germans in 1940, the only part of Great Britain to be occupied. You might think they could have been a useful outpost for the enemy, a springboard for operations against this country, but that's a miscalculation. In fact, they have turned out to be just the opposite, what the English would call a dead loss. They are out on a limb, away from France, and a hundred miles from this country. When the invasion comes they could be the first place in Occupied Europe to be liberated – or they may be the last.'

The young pilots continued to regard him almost sullenly. This was his big idea. 'Because they're out on a limb – and you can't defend them – the enemy has neglected his garrison there. The latest intelligence estimate gives its strength as one-third of the number it is supposed to be and the troops are not grade one. There are no fighting planes at the airport and the anti-aircraft defences are little league.'

He looked from face to face. There were a few signs of reassurance. 'The situation,' he confirmed, 'has been pretty much static for four years. The British have never tried to bomb the islands, not even the airport in Jersey, for the good reason that the civilian population are their own people.'

'They've bombed French civilians,' put in a voice which added: 'sir.'

'They have,' said Miller. He could see Pitt was looking uncomfortable. Miller added nothing but tapped the island with his finger. 'For these reasons we have chosen Jersey as the enemy territory which we are going to overfly in this exercise, or operation, if you want to call it that. Maybe we'll all get a medal.

As it is lightly, probably incompetently, defended there should be no trouble avoiding anti-aircraft fire.'

'How about those Messerschmitts, those Me.109s, sir?' asked one of the young men. 'They have them in northern France.'

Miller tried to sound confident. 'The British are going to stage a diversionary raid in this area,' he indicated the map again. 'In the region of Caen . . . here. If any enemy fighters are going to take off they'll be heading in that direction. In any case, the Me.109 has severely limited flying time. I don't anticipate there will be too much trouble with those guys.'

A pilot put up his hand and recited his name: 'Caldy, sir. What about an escort? We're unarmed. Those Daks don't carry a peashooter.'

It was Major Pitt who said: 'I'm hoping to fix an escort.'

Butterfield asked the next question: 'Why is this er . . . operation . . . necessary?' He looked about him. 'Am I allowed to ask that?'

Major Pitt was watching carefully. The young pilots eyed him momentarily and then turned their attention back to Miller. 'Yes, sir,' said another. 'Why are we doing it?'

Miller said bluntly: 'Because it's an order. It will give you the confidence of flying over Nazi-occupied territory so that when the big night comes you will at least know that you've done it before. It will just be a taste of the real thing.' His mind went back to Devon and the men who died in the sea. 'Even exercises have an element of risk.'

Butterfield asked: 'When, sir? When do we go?'

'Depends on the weather. Maybe tomorrow.'

There was silence, a long silence it seemed to Miller. He said: 'This time, of course, there will be no passengers, no paratroops.'

'It might give them . . . experience also, sir,' said one of the pilots.

Pitt intervened: 'Let's not get too clever, son. The top command has sanctioned this show. There'll be no cargo. Any further questions for Captain Miller?'

It was Butterfield who said to Miller: 'Are you coming with us, sir?'

'Sure I am. I need the experience too.'

Pockets of the next morning's mist had edged away by the time they walked across the airfield towards the Dakotas. If it had not been for the circumstances it would have been a nice day. One aircraft had its two bulbous engines stripped down, looking oddly naked, so only eight were going. Major Pitt came from his office as they assembled below the wing of the leading plane. Even at a distance there seemed to be a lightness in his step and he was waving a square of paper.

'We got our escort,' guessed Caldy, the one who had asked about it.

'A World War One biplane,' said Butterfield and they all laughed, some of it from relief.

'Okay, fellas,' said Pitt. 'The US Air Force is giving us an escort. Three mustangs, so they say. But maybe only one. The best aeroplane in the sky. Anyhow, between one and three. They aim to rendezvous with you in mid-English Channel, as you approach Jersey. They'll see you're okay.'

Two of the airmen were standing a few paces apart, as if keeping quiet, and were not in their flying suits. 'You guys on leave?' he said. He glanced at Miller.

'We don't have a plane, sir,' said the first youth. The other nodded to the aircraft being repaired. 'That's our cow.'

Pitt grimaced, then said: 'Get yourselves ready. You can go as passengers. There's plenty of room. You can tell the others what to do.'

Disconsolately, the pair turned back towards the huts. 'Maybe they figured on cleaning up the garden,' said Pitt. He turned to Miller: 'They could fly with you.'

'Sure, major.'

'There's plenty of space in the back now we don't have the soldiers,' said Butterfield.

Miller changed his mind. 'Maybe I should fly with somebody

214

else. I've already had a trip with Butterfield. How about you, son?'

He pointed at Caldy who said: 'Okay, sir. There's room.'

Mechanics had been fussing around the blunt-nosed white-striped transports. The two men returned wearing their flying gear and the major, having shaken each man's hand, turned and strode back to the perimeter. He stood contemplating them as they boarded the aircraft and the clumsy propellers began to turn with their initial puffs of smoke. The rustic Suffolk morning was rent by the harsh sound of the engines warming. Then the planes began to move into a queue for the runway like obedient circus animals.

Caldy was chewing gum. 'It's going to be great,' he said over his shoulder to Miller. His navigator was already muttering into the mike at his mouth. 'He's called Blumenthal,' said Caldy. He laughed. 'I can't always say it early in the morning.'

'I'm glad you're feeling good,' said Miller. 'It will be okay.'

'I didn't sleep much but I'm real glad about the escort. Once I actually see those mustangs on our wing-tip I'll be even happier.' He glanced back at Miller, his young face full of doubt. 'I'm not a naturally brave guy, sir,' he said.

'Who is?' asked Miller. 'If only brave men had to fight a war there wouldn't be enough to have one.'

They were third in line to take off. The engines were grunting strongly. 'Butterball's going,' said Caldy. They had to raise their voices, sometimes to the point of shouting. The first Dakota, as though gathering itself for the attempt, gave a couple of clumsily playful jumps on the runway and then roared confidently towards the morning sun.

The second plane hesitated, then straightened itself out and followed Butterfield's lead into the sky. Caldy took the third aircraft off easily, almost lazily, as if tempting a stalled engine. Miller was once more aware of the differences in styles, in temperament, in technique, of pilots and the aircraft themselves. They were never the same.

'England sure looks pretty today,' said Caldy, chewing gum like a machine. 'So green and not so crowded.'

'From here,' agreed Miller. They were taking a course north of London, then to the south-west and eventually turning south over Dorset and across the widest breadth of the English Channel. 'This place we're going, Jersey, was named after Jersey in the States,' suggested Caldy. 'Right?'

'The other way around,' said Miller mildly. 'Since ours is New Jersey.'

'They follow us in everything else,' said the young man. 'This country was way back a hundred years out of date, before Uncle Sam got here. I think they've learned a few things from us.'

'Probably so,' said Miller. 'Jitterbugging, hot dogs, chewing-gum.'

'I can't wait to get home,' said Caldy, looking over the nose of the plane. 'To good old Nebraska. To Omaha.'

'Never been there,' said Miller. He was watching Butterfield's aircraft in the lead. The others had spread in a fan formation. The day continued clear and he could see for miles.

'Insurance,' said Caldy proudly. 'Omaha, the insurance capital of the United States of America, which means the world, I guess. That's what I'm going to do. Go straight into insurance. Make a few bucks.'

'Get married?' suggested Miller.

Caldy sounded surprised. 'Maybe married. After a while.'

'Have any of you guys got British girlfriends?'

'They're the best thing about this cold, wet place. They're so . . . well, willing. I've got a great girl. In Sudbury. Doris. It was quite some while before I could figure out anything she was talking about. I didn't know whether she was saying "yes" or "no". But we're okay now. She wants to come back to the States with me.'

'Are you going to take her?'

Caldy chewed thoughtfully. 'I don't know. I just don't know. Maybe not. I think it would be all too big for her. She says I talk like a movie star. I haven't told her I don't have no fancy apartment like she imagines and that I've never been within a hundred miles of New York City. We live in a wooden house thirty miles from Omaha. Somehow I don't think she'd fit in there. We got dogs.'

'There's going to be any number of mistakes made after the war,' said Miller. 'Misunderstandings.'

He looked through the small triangle of window available to him. The navigator had said nothing in his direction, only muttered into his mouthpiece and sometimes spoke briefly to Caldy. They were flying over the northern outskirts of London.

Caldy nodded downwards. 'This must be the view the Nazi bombers get. My girl has never visited the city, and she says she don't want to go. She says it's full of sin.' He grinned. 'And is she right! I spent my last leave there and I know. That's some place. Almost as good as Omaha.'

Miller could see the two leading Dakotas and he knew that the others would still be arranged around them in the fan shape. The morning continued lucid, the toy fields below, rivers reflecting the pale sky, and, when they had cleared the London suburbs, the spiders' webs that were the small towns and villages of England.

'About here we should turn to port,' said Caldy casually. He glanced at the navigator who pretended not to hear him but after an interval said: 'Any moment.' It was the leading aircraft, Butterfield's plane, which gave them the signal, banking unhurriedly to the left. The formation obediently tilted behind him. Now they were heading south-west, the land below brightly green with small puffs of cream clouds making shadows on the ground. After twenty minutes the coastline appeared in the distance, a wriggling edge, with the pale sea beyond.

'We won't have such a pretty ride on the night,' said Miller.

Caldy caught the inference and, chewing furiously, turned and looked directly at him. 'You'll be coming, captain? On the real show?'

'I certainly hope so,' said Miller. 'I don't know yet whether they'll let me jump. I'm qualified but I get the feeling that they're scared I could screw up the whole invasion. I'd have to know the exact drill, the tactics on the ground, the target area – all that detail. Unless they can release me from my present assignment and I can get a few practice jumps, and learn what the other paratroopers know, then I don't think they'll even give it a thought. The last thing I want is to be a handicap.'

They were flying over Southampton, its glinting harbour tightly packed with sea-going craft, warships slim and grey in the sunlight. Miller went on: 'But if they won't let me jump, then I want to be up front with you guys. I don't take up much space.'

Caldy laughed nervously. 'You can take my place, sir. I'll head home to Nebraska.'

Miller patted his shoulder. 'It's going to be okay, son. Everything is.'

'Do you think they'll just fold up, the Nazis?' asked the youth. 'Run away? Go down in a heap?'

'None of those things,' said Miller. 'They'll fight, they'll fight like hell, but they'll lose in the end. We'll be stronger.'

The navigator said his first conversational words: 'They got the Russians one side, and everybody else closing in, they should quit now. Where the hell do they get the men to keep getting killed, taken prisoner? And how do they get hold of the gasoline?'

'Why don't you ask them yourself?' Caldy pointed: 'Those Nazis are right ahead of us.'

All three men leaned to peer through the bevelled glass. From that altitude France was misty, the Channel Islands mixed with the mainland; then a flash of sunlight came like a signal from some window or windscreen. 'There they are,' said Miller. 'Jersey is the big one.'

Caldy gave anxious stabbing looks around him. 'Where's the escort?' he muttered.

It was only by chance that the Messerschmitt 109 was on the tarmac at Jersey airport. The wonderfully agile fighter plane had proved itself throughout the war, but only for a few minutes at a time. Even during the blitzkrieg summer of 1940 it could only

218

escort German bombers over England, or join in dogfights with Spitfires, for half an hour before turning back to France. Its fuel tanks were tight.

Luftwaffe captain Berthold Rainer was well aware of the Me.109's shortcomings and the previous evening he had come in to land at Jersey, in preference to trying to reach his base in northern France with a fuel gauge showing empty. Now in the lucid Channel Islands morning he waited while his machine was refilled. He considered what a pleasant place the islands were, in the front line and yet a peaceful backwater. He had a French girlfriend in Amiens, ten years younger than his wife in Düsseldorf, and he hoped to have her company that night.

He was in his flying kit, his helmet strap loose about his chin, sniffing the day and mentally approving of the airport which in 1940 had been conveniently delivered almost new to the occupying Germans. An airman came from the central building and approached him at a trot, saluting even as he halted. 'Captain, a formation of American transport planes is approaching Jersey from the North. There are eight, flying at three thousand metres.' He handed over the transcript of the message. Rainer's face glowed. Quickly he began to fasten his helmet and shouted at the mechanic refuelling the plane to hurry. 'Transports?' he said to the messenger. 'You're sure they are transports?'

'Correct, and they have no escort, captain,' said the grinning man.

At that moment the formation of Dakotas announced itself with a steady celestial roar. The Germans looked up. The planes were outlined like crosses in the sky.

'Eight,' counted the *Luftwaffe* pilot calmly. 'What a beautiful sight.'

They had encountered their first anti-aircraft fire as they crossed the Jersey coast. It appeared to be coming from a ship in St Helier harbour and was exploding far below them, a group of harmless dandelion puffs. Caldy looked concerned but then realised and gave a whoop. 'Wow! I've seen action. I've seen combat! I'll get a citation.'

'There's some more,' said Miller, nodding ahead. 'But they'll never hit us like that.'

'Can we go home now?' asked Blumenthal solidly.

Miller laughed. 'Before they get our range, you figure?'

'I mean *now*, sir.'

Caldy was still searching for the promised escort. Then he thought he saw a plane, circling above them, vanishing from their view into cloud. 'Is that a mustang?' he repeated several times. 'Is it?' Then they realised it was not. The black crosses below the diving wings were clear. 'Christ, it's a Nazi!' squealed Caldy so loud through his mike that Blumenthal clutched his ears. 'Okay, okay. Quit screaming, will you.'

Horrified, Miller traced the yellow-nosed Messerschmitt as it rolled above the leading Dakota, easily, even lazily, as though sizing it up, smacking its lips. It began a steep climb. 'He's going for Butterball,' whispered Caldy. He looked wildly around. 'Where's the fucking mustangs? They promised. The colonel promised us, didn't he?'

The German fighter, as if delighting in showing off, rolled on to its back and then smoothly swooped in on Butterfield's aircraft, coming from behind and hammering it with machine-gun fire. Smoke spurted from the transport.

'He got him,' muttered Blumenthal. He turned his shocked face to Miller. 'He got Butterball.'

'He couldn't miss,' said Caldy. He, too, turned and stared at Miller.

Miller knew they were going to blame him.

Then a second shadow fell across them, and a third. 'It's the escort,' Miller said, knowing it was too late. 'They got here.' Two US mustangs, showing their white star emblems, flipped over them and went for the Me.109 like starving dogs at a pigeon. The German saw them coming and curled up and away into the sky.

'Get him, get him,' Miller was muttering. 'Go, get him.'

'Kill the bastard,' said Caldy.

'Butterball is going down,' said Blumenthal in an almost conversational tone. 'He's burning.'

Caldy said: 'Four of our guys.'

The sky was stained with smoke. The noise of the fighter planes drowned even the Dakota's own engines. Then there was an orange explosion high above.

'They hit him,' said Miller. 'Look, he's falling.'

The German plane descended, slowly and gracefully it seemed; pieces fell away from it, and then a finger of fumes came from behind it which spurted into bright flame. It dropped past them.

They turned to see what had happened to the Dakota. It was coming down, belching smoke, but in a steady descent as though making a controlled landing. Then one of the engines dropped away.

Underneath his flying goggles, Caldy began to weep like a boy. 'Let's get out of here,' he said. The other aircraft were wheeling away, in no particular formation now, heading back as fast as they could fly.

As he almost bent the plane around Caldy snivelled. 'Look, there's a parachute. It's going down into the sea.'

Chapter Seventeen

'Look, there's a parachute,' said Sergeant Fred Weber. 'It's going down into the sea.'

Gino attempted to see over his own shoulder but then splashed the oars to rock the little boat around. They had not caught many fish that morning. Their hearts were not in it because Weber was going and it could be their final time. They were about to pull back to the harbour.

Now they could both look. The parachute was at about two hundred feet and was descending sedately into the sunny waves. Weber searched the sky as though the plane might still be up there. 'Too small for an invasion,' he said. 'One parachutist.'

'It only took one German to capture Jersey,' Gino reminded him. 'But I think you are right, Fred, it's no mass landing.'

The man on the end of the parachute could have been surveying them. They were only two hundred yards away when he splashed into the sea. They heard his shout as he hit the chill water. Gino turned the boat fully in that direction and began to row.

Butterfield was floating, trying to get rid of the parachute. He cut the cords, then swam three strokes to the side of the boat and asked: 'Are you going to shoot me?'

'We haven't got a gun,' said Weber.

They almost fell into the sea themselves as they hauled him over the side of the boat and extricated him from the rest of his harness. Weber made room for him on the seat. The big, blond, soaking wet American slumped forward with a subdued sob. Weber patted him and Gino began to pull on the oars. Butterfield looked up. 'Are you Nazis?'

'German,' corrected Weber.

'Italian,' said Gino.

'American,' said Butterfield. 'If you're not going to shoot me I'd better give you this,' he said, pulling a long and ominous-looking knife from his flying boot.

Weber accepted it as if it were a ceremoniously surrendered sword. 'That's very nice,' he said. 'For a knife.'

'Good for gutting the fish,' said Gino. He looked at Butterfield. 'Can we keep it?'

Butterfield said: 'I guess so.' His cheeks quivered and he began to weep. Weber again patted his soaked flying suit. 'My buddies,' said Butterfield. 'Three guys. They went down with the Dak.'

Neither Gino nor Weber was sure what a Dak was. 'The aircraft,' said Butterfield, sensing their uncertainty and pointing upwards. He sniffed. 'Real good guys, all of them.'

'There are a lot of good guys,' said Gino thoughtfully. 'Millions.'

'Missing,' agreed Weber. 'Everywhere.'

Gino tugged the oars. Weber said: 'We didn't see any plane crashing.'

'It crashed all right,' said Butterfield. 'God-dam Messerschmitt got us. I'm married, you know. So were two of the others.'

'I didn't know we had even *one* Messerschmitt in these parts.' Weber shook his head. 'He must have come in on the quiet. We heard some bangs but we thought it was at the quarry.'

'They get a lot of stone from the quarry,' put in Gino. 'They use it for gravestones.'

Butterfield looked distraught and cold. Weber put a sheet of canvas around his shoulders. The airman gazed about him at the blinking sea and then considered his two rescuers. 'We were unarmed,' he said. 'Some crazy officer thought it was a good idea to fly us over here. To give us experience, he said. Experience of what?' He looked appealingly at Weber. 'What happens to me now?'

Weber shrugged. 'You can't escape. You will have a nice time as a prisoner until the war is over. Which won't be very long, the way things are going.'

'Where?' asked Butterfield. 'Where will they put me?'

Again Weber shrugged.

'Try and avoid Berlin,' said Gino.

They reached the harbour mouth. There was a military ambulance on the quay and a group of soldiers with rifles. Butterfield's eyes were frightened but Gino said: 'Nobody's going to shoot you. There are rules.'

They reached the seaweed-covered slipway and the soldiers moved to meet them with two men bearing a stretcher. Everyone was eager to join in. A group of civilians stood at a short distance, mostly women, and they began to applaud as Butterfield was helped from the boat. The sergeant in charge of the soldiers glanced at them but a woman shouted: 'Well done the Jerries,' which eased his doubts.

Although he protested that he did not need the stretcher, Butterfield, in his sodden flying suit, was laid on it and carried up the slipway to the ambulance. He half sat up, water draining from him, and waved gratefully at Weber and Gino who tenuously waved back. 'Out of the war,' said Weber. 'Lucky boy.'

They went back to moor the boat and take out the fishing tackle. The three fish they had caught that morning they gave to the civilians who appeared disgruntled that the catch was so small.

'This is the last time I shall see this boat,' said Weber lugubriously. 'Tomorrow, maybe, I go. Remember how we found it here? After the war the owner will come back for it.'

'They won't let me take it out alone,' grumbled Gino. 'They'll think I'm rowing to England. And, in any case, it would never be the same without you, Fred.'

Impulsively, emotionally, they shook hands. 'Where my duty takes me, I must go,' recited Weber, making a long face. 'Who otherwise will cook my general's food?' Sadly they began to walk up the slipway and Weber turned and saluted the boat. He then glanced sideways at Gino. 'You perhaps could come to,' he said shyly.

Gino at first looked shocked. 'But France, Fred? It's soon going to be a battlefield. And I'm a civilian, a neutral. Italy surrendered two years ago.'

'Best thing you can be in a battle,' said Weber. 'A neutral. You can hedge your bets. And there's a little port not far away from my posting. There must be some fishing. As good as here maybe. I think I can fix it, you know. I'll tell the general that we always work together. See what happens.'

That night, when the occupying officers had eaten dinner and gone to their quarters, Gino was sitting alone in the kitchen; the women washers-up had all gone home. He had just opened a bottle of schnapps at their thick table when Weber appeared. 'In ten minutes I have to see the general,' he said. 'He wants a bedtime drink.'

'This stuff?' asked Gino, picking up the schnapps bottle and thumping it lightly on the bare table.

'Ovaltine,' corrected Weber. 'The English drink it. He had never heard of it until he came to Jersey but there was a store of the stuff in tins and he likes it sometimes. He says it helps him to sleep.' He got to the point. 'Do you want to come to France with me or not?'

'Fred, my family . . .'

'You haven't got a family.'

'In Italy. If I died in the fighting they would miss me.'

'You haven't seen them for years. A couple of old aunties.'

Weber took the bottle and poured a glass each. 'All right, Fred,' said Gino with a thoughtful sigh. They shook hands. 'See what he says. Whatever he decides, I will do. Why don't you go now and get it over with.'

Weber nodded and as part of the movement he swallowed the rest of his schnapps. He stood up as straight as he could, smoothed down his mess uniform and with a mocking and silent

'*Sieg Heil!*' with his single right-hand finger went from the room.

'*Sieg Heil*,' muttered Gino. He glanced around. 'Bloody Hitler. It's all his fault. And bloody Mussolini.'

The evenings were very light now. It was May and outside the kitchen window there was a remaining glow in the sky. He wondered what being in a battle was like, if there would be places to hide. War was hell.

Weber came back after ten minutes. 'We must have a toast,' he said triumphantly. 'We are *both* going to France.'

Gino's heart fell and rose in almost the same movement. 'You fixed it,' he said flatly. 'How did you do it, Fred?'

'At first he would not hear of it. But then he said okay. I told him we were lovers.'

At dusk the next day they went to the port, Weber in his *Wehrmacht* uniform and with his army kitbag, and Gino wearing his shabby best blue suit and carrying his once-smart suitcase. They looked down from the jetty at the bulky tugboat flying the French tricolour. 'At least she's flying the right flag,' said Weber. 'Keep the British away.'

'In their hearts the British still like the French,' agreed Gino. 'Even if the French do not return the compliment.'

A fussy St Helier port official with an extravagant badge on his cap told them to wait before boarding the tug. He was a Jersey man, his accent curiously South African. There was another important passenger. They watched as he arrived, with an armed escort in a military truck.

'The American,' smiled Gino. 'He is coming too.'

Weber shrugged. 'There is nowhere to keep prisoners here, except in the prison. And you cannot put a man captured in a war in a common prison. That is for criminals. So the Yankee comes with us to France.'

Butterfield was confused as he climbed from the car and he did not immediately realise who they were. He was wearing a grey

226

boiler suit with a large orange circle on the back. They moved towards him and almost formally introduced themselves. 'You guys,' he breathed. 'You saved my life. Thank you.'

They laughed and said it was nothing. The two guards were concerned with getting their own kit aboard the tug so all three of them shook hands. 'I think I'd rather stay here,' said Butterfield, looking about him. 'It seems a real nice little place.' His face remained sad. 'The plane crashed in the sea,' he said. 'And they didn't pick up anybody.'

Gino asked: 'Did they give you plenty to eat?'

'Enough,' corrected Weber. 'Nobody gets plenty these days.'

'Fine. I did okay. I hope my wife gets to hear I'm alive. A Red Cross guy came to see me and said he would make sure she got news. And the fellas at my squadron as well. I don't want them sending letters to her.'

He peered over the edge of the jetty and saw the tugboat for the first time. 'Good and strong,' he said.

'And she flies the French flag,' added Weber. 'It will stop your friends from bombing you.'

Their conversation was halted by the arrival of a motor hearse. It stopped and the harbour official directed the driver further down the quay. The escort soldiers came to polite attention.

'This man was very important in Rouen,' said the official. 'He died when he was taking a vacation here. So now he goes home.'

'Nice coffin,' said Weber.

'The coffin supplies are going down like everything else,' said the official. 'This must be one of the last.'

Weber suddenly realised. 'He's not coming with us, is he? On this boat?'

The harbour man shook his head. 'No, no. The crew won't have him. A cadaver is bad luck. He is going on the barge the tug will be towing.' He pointed.

'With the dead wagon, by the look of it,' said Butterfield, joining in. 'That's quaint. The funeral car's going too.'

Gino said: 'They could not just put the coffin on. Not by itself.

That is no respect.' They watched the hearse slowly descend the open ramp at the front of the barge.

There was a man standing near, so unkempt they thought he was some harbour tramp until the official saluted him and told the others he was the tugboat captain.

'Cargo,' the captain said. His name was Henri and he was smoking what seemed to be a sliver of brown paper which stuck to the corner of his mouth. 'We come in with cargo and we go out with cargo.' He indicated for them to follow him and the entire party, including Butterfield and the escorts, went a hundred yards and looked down into the barge. The hearse, with the lid of its coffin in view, was now settled on the deep deck, separated from the rest of the cargo by a wall of wooden crates.

There were two damaged military vehicles, several motor-cycles, and among the pile of crates a rough cage containing a big, restless, black dog. A solemn man climbed a ladder from the interior of the barge. His suit had been pressed so many times it was almost threadbare, his black tie creased and his white collar frayed. He patted the hearse fondly when he was at roof level.

'Take good care, captain,' he said in his Jersey accent.

'He won't be seasick,' said Henri in familiar English.

The man said: 'I mean the hearse, captain. We only have two now and the other one has to be pulled by a horse.'

Gino said: 'I have seen it. Very pretty.'

'The horse keeps dropping his dollops on the bonnet of the car.'

The captain said: 'If you're worried about your car, why don't you come with us?'

The black-suited man looked shocked. 'Out there? You'd be lucky. I don't mind death, I'm used to it. It's dying I can't stand.'

He went off at a quick shuffle. Henri sniffed the dusky air and as though he had received a signal in this way he indicated that they should follow him back to the tug, down the gangway and on to the deck. The harbour official saluted them as they went. 'Best of luck,' he said.

*

Everything aboard the tug stank of leaking engine oil. In the main cabin, optimistically called the salon, there was a bottle of Armagnac on the round and rough central table and a dozen greasy glasses. A pygmy-sized black man busily filled the glasses. When the captain nodded to him curtly he went out and returned with some pig's trotters and bread.

They grouped around the table, crowded into the grubby dimness. There were Weber and Gino, Butterfield, less downcast than he had been, the two German guards who had only talked between themselves, and a primitive-looking ship's engineer.

Henri the captain said: 'Because nobody here is French but you all understand some English, except the two Hun guards,' he glanced disparagingly towards them, 'I will speak in English. I worked for twenty years in England. Folkestone.' He raised the first glass. The black man was standing near the door, also holding a glass. They all raised their drinks. Butterfield choked over his.

'We must have a lifeboat drill,' Henri continued. 'Because the maritime regulations say so when passengers are aboard. Well, my advice is, in an emergency, to keep away from the lifeboats. They cannot be used because of woodworm and rust. There is a small boat on deck, a jolly boat, which will float free if the ship sinks, but the chief engineer here and our two deck-hands sleep very near to it and would be the first in it, followed close behind by me.' He raised a congratulatory toast to the uncouth engineer who responded and then grimaced about him as if he was prepared for anyone who argued.

'There is a locker on deck, near the gangway,' continued the captain. 'It contains life-jackets but only some are in good condition, very few in fact, so I think that you should go to the locker after this and each search out a suitable one, no holes.'

He drained his glass. The black man wriggled his way through and refilled it and the others', whether or not they had been finished. 'Are we expecting trouble, captain?' The voice was Butterfield's. 'Could we be attacked?'

Henri shrugged. 'Oh, I hope not, Mr Yankee. We fly the

French flag and if an aeroplane tries to attack us we will wave white flags also. Like hell. It is a pity that you do not have a spare Stars and Stripes with you. They would take some notice of that.'

'I don't carry one,' said Butterfield.

Henri went on: 'The danger on this voyage is not from the sky. The British and the Americans know we sail between St Malo and Jersey once a week and they have never attacked us yet. If they see us they flap their wings. No, the danger is from little things that cannot see our flags. They have no eyes, only pricks. All over them. I am talking about mines, round things with spikes. Big regions of la Manche, the English Channel, are laid with these mines, British and German. There is a swept passage near the French coast which is free and this is the way we go. That is why it takes so long. But there is always the risk of some drifting mine finding us. And we must know this.'

'How will we know?' enquired Gino nervously. 'There is some warning?'

'There is a fucking great bang,' said the captain.

Late that night in the shadowed salon they began to play cards. Outside it was calm. The cook had produced a prodigious cauldron of cassoulet, thick with everything, and they had emptied the dish, the German guards gobbling three helpings each and then scraping the iron container. They drank a lot of *vin ordinaire* and two more bottles of Armagnac. Butterfield produced a roll of American one-dollar notes and one five-dollar note which caused the others around the table to gaze at him and ask to examine the money.

'The dough got caught in my boot,' he said, smiling a little. 'The guards just didn't find it.'

The German soldiers asked to hold one green note and having done so and examined it, returned it with deference. Henri put some grisly francs on the table and the chief engineer produced a filthy bundle of money from various countries, some of it current. One of the guards played for both of them because they did not have enough Jersey occupation notes to play singly. Gino shrugged that he did not know how to play and he went with Weber up to the deck and into the mild but misty night.

The sea was slopping indolently against the hull of the lumbering tug, the mist hung around them like a shroud, and they could hear the dog barking aboard the barge rolling invisibly behind.

Below decks the captain had just said: 'Pontoon,' with quiet triumph. He laid the cards down and added: '*Vingt-et-un*,' to make himself fully understood. As if slapping the king and ace on the table had triggered it, there was a huge explosion which tipped the vessel sideways and sent a cannon-ball of flame through its hull. None of them had time to scream.

On deck, Weber and Gino were flung to the rail and then overboard as the ship staggered sideways into the water. Both were stunned but the coldness of the sea jerked them back to consciousness. They were splashing around in a circle. They could both swim but Gino not well, having last been in the sea at San Remo in 1938.

The tug was on fire amidships. They watched, stupefied, as the burning bridge collapsed, making the sea steam. Weber caught hold of Gino and they hung together desperately in the small waves. Then they saw the empty jolly boat from the deck, bobbing towards them through the fog as if wanting to help.

Neither man ever remembered how they managed, gasping as they were, to get over the low side of the boat. Weber slid aboard on his belly and sucking in air got Gino over the side too. They lay sobbing in the bottom of the craft for several minutes before Weber managed to straighten himself and pull himself upright. He tugged at the Italian until he was able to sit up also. 'He said it would be a big bang,' shivered Gino.

There was a locker at the bow of the boat. Gino opened it and pulled out two blankets and a half-bottle of Scotch. They thanked God, individually and together, wrapped themselves in the blankets and swigged the Scotch.

They drank half each. It warmed them as much as the blankets. Softly and sadly Fred Weber began to sing:

> *'Auf einem Seemannsgrab,*
> *da blühen keine Rosen . . .'*

Gino regarded him dolefully and said: 'I wish you wouldn't sing that.'

Nothing could be seen of the tugboat now, only pieces of wood, some smouldering, lying on the water. Then they saw Butterfield. There was no mistaking his fair hair and the bulk of his body. 'The Yankee,' said Weber. 'Get him out.'

There were no oars in the boat and they manoeuvred it with their hands until they had reached the young man. 'Don't spill us over,' warned Weber as they got their hands under his armpits. Then, as an aside: 'Every day we seem to be getting this man out of the water.'

But this time they were too late. He was really dead now and they let him slip back into the sea. 'Now his wife will get another message,' said Gino. There was no sign of anyone else.

They sat, sad and shivering, beneath the blankets in the small, bobbing boat. It was like the times they had spent fishing, although they were happier then. Then the boat began to leak.

The water came in regularly. 'Another half an hour and we will be swimming,' said Weber. 'Bail with our shoes.' He looked at Gino's flimsy pre-war footwear. Use mine. They will hold more.'

He took off his German Army boots and they began to bail, although some water escaped through the lace holes. After ten minutes they were exhausted. Then they heard a dog barking.

'The dog, the barge,' said Weber, cupping his hand to his ear. 'It must be near. We must find it.'

It found them, floating mysteriously towards them through the mist, the dog howling as if to guide them. They each croaked a sort of cheer as it obligingly came alongside. There was even the metal ladder so that they climbed aboard easily. The dog was ecstatic. The hearse was travelling undisturbed.

They made a fuss of the dog and Gino found a few biscuits in a container next to the improvised kennel. He put the biscuits through the bars of the cage. 'Not so many,' warned Weber. 'We may need them.'

But they did not. They had only been aboard, crouching under some sacking, for half an hour when it began to get light and the mist started to thin with the growing dawn. Then a noise like a grunt made them climb the ladder to the deck level. Another tug was lying half a mile away and someone was waving. 'We are saved,' Gino said. 'Thank God.'

Weber said: 'Yes, thank you, God.'

Two hours later they were in St Malo in dry, odd clothes donated by their rescuers. No one on the quay took any notice of them and they both felt left out. 'You would think that somebody would mention it,' sniffed Weber. They did give a statement in German, French and sign language to a French official who seemed only mildly interested. Acidly, Weber asked him if they were taking up too much of his time. 'No, monsieur,' said the man, pushing his cap back. 'This will take only one page in my book.'

More interest was shown in the hearse and the occupant of its coffin, which were unloaded just after the dog. Gino waved to the dog who was being put on a cart pulled by a donkey.

'He was a well-known man,' said the French official as they watched the hearse. 'They will take him home to Rouen.'

Weber said: 'Well, he wasn't disturbed. There was a fucking big bang but he didn't even stir.'

Two hours later they were aboard a halting, wooden-seated train going to Caen. They had been given breakfast at St Malo – a special breakfast, apparently, which included an egg and some horse-meat sausages kept for heroes or survivors of battles – and then taken to the train. 'I hope nobody drops a bomb on this train,' Weber had said lugubriously as he climbed, stiff and tired, aboard. 'Or that terrorists don't remove the railway lines. We've had enough war for a while.'

He wedged himself into a corner and dropped into an exhausted sleep. On the opposite seat Gino surveyed the passing countryside, grey-green under the sullen sky, and wondered what was going to happen to him. He was deeply fond of Fred Weber but the experiences of the past few hours made him think that he might have been better off marking time until the end of the war as waiter in the officers' mess in Jersey.

They stopped at every insignificant station. At one, a grumbling priest puffed into the compartment, a man so begrimed and ragged that Gino almost asked him if he needed help. His shabby cloak just encircled his fat body, his eyes were deeply ringed below the threadbare hat, his fingernails were black moons and even his rosary, which he produced and fumbled, was greasy.

When his panting had subdued he peered at Gino through sticky eyes. Weber was snoring. The priest looked irritated. 'This man is snoring,' he said to Gino.

'He is asleep, Father,' the Italian pointed out.

'I don't like men who snore,' said the priest. He seemed to realise that the statement might compromise him. 'I have heard them in workhouses.'

'This man is a sergeant in the German Army. He is wearing civilian clothes because we have both been swimming in the Channel.'

'Early in the year for that,' grunted the priest.

Gino scowled but not directly at the priest. 'We were in a ship and it was blown up by a mine. Everybody else was lost. We were lucky.'

'God was good to you,' said the holy man taking out his filthy rosary and calculating the beads through his dirty fingers. 'He wanted you to live. Perhaps he has some gallant destiny for you.'

'With due respect, I hope not,' said Gino. 'I am too old for war.'

'So am I,' said the priest, as if he had been in the thick of it. Suddenly his eyes glimmered in their pits. 'Great things are coming,' he said.

'The invasion,' nodded Gino. 'Let's hope it is soon, and all over in no time.'

A look approaching contempt contorted the priest's face. 'Invasion?' he growled. 'Who cares about invasion? That's all people talk about. Something much more important than a trivial battle is coming – the procession of Our Lady of the North.'

Weber began to snore again and Gino leaned over and prodded him gently. Weber murmured: '*Scheisse*,' and half turning into a different curl continued his sleep. 'This is a big event?' asked Gino politely.

'Big? Big? It is the greatest event ever in France. Every year there is the procession of the Blessed Virgin,' manically he crossed himself three times, 'but this year there have been *visions* and *signs*. Every year the likeness of the Blessed Virgin is taken in procession through all of northern France and thousands, thousands, monsieur, follow. Sometimes it stretches for miles, village to village, town to town, people joining in.' He smiled greasily. 'Big collections.'

'It sounds really nice.'

'Nice? Is that all you can say? It will be the *greatest thing* in France's recent history. It will stop this mad war in its tracks. Be prepared for it.'

'Do you have a date?' asked Gino uncertainly.

To his surprise the priest found it necessary to produce a shabby diary. 'June the sixth,' he said. 'It will be a day no one will forget.'

Evidently he had afforded Gino enough time. He replaced the diary with a tattered prayer-book and hung low over this, working his lips for the rest of his journey. He rolled out at a small station, turning on the platform and dismissing them with a sharp blessing.

Weber stirred. 'I heard him,' he groaned. 'God himself couldn't talk as much as that prat.'

'It seemed very important, Fred,' said Gino uncertainly.

'*Scheisse*,' said Weber.

At Caen a small army truck was waiting for them. 'That's very prompt,' said Weber. 'Has the *Wehrmacht* suddenly become efficient?'

'The general wants his dinner tonight,' said the driver. 'He says only you can cook like his mother.'

'Depends on the supplies,' said Weber, nevertheless pleased.

They climbed into the vehicle. 'Any baggage?' asked the driver.

'At the bottom of their sea,' said Weber. He was disappointed that the soldier did not ask how it got there. Instead, as they drove away, he said: 'The supplies are not good. The bastard French charge so much money for their rotten farm stuff, and anything good they hide away for themselves. They are waiting for the Americans to feed them.'

'No one here seems very confident of victory,' pointed out Gino carefully.

The driver snorted. 'Victory? It's too late for victory. All people think about is the best way to get out, to run.' He leaned towards them confidentially. 'For myself, I keep a supply of gasoline hidden so that I, with one of the superior officers, can make my escape. I will just go home to Bremen and hide in the attic.'

It was twenty miles before they reached an ancient arch by the side of the main road. The villages they passed seemed subdued, with few visible people, only squads of German soldiers making vague barricades and digging hopeful trenches. They turned in under the arch and drove down a long single road, straight as only a road in northern France could be, lined most of the way by upright poplars now coloured with May leaves.

They came to another gate guarded by sentries. There was an armoured car which looked as if it had not moved for some time – dock leaves sprouted around the wheels. The crew were sprawled on the turret, faces turned up to the sunshine. A sergeant came forward and did not appear worried that Weber and Gino had no papers and were wearing odd clothes. 'Good that you are here at last,' he said. 'The general needs you.'

Weber said: 'Watch out for June the sixth.'

'The invasion?' asked the sergeant casually. 'Is that when they say it is?'

'Much more important,' put in Gino. 'The procession of Our Lady of the North.'

'Oh, good,' grunted the sergeant. 'I'll watch out for it.'

They went into a large, fine house, old and red with turrets peering over the countryside. In a cavity on the roof was a light anti-aircraft gun and they could just see the toadstool helmets of the gun crew. To their amazement, General Bergensdorf came into the reception hall as they entered, almost as if he had come to greet them. Weber came to an awkward attention and Gino shuffled his feet together. The general raised a flat hand in an absent-minded salute. 'Where have you been, Sergeant Weber?' he said good-humouredly.

'In the sea, sir,' said Weber. 'The boat struck a mine.'

The general did not seem surprised. 'Well, I'm glad you survived. Nobody here can cook.' He glanced curiously at Gino. 'You two must look after each other.'

As he went away, at a slow march as if he had a lot on his mind, Gino regarded Weber dolefully. 'He really believes we are . . . you know . . . lovers.'

'Whatever he thinks, he thinks,' said Weber. 'But we must stick together, Gino. Because of when this war is over.'

Gino smiled bleakly. 'You mean our restaurant in Jersey, Gino and Fred's,' he said wistfully. 'It seems a long way away.'

The German looked doubtful. 'Yes, our restaurant, sure,' he agreed. 'But that is in the far distant future. I was thinking of *right* after when the war is over. I'll need a reference from you.'

'From me?'

'You are neutral and you can tell the Americans or the British that I am no friend of Adolf Hitler's.'

'I see. If they'll believe me.'

A sleepy-looking soldier appeared. 'I must show you your quarters,' he said.

'And the kitchen, please,' said Weber. 'We would like to see where we will work.'

'And the officers' mess,' said Gino.

The soldier looked uncomfortable. 'The orders were just to show you your quarters.'

Weber regarded him caustically. 'If all you do is obey orders you won't last very long in this army.'

'Who will?' shrugged the man. He turned and they followed him first to a fine lofty panelled room with long, polished tables laid around three sides, and a round table for six on the fourth. 'The top brass sit at the round table,' said the sleepy soldier. He assumed the faintest touch of pride. 'We had Field Marshal Rommel here last week.'

'This table is my responsibility,' said Weber. He glanced at the man. 'Is he coming again?'

'Maybe. It depends when the shooting starts, I suppose.'

Food to the dining-room was delivered by two small lifts from the kitchen below. 'Dumb waiters,' said Gino. 'Very useful.'

'All the waiters here are dumb,' said the soldier.

'This sort doesn't speak. They don't tell tales,' said Gino, pointing to the lift.

The man merely nodded his head and led them through a panelled door and down a curved staircase to a kitchen in the wide stone basement. Weber went around testing surfaces with his finger, crouching to look at the gas stoves. 'Is there an emergency supply?' he asked.

'Wood,' said the soldier. 'There is plenty of wood. The French sell it.'

Weber, followed by Gino, went to the cool larder and then looked carefully around the room. 'How many cooks?' he asked.

'Too many. They get in each other's way. That is why the food gets cold.'

'I am only dealing with the general and his staff at the round table,' said Weber firmly. 'They must not have cold food.' He put his head into the aperture of the dumb waiter, sniffed and looked up like a man peering up a chimney. Then he explored the second lift.

The soldier led them up the stairs again and then from the mess up three more flights to the top of the tall house. Gino wondered who had once lived there. They had two small rooms in the turrets that they had seen projecting from the roof. The wooden latticed shutters were open and a breeze filtered in. From the window of his room Weber could see the coast and a small village wedged in the cliffs. 'Is there any fishing nearby?' he asked.

To his surprise the soldier brightened. 'Cod, sea bass and other fish,' he said confidently. 'You can go out with the Frenchmen from the village or they will hire a boat to you if they think you won't sink it. The catches are not bad.'

Weber gave Gino a pleased prod. 'I told you. We must make arrangements.' He glanced at the soldier. 'The general is partial to cod,' he said.

The soldier departed.

They looked around the room and then went into Gino's quarters which were identical. 'Not much luxury,' said Weber. 'But the view is fine.' He went to the window. A green, peaceful evening was lying across the French fields and the Channel beyond.

'Gino,' said the sergeant, 'it's not at all bad. The view is good. The sea is no distance.'

Gino looked disconsolately at the same scene. 'Fred,' he said, 'you realise we are in the front line.'

Chapter Eighteen

Again Paget had to walk up the Baker Street stairs. 'You're still waiting for them to mend the lift,' he said to the FANY at the reception desk.

She hardly looked up from the telephone directory she was searching. She kept her finger on the page and said: 'Bootmakers.' Then she turned to Paget. 'It's been done,' she said flatly. 'But it's up the spout again. Apparently it's down to the war.'

While he waited she rang through to the inner office and then, with a stiff smile, said: 'Fairy will see you now.'

Colonel MacConnel, wearing a pained expression, was at his oriental desk. 'It's buggered my back climbing those stairs,' he said. 'I had to have a week off sick. How is that helping to win the war, I ask you?'

Paget merely shook his head sympathetically.

'All a bit of a mess-up in France, wasn't it?' said the colonel, lifting a file from the desk and sniffing as he opened it. He then stood up and shook hands as though he had previously forgotten.

Paget took a chair. 'More or less,' he said. 'I was almost caught red-handed. It's a good thing the Germans are so lax. By the time I'd got to the Bookbinder Circuit those resistance people under the death sentence had been sprung from prison by the bombing and gone home. That bombing apart, it's all hit and miss over there. If it wasn't so tragic it would be funny.'

MacConnel lowered his head pensively. 'What would resistance have been like in this country if we'd been occupied by the Germans in 1940?' he asked. His eyes came up. 'It would not have been wholehearted, you know. There are some . . .' He paused. 'Some in this building . . . who would have come to an accommodation with Hitler. Resistance groups would have been splintered, just as they are in France. There might have been betrayals, assassinations even. The French don't have a monopoly on inward hatreds. They always emerge at times like this.'

'I imagine so,' said Paget.

'In France, sometimes it works,' MacConnel went on. 'And we hope very soon it will work very well. The trouble is there are so many factions in the French resistance. Each plays the game as they see fit and half the time the Germans just sit back and wait for a betrayal. On the other hand, miles and miles of France is now virtually out of the enemy's hands.'

He sighed and pressed his fingers together. 'It's not been an outstanding show over there,' he admitted. 'Belgium is worse. We've lost almost a hundred people – out of, say, three hundred.' His face brightened a little. 'Our big success has been in Norway, you know. It's still secret but I've got to boast to someone.'

'What was that, sir?'

'We blew up a heavy water plant. With the help of the locals, of course. But it's going to stay blown up.'

'I don't know what a heavy water plant is,' said Paget.

'I'm a bit vague myself, to tell you the truth. But it really was a big success. It's got a lot to do with atomic energy, however that works. Anyway, it was a brilliant operation and it's put the Germans in the mire.' He paused. 'In France there are other objectives.'

He took out a tattered atlas and turned to France. 'Did you ever get around to that poet chap . . . What was . . .?'

'Verlaine,' said Paget. 'The sobbing of the violins in the autumn.'

'Terrible stuff. But good, you know all about it anyway.'

'So does everybody else. The resistance know it and, therefore, the Germans know it.'

'Someone always sneaks,' said the colonel with no surprise or disappointment. 'We'll still use it, I expect. They'll think it's a double bluff. When the BBC recite that rigmarole some will twig it's the invasion and some will say it's a bluff.'

'There seems to be a lot of activity like that,' said Paget.

'Double bluff? Yes, it's a useful excuse when the enemy finds out. Anyway, Verlaine and his sobbing violins is still in place. Once the troops are ashore, the priority for the resistance will be to block the railways and if possible the roads. Someone has come up with a wheeze, someone in France for a change, and what's more they've informed *us*. In a roundabout way, that is. Have you ever heard of Our Lady of the North?'

'I can't say I have.'

'It's a huge traditional religious procession. One of those plaster saints, you know, like they have, hoisted through the countryside for days on end and followed by thousands, priests and peasants most of them.' He paused cautiously. 'You're not a Roman Catholic, I take it, Paget?' Paget said he was not. MacConnel continued: 'It's due to drag itself across northern France at the beginning of June. If we could arrange it so that it got in the Germans' way . . . even for a few hours . . .'

Paget said: 'It sounds like the sort of thing that could happen in France. As long as it doesn't get in *our* way. The Allies.'

MacConnel regarded him sternly. 'Then we'd have to move the silly sods on,' he said. 'And sharpish.'

Now that it was almost summer the village looked much as he remembered it in boyhood; the heavy green oaks and horse chestnuts by the station, the renewed fields, the flowers crowding the cottage gardens.

'You wouldn't know there was a war on, would you, Mr Paget?' said Hughie Skinner, pedalling his wavering bicycle hung with a brace of rabbits. Paget walked from the station, in uniform, carrying one bag, feeling the West Country morning warmth on his face. Reaching the cricket ground he saw that Charlie Merry, who for years had tended the pitch, was out there with his grass cutter and garden roller. There were daisies on the outfield.

Then a haphazard formation of Italian prisoners of war rounded the curve in the road, languidly marching, wearing their chocolate-brown uniforms patched with gaudy colours, and hats of various shapes at jaunty angles. They did not look as though they had escape on their minds; it was an untidy squad, cigarettes in the edges of mouths, guarded by a solitary soldier, his rifle slung, his step as lazy as theirs and with his own fag dangling. When he saw Paget's rank he panicked and somehow concealed the cigarette in his mouth, then attempted to shoulder and slap the rifle butt in a salute which Paget acknowledged. The Italians smirked, made rude, subdued remarks and continued shuffling.

'They're up at the Grange,' his father told him after they had greeted each other. The old man was in the small front garden trimming his privet hedge for the first time that year. He did it annually on the same day. The deep scent of the commonplace shrub was like that of a tropical plant. His mother came from her shopping and embraced her son gratefully. She then examined his face, stepping back to do so, and saying: 'Let me see you, Martin.'

'She thinks that some bits may have fallen off,' laughed his father when she was making coffee.

'It's perfectly all right,' his mother called from the kitchen. 'I can see he's in one piece.'

'This has got to be a quick leave,' he told them. 'Three days at the most.'

His mother looked hurt. 'But you haven't been home since Christmas. You must be most important.'

He smiled. 'It won't be long now. Not too long.'

'Peter Branscome has been home three months,' she said, as if it were unfair. 'And he was a prisoner in Germany.'

His father said: 'Repatriated. He was ill, in and out of hospital. He says he was coughing so hard he was keeping the guards awake.'

'At least he's home,' she said stubbornly. 'His mother told me he's going to get married as soon as his TB has cleared up.'

The two men laughed. 'I can do without the TB,' said Paget. 'But if you want a cushy war, become a prisoner. Those Italians I saw on the road. They looked happy enough.'

'Glad to be out of it,' said Geoffrey Paget. 'Don't blame them. They were always on the wrong side.'

His mother poured coffee from the pot. 'Nice fellows, too. They work on the farms and there have been no complaints. The local girls think they're handsome.'

His father said: 'The rumour is that the Grange is going to be a refugee centre once things get going in Europe. That house has had a lot of lodgers in this war.'

'And nobody is pleased about it,' said his mother. 'Refugees. As Betty Forsyth was saying the other day at the Women's Institute, who knows where they come from, what their background is, what they'll do here and how long they'll stay? They're not going to be very popular. Betty thinks they'll be riff-raff.'

'Not good-looking like the Italians,' mentioned her husband.

Emma turned to her son. 'Bert Hannaford died,' she said with a sort of embarrassment. And, as if it were necessary: 'From Hannaford's Garage.'

Paget was shocked. 'Bert? That's terrible . . . Oh, how sad.'

His father said: 'Even in a war death goes on, just as life does. Ordinary everyday death.'

Slowly Paget said: 'Of course, but you don't think of it like that. Poor Bert was looking forward to after the war. Listening to the cricket on his wireless. And he put together my car and looked after it. I must go and see Mrs Hannaford.'

Emma said: 'She told me she's expecting you to see her when you can. About the car.' She paused. 'That girl Margaret Carne who you know – I can't remember her married name – she's back from London, been at her parents' house for some time. I've seen her with her two children, no husband in sight. Goodness knows what's happened there.'

'Refugees,' said her husband. 'The place is full of them.'

Summer weeds were growing energetically through Bert Hannaford's path. Paget bent and pulled out a couple of handfuls of dandelions while he waited for an answer at the door, and hid them behind his back when Mrs Hannaford opened it. She looked frail and sad, but she made herself smile when she saw him.

'I can't say how very sorry I am to hear about Bert,' he said inadequately as she invited him into the cottage. Secretly he threw the dandelions aside before he entered, then leaned forward, put his hands gently on her shoulders and kissed her on her cheek. 'He was a great man.'

'In his own way,' she agreed. 'It was quite sudden, quick really – one day he was in the garage and the next he was in Taunton hospital and then the day after that he was dead. He asked me to look after your car for you. Almost the last thing he said. It was important to him, that car. It kept him going through the worst times, the bits to put into it arriving after waiting weeks, and the building it all together.' She offered him a cup of tea and he accepted. She needed someone new to talk to. They discussed Bert for half an hour. 'It was a pity the boys couldn't be at the funeral,' she said. 'But they're away at the war and that's all there is to it.' She smiled.

'I'll come tomorrow. If that's possible,' he said, unwilling to impose on her. 'I may not be home long and I'd like to take the car out just once. Will that be convenient?'

'Bless you, of course,' she said. 'You can leave it here until you need it when the war is all over. I like it being there, Mr Paget. We was married for fifty-five years and it's something he liked.'

Sadly he left the cottage and walked in the sun towards the village centre. The pond which had been iced over at Christmas was now thick as cabbage soup, fish in its shadows, the ducks noisy. Margaret was leaning over the iron rail while her small sons threw bread. She looked up and saw him without surprise.

'I heard you were back, Martin,' she said quietly. 'I am so glad to see you.'

They both looked up and down the street and then at the preoccupied children before exchanging a brief kiss. He held her hand. 'I'm sorry I had to go away after that night,' he said. 'I couldn't get in touch.'

She giggled. 'When we were bombed.'

'The next morning I had to go. I've been trying to contact you but it was difficult. For both of us.'

She said: 'I've finally left now and brought the children down here. We'll have a divorce. Divorce goes on even in the middle of the war. In fact, it's thriving.'

Paget said: 'Old Mr Hannaford died, you know.'

'Yes, I heard. I remember him being here for ever. Apparently when they took him to hospital it was the first time he'd been to Taunton since the King's Jubilee.'

'I've been to see Mrs Hannaford. I'm going to get the car out tomorrow. It may be my only chance.'

'*Our* only chance,' she smiled. 'Again.'

The Somerset hills, the Quantocks, were backed with a peaceful haze; sheep grazing on their flanks, pockets of soldiers lying in the sun by their tanks and guns, everything quiet and ready.

'Where will we go?' asked Margaret as the red car crested a hill and the rich summer scene spread in front of them as if a curtain had been raised.

Paget did not know. 'There's a ten-mile exclusion area around the coast now and a car like this turning up is not going to go unnoticed,' he said.

She leaned closer to him in the small seat. 'Martin, I want to go to a small inn with a big bed,' she said.

'Great Bedly,' he laughed and turned the car off at a right angle. 'The Little Angel.'

They dipped into the warm valley, and the narrow road ran into the village square with the inn at its corner, built with the same ancient stones as the square itself. 'I hope they'll give us a room,' she said.

'I'll say we are married.'

'No. I'll say *I* am married because I am. And I'll show them my ring if they want proof.'

'Isn't it madness that we're in the middle of battles and deaths and they are still snotty about you sharing a room if you're not man and wife.'

'How do those Americans manage?' she said as they went in.

As if he'd heard them, the shabby porter at the desk muttered: 'Those Yanks. There was wenches climbing through the windows. In and out. We found one hanging on to the ivy outside. Not much on her in the way of clothes, either.' He looked at Paget's identity card. Margaret said she had forgotten hers. She waved her gold wedding ring under his narrow nose. 'I'm Mrs Paget,' she said.

'Of course you are, madam,' said the porter. 'And I'm Mr Sealy. Anything you want, just ring the bell on the landing. I generally hear it.' He glanced up at Paget. 'Just one night, is it, sir? I expect it is. Nobody seems to have time for more than one night these days.'

Paget said: 'I'm afraid I have to get back.'

'Very important, the war, sir. Top priority, you might say.' He took a huge key from a board behind the desk and asked if they had any baggage. 'In the car,' lied Paget. 'I'll get it later.' Margaret was already going up the dark staircase. Mr Sealy lowered his voice. 'Those Yanks, sir. I'll be glad when they're all gone.' He reduced it to a whisper. 'Making water, urinating that is, in French letters, tying the tops up and throwing them from the bedroom windows. The ruddy things was exploding like bombs or bouncing outside like hobgoblins, frightening the life out of people.'

He ponderously opened the wide oak door. 'Oh, it's a huge bed, darling,' said Margaret. 'What a size.'

'Two centuries old, that bed is,' said the porter. 'There's a lot of people been in there.' He guffawed. 'Though we 'ave changed the sheets now and again.'

He was still laughing at his own joke when he left them. Paget tipped him two shillings and he said that if they rang the bell he would bring them a tray of tea. 'We got some digestive biscuits in from Bath,' he said.

Margaret sat quite primly on the bed, her knees together, her smile quizzical. 'I wonder if we will manage it this time?'

Paget moved in front of her and she put her arms around his waist and pressed her face to his stomach. He kissed her hair and placed his palms on either side of her face. 'Enough of the preliminaries,' she suggested. 'Lock the door, Martin.'

'What about the tea and biscuits?' he smiled.

'I can wait. Even for the digestives.' Decisively she looked up at him. 'Well, I'm going to start taking my clothes off. You can just amuse yourself, if you like.'

They stood close to each other while they undressed. She carefully unfastened her blouse and her brassière. Her breasts looked creamy.

'Say hello again,' she said. He cupped them in his hands and kissed them.

She was pulling down her skirt and her knickers at the same time.

He was naked now, too. She slipped her hands between his legs and began to caress him. She encouraged him into the bed, pushing back the counterpane and the sheets with one house-wifely hand while she still held him tethered with the other.

They rolled into the cool sheets. Outside the window there were afternoon birds singing. She suddenly released him, eased herself from the bed and closed the old shutters, then drew the frayed flowered curtains against the sunshine. 'There's a time and a place for birds,' she said.

Now they lay naked together at last, rolling in the luxury of each other's friendly flesh. He kissed her and entered her deeply. They made love and then lay still against each other. 'Don't let's promise anything, Martin,' she said. 'Like being faithful. There'll be plenty of time for all that when the war is over.' Eventually she opened her eyes and surveyed the cracked and yellowing plaster above them. 'At least this time, darling, the ceiling stayed up.'

'I'm afraid I have to suddenly report for duty,' Paget told the porter as he paid the bill.

'Of course, sir. It's all rush, isn't it,' said the man. 'Sorry you didn't have time for the digestives.' Paget gave him another two shillings. 'God bless you, sir,' he responded. 'And your wife.'

They drove back, mostly in silence. It was now early evening and the war seemed at a great distance. A man drove sheep over the slope of a green hill and there were children playing hopscotch in a village street.

'I wonder if it will all be the same again,' he mused. 'Everything back in place like it was. I doubt it.'

He pulled over and they kissed fondly before they reached the village. She got out of the car two hundred yards from her gate. As he drove away he looked in the mirror and saw her two sons hurry from the house to greet her.

His father was at the gate. 'PC Wottle came around,' he said. 'You've got to go back. They're sending a vehicle for you.'

'Damn it,' muttered Paget. 'I'll take the car back to Hannaford's.'

An air force saloon with a uniformed driver was there within half an hour. Paget kissed his moist-eyed mother. 'Would you like me to tell Margaret Carne you've been called away?' she asked. He said yes. He shook hands with his father. The couple stood at their flower-hung gate, waving in slow motion.

'Don't you hate this war, sir?' said the young driver.

'All the time,' said Paget.

By midnight he was at Tangmere in Sussex. It was a calm, half-moon night, with the beams outlining the clouds. He walked in his worn French civilian clothes to the runway where the Lysander was already warm. A man who came with him, whose name he did not catch, shook hands and wished him good luck. Ten minutes later he was aboard the rattling aircraft and heading south below the moon.

Chapter Nineteen

By the last week of May everything was ready, except the weather. In the early part of the month it had been promisingly warm throughout southern England – on Whit Sunday the temperature had touched eighty degrees – but as June approached, days became sullen with low cloud, rain and a choppy English Channel. The tides also needed to be timely to land the massed army safely and fit to do battle; the skies had to be right for the airborne assault. The expansive plan was to send a great fleet of ships to the beaches of Normandy to land, in the first day, battalions of fighting men, tanks and armoured vehicles, and machines of bizarre design which threw up explosive mines with their flails or laid out their own road as they moved forward. It was the most ambitious, imaginative and widespread strategy of any war in history, scientific, mighty, awesome.

Harris and his men set out by bus.

'It's a ruddy *bus*, sarge,' complained Blackie loudly when they confronted it, standing red, commonplace and expectant on the Salisbury Plain road.

'Southampton Corporation,' Warren read ponderously from the emblem at the side. 'Will we 'ave to pay fares?' He laughed, equally ponderously, at his own joke. Nobody else did. He was not adept at jokes but he tried again. 'Thirty tuppences, please.' Still nobody laughed.

The platoon began trudging towards the bus. Harris looked briefly back over his shoulder at the shabby camp with its hump-backed huts, the grey-green plain and the washy sky rising behind it; his home for four years. Now the games were over, the reality was about to begin. 'Packs on the bottom deck,' he instructed briskly. 'Men upstairs.'

'A bus,' said Jock Gordon, taking up the grumble. 'It's like goin' ta school.'

Harris ushered them aboard. 'Go on the top deck and you can have a fag.'

That cheered them. They took seats on the upper deck and began to drag at the Woodbines which they had shared out. 'Snout?' 'Wanta snout, mate?' 'Ta. I owe you one.'

The driver appeared up the stairs, a warm-faced man with a dangling moustache. His buttons and badges were bright and his uniform pressed like a guardsman. He doffed his peaked cap before he spoke. 'Gentlemen,' he said in a rounded Hampshire voice. It was as if he had rehearsed his words. The soldiers viewed him with surprise. 'It's my privilege to be driving this bus this morning. I would like to be with you going to fight, but I'm too old and I've only got one lung.' Then he looked lost for words.

May said: 'Nice bit of bull you've done on your kit, mister.'

Looking suddenly pleased, the driver gave his buttons a rub with his sleeve. 'Well, I did it specially. I thought I ought to look smart even if I'm not doing much. It's my invasion outfit.'

He prepared to retreat down the stairs. 'Anyway, good luck to you.' He put on his cap and gave them a shy salute.

Harris said: 'Thanks.' He called to his men: 'Three cheers for the driver!' They cheered.

'He can go instead of me if he wants,' said Blackie.

Treadwell said: 'He's the first bloke I've heard who reckons all this caper is serious. Every other bugger thinks it's just a game.'

The bus quivered strongly as the engine started. 'He's tuned it up as well,' said Gannick, who had lit his pipe and began to puff.

'Sit back and enjoy it, lads,' suggested Harris. 'We're on our way. Hitler's already quaking in his boots.'

Hitler was, in fact, insisting with his customary bile to his commanders that the invasion would be launched in the Pas de

Calais at the narrowest neck of the English Channel. Normandy, he told them with the conviction of a man who had never been wrong, was out of the question, just a bluff. He knew best. The commanders saluted and went away knowing the game was up.

The corporation bus drove south away from the plain. 'Goodbye, ye hilly bastard,' called Gordon. 'France can only be flatter.'

A silence fell upon them as if they now began to realise where they were going. Harris broke it: 'Well, the first stop is Lyndhurst, in the New Forest. They call it a holding camp. And hold you is what it does, so don't ask for leave or even time to go to the pub. Because once we're there, nobody moves until we go to the boats.'

Throughout the south and south-west of England almost every park and open space had become a tented camp with guards at its gates. The soldiers who were destined to give Europe freedom were confined behind wire. The mass of the Americans was joined by a British army together with a Canadian division that had been in the country since 1940 when it was rushed across the Atlantic to help stem the expected German invasion. The enemy had not come and it had been training for four years. Now it was keen for the fight. There were Frenchmen unsure if they and their leader, General Charles de Gaulle, would be welcome in their own country, openly bloodthirsty Poles out for revenge, and others. War had been an odd mixer. Across the Channel, ready to face the assault, were Indian soldiers whose hatred of British rule had persuaded them to fight for Nazism.

In Southampton, the major port for the invasion, the city common had become a military base. American soldiers threw their spare small change over the fence to local children hanging against the wire. Some of the boys had American badges and insignia sewn by their mothers on their sleeves and pockets. A thin-legged child on an old bicycle flaunted the emblem of the US 2nd Armored Division with its motto: 'Hell on Wheels'.

Half an hour's journey away was Southwick House where

General Eisenhower was headquartered, like all his soldiers waiting for the day and knowing he had to make the lonely decision as to when it would be. It was his choice, his voice that would give the order. Tents spread east into Kent and west as far as Cornwall. On the moorland of the New Forest were extensive enclosures where soldiers were assembled behind wire, and wild ponies, deer, pigs and cows peered through fences at men in cages.

Into this massive military realm that morning chugged the red bus carrying Harris and his squad in convoy with trucks, jeeps and other everyday omnibuses. Through the forest town of Lyndhurst they drove.

Gordon had acquired a local guide-book. 'The real Alice in Wonderland is buried here,' he announced loudly. 'Alice Liddell, she was called.'

'It's us who's in Wonderland, something like it, anyway,' said Treadwell, staring through his glasses.

The town's inhabitants were going about their daily business, and taking little notice of the soldiers or the vehicles. The squad peered busily like day-trippers from the bus windows. The driver drove them proudly, performing elaborate hand signals, a set distance behind an armoured vehicle, and sitting upright as a guardsman.

The transports were going to different destinations and the convoy split up. Harris had to ask for directions from a snappy British military policeman at a crossroads. The redcap said nothing, just pointed. They turned through gates made from tree-trunks, flanked by men with bayonets and grim expressions. Eventually the hastily laid road terminated. Harris called his men to disembark; they unloaded their equipment and humped it to a tent.

'Now Oi used to loike camping,' mentioned Blackie as they walked below the smelly canvas. 'Did you never go, Bunny?'

Warren said: 'S'posed to but Oi had them mumps.'

There was an oil-lamp on a table and a row of beds and metal lockers. On each bed was a pile of blankets and a tough pillow. On the table were some books: a Bible, a French dictionary, a warning leaflet about leaving litter on the battlefield ('It will give your position away') and another on the dangers of venereal disease. There was also a notice on the soldier's rights if he should be taken prisoner of war.

'I wouldn't mind gettin' taken prisoner, sarge,' said May, as if he were showing initiative. 'It's dead cushy and you don't get shot or nothing.'

Harris regarded him caustically. 'You'd better read the Bible, mate. Or the thing about getting the pox.'

Within the holding camp were ranks of camouflaged tents and two big prefabricated mess halls. The soldiers explored the vicinity within the wire in cautious pairs as though they were reconnoitring enemy lines. They called to men in other compounds. Treadwell and Gordon returned to the tent, ducking under the stiff canvas door.

'There's a big skive on the go,' reported Treadwell. 'Blokes going sick.'

'Malaria,' confirmed Gordon.

'Malaria!' Blackie was outraged. He jumped from his mattress. 'How's there malaria around 'ere? It b'ain't bloody Egypt. It's a dodge to get off the invasion.'

Gordon said: 'It's damp and humid here. It's those stationed in India and places east, afore the war.'

'The Yanks have caught everything,' said Treadwell. 'One of the medics says they're going down like flies. Everything from the flu to the shits.'

'Aye, crapping themselves grand,' confirmed Gordon.

'Pox,' said Warren. 'Pox is the best bet.'

They watched him cleaning his rifle barrel with a cord pull-through. 'Bit hard to catch in 'ere,' he said.

One side of the compound bordered a village road with a clutch of cottages and a school on its far side. Blackie and Warren went to the edge of the cage and watched the children in the

254

playground. 'Jus' loike we used to be, eh, Bunny,' said Blackie fondly. 'Boys and maids. Little bastards.'

'Jus' like,' agreed Warren. He peered along the street. 'That next camp up there on the other side,' he said, 'looks like Yanks. See, they be standing against the fence starin' out.'

'Just loike we,' said Blackie. 'Same as a zoo.'

It was half past twelve and they were about to turn towards the cookhouse when the school gate was thrown open and a stream of children came out, a hurrying crocodile, making for the American enclosure. The British soldiers observed them with an annoyed wistfulness. 'Where they think they be goin'?' asked Warren.

'Where they'll get most,' said Blackie.

He was right. The boys and girls reached the margin of the American perimeter fence and began to shout and jump. The men inside the compound laughed and called to them, throwing chocolate bars and packs of chewing-gum over the top of the fence. The children fought and tumbled.

A soldier who with three others had appeared behind Blackie and Warren joined in watching the scramble. 'Fucking greedy, I call that,' he said.

'We was fighting this war for those kids a long time before them Yanks got 'ere,' one of the others added.

'Same as the last war,' agreed Blackie. 'Didn't get there till it was nearly over.'

They could hear some orders being shouted in the American compound and the GIs near the wire backed away. The children cautiously did likewise, turning back towards the school. 'Hey, you! You kids!' called the first soldier behind Warren. The children paused and looked towards them without enthusiasm.

'Come and talk to *us*,' urged a second soldier. 'Come on.'

'What be the matter with us, then?' Blackie joined in.

To their surprise some of the children, four boys and two older girls, came unhurriedly towards them. 'Why was you shoutin'?' asked one of the girls.

None of the soldiers answered until Warren said: 'You went over to the Yanks all right, di'n you? What's the matter with us?'

One of the boys ran his coat sleeve fiercely across his nose and said: 'Cos they gives us Hershey bars.' He pulled half a dozen chocolate bars from one pocket and then a further handful from another and held them out in a fan shape like a gambler with two hands of cards.

'And gum,' put in one of the girls, holding up a white packet. She giggled: 'Got any gum, chum?'

'S'pose you don't want to be talkin' to the loikes of us, then?' said Blackie.

'You talk funny,' said the boy with the handfuls of chocolate. 'You one of them Poles?' The others produced bars from their pockets, tore away the wrappings and began to eat them furiously. The soldiers' faces narrowed. The children, chocolate oozing around their mouths, kept their eyes on the soldiers.

'Are you all going to get shot?' asked one of the girls.

'Killed?' asked a boy. He played at firing a machine-gun. The rest began to snigger.

'*You'll* be getting killed,' retorted one of the soldiers. 'I'll come over this wire and do it myself.'

The children hooted. 'But you can't get out!' exclaimed the elder of the girls. She produced a stick of chewing-gum and began to unwrap it teasingly. 'You're locked up.'

'Cos you might run away!' shouted the second girl.

The soldiers were clutching the unmoving fence, pushing against it. 'Bloody little swines,' said one of the men.

'Ooooh, I'll tell my dad about you,' responded the other girl. 'He's a butcher.'

The children broke into further mirth and stuck out their chocolatey tongues. A bell sounded from the school. The boy with the most Hershey bars selected one and tossed it over the fence. It fell in the middle of the soldiers and for a moment no one moved. Then Blackie bent to pick it up but was pushed aside by one of the others.

The youngsters jeered and began tossing chocolate bars over the fence. The soldiers fell into an undignified scrum as they tried to claim them. Warren had his Hershey bar snatched from his hand and he snatched it back angrily. They scuffled and swore.

The children were trotting back across the road to the school. One of the girls returned for a moment, and blew them a raspberry before lobbing a packet of chewing-gum over the fence. The trapped soldiers stared after her, one picked up the gum and the others began to eat their Hershey bars.

It rained for two days and drizzled on the third: thick, summer rain diminishing to a misty dampness that spread across the waiting regiments. Forest trees dripped like a hundred ticking metronomes ticking, forest streams were glutted and ran swiftly, marsh moss stuck to the soldiers' boots.

'It be a soddin' bog,' complained Warren, splashing into the tent. 'Worse than a farmyard.'

The rivulet of rainwater trickled its way between the beds; the oil-lamp, alight although it was midday in May, glowed, giving an illusion of heat as well as a glimpse of light. The men were damp and bored. 'I can't play at yon snakes and ladders any more,' grumbled Gordon. 'Nor yon draughts.'

Harris pushed through the wet flap, displaying a sheaf of blue papers and a single white sheet. 'Which do you want first?' he asked. 'General Montgomery or Entertainments?'

Gordon put out his hand for the white paper. The blue papers were left ignored on the bottom of Treadwell's bed.

'Tomorrow night,' the Scot announced, 'there's going to be marionettes.'

'French dancers?' asked Blackie, beginning to smile.

'Puppets,' Treadwell told him. 'Like we are.'

Blackie looked affronted. 'Things on strings? Christ.'

Gordon studied the sheet. 'But tonight sounds better. Songs at the piano, it says. Some folk called Teresa Concetta and Andre Brech.'

'A bit of a singsong,' suggested Warren.

'I doubt it,' put in Harris. He had been frowning over the message from Montgomery. 'Not with names like that.' He handed around the blue leaflets. 'This is addressed to all troops,' he said. 'From the man at the top.'

'But no' at the front,' muttered Gordon. He took one of the pamphlets.

'Read it out, Treadwell,' Harris said. 'You've got the glasses.'

'It's seeing any ruddy thing in this tent,' grumbled Blackie. 'What be the use of a message from Monty if you can't see what it says?' He looked up with a slice of hope. 'Or it might be moi eyes be goin'. Off to the MO Oi ought to be.' The sergeant laughed and went out. He was going to write to Enid.

Treadwell coughed. 'All right, here goes.' He moved closer to the oil-lamp and began to read, slowly and aloud: 'The time has come to deal the enemy a terrific blow in Western Europe . . .' He looked up as if to make sure they were listening. They were attentive. But why would Montgomery send a message to them? They would do as they were told anyway.

Clumsily he continued: 'The blow will be struck by the combined sea, land and air force of the Allies, together . . .'

'Look, a mouse!' Warren pointed.

Everyone looked. Treadwell stopped reading Montgomery. The mouse was sprawled in the muddy water trickling through the tent, half dead, its back legs moving fitfully as if it were trying to swim.

'Puir thing,' said Gordon.

Blackie said: 'Some bastard's stamped on 'im. Look 'ow flat 'is arse be.' He took Montgomery's proclamation from Treadwell's hand and leaning over, scooped the creature into it. The soaked field mouse lay on the general's fighting words and, rolling its eyes, gave up its own fight.

'Snuffed it,' said May.

'Buggered,' said Chaffey.

'Bury it proper,' said Warren.

He went to his bed and slid his bayonet from its scabbard. 'My dad used to dig graves a bit,' he said. ''Member 'im, Blackie?'

'Delver, weren't 'e called?' responded Blackie surveying the dead mouse.

'Delver Warren,' said Warren fondly. ''E tucked a few away.'

'Where we goin' to bury yon mouse?' said Gordon. 'Not in the tent.'

'Yeah, might niff,' said Chaffey.

Warren put his head out of the tent to see if it had stopped raining. Harris came back to find out what the excitement was about. He saw the mouse stretched on the blue paper of the proclamation. 'Don't take him near the cookhouse,' he warned. He went back to his own tent.

Warren with his bayonet and Gordon, respectfully carrying the mouse, went between the guy ropes and found a corner where some grass had survived. The other men came after them. 'That'll do,' said Warren. 'Just the job.' They stood like children playing at funerals while he cut a small oblong from the ground. Gordon wrapped the mouse in the proclamation and inserted the body into the hole. 'Wee, sleekit, cow'rin', tim'rous beastie,' he recited. The others glanced at him. 'Rabbie Burns,' he said as if it were a close friend. 'Ode "To a Mouse". Learned that in school. I allus thought it might come in useful.'

Back in his tent, Harris wiped the drizzle from his cap badge and wondered who cleaned Montgomery's two cap badges. How could a man wear *two* cap badges?

The tent which he shared with the other three sergeants was square. All night the rain had been tattooing on its taut roof, and they had tossed a coin to select which one of them would get out of his camp-bed and ease the guy ropes. The sergeants were all strangers. One of them, from Aldershot, had been a soldier twenty years. He tossed the coin by dim torchlight and told Harris that he had lost.

Now, for a while, Harris had the luxury of the tent to himself.

He sat on his damp bed and by the light coming in from the sullen day began to write:

Dearest Enid,

I thought I would drop you a line now because I don't think there's any chance of getting leave and coming home to see you. Because of the censor I can't tell you hardly anything except that my ankle now seems to be okay. The medics say as long as I don't put too much weight on it. Anyway I'm fit for duty.

I know that you and I will never be the same. You are so lively and I know I'm a bit stodgy but when the war is over we'll be able to spend more time together and work things out.

But I just want you to know that I love you now the same as I loved you when we got married. It will never be any different for me.

Your loving husband, Harris.

The rain had moved tardily away, leaving a pale Maytime sky over the endless canvas roofs. Only a few miles distant, in the southern harbours, ships were being shuffled, shifted, loaded, made ready. It would not be long now.

Each soldier was permitted one bottle of beer a day; non-commissioned officers were allocated two. They were on sale between six and seven o'clock each evening in the prefabricated buildings that served as a canteen and a sergeants' mess.

'Right you be then,' said Blackie, squinting down the neck of his beer bottle to the empty interior. 'Weem ought to go and see this couple, whatever they call theirselves, and their . . .'

'"Songs at the Piano",' provided Gordon.

'It might not be so bad,' said Treadwell. 'There's bugger all else to do.'

Determinedly they strode out across the muddy camp to the larger of the mess halls. Other soldiers were making their unhopeful way towards it. By the time a wan, overfed woman and a stringy man in an ancient dinner suit were in place on the makeshift stage and the scarred lid had been lifted from the piano, most of the chairs were occupied. 'Madame Concetta will begin her performance with two *lieder* – two songs from Schubert,' announced the stringy man. He began to play, frowning at the piano's notes.

The lady expanded her black-curtained bosom and began to sing. The men who were waiting to go into battle sat in deepening gloom. Blackie was transfixed. He put his small head into his rough hands and moaned: 'Fuck me gently.'

By the first of June the American holding camp on Southampton Common was so tight that there was little room even to walk. No drills were held, there was no space for training nor even volleyball. The soldiers sat in their wet tents and relentlessly played poker, the doomsday version of the game, with stakes, on paper, as high as twenty-five thousand dollars.

A jeep was waiting for Soroyan. He climbed aboard. 'Those guys,' he sighed. 'How they gonna pay out that sort of dough?'

'They're reckoning on being dead,' the driver said casually. 'Somebody must like you, pal. Second time you've been sent on the mail run.'

'They've figured I can read,' said Soroyan. The driver headed the jeep for the guarded main gate with its clutch of girls and children outside, the sentries ignoring them. Bull, the driver, said: 'We could make a killing, more than cleaning up at poker, if we could somehow smuggle those molls into camp.'

'No hope,' sniffed Soroyan. He flicked a packet of chewing-gum at some boys who scrambled for it. 'Nobody gets out and nobody gets in.'

'Except us,' said Bull. He turned the car towards the docks.

'They owe me,' said Soroyan. 'Uncle Sam owes me. Once you've been in action and wounded, then they got to send you back Stateside. Home. That's the rule. Right?'

'Sure is.' Bull looked interested. 'You been in action?'

'Exercise Tiger,' said Soroyan. 'Screw-up beach landing. Some Nazi E-boats. D'you hear about it? Seven hundred GIs dead.'

'Who ain't heard?' Bull whistled silently. 'Were you in that shit?'

'Certainly was. Trouble was, I wasn't wounded *enough*. I survived in the ocean. I was just wounded up here.' He patted his forehead. 'In my brain.'

Bull eased the jeep to traffic lights. He waved to some schoolboys in a bus going to the public swimming baths. They waved their towels. 'If you want to stay alive,' muttered Soroyan, 'learn to swim.'

'So they're giving you a second chance,' Bull said.

'To die,' breathed Soroyan.

Bull steered the vehicle off the main road and took the long street to the docks. Enid was walking back to her house. Soroyan sat up from his slouch. 'Jeez, did you get that ass?'

'It was some ass,' agreed Bull. 'Some tits at the front, too. I saw in the mirror. Nice legs. Nice-looking blonde.'

'Drop me off here,' said Soroyan decisively. 'You can pick up the mail. I saw the house where she went.'

Bull was astonished. 'But you're on this duty too. You can't just hightail it after an ass.' He stopped the jeep nevertheless.

'Be a pal,' urged Soroyan. 'It's only frigging letters. Wells Fargo it ain't. I'll meet you here, on this street, in half an hour.' He hesitated. 'Forty-five minutes.'

'Okay,' said Bull, still full of doubt. 'So what if that sergeant in the mail section wants to know where you are? Do I tell him you've gone to pray?'

'Great idea,' said Soroyan, climbing from the jeep. 'And I sure will be praying. For some luck. See you, buddy.' He banged his hand on the roof frame and Bull, shaking his head, drove off. 'You'll be dumped in the brig!' he called over his shoulder.

'Might be an idea!' Soroyan shouted back. He loped along the street, wishing he had thought to bring a packet of the nylon stockings which so often came in useful. He arrived outside the house, straightened his uniform and his cap, marched up the short path and rang the bell.

Enid's eyes widened when she saw the tall, tanned young man.

'Was there something?' she enquired, moving seductively against the door frame.

Soroyan had his speech ready but in the end he ad libbed. 'Oh . . . oh, yes, ma'am.' He even manufactured a blush. 'Wow . . . I'm sorry. You're so beautiful . . .'

'Thank you.' She had seen him in the jeep. 'So are you.'

'But . . . wow . . . but I seem to have come to the wrong address. I was looking for the Metcalf family. Mr and Mrs Metcalf . . . and all the little . . . Metcalves.'

'Metcalf?' wondered Enid, looking up and down his tunic. 'I don't know anybody of that . . . Would you like a cup of coffee?'

Soroyan succeeded in continuing to blush. 'Well, ma'am, thank you. I seem to have gotten the wrong street. These little streets all look the same.'

'I expect you have much bigger streets in America,' said Enid, opening the door and letting him in. 'Everything's bigger, isn't it?'

They were close in the passageway, his handsome olive-skinned face only inches from her powdered nose. 'Most things,' he said.

She led him through to the kitchen. 'My husband's away.' She opted for the half truth. 'On war work.'

He sighed and sat on the chair she offered. She thanked God she had done her hair and make-up before she went to the shops. 'Looks like everybody's got war work,' said Soroyan, taking in her legs as she walked towards the kettle. She had the seams of non-existent stockings etched up the back. The ink had smudged on her calf. Why hadn't he brought the nylons? 'At this moment, I'm one of thousands of guys stuck behind wire. The first smell of freedom we'll get is when we hit those killer beaches in France. Yes, ma'am.'

Enid turned her full, sympathetic face on him. 'It's just terrible, I think. Herding you together like that just before you go off to fight.'

'And maybe die,' he muttered, looking directly at her.

A genuine dampness came to her doll-blue eyes. 'You could, easily,' she said. She was ashamed that she had told him that

Harris was on war work. His letter had arrived that morning and it had made her very sad. She told herself she needed cheering and here was the very person to do it.

'Will it be very dangerous?' she asked. She stood by him as he sat tall in the chair.

'I guess it will. I've already got lucky once. I ended in the English Channel which was on fire all around me at the time. Lots of guys died.'

Enid caught her breath. Her breasts heaved below her blouse. 'Poor you,' she said. Her hands went halfway to his head in a motherly gesture. She halted and began to withdraw them but he nodded his head back into them.

'I'm scared as hell,' he said. 'I need . . .'

'You need what?' she asked. 'I'll try and get it for you.' The kettle was boiling and she attempted to ignore it but it began to whistle. Reluctantly she went to the stove and turned it off. Soroyan had risen from the chair by the time she turned back.

'You're very tall,' she said. Her chin was almost on his uniformed chest.

'And you're very beautiful,' he repeated. 'I just . . . . God, I just wish we had time to get to know each other.'

'There's time,' she assured him. She was enjoying the feeling. It was just like the pictures. 'There's always time. What's your name?'

'Soroyan,' he told her. 'Ben Soroyan. My family came from Armenia.'

'I don't know where that is,' shrugged Enid. 'This war is like geography, isn't it? My name is Enid Harris. I'm originally from Eastleigh.'

They were inches apart. 'Armenia is in some different part of the world that is miles away just now,' he said throatily. 'Miles and miles.' He could not believe how well it was going.

'And you're here,' she whispered. She moved against his tunic feeling the hard, fit body beneath it. She bit one of his buttons and then turned her face up. As they kissed voluptuously and she withdrew to get some breath, she caught sight of her husband's simple letter on its lined paper. She had read it twice. It was not long enough to read it more than that. Oh, Harris.

Soroyan was kissing her again. He pressed against her breasts. He checked his watch as his hands went over her back and down to her buttocks. Half an hour left. 'I'll feel so much braver for this,' he said. 'I won't care what happens to me.'

Furtively she glanced at her husband's letter again. Then the doorbell rang. Soroyan said: 'Shit.' She put her finger to his lips as she disengaged herself and glanced about the kitchen. 'Just in case,' she cautioned, 'you'd better get into the pantry for a minute. I'll see who it is.'

He began wildly looking about him for the pantry. She opened the cupboard door and gently pushed him in with the sugar ration and that day's loaf of bread. There were tins on the shelves and he prudently selected a can of Spam and held it like a hand-grenade.

Enid rearranged her hair and smoothed down her skirt and blouse as she went along the passage.

It was Maggie Phillips and she was sobbing. 'Oh, that bastard,' she wailed. 'He's gone off with a lump of a land-army girl.'

'Your Brian?'

'Who else would it be?'

'What a pig. He's only just let you know, has he?'

'This bloody morning. And it's my birthday, Enid, like you know. I thought it was a card.' She began to sob deeply again.

Enid gently encouraged her into the house. 'Don't worry, love,' she said. 'Forget your Brian. Come into the kitchen. Have I got a present for you.'

Chapter Twenty

Harcourt drove Miller south-west from London to Winchester, with its strong, old cathedral, to the headquarters of the US 9th Infantry Division, through a placid early summer day. 'I just don't know, sir, how England can be so beautiful and yet not warm,' Harcourt said as the road curled through the green, gently hilly countryside. As they neared the grey and solemn city they saw the roads were taken up as parking places for bulky Sherman tanks with their ominous guns, veiled in camouflage netting.

From Winchester a flow of military traffic was crawling east. A British military policeman, his boots glowing in the sunshine, was at a crossroads. 'Cheesefoot Head, sir,' called Harcourt from the car window. 'Follow the rest,' waved the MP. 'And you don't have to call me sir, soldier. Up to now I'm only a corporal.'

'Just politeness,' Harcourt muttered, withdrawing his head. He half turned to Miller. 'He just looked like a sir, sir.' Miller laughed. Harcourt, as if he had been waiting, said: 'When they start this invasion, captain, I want to come with you.'

Miller patted his shoulder. 'Right now, Benji, I don't know whether I'm going to get there myself. I'm still pushing for it.' He grinned privately. 'How do you feel about a parachute drop over France?'

There was a pause before Harcourt said: 'Maybe I'll wait a little.'

Cheesefoot Head was a sumptuous natural amphitheatre, a great grassy bowl set in endlessly curving Hampshire countryside. At the top the wind was blowing the long grass. Even today, sixty years later, it is not difficult to picture the scene that afternoon, the steep green slopes lined row above row with khaki soldiers. Above them a blue sheet of English sky spread and in the air singing skylarks rose. Miller stood amazed.

General Dwight Eisenhower, the Supreme Allied Commander, was due. He arrived on time and a low murmur went up from the galleries of soldiers, every one of whom thought of him like a friend and called him Ike. He turned a full slow circle on the wooden platform to take in the massed and expectant faces of his men. Senior officers on the platform sat down and took in the scene in silence, perhaps in awe. When Eisenhower, a neat, unmilitary figure, was announced by a tall captain from Texas, and stepped two paces forward to the central microphone, all the ranks began to applaud and shout, the men rising to their feet, the acclaim growing and going like a travelling wind over the sweeping countryside, sending distant sheep bolting and stirring farm horses.

The applause continued until Eisenhower, with his wide, half-melon shaped grin visible even from the top tier of troops, held up his hand to end it in an instant. He began to speak into the microphone.

'Men, you are embarking upon the Great Crusade, toward which you have striven these many months . . .' The words rose up through the green basin.

'I saw Joe Louis box here,' said the officer next to Miller in a soft conversational voice but not a whisper. Miller glanced at him in astonishment. He saw he was a full colonel. 'You did?' he answered politely. Eisenhower was saying: '. . . The hopes and prayers of liberty-loving people everywhere march with you . . .'

'Sure I saw him,' said the other American. 'He was the finest human being I ever did see. He came to fight, right down there where the man is speaking from, and it was a great experience.'

Eisenhower said: '. . . Your enemy is well trained, well equipped and battle hardened. He will fight savagely . . .'

'It was no great fight,' said the officer. 'Only exhibition stuff, a couple of punk boxers to fight him. He could have handled both at the same time. My God, what a fighter . . .'

The other men around them were intent on Eisenhower's words. Miller's neighbour was speaking directly to Miller as if he had to tell someone. 'And Judy Garland,' he continued. 'I saw Judy sing here also. What a day that was. The guys loved it . . .'

'I have full confidence in your courage, devotion to duty and skill in battle.' Eisenhower's voice rose.

'Judy, she sang "Over the Rainbow".' When he laughed it was like a small grunt. 'You know "Over the Rainbow"?'

'I do,' muttered Miller.

'And "There'll Always be an England"?'

Eisenhower raised his voice: 'Good luck! And let us all beseech the blessing of Almighty God upon this great and noble undertaking!'

Miller's neighbour said: 'Gee, you know how these dumb censor guys, how they cut out everything they can from your letters back home?' Miller found himself nodding. 'Well, I wrote to my wife about Judy, saying how great, how heavenly she was, but the fuckers cut half of it out, including the fact that it was Judy *Garland* I was raving about. She thought I was writing about some English girl called Judy I'd met. What about that?'

Miller glanced around. The men were sitting shoulder to shoulder, rank upon rank, on the sloping grass, intent on Eisenhower's words. No one else seemed to have noticed his neighbour's strange commentary. Then the Supreme Commander finished. He folded his notes and stepped back. The cheers and the clapping resounded around the amphitheatre, as again the soldiers rose.

'I have to go,' said the infantry colonel. 'I have to be with Ike. I'm on his staff.'

Miller's eyes rose. 'I didn't hear much of his speech,' he said.

'It was okay,' said the man easily. 'Inspiring. I helped to put it together.'

The soldiers were dispersing. Miller walked with the crowd, like spectators from a ball game, up to the car park where Harcourt was waiting with the other drivers. 'We heard it loud and clear,' said his driver. 'Stirring words, sir.'

Miller grunted. 'That's more than I did, son. Some crazy colonel – a colonel, for God's sake – kept talking in my ear about Joe Louis and Judy Garland.'

'Oh, gee, that's a pity,' said Harcourt, opening the car door. 'Maybe there'll be another show sometime.'

'I don't think so,' said Miller.

Every road was clogged with military traffic. There were tanks, their gun barrels pointing unerringly up village streets, their crews handing candy to children and laughing and acting up to their sisters and mothers. A woman with a Brownie box camera took a photograph of a wide-grinned American soldier with her dog sitting on his tank alongside him.

'Nice picture,' said Harcourt. 'But against security, I guess.'

Miller said: 'It's too late for security now, Benji. If they don't know we're coming they never will.'

Roadblocks checked every vehicle going into or coming from the ten-mile southern exclusion zone. The civilian population was hemmed in. Only in an emergency could any local people pass through the barriers. All civilian travel to neutral Southern Ireland was forbidden.

'Dorchester,' ruminated Harcourt. 'That's where we're going. I checked it out, sir. There's two Dorchesters in England. I hope we're heading for the right one.'

'Dorset,' said Miller, unfolding an order. 'Then who knows where.'

'Berlin maybe,' said Harcourt. He sighed. 'I hope soon. I want to go home.'

'Missing your folks?'

'Sure thing, sir. My mammy's missing me too.' He laughed. 'That'll be some day – when Benji comes marching home. Everybody on the block will be out to see me. All those folks listening to what I've got to say. I ain't done nothing great, no heroism, no danger even, not yet, but they'll all be in that place just the same. Then all I need to do is to get a job. I hope somebody has got a job for me.'

'You're a good man, Benji,' said Miller. He meant it. 'You make sure you're waiting with the car when I get back from France.'

'I'll do that, sir. You'll never see an automobile so polished and shining. You've been a good boss too, sir. I been proud to drive you.'

They reached Dorchester in the evening. 'Another fairy-book town,' commented Harcourt. 'I just don't know how they built them like this.'

They drove up the old, rising street. 'Over a long time,' said Miller.

The American camp was a few miles north of the town, below a green hillside decorated with a giant white figure of a naked man, cut centuries before in the downland chalk. Harcourt whistled. 'Phew, that guy sure looks healthy.'

'He certainly does,' grinned Miller.

'Nobody ain't gonna beat that,' said Harcourt.

They turned in to the camp. At once Miller saw Colonel Jeffries. It was as if he had been waiting. 'Captain, you okay to take a walk?' said Jeffries.

'Yes, sir. Right away.'

They strolled to the fringe of the camp. It was a mild evening but the sky was overcast and disturbed. The carved giant with his long penis lay on the hillside in front of them. 'He's really impressive,' said Miller.

'No doubt about that,' nodded Jeffries. 'Can you see that in the United States? They'd soon have a pair of pants on him. It's given our guys here an inferiority complex.'

Jeffries looked better than when Miller had seen him after the landing exercise tragedy off the coast of Devon – less tired, less fraught – but he still seemed as if he would prefer to be somewhere else, anywhere rather than the war.

'Colonel Hendy, the commanding officer here, is going to

parade his troops tomorrow,' said Jeffries. 'I thought it would be a good time to catch up with you. We've done just about all we can from the training angle. That's finished. Some of it worked, some of it didn't. It's just going to be days now – only the weather is in doubt, and with all those men in the holding areas, well, there's no room for basketball never mind training. Those guys, they're trained as much as they'll ever be. All they'll get from now is the real thing. I think you and the other overseeing officers have done all you can, Miller. A good job.'

Miller said: 'It remains to be seen, sir.' He waited, then asked: 'Am I going, sir? Or have they turned me down?'

'You're going,' said the colonel.

'Great, good.'

'But you won't be jumping by any parachute. They can't accommodate you. You can ride the plane, if that's what you still want to do, captain.'

Miller said: 'I owe it to them. You know what happened with my big idea?'

'Sure, I do. Things like that will happen. Men get killed in training. As we know too well.'

'It didn't make me popular,' sighed Miller. 'It was just lousy luck that Dakota was shot up. A fluke. That Messerschmitt just happened to be there. But you trying telling those boys that, sir. Four of their buddies didn't come back. One came down by 'chute but has since been reported dead.'

'A sad tale,' said Jeffries with no emphasis.

'That's why I owe them,' said Miller. 'I'm not top of their popularity poll but they want me to be with them, to take the same risks.'

'You have a wife,' said Jeffries. It was not a question.

'I do. She looks after our dogs. The young pilot who died, he had a wife too. A new one.'

They began to walk back to the mess. There came the sound of male conversation from inside. 'Why the parade tomorrow?' asked Miller.

'Colonel Hendy wants to show his men off,' said Jeffries. 'He wants to show the folks around here that they're fighting men and soon they're going to be doing just that – fighting. He thinks the English here don't have a high opinion of the Yanks, as they call us. In some cases it's become a term of contempt: Yanks. He wants to march them down the street just to show that we mean business, that they're not a bunch of toy soldiers.'

They went into the mess where each had a drink and then another. 'After the parade, Miller, I suggest you get out of here real quick. Get up to your Dakota, boys. You wouldn't want to miss the show and it seems like the curtain is going up soon. Very soon.'

He made a telephone call to London that night. 'Use this one, sir,' said the sergeant of the guardroom. 'The nearest public booth is in town, and it's off limits tonight anyway because the colonel wants the fighting to be in France, not in Dorchester.' He pointed to the receiver. 'Uncle Sam can afford it.'

Kathleen answered. He heard her draw her breath. 'I thought you'd never call me again. I'm so glad you rang,' she said. 'I must have been mad, or drunk, probably drunk, that night. And you'd had a bad day.'

'Some men were killed,' he said simply.

'Oh, God. What a selfish bitch I am. Blame the booze. Can I see you soon?'

'It will have to be soon,' he said. 'I'm away from London just now but I have to come through tomorrow night.'

He sensed her disappointment. 'But I won't be here. I'm just back sorting some things out. The play is touring and we're at Reading.'

'I know where Reading is,' said Miller. 'It's on my route from here.'

'Oh, good. I'm so glad you called. What time?'

'I'm not sure. Things are confused just now. It will be late evening, I guess. I'll find the theatre.'

Kathleen said: 'It's in the middle of the town. Come to the stage door. You won't need to see the play.' She paused. 'It sounds like you've had enough drama.'

They were in Miller's car, mounting the hill to the crossroads at the top of Dorchester town. Harcourt pulled up at a red light. The traffic was entirely military except for a farm wagon drawn by two nodding horses moving sedately in the middle of the jeeps and trucks. The horses stopped, tossed their manes and snorted in the hold-up. A boy in short trousers and a grubby khaki shirt held the reins and shouted unnecessarily in a country voice at the horses. Squatting on a bale of straw in the open cart was a wrinkled woman wearing a straw hat who surveyed the soldiers with indifference.

'She don't give a shit,' said Colonel Jeffries, sitting beside Miller. 'War's all the same to her.' He glanced to the left where there was a statue on a plinth. 'This Thomas Hardy,' he said. 'Are you familiar with his writing?'

Miller admitted he was not. '*Gone With the Wind* is about my level,' he told the colonel. 'And I've never gotten to the end of that yet.'

Jeffries laughed, a rare occurrence. '*Gone With the Wind*, that's an old war,' he said. 'But old wars often won't lie down. Where do you hail from, Miller?'

'Bismarck, North Dakota.'

'I come from Virginia. They're still fighting the Civil War down there.'

The car began to move. Miller said: 'In not too long they'll be writing books about this war,' he said.

'And getting it all wrong,' said Jeffries caustically. 'Men who never fired a shot putting it all down on paper – making money.'

They were now in the steep street of the town. Miller could see Harcourt, who never spoke conversationally if another officer were in the car, shaking his head privately at the grey quaintness. The pavements were already lined with people. There were schoolchildren in summer clothes waving Union Jacks and Stars and Stripes. 'The kids seem like they've got the message,' said Miller. 'They've come to cheer the Yanks.'

'It won't harm them,' muttered Jeffries grumpily. 'If those Goddam Nazis had gotten here then they'd have been *ordered* to turn out. Maybe they'd be waving swastikas. People here don't seem to realise what's about to happen, and happen real quick, that these young guys marching along in their pretty uniforms are going to be battle veterans pretty soon.'

'Maybe our boys should march in battle kit,' suggested Miller. 'Bazookas, everything.' The parade, not even carrying rifles, had been forming up at the camp in their smooth dress uniforms.

'Could be,' said Jeffries. 'Maybe they don't want to frighten the kids.'

'The kids would dig it. Boys like guns and girls like soldiers. Girls in Paris turned out to see the Germans marching in. But like you say, could be that they had to.'

There was a saluting base halfway up the lopsided street and the mayor in his scarlet robes and chain, a bishop in his ecclesiastical hangings, and other civilian men in tidy suits, some with bowler hats, were already on the platform. Jeffries and Miller saluted them at the dais and there was more ceremony when a US lieutenant general and a British brigadier arrived with the colonel of the local American unit. The bishop stepped forward and said a prayer and a blessing although it mostly went unheard for there was no microphone, and the crowd did not stop indifferently chattering. The lines of spectators had grown three deep on the pavements and there were others standing in shop windows and gazing down from the upper rooms of offices.

Then from the distance, from the upper part of the hill, came the surprising sound of bells – happily tinkling bells, as if fairies, not soldiers, were marching. 'Great,' breathed Jeffries with pleasure. 'We've got a Jingling Johnny.'

The people on the platform turned expectantly, the faces of the crowd looked that way, the children's flags drooped as they craned their heads and stepped out into the road to see. The distant tinkling became jangling.

Miller, who had never seen a Jingling Johnny, nor even heard of it, peered up the hill with the rest. The British brigadier whispered to the bishop: 'Trust the Yanks to do something different.'

Down the ancient, stone street came the parade. From the platform they could hear the swelling voices of the watchers and the clapping of their hands as the soldiers marched, and before them the loud and undulating ringing of the bells. Then they came into sight.

In the front, a dozen paces ahead of the first rank of soldiers, pranced a tall, bulging black man festooned with bells which rang to the rolling movements of his body. He sounded more bells with his hands and legs. He bore a pole on which was a silver cone and the shape of a crescent moon; horse tails hung from it, and more bells and other jingling devices. The man knew how to play it and he played it with his entire body, wriggling and swinging and pirouetting in the street. Every movement sounded the bells. He had bells on his fingers and bells on his toes. His knees bent and he jumped and he rang. He leaped jangling into the air and in the next movement squatted down almost to the level of the street. He went dancing and jingling from one pavement to the other. 'Beautiful,' Miller heard Jeffries say to himself. 'Just beautiful.'

The townspeople clapped and shouted, the children cheered, old men grinned and round countrywomen jogged to the music. Miller saw tears running down Jeffries's face. At last he was proud.

Behind the Jingling Johnny came the American soldiers, not marching like a conquering army with weapons, firm boots and rigid arms, but almost sliding along. Their uniforms were sleek and smart, their faces set, and above their faces caps all fixed at the same angle. There were five hundred unarmed soldiers, marching to the music of the echoing bells, and at their centre the banner bearer carrying Old Glory, its Stars and Stripes glinting in the Dorset morning.

'Sir, I never did see anything like that. It made me good and proud to be an American,' said Harcourt as he drove the car from the town.

'It sure was something,' agreed Miller. 'That guy with the bells . . .'

'Johnny Jingle,' said Harcourt. 'It was better than a whole band, sir, better than a band.'

'That commanding officer wanted to demonstrate to every-body, mostly the British, that we could put on a show,' said Miller. 'Any day those soldiers are going to have to put on another.'

'They going straight to France, you think, sir?'

'They'll be there before too long.'

'There'll still be plenty of war left,' said the young black man pensively as he drove. 'Soon, sir, I guess we'll be going our ways.' He paused. 'Are we going direct back to London?'

'No, not direct. I don't have to be in Suffolk until noon tomorrow. On our way is a town called Reading – it's pronounced Redding – and I'd like to call in there tonight.'

'Sure, sir, I know Reading,' said the driver. 'I went there. On the train. They got a Baptist church and I went for a whole Sunday. They're friendly people and we had a fine time, a picnic, except it rained and we had to go in a hall. They invited me back anytime.'

'This could be the time,' said Miller. 'I'll be there a couple of hours, maybe three, visiting a friend. Could you go and see your church people?'

'Sure could,' said Harcourt. 'I'd be very happy with that, sir. Maybe it will be the last chance.'

He went into the theatre for the final fifteen minutes of the play. *The Seagull* was not getting big audiences in Reading. Kathleen, as before, was slim and aloof and deeply intense. There was a profound sense of failure, in love and in life.

'It's a moody last act,' Kathleen smiled when she saw him. They did not say where they were going but just walked a little apart down the empty street. It had been raining and the pavements glowed dimly in the blackout. 'I've heard people sobbing in the stalls,' she said. 'One woman walked out, staggering almost and crying her eyes out. Mr Chekov did not intend to cheer anybody up.'

She linked her coated arm through his. 'Are we just going to wander about the town like this?' she asked. 'Or would you rather come to my house?'

'You have a house?'

'It's been lent to me. A small terrace by the station. They used to be houses for railwaymen. I only moved in on Saturday but if the play doesn't fold I'll be there for a couple of weeks. How about you? Are you going anywhere very soon?'

Miller nodded. 'In a few hours.'

He felt her sag. 'It's that close, is it?'

'It won't be long. I'll need to leave tonight at some time.'

She sighed. 'Acting doesn't help with real life,' she said. 'The war seems strangely remote when you're up on that stage in the lights, and even when you get off it you don't return to reality. I imagine you must have seen a lot more drama than me.'

'I think I have,' he said. 'Recently.'

She took her keys from her handbag as they approached a terrace of low-roofed brick cottages. 'Oddly enough they belong to the theatre,' she said. 'It goes with the job.'

She opened the door. Inside was a long curtain, the texture of a blanket, and she pushed it aside so they could enter a tight passage and then pulled it over the door again before switching on the light. A central ceiling lamp cast a doleful shadow over elderly wallpaper. There was a picture, a vague mountain view, on one of the walls. It was askew and she righted it as she passed.

'The decor is from the railwayman's time, I imagine,' she said as she went beyond a second door. She put down another light switch. 'Also the furnishings.' She swept her hand around the tight, low-ceilinged room. 'Railwaymen must have been very small,' she said.

She moved against him and they kissed deeply, almost wrestling into each others' bodies. Their arms held each other hungrily. Then she eased herself up so that she was sitting on the sturdy table with its worn covering. She opened her legs and pulled him to her. 'I'm sorry for what happened,' she said. 'I'm so sorry. I drink too much. Some men were killed, you said.'

'A lot,' he confirmed. 'And they were only practising. Most of them drowned during a landing exercise.' He wanted to tell her. He was weary of keeping secrets.

Kathleen whispered: 'How terrible.'

'Certainly was. More than seven hundred.'

She put her slim hands to her mouth. 'Oh, my God.'

'Sure. Just rehearsals. Just think what the real thing could be like.'

'And you'll be there.'

'I'll be there,' he said. 'But removed from it.' He pointed at the ceiling.

'In a plane,' she said. She moved against him again as though needing to get rid of the image. 'I can't talk about it any more,' she said.

'Nor me,' said Miller. He was sniffing against her face, taking in the smell of the woman in her. She said: 'I have some supper for us. And some wine. Would you like to go to bed first?'

'You know I would.'

She smiled as if in relief and they held each other again. Then she slid from the table and her slim fingers took his hand. Saying nothing, she moved towards the passage and they went domestically up the straight narrow staircase. 'There's no light on the landing.' For some reason she was whispering again. 'They probably thought it was excessive.' There were two shabby bedroom doors, both closed. She opened the second one. 'The posh room,' she said.

The bed occupied most of the space, a big lumpy bed,

patterned with shadows when she turned on the light of a bare bulb. 'I can't gaze up at that,' she said firmly. She pushed the switch off and leaning over an untidy dressing-table, opened the curtains at the bay window which took up most of the front wall. The pale light of midnight filtered into the confined room.

Kathleen took a stride to a picture on the wall to one side of the bed. 'This old chap with whiskers,' she said. 'He's not going to watch.' She unhooked it and put it on the floor facing the wall, and then went close to Miller again. 'Undress me,' she said quietly. 'You know I like that. Take all my clothes from me.'

He did as she asked, taking her garments one by one. She held out her hand to take each item and placed them on a single chair at the side of the bed. She was still wearing her skirt and her small exposed breasts pointed eagerly. He rubbed them gently, working the nipples between his fingers. She said: 'That's a novel one.' Her hands began to undo his buttons, on his tunic first, then on his trousers. In a few moments they stood naked against each other. Almost miraculously a ghostly touch of moonbeam came into the room. 'Limelight,' she murmured. Then: 'Come to the bed. I mustn't scandalise the neighbours.'

She pulled away an old patchwork counterpane and folded back the sheet. 'I always bring my own bedlinen,' she explained conversationally. 'I don't mind anything else but I must have that.'

She seemed even more frail than last time. Her hip-bones were hard. But her intensity was full and sensual. He had a passing image of her on the stage that night, tight and edgy, full of hopelessness. Now her lovemaking was hard but not happy. It was as though it was something she had to have, to eat up. He felt clumsy and simple when he was with her. Perhaps that is how he was. Clumsy and simple.

She worked at it, drawing him into her, moving her hips and thighs to pull him in further, deeper. She came to her climax, her mouth open in a silent scream as if she had come unexpectedly. She held his upper arms with hands like narrow iron bands, biting his chest and then panting and opening her mouth to suck in breath as he ended. They fell against each other and lay spent. 'Wherever you're going,' she whispered, 'wherever it is. Try and come back.'

Then the strangest thing happened.

Kathleen said: 'I will get a glass of wine,' and she put on a flimsy robe and went from the room. She returned with two flutes of white wine and they sat together in the bed drinking and looking out at the indifferent moonlight over the slates of the town. Then she said: 'I want to show you something.'

She put down the wineglass as she rose, opened the bottom drawer of the dressing-table and returned to the bed. 'Do you see this?' she said.

It was a ring. Even in the dim room he could see it was exceptional, a large diamond and ruby that caught even the poor light from the window. 'I wish you could see it properly,' she said. 'It's so beautiful. It's worth thousands of pounds.'

'Should you be leaving it in a drawer in a strange house?'

She gave a croaky laugh. 'You are such a practical person. If somebody stole it, then it would be only justice. That's how I got it.'

His glass was almost to his lips. He paused, then drank the remainder of the wine. 'How?' he asked flatly. 'Is this one of your stories, Kathleen, one of the fantasies you make up, that you told me about?'

She seemed flattered that he had remembered. 'But it isn't,' she said almost smugly. 'It's true. And I pinched it in the most terrible circumstances. So terrible I feel quite proud in a grotesque sort of way.'

'Tell me.'

'Have you heard of the bomb that hit the Café de Paris in London?' Miller had not.

'It was three years ago. The Café de Paris in the West End, the most popular night spot and, so they boasted, the safest, because it was down below the ground. That night it was packed and I was in there with a naval chap I knew. The bomb came straight through the roof when everybody was dancing. The singer was at the microphone and this thing came through the ceiling.

'It killed nearly two hundred, including the man I was with. His name was Barry . . . or was that his surname? Anyway, I never saw him again. One moment it was a foxtrot and he was holding me, and the next nothing.

'I don't remember anything until I woke up, trapped under a table. I could see the open sky through the roof. I felt okay, apart from a splitting headache. I lay there thanking God for saving me. All around were mountains of debris. The dust was choking. Rescuers were climbing in. I moved different bits of my body, my arms and my legs, and then my head – and when I moved it to the left and pushed some bricks away I saw a woman's hand and this ring, this beautiful, rich ring was on her finger.'

He stared at her in the shadows. 'And you took it.'

'Looted it, would be the technical term,' she said. 'There was a lot of looting going on in the Blitz, believe me, a lot went on that night and the next day. People pocketing stuff.'

'Why did you do it?'

'Instinct, pure opportunism. But why not? It wasn't going to be any use to that poor wealthy woman. She was dead. And her insurance would have covered it, if she had any sense, that is. So I took it. It is the most valuable thing I have.' She turned to face him. Her bare breasts hung small. 'I've never told anyone else,' she said. 'No one.'

It was one thirty when Miller left the small house. He turned and waved to her at the window, then walked to the US military car park by the railway station. Harcourt would be getting some sleep in the car. He showed his identification to the sergeant in the guardpost at the gate and walked to the car. Harcourt was not there.

Going back to the gate he asked if the guard had seen him. The man looked at a list on a clipboard. 'He left just after you drove in here, sir,' he said. 'You went and he followed ten minutes later, at nine forty. He ain't come back yet.'

Miller returned to the car and looked in the window. The guard had the keys and he walked back to get them as a local police car came slowly along the street, then stopped outside the compound. Miller observed it, his eyes narrowing. A uniformed sergeant and a middle-aged man in civilian clothes got out. Miller was fifty yards away. He watched. The guardhouse sergeant turned and pointed in his direction and, his heart going cold, he went towards them.

The British plain-clothes policeman said: 'I'm Detective Constable Donald Fareham, sir. Reading police. There's been an incident.'

Miller said: 'What sort of incident, detective?'

The plain-clothes man, grey haired and weary, said: 'A young black man was involved. He was attacked and I'm sorry to tell you he has died.'

Miller thought he was going to fall down. He felt the life drain from his face. He stood unbelieving. 'Harcourt,' he mumbled. 'How can he be? He was here . . .'

'He was your driver, sir, so I understand,' said the uniformed sergeant. He made an attempt at hope. 'There might be a chance that it's the wrong fellow.'

'He's tall and black,' Miller told them. He felt his voice separate from his body.

'He's black,' answered the sergeant. 'He was lying down when I saw him but he looked tallish.'

For a moment Miller thought he was being flippant. But his police face was loaded with genuine sadness. 'It happened quite near here, sir. Just around the corner. About two hours ago.'

'Who . . . who would have killed Harcourt?' muttered Miller to himself. His face came up from his chest. 'Jesus Christ, he was the most inoffensive . . .'

'Unfortunately the others weren't,' said the detective. 'Inoffensive. Witnesses, people in the flats over the shops, saw him being attacked by up to six of your white American GIs. Some of these residents went down in their night attire but they were too late. The victim was taken to hospital where he was pronounced dead on arrival.'

Miller began to cry into his hands. 'Almighty shit,' he said. His tears were running through his fingers. The guard looked embarrassed. The plain-clothes policeman said: 'Would you feel up to coming with us and see if you can identify him, sir?'

'Sure,' said Miller, trying to wipe his face with his hands. 'That's the least I can do for him.'

They moved towards the police car and Miller went with them. 'Has the US Provost been informed?' he asked. He was trying to think rationally. He had to get to Suffolk.

'We've told them,' said the sergeant. 'They'll be along soon, I expect. But they're all tied up with this invasion business.'

'So was Harcourt,' said Miller sadly. 'He was driving me to join a unit tonight. We . . . we would have been on our way now.'

Christ, he thought, it's my fault again. Butterfield and his buddies, and now Harcourt. Because he, Miller, had made the wrong choice, been in the wrong place. 'I'll have to write to his folks,' he mumbled. 'What the hell can I say to them?'

They drove through the vacant streets. 'Here's the hospital,' said the sergeant. 'The mortuary is around the back.'

They took him to the police station afterwards and they gave him some British coffee. While he was making his statement a lieutenant in the US Provost Marshal's department arrived with two snowdrops. 'My sympathies, captain,' said the young officer.

Miller nodded. His mind was crammed with the nightmare. The walking into the hospital mortuary and being led to one of the two bodies laid out there. Someone had put a small American flag on the sheet over Harcourt. Miller had steeled himself for the moment when the sheet was pulled back but all he saw was the same Harcourt, stretched out with his everyday serene expression. Miller put out his hand and tenderly touched the black man's cheek, then said: 'Yes, that's Private First Class Benji Harcourt. My buddy.'

At the police station the provost lieutenant said: 'We have arrested a suspect. The guy is still drunk. It won't be difficult to pick up the others. They'll go to prison, captain. Maybe face the death penalty.'

'And miss the rest of the war,' said Miller.

'I guess so.'

'Well, I can't,' said Miller, straightening up. 'I have to be a hundred and something miles away by morning. I'll drive myself.'

The officer shook his head. 'I don't think you should, sir. You need some sleep.'

Miller regarded him aggressively. 'I need to be there.'

'We can provide a car and a driver, sir.'

'Okay. Okay, thanks. I need to go back to my car before that.'

The two snowdrops were standing in the embarrassed manner of big men in a difficult situation, their hands behind their backs. They began to survey the interior of the British police station as if they thought they might learn something interesting.

The officer said: 'We'll take you back, captain, and get you transportation. Where is it you were heading?'

'I still am,' said Miller grimly. 'It's a US airbase in Suffolk. That's north-east of London.'

'Yes, sir, I know. I was in Suffolk.'

Miller said: 'I must get there by noon.'

'We'll get you there. We need a statement but if you authorise it we can get it from the police here. We can go now.'

They went out. The night was becoming pale. On the way back to the military car park, as Miller sat beside him in the jeep, the lieutenant said: 'Those rednecks had drunk a gutful. Bartenders are under orders not to provide drink like that. They told him they were celebrating the invasion. Eventually he threw them out and they saw a black man, alone, and they attacked him. It's too God-dam bad when you think about it.'

'I *can't* think about it any more,' said Miller. 'I don't want to now.'

They pulled into the compound and the lieutenant went into the guardhouse to telephone. The guard handed Miller the keys to his car and he shuffled towards it. There was a faint glow of the early dawn on its roof. He unlocked it and stared in the shadowy interior as if he half expected Harcourt would be there. He climbed into the driver's seat and sat there with his face in his hands, exhausted, broken. He was stirred by one of the military policemen tapping on the window. 'Your transportation's here, sir,' he said when Miller opened the door. He looked at his watch. It was five o'clock and full daylight. 'I'll be right along,' he said. The man went and Miller carefully opened the glove compartment on the driver's side. There was only one thing, a thin book with the words: 'Baptist Prayer-book.' He slipped it into his pocket. He would send that to Harcourt's mother.

He sat deeply in the rear seat. The driver woke him as they were entering the gates of the Suffolk base and he had to show his identification. The terrible realisation came back to him. It was eleven in the morning. He took his personal kit from the car and watched it drive away. He turned and in the dull daylight directly entered the main wooden building.

He opened the outer door and then the one at the end of a passage, almost knowing what to expect. They were all in the room, their flying kit around them, sitting in chairs, drinking coffee and trying to read magazines. The Dakotas were out on the tarmac. The pilots, Butterfield's buddies, looked up and then looked down again. No one said a word. Suddenly he wanted to tell them about Harcourt. But he knew nobody would listen.

Chapter Twenty-one

Gilbert's nightclub, Le Coq Noir in the centre of Rennes, had been reduced to charred rubble, which the rain then turned to a pile of black mud. '*C'est la guerre*,' muttered the taxi-driver when Paget asked.

'*La guerre*?' sniffed Gilbert in his secret room within the clothing factory. They were making hats for German uniforms. It had taken the opening of several mysterious doors to reach him. 'Not the everyday war, monsieur, the war we know. No, this was the black-market war. My club was burnt down because some criminals thought I was making more money than them.' He frowned towards Paget as if he had just realised who he was. 'What do you want now?'

Paget said hopefully: 'I've been sent over to coordinate – well, *help* to coordinate – your people as far as sabotaging the railway links to the north when the invasion begins.'

'A matter of days now,' shrugged Gilbert. 'The air waves are a babbling of secret messages. That ridiculous poem, "The sobbing of the violins in the autumn," has been everywhere. I hear the Germans have been looking it up at the free library. Why couldn't they have picked a couple of lines by Voltaire? Even if everybody knew what the signal was about – which most people do – we could at least be proud of it. Verlaine . . . pah.'

There was a pile of German hats in a corner of the dishevelled room. Gilbert put one on his head and sat reflectively on the single chair. He had a sudden idea and began studying Paget. 'There is,' he said eventually, 'something you *could* achieve.'

'What is that?'

'Four of our people are in the local police station. One is Antoinette Barre.'

'Antoinette . . . oh . . .'

'You know her, I believe.'

'We hid together.'

'Ah, yes, when you first came to France, wasn't it?'

'Is she in danger?'

'Not at this moment. But she will be by tomorrow unless we get her out. The police, the French police, are only holding them on a vague suspicion at the moment. All the local Gestapo, except for a couple of unintelligent underlings in their office, have gone to Paris. Someone's retirement dinner and they are not due back until tomorrow. But if they get their hands on any of our people in the police station then it could be serious. Between the four they know a lot. Fortunately, the Gestapo are not yet aware how important Mademoiselle Barre can be to them. She is, as you know, very beautiful in a wild sort of way. The boss Gestapo man would enjoy the interrogation.'

Paget felt himself shiver. 'We've got to get them out.'

'*Exactement*, monsieur.' He drifted into pensiveness again. 'The police station is not a fortress, just a police station, with French policemen, you understand, but next door is the German town barracks. This is not high alert or anything, just another group of troublemakers brought in for questioning. But it soon will be when they realise.'

'How do we do it?'

'We go in and snatch them,' said Gilbert easily. 'In five minutes they could be out. The fly on the appointment is that in the reception office is an alarm bell connected to the barracks next door. If somebody rings it then we could be trapped.'

Paget said: 'What about the phones?'

'We can deal with the phones. We have friends at the exchange who will need jobs after the war, and the phones can be conveniently jammed. But we need somebody who can pass as a

German officer to go into the reception area and stop them sounding the alarm.' He treated Paget to a stare full of meaning.

Paget muttered: '*Heil Hitler.*'

'We have a smart uniform that would fit you perfectly. Some of the badges and that sort of thing are not correct but it will pass mustard.'

'I don't speak German.'

Gilbert's shoulders drooped. 'Now you say. I wonder why they send you people here.'

'I wonder that myself,' said Paget.

'All you need is a few guttural words. *Achtung!* and that sort of thing.' He looked exasperated. 'You could try the sobbing of the violins in the fucking autumn.'

'Do you want me to do this?'

'You are the only one available at this moment.'

'And expendable.'

'The uniform will fit, with a little alteration here and there, and nobody will recognise you here.'

'When does that happen? Soon, of course.'

'Now. *Maintenant.* I will get someone to bring the uniform. One of the girls here can do the tucking in. In no time you will be transported to be an *Obergruppenführer.*'

'Thanks,' said Paget. 'I'm really looking forward to this.'

'*Bon,*' said Gilbert half an hour later. 'Excellent.' He surveyed Paget in his German colonel's uniform and nodded approvingly.

'This revolver is loaded?' Paget asked.

Gilbert said: 'Of course. What good would it be otherwise? You cannot point it and say: "Boom!" Do not forget to release the safety catch.' He sat on the single chair again. The girl who had been sewing the tunic of the uniform while Paget stood to attention had left. 'She will want overtime for that,' grumbled Gilbert. 'Patriotism is not known here, only greed.'

He made the points on his fingers. 'So, you march into the front foyer of the police station, and don't forget *Heil Hitler*, the short version.' He demonstrated bending his arm at the elbow and jabbing it upwards. 'And performed while walking. There is no need to stop. The less time they have to study you the better. What next? Ah, yes. The reception office is on the right. In there the alarm bell is on the side of the filing cabinet to the right, against the window. Nobody must be allowed to go near that.' One eyebrow went up. 'If they do you know what to do.'

'Shoot them,' said Paget.

'Quietly as you can. It's a pity the gun does not come with a silencer. You keep them from the bell while the rest of our men, three and myself, go into the police station and overpower any resistance.'

'How will you do that?'

'Stabbing,' said Gilbert as if it were obvious. 'It is quieter. As I told you they are mostly French police, so we hope it will not be necessary. But that is not your concern. You must just keep the men in the reception office away from the bell connected to the barracks. We have already arranged for the key to the cells. When you see or hear us make our escape with the prisoners, then you come after us. Only shoot somebody if necessary. Close the door of the room behind you and lock it. Outside will be two cars. Get in the second car and get away. It's a simple plan.'

'It sounds very easy,' said Paget, unconvinced. 'When do we start?'

Gilbert looked at his watch. 'Now,' he said.

He led the way from the inner room and they progressed through the several doors and work areas hung with materials and clothes, mostly hats and uniforms. When they were about to go out into the street Paget said: 'You haven't told me where the police station is.'

Gilbert's eyes became dark. Then he said: 'Through the market, straight up the street and you'll see it. Outside the German flag is flying. Don't go into the barracks by mistake; that would really put the cat among the pigeon shit.'

Paget straightened himself, smoothed the uniform, took a

breath and went at what he hoped was a relaxed stride down the pavement. They had never taught them German marching. He must suggest it in a memo. The boots squeaked. Shopkeepers nodded pleasantly, he imagined knowingly, to him from their doorways and two German soldiers buying muddy potatoes in the market dropped some in their attempts to salute him.

Gilbert had vanished, but he almost comically reappeared behind one of the market stalls and handed a small turnip to Paget. 'If you get into big trouble,' he whispered, 'pull the pin and throw it.'

The grenade had been fitted into the hollowed-out vegetable with the metal pin a little inset. Paget wondered if a German officer carrying a turnip might look conspicuous but he only received more nods from the market people as if to say what a nice turnip it was.

He walked the three hundred yards up the street to where the German flag was hanging beside a more modest tricolour outside the police station. In front there was a small courtyard surrounded by iron rails but there were no guards in the forecourt. Nor were there soldiers inside. The Germans clearly did not appreciate the value of their prisoners.

At a desk inside the lobby sat a French police sergeant, an oldish man with a philosophical demeanour, who stood as Paget came through the door. Keeping the turnip half-hidden in his left hand, Paget put up a stiff but hesitant salute with his right and mumbled: '*Heil Hitler.*' The Frenchman nodded approvingly at the turnip.

Marching through, Paget turned sharply right into the reception office. There were three blue-uniformed French policemen and one German junior officer in there, grouped in a corner sniggering over some confiscated pornographic pictures. There was an overalled Frenchwoman, stubby, elderly, holding a mop like a support as she cleaned the office floor and mechanically worked her jaw in time with her mopping.

The four men straightened as he entered and one of the

Frenchmen attempted to conceal the photographs in a drawer. One picture flew out of his reach and landed near the charwoman who picked it up, snorted and, as though aware of her duty, handed it to Paget. It was a nude girl apparently milking a cow. He sniffed and put it on the reception counter. He could see the alarm signal, a single white button, on the far right of the room. It was fixed, as Gilbert had told him, to a filing cabinet.

Paget threw up a belated '*Heil Hitler*' and the young German officer saluted in the same way while the Frenchmen, each guiltily eyeing the photograph, came to a shambling attention. The eyes of all four men now moved to the turnip. The officer seemed to be feeling some suspicion. He was examining Paget's uniform and then looking at the turnip again. He spoke in German and Paget grunted as though the question was beneath his need to answer. He was aware of some commotion behind him in the entrance lobby. The young officer stood on his toes, looked beyond Paget, and saw whatever was going on. '*Gott!*' he said and made to move forward.

Paget took out his pistol. He would have thrown the grenade but the charwoman was in the way, her jaw still ruminating. The officer was unarmed but he now rushed bravely towards Paget. On the way he fell over the charwoman's bucket, sending it clanging across the floor with the water flying. He ended on his knees with the woman standing over him, still blank-faced but with her toothless mouth working even more furiously. Paget pointed his pistol at the man. He motioned one of the frightened French policemen forwards and told him in French to disconnect the alarm. The man went across the room and with one glad pull parted the button from the cabinet.

The German was still on his wet hands and knees. Paget kept his pistol fixed on him. From behind came a male voice: '*Partez.*' He backed towards the door. Once outside he shut it and was surprised when the oldish French police sergeant, who had sat so thoughtfully at the lobby desk, appeared and handed him the key. He locked the door, and made to return the key to the Frenchman who, suddenly vigorous, shook his head. Paget kept the key and made for the main exit.

Outside everything was normal and sunlit. He could hear the traders in the market. Under the trees opposite were two Citroëns. As he made for them one moved away. The door in the rear car opened and he threw himself in. Antoinette Barre was sitting in the back seat. 'That's a nice turnip,' she said.

The pigsty had not housed pigs for some time; it was clean and sweet-smelling with shafts of sunlight streaming on to bales of fresh straw through apertures at the tops of the walls, below the corrugated-iron roof. There was room for them to sit agreeably between the bales.

'This estate,' said Antoinette, 'belongs to a lady aristocrat who is sympathetic. She is a widow and the Boche do not trouble her, except by appointment. She lives in the big house, about three kilometres away.'

'Is this Madame Dupard?' asked Paget. 'If so I know her. I was in the house a few weeks ago. On my last visit.'

'That is correct.' She turned in the straw and studied his face. 'Have we met before? It seems that we have.'

'Last year,' he said, disappointed. 'You hid me. You stayed with me in a house.'

She still had difficulty. 'In October,' he prompted.

'Ah, yes,' she smiled. 'I remember a little. So many things happen in this country now, especially to me. I cannot remember everything.' She turned and studied him again. 'Did we make love?'

She shrugged as if the reply did not matter. 'That house,' she said. 'It was always dark. We were shut away in the dark so I did not see you much.'

Paget said: 'Does Madame Dupard know we are hiding here?'

'I don't know. If she does not, then it is better to continue that way. We should be safe although we will move on soon. The time is almost here for the invasion. We have heard the message.'

'Verlaine,' nodded Paget.

'What a beautiful poem. "*Les sanglots longs des violons de l'automne*". I am glad it was chosen to signal that the battle is soon. Everybody is misquoting it.'

'It's supposed to be secret,' he pointed out.

'There are no secrets in France any more,' she said. 'We are not good at keeping secrets.'

He was still wearing the German uniform. 'Soon you will have something more comfortable,' she said. 'Those boots make a noise like a mouse. They will bring clothes with the food and, I hope, the wine. Madame Dupard has some good vines here. We may get some from this estate.'

'How will the Germans search for us?' he asked. 'Very thoroughly?'

'I do not think so. They did not realise that they had four resistance people in the police station. They are always picking up people. And the Gestapo were away in Paris. They may not even know. They may not be interested. They are busy planning to save their own skins. Nobody likes the Gestapo and especially not the German army and the French police. If they can keep it quiet and not cause any disturbance about the incident then they may do that. They think it is a small case, not of importance, and it would only make trouble for them. Also, I think everybody will have plenty to do, to think about, when the parachutes start falling from the sky.'

He said: 'I understand you have married a German officer.'

Antoinette laughed outright. 'You understand a lot that is incorrect about me,' she said. 'Who told you this?'

'I heard,' he said. 'Is it true?'

She pouted. 'A little true. But it is not a real marriage, not even legal, but it is – how shall we say – an arrangement. He is a good German. He hates Hitler and the Nazis. He works at the headquarters in Marseilles and he is able to tell me things I would not otherwise know.'

'He might have been in danger if you hadn't been sprung today,' he said. 'If the Gestapo had interrogated you.'

Her face darkened, or the sun might have gone in. 'I do not even think about that,' she said. 'I would only do what was possible. I have several choices of dying. But before that I would spit in their faces.'

Chapter Twenty-two

By Sunday 4 June, the day had almost arrived. The churches were not particularly full; it had been a long time coming and there had already been several National Days of Prayer. Rain had spread across southern England, it came with a choppy wind and there were four-foot waves off the coast, poor prospects for an amphibious landing on a hostile shore. The *Daily Mail*, after years of silence about the weather, quietly printed a report of the poor conditions in the Channel.

General Eisenhower's headquarters was in a convenient position to view the English sky and sea. When he came out from Southwick House, near Portsmouth, the dark and hurrying sky told him enough; he did not need his experts. 'We have to wait,' the Supreme Commander said. 'Or move the invasion to California.' A quarter of a million soldiers crouched in their camps.

In his camp twenty-five miles to the west of Eisenhower, Private Blackie was fuming. 'Jam sandwiches,' he complained to the others in the tent. 'That's what they're giving us to go into action – jam fucking sandwiches.'

'Hope they're not strawberry,' ruminated Gannick, taking out his unlit pipe and staring into the burnt bowl. 'I can't abide strawberry. Plum's all right.'

'Any sort,' said Blackie sitting on his bed. 'Christ, this dump be bad enough. Stuck in 'ere loike bloody convicts in a cage. No women. 'Ardly a drop of beer. You can't even talk to the NAAFI maids cos it be against orders and they won't answer you. What 'arm is that goin' to do, talking to they? Oi ask you?'

Nobody replied and he put his thin head into his thin hands. 'And then they ship you off to go and fight – and 'and to 'and.'

Warren came ponderously and sat on his bed opposite. 'It'll all be over soon, Blackie,' he said. 'Couple of months at most, Oi reckon. We'll all be 'ome by Christmas.'

'There's something on tonight,' put in Peters, the eighteen-year-old, with an attempt at hope. He studied a square of paper. 'A gospel meeting.'

Very slowly Blackie raised his head. Warren was surprised to see his cheeks smeared with real tears. He almost moved his meaty hand to wipe them away but Blackie glared at him and did it himself. 'Now that be bloody good news,' breathed Blackie. 'A gospel meetin'.' He looked at Warren for a moment and smiled crookedly through his unhappiness. ''Member how we used to fart in Sunday school, Bunny?'

'So did the teacher, 'member,' said Warren. 'Windy Willis, we called 'un. We used to try and match 'er, di'n we, fart for fart. An' she made out she di'n notice.'

''Twas loike a farmyard,' said Blackie with a distant satisfaction.

Harris came into the tent. 'We've been stood down,' he said. 'For twenty-four hours.' He surveyed them. 'Put that snakes and ladders away, Gordon, if you've finished playing with it.' The Scot looked offended. 'I wasna playing snakes and ladders, sergeant,' he said disdainfully. He took the board and the counters and handed the lot to Treadwell who put them in his bedside locker, looking ashamed. 'It takes brains to play snakes and ladders,' Treadwell said defensively. 'There's a lot to it.'

'Take it on the ship,' suggested Harris. 'We might be out there for days.'

'Sarge,' put in Blackie. 'Did you hear they're giving us jam sandwiches?'

Harris nodded to outside. 'If the sea's like it is we won't want them,' he said.

'How's your missus, sergeant?' asked Gordon. 'She all right?'

Harris said: 'She's fine, Gordon.' He frowned. 'You haven't been around there, have you?'

They all laughed and Gordon blushed. 'I just thought I'd ask,' he said. 'Only being polite.'

Harris patted him on the shoulder. 'I know, son.' He studied the gaunt faces, hardened but still young. 'Everybody ought to write home,' he said quietly. 'There's no knowing when you'll get another chance.'

As though he had been waiting to ask, Treadwell said: 'What d'you reckon it's goin' to be like, sarge? Over there. Got any idea?'

The others leaned forward trustingly. 'God only knows,' he told them. 'I don't. If I did I'd be in conference with Ike and Monty with a line of pips instead of stripes. Then I wouldn't need to go at all.' He sat on a bed and they grouped around. 'I've been trying to get some idea from anybody in the sergeants' mess who's been on an amphibious landing, the real thing. There's two Hampshire blokes who were in the Italian landings at Salerno. And that was no picnic. They reckon the best thing you can do is run.'

'Funny thing,' said Gannick, taking his unlit pipe from his mouth. 'Telling a soldier to run.'

'Forwards,' said Harris firmly. 'You can't run away because the only place is the sea. But they say you run like mad for the first bit of cover.' He studied their faces. 'And you watch out when you jump from the landing-craft. Like they told you when we did the training, *don't jump too soon.* Otherwise the bloody boat runs over you, just like a bus. And you're under it and you get drowned.' Each face looked drawn, as if pulled together by string. How would they do it when the moment came?

Blackie eventually spoke. 'In that case, sarge, I'm goin' to be last on the bus. I'll wait till every other bugger 'as got off. Then I'll go.'

That Sunday the military padres were kept busy. In the American camps there were long files of soldiers waiting to make their confession, although, having been confined behind the wire for so many days, they had little to confess. Private Ben Soroyan did mention that he had sinned during his postal run duty but the padre was wondering how many men he still had to absolve before lunch and handed out a couple of 'Hail Mary's without even asking the nature of the trespass.

In the tents and huts of the wire-enclosed compounds the GIs, like the British Tommies a few miles away, could do little but wait and listen to the rain on the canvas and the tin roofs. The tents were more popular because the sound was softer. Some men still crouched at poker, the stakes now risen to the many theoretical thousands of dollars with grim side bets on who would be alive to collect the winnings. All the songs had been sung by now, the songs of home places: 'Carolina, I'm Coming Back to You', 'Deep in the Heart of Texas', 'Avalon' and 'My Little Grass Shack in Hawaii', although few of the soldiers had ever been anywhere near Hawaii. They had become weary of the false enjoyment of singing and the guitars, harmonicas and ukuleles had been shoved away.

In the next bed to Soroyan was a man who knew Avalon for real. He used to sing to himself: 'I left my love in Avalon and sailed away.' Stretched out with his eyes shut and the English rain on the roof, he said to Soroyan: 'It's a few miles out in the ocean, Santa Catalina, off Los Angeles, but it ain't like anywhere else. It's real small and quiet and plenty of sunshine but this great ballroom where all the big bands play, Tommy Dorsey, Bob Crosby, they all take the boat across. I can just see it now. All them people dancing across the floor. I can hear the bands playing.'

Some men continued to go to the perimeter fence to talk to the local girls between the times when the females were periodically chased off by the military police, only to return. Few of the soldiers and the inarticulate girls, however, could sustain conversation through chicken wire for long, although they were youthful and pledged their love after a few literally touching meetings. They had touched fingers and breasts and even fly buttons and some had managed a contorted kiss, but banal conversation lapsed into jokes and tears and unkeepable promises before the men retreated to their tents to wait for action and perhaps death, and the young girls went home to their mothers.

Rumours ran rife through the camp. Most were about the war and what was going to happen. But there was one secret story that two professional women were offering sex through the gaps in the chicken wire in a secluded area behind the church. Two queues had formed, one for intercession and one for intercourse, but the military police arrived and the women vanished.

It was just dark that night when Soroyan quietly left his tent. It had stopped raining and there were traces of moon among the clouds. Perhaps the day after tomorrow really would be the day at long last. The tents were stirring in the darkness, voices and suspicions of light; there were sounds from the huts, too. Someone had taken up a guitar again and was playing a reflective melody, not quite mournful, but enough. There would not be much sleep.

There were guards standing slackly outside the wire but Soroyan merely walked more carefully on the wooden duck-boards. Some men were loitering in the areas around the tents, smoking and talking in subdued voices. The path bent around the church where he had so easily unburdened his soul that morning. Now he became stealthy and went to the shaded area below some branches. Two other soldiers were standing there. They turned as they heard him. 'They ain't coming,' said one.

The other, a very short soldier, spat on the nearby ground and said: 'God-dam it, nothing works out with women. Not ever.'

'We *fixed* it,' said the first man sulkily. 'They promised. You can't trust the fucking English.' They began to move off around the church path.

'Maybe you'll be lucky, buddy,' said the small soldier.

'Yeah, good luck,' muttered the other as they moved away.

Soroyan waited, moving away from the dripping trees. Almost at once the reason for the other men's disappointment was righted. A bus arrived on the road a hundred yards away. It came darkly to the stop and then drove away, leaving a solitary shadow at the side of the road. She waited, tidying herself, then stumbled over the rough ground towards Soroyan. He moved towards the fence.

'Oooo-er,' she said, stopping but then moving closer. 'You gave me quite a fright.' She peered along the length of the wire. 'Are you the only bloke here?'

Soroyan said he was. She was not by any means choice, he could see that even in the dimness: stumpy, solid, and for some reason wearing a brimmed hat, perhaps to hide her face.

'There were some other guys,' he said, keeping his voice low. 'But they went back.'

'I *said* eleven o'clock,' she grumbled. 'That's when the bloody bus gets here. It was five minutes late, that's all. Do you want it, then? It's five dollars. Before.'

Why not, he thought. He had not kidded himself that Rita Hayworth was going to stumble to the fence. Tomorrow, the next day, he might be beyond sex, beyond everything. He pushed a five-dollar note through the chicken wire. 'Thank you,' she said politely. 'Promise, I won't bunk off.'

'How . . . how do we do it?'

'Through this bleedin' wire,' she said. 'It's the only way. You put your dick through one of the holes and I sort of get myself hooked on to it this side.'

'These holes are small,' he said. 'Have you tried it out?'

She seemed confused. 'No, I 'aven't, but one of my mates 'as done it. She told me. Must have been a bloke with a thin dick.' She opened her handbag. 'I brought these just in case.'

'Jeez,' he said, seeing what she had produced. 'Wire-cutters.'

'Right. They're my old man's. He's an electrician but he's poorly just now. That's why I'm doing this. I packed it up once.'

Soroyan said: 'But, this wire is US property. There'll be all hell. They'll court-martial me.'

In the dimness she regarded him squatly. 'Do you want it or don't you?'

'Sure, I do. But there must be some other way.'

'I'm not doing *that*,' she said firmly. 'Gamming. No, I don't like the taste.'

Soroyan looked about him nervously into the darkness, worried about their voices.

'Look,' she said. 'I can only stay until the bus comes back. It's the last one.' She took the decision into her own hands and began to snip easily through the chicken wire. Soroyan watched, horrified, but the wire parted easily and no alarms sounded. He began to unbutton his fly.

'Wire-cutters?' said the captain. He glanced at the white-helmeted guard. 'She had wire-cutters?' He was young, no older than Soroyan.

Soroyan stood with his eyes closed. He was aware that two of his buttons were still undone. The captain had been summoned as he was about to go to bed. There was toothpaste on his chin. He sat behind the desk in the bleak light of a hut.

'What do you have to say about this, soldier?' he demanded.

'She had the wire-cutters,' Soroyan said. 'She brought them with her.'

'She came all prepared.'

'Yes, sir.'

'Did you make a date to see this woman?'

Soroyan said: 'No, siree. I was just strolling there, getting some air before the invasion, thinking about things, you know, sir.'

'Yeah, I know. We've all been thinking about things. But with most of us no prostitute has come along with wire-cutters.'

'No, sir. Well, there she was and she made the offer.'

'How much did you pay?'

'Five dollars, sir.'

The officer turned his eyes at the snowdrop and they both shrugged as if it were not unreasonable. 'And the idea was you stayed this side of the fence and she stayed the other and you did it through the hole she cut?'

'That was it, sir. But the guard showed up before we got started.'

'Did you . . . Were you going to wear a prophylactic?'

'No, sir. I figured that this might be the last time I do it in my life. We're going into action. So I didn't.'

The captain put his head in his hands. He stared at the guard's report on the desk in front of him. 'You have an interesting name,' he said. 'Soroyan.'

'Yes, sir.'

The captain looked up. 'Now get this, Soroyan. I could be throwing you into the brig. Damaging, or causing to be damaged, US Government property, a wire fence. But I don't want to do that. You might not be released for weeks, and we need you on that beach, soldier.'

'Yes, sir.'

'So you'll make up for the fence damage out of your pay. Otherwise get going, back to your quarters. We may be moving tomorrow.'

'Yes, sir.'

'And you're improperly dressed. Finish doing up your fly.'

On that rain-beaten Sunday, in the British compounds the clerics were not so busy as those ministering to the Americans. Anglicans prayed at one service, and Roman Catholics at another, but it was the evening gospel meeting that attracted the troops. By that time the penned-up, pent-up soldiers would have gone anywhere for anything, and there was a rumour that the organist was a glamorous woman, that there was a girl choir and that later there would be free refreshments and no collection plate.

The soldiers had cold showers, shaved in lukewarm tea saved from the canteen, and brushed their hair; only a few cleaned their teeth, the practice not being general. Then they trudged through the mud to the gospel meeting. By the time the tubby minister came busily on to the platform and the organist, not uncomely but older than expected, had set up the miniature portable organ, every chair had been taken. The girls' choir consisted of six females of varying ages, sizes and, less to the point, singing ability. There were some groans.

After a prayer and the exhortation: 'Let's have a truly wonderful time tonight, let's sing to the Lord and make sure He hears us.' The minister, so young and pink that some of the troops wondered why he wasn't a soldier like them, announced that the first hymn would be 'What a Friend We Have in Jesus'.

Before the organist had finished the introduction Blackie and some others had recognised the tune. They sang their own words. Harris had Gordon standing next to him and Gordon sang dutifully from the hymn sheet but the sergeant had a suspicion that further along the line the words were being changed:

> *'When this blinkin' war is over*
> *No more soldiering for me*
> *When I get my civvy clothes on,*
> *Oh, how happy I shall be.*
>
> *'No more cleaning out my rifle,*
> *No more asking for a pass.*
> *Then I'll tell the sergeant-major*
> *To stick his bayonet up his arse.'*

The minister on the stage was ecstatic. 'Wonderfully sung,' he enthused. 'The Lord would have been very pleased.'

Chapter Twenty-three

General Dwight Eisenhower was a simple man and it was with simple words that he gave the signal for the great invasion to start. It was 5 June. On that day, in Italy and after a long campaign, the Allies had taken Rome. The weather in England was tardily clearing; perhaps it would be fine for a day, or even for a few hours, but he sensed it was time, the only time. The winds and the tides would not be right again for almost a month and although it was a risk, he had to take it. He came from his headquarters, not on the face of it a man of destiny, more a man of care; a neat and thoughtful man. He walked towards his senior officers, American and British, Canadian and French, standing on the wet lawn, and said without emphasis: 'Okay. Let's go.'

At these words, 287,000 men, 10,000 aircraft and 5,000 ships moved into their places for action, for the most immense military assault ever known.

The words of Sergeant Harris were, like General Eisenhower's, simple: 'All right you lot. We're off.'

The soldiers looked at each other, some abruptly nervous, some already gritting their teeth, others hoping for someone to make a joke. They got into their kit and slung their rifles over their shoulders. 'What bastard 'as pinched my bayonet?' demanded Treadwell seriously.

Gordon found it for him. It was under his pillow. 'Ye've been frightened in ya' dreams, have ye?' said Gordon. 'Ta keep the boonie men away.'

They trooped from the tent. All over the camp and the other

muddy miles of compounds to the east and to the west, men were on the move. It was ten in the morning. 'Anyhow they gave us a lie-in,' said Warren in his ponderous way.

No one looked back at the tent for they had no affection for it. There were lorries revving on the road and the children in the school playground watched them climb aboard and gave them a half wave. Some boys began playing soldiers, shooting each other with imaginary tommy-guns.

The day remained damp but with the wind diminished. Warren put his hand out of the lorry and forecast: 'The sea'll be flatter now.'

'Oi hope bloody well so,' sniffed Blackie. 'Bad enough being sick with fright.'

Harris, sitting by the tailgate of the vehicle, glanced towards him. 'Pack up the gloom, lad. Why don't you start a singsong?'

Blackie returned the look bleakly. 'Is that an order, sarge?'

'No, it's not an order. Even I can't order you to sing. Fight, yes.'

'Can we just hum?' suggested Chaffey.

'Shut up,' said Harris, grinning. They were like a grown family to him, naive, unruly, friendly, dependent on him and on each other. That morning he would be going past his own front door; perhaps Enid would be waiting to see him march away.

In Southampton the lorry pulled into a sports field, goalposts sagging redundantly among rows of military vehicles. Troops were jumping down, standing in squads, and forming into marching columns under the bawled orders of a warrant officer, flushed with importance and lack of breath, who was not going with them.

They were mostly Hampshire Regiment, local soldiers; like Harris, some of them would be marching past their own homes. Platoon by platoon they formed up on the grass. Gordon went to one of the sets of goalposts marooned among the lorries and Blackie pretended to head an invisible ball past him. 'Offside,' said Harris.

He called them to order and they formed up. He growled:

'Squad – squad,' in his best fashion. There were other soldiers watching. 'Squad a-tten-tion!' The heels of their polished boots came together. Harris glanced towards the warrant officer but he was pacing and bawling in the distance. Harris ordered: 'Squad – right turn – by the left – quick march!' The thirty men moved sharply, performed a brisk wheel and joined a column that was leaving the field for the main road. Then they headed for the docks, through the grey and damaged city, between the shops and houses. The civilians in the streets scarcely gave them a glance. Marching men were nothing new.

The head column disappeared into the city distance. For a moment Harris feared that they would be taking a new route, that they would not be marching down his street, that he would not see Enid. But the order was called as the first formation reached the junction. Would she be there? How many men had marched by in the last few hours? How could he expect her to keep watching from their window? And how would she be able to pick out one soldier from so many, even when the soldier was her husband?

As they marched towards the house he could see that she was not in the window. He grunted, fixed his eyes ahead and continued in stride. Then over the tramping feet he heard her girl's voice calling: 'Harris! Harris! Come back!'

She sped along the pavement on woolly bedroom slippers until she had caught up with him. The troops were hooting and whistling. She was wearing an RAF greatcoat over a nightdress. Her fair hair was tussled, her face pale without make-up. 'Oh, Harris, darling, come back soon!'

Harris did the only unmilitary thing he had ever done. He broke ranks and stumbled towards her on the pavement. His men closed up and urged him on. 'Go on, sarge, give 'er a kiss!' She was half trotting in her bedroom slippers, trying to keep up. He caught her in his arms and they did a sort of dance alongside the marching troops. Pushing his Sten gun aside he kissed her, and she kissed him all over his hard face while the marching men cheered. They pulled apart and looked at each other at arm's length. 'Nice coat,' he said.

'Four quid,' she replied. He kissed her again and then did another clumsy dance step to regain his place at the fore of the squad. She continued her flapping run alongside. 'I've got to tell you!' she called breathlessly. 'I'm having a baby!'

Harris tried to look at her between the heads of the moving men. His eyes swivelled. The soldiers cheered louder. 'I'm pregnant!' she called again. She was breathless by now and she stood panting and holding on to someone's garden fence. 'Harris!' she managed again. 'Did you hear me?'

'Yes!' he shouted back over the heads of his men. 'Lovely!'

She tried to regain her breath, the air-force-blue coat heaving. 'It's ours, Harris!' she finally shouted: 'It's all ours!'

Some men of the Hampshires had been aboard the troop transports for three days in Southampton, waiting for the weather to change. But when Harris and his section went aboard their designated ship they set sail two hours before the light faded.

The English Channel remained sullen and the transports were not meant for comfort. They were scheduled to be in position off the Normandy coast by four in the morning. There they would transfer the soldiers, scrambling down nets over the sides into landing-craft to take them to the dawn shore.

The troops sat or half lay throughout the night, their equipment and their cumbersome rifles stacked around them. There were some sleeping in the gangways with other men clumsily stepping over them with oaths and grunted apologies. There was a smell of engine oil below decks and the floating aroma of sausages, bacon, fried eggs and chips from the galley.

'Christ, Oi wish it *was* jam sandwiches,' said Blackie, hunched in the half-light of the crowded troop deck. 'Jam don't niff like that.'

'Why you grumblin' again?' said Chaffey, swaying as the ship pitched and creaked. 'Don't you like a nice fatty sausage?'

'Oh, shut up, mucker,' pleaded Treadwell who was sitting on the other side of the bench. 'You're turning my guts.' The vessel trembled at its seams.

'After this,' breathed Gordon, 'gettin' ashore on that beach is goin' to be pure pleasure, Germans or no Germans.'

'There'll be Germans,' May assured him morosely. 'Plenty of them.'

'It's not going to be like a day at Southsea,' said Harris at the end of the line, hunched against the bulkhead. He tapped his Sten gun as though ensuring it was still there. His mind was full of Enid. He could see her now, running and funny in that air force coat. A baby. She had told him that his body was hard enough to stop a German bullet. Now he would *have* to survive.

The soldiers dozed against each other. Somewhere, dance music began to play on a loudspeaker and a chirpy singer sang: *'They've blown all the feathers off the nightingale in Berkeley Square.'* Someone bawled: 'Turn it off, for Christ's sake.'

One of the crew, an old, grey seaman, asked loudly: 'Anybody for dancing?' There were more curses. He turned it off.

Harris wondered whether he would get home before Enid's baby was born. Would he get home at all? He tried to shut out the smells of cooking and the men being seasick and the thoughts of what might happen the next day. He tried to sleep.

An authoritative voice came over the loudspeaker. 'Any ranks feeling unwell go on deck for ten minutes. No longer. Make room for others.'

Blackie sat up, groaned, and staggered between the sleeping shapes and up the ladder to the open deck.

Out there other men were sitting and standing, taking in the breeze of what was now a balmy night. Blackie gulped the air. He was surprised how easy the sea looked, not like it felt below. It was faintly luminous. He could see the shapes of other ships close around, showing no lights. He breathed deeply and sat next to another hunched soldier who said: 'Fortnight ago I 'ad bastard malaria. I was in India once. But they got me better too quick and now I'm 'ere, bugger it.'

After five minutes Blackie moved towards the back of the ship. There were fewer men there, standing without speaking. Against orders one shielded a cigarette with his hand and lifted it to give a drag to the soldier next to him.

There was a sailor, wearing a hood like a monk, standing near a coiled rope. 'Nice night for a cruise,' said Blackie. The man snorted and offered him some chewing tobacco. 'No thanks, mate,' said Blackie. 'Don't want to start any more bad habits. What you doing up here then?'

'Waiting for the day,' said the man, pointing towards the east.

'Like we been doin' for a long time,' mused Blackie. 'Bloody months.'

'It's nearly here,' said the sailor.

By their own methods Sergeant Fred Weber and Gino knew almost as much about military affairs in northern France in early June 1944 as did the German High Command.

Gino picked up shreds of information just as conscientiously as he supervised the officers' mess dining-room, and Weber over-heard even more detailed secrets, sometimes reduced to whispers, by inserting his head into the aperture of one or other of the dumb waiter lifts which took the food from the kitchen to the senior officers' table and transported the dirty dishes back.

It had to be done with discretion but the openings for the lifts were in a partially private corner, near to Weber's chef's desk, and he could insert his head and eavesdrop at most times. The lifts amplified the table conversations. He gathered that Hitler was not popular. The only time that he was seen listening by one of the cooks he told him that the ropes operating the lift had become entangled.

'Everyone is gone,' Weber said to Gino as they finished their tasks on the night of 5 June. 'I hear that Rome has fallen. It won't be long now.'

'None of the top brass were at dinner tonight,' added Gino, keeping his voice low. 'Your boss is somewhere overseeing something . . .'

'Manoeuvres,' said Weber. 'Miles from here. Why they need to practise now I don't know. The time for practice has gone.'

'If they don't know now they never will,' agreed Gino under his breath. The kitchen was empty except for a local woman bad-temperedly washing up pans. Weber called for her to make less din and she replied grumpily. 'She knows she'll be out of a job soon,' forecast Weber.

'She'll get another job with the Americans,' said Gino. 'They won't bring washing-up women with them.'

'Don't raise your voice, Gino. It may be taken as defeatist.'

'But where are all the top brass gone?' said Gino.

'I heard that Field Marshal Rommel has left Paris, gone home to see his wife. It's her birthday.'

Gino nodded approvingly. 'That's nice. Not like someone else I could name who was sitting at that table last night and is this evening dining with a lover, or by now has progressed to the bedroom, in Paris.'

Weber said: 'They don't believe there will be an emergency. Not just now. The weather is not right. Although it seems calmer tonight. Still, they know best, they are the command.'

'Perhaps they've all deserted,' joked Gino. Weber took an alarmed glance around the kitchen. 'No jokes, Gino, please,' he said. 'German officers may go to see their wives and their mistresses, but they do not desert.'

The washer-up woman walked out, flinging her dishcloth aside, and Gino said: 'I wouldn't be surprised if *you* are the senior man here tonight, Fred.'

Weber looked pleased. 'At last, in command.'

They had been drinking steadily. 'War affects people in different ways,' philosophised Weber, looking at the light in another glass of calvados. He preferred schnapps but there was more calvados. They had kept a bottle of schnapps in case they were captured.

They sat and drank and talked. It was surprising how easily and swiftly the bottles were emptied. At one in the morning they decided to go fishing at first light if the weather continued to improve. They went drunkenly to their quarters, neither conscious of the sounds of many heavily laden aircraft passing overhead.

Gino had an alarm clock and, even confounded by calvados, he opened his eyes at its summons. It was three thirty and dawn would not be long. Just enough time to get to the harbour. He knocked on Weber's door and heard him groan but he knew he would get up. He went to the kitchen and made a pot of coffee.

At four o'clock they were in the enclosed harbour with old Clovis, a deaf but deft local fisherman. None of the three men had heard anything in the hours of darkness. Even now Weber and Gino, with their aching heads, were only distantly conscious of the sounds in the sky. Clovis heard nothing. He never did.

They took the small boat from the harbour. Grey light was showing in the east. The fishing gear was in the stern. Clovis rowed strongly. The German and the Italian thought sadly that this might be the last time they would be able to go fishing.

When they were clear of the harbour and the short promontory that sheltered it from the east, Clovis sniffed the air and decided this was the place to fish. Weber and Gino began to bait the hooks. Then Clovis sat up. They looked at him, then in the direction he pointed – to the lifting mist in the Channel. 'They are here,' he said without emphasis, then in an even flatter voice: '*Vive la France.*'

All three men stared east and then north. The curtain of mist was rising quickly and they saw that there were hundreds of ships out there; every piece of the sea seemed to be covered with their shapes, their shadows. Ships on ships. Then they saw and heard the planes for the first time. Distant big guns sounded.

'*Regardez,*' muttered Clovis.

'*Mama Mia,*' said Gino, crossing himself.

'*Scheisse,*' said Weber grimly.

*

It had been one in the morning when the Dakotas took off. They moved heavily and noisily down the runway, their engines clamouring in the Suffolk night, loaded with paratroops.

'You don't mind me flying with you?' Miller said to Caldy.

Blumenthal, intent on his listening, bent forward encased in his earphones, glanced up and nodded at Miller. Miller returned the nod. 'Sir, I requested that you be sitting here with me,' said Caldy.

'I thought maybe you'd calculate I was bad luck.'

'No, sir. Some of the other guys kinda thought that but not me. Could be I'll be needing you.'

'I'll take that as a compliment. Thanks,' said Miller.

'Don't mention it, sir.'

The boyish pilot straightened the cumbersome plane, its lights full on. It was a settled June night now, after all the rain and wind, cloudy but steady. As they taxied Miller picked out the outline of the trees along the rim of the airfield, the dark patches that were buildings, barns and houses where civilians were deep in their every-night sleep.

The pilot, with his fair hair protruding from his flying helmet, was concentrating on the aircraft in front. They were to be number three to take off. The rest of the squadron was strung out, back into the darkness. A door opened in a hut at the edge of the airfield and a flitting shaft of light came out. It was Major Pitt's office. He waved but no one saw him.

Each of the Dakotas had a full load of paratroops, fifteen to each aircraft, sitting unspeaking in rows along the dimly lit hull, their parachutes, their weapons and their heavy kit piled around them. To every man's left leg was fastened an extra bag, packed with tools and ammunition. Slotted in each man's boot was a long dagger. By morning they intended to be in occupation of defence installations, communications posts, concrete strongholds, and emplacements of heavy guns whose long barrels traversed the landing beaches.

After their normal waddle to the end of the runway the transports took off, each with a shattering roar, three minutes apart, and rose to five thousand feet through shredded cloud and into the clear places below the unhidden stars. Everywhere was placid, airy, calm, and they were floating through a flat sky. Carefully Caldy observed other planes in the formation; there would be many other squadrons at the rendezvous above England's southern coast. 'We have a lot of people up here,' he said casually as if to himself. The paratroopers in the back could scarcely stir. Some drifted into dozing, some nibbled at chocolate. Some merely stared ahead. This is what they had come for.

'Nice night for it,' said Caldy, peering at the stars.

'After all the rain,' said Miller. It was like two men, father and son perhaps, conversing in an ordinary place; safe, on the ground, at home.

'Maybe we'll see the ships,' mentioned Blumenthal. 'Down there somewhere in the ocean.'

'They had just better be there,' said Caldy.

The sergeant loadmaster, who would be overseeing the paratroopers' jump into space, came from the rear and offered them chocolate. They each took a piece. He said everything was fine at the back. He had not asked the airborne men but he knew they were fine. They knew what they had to do. 'At times like this I wish I was jumping too,' he said. 'Getting out of this crate.' He went back to his men.

The south coast was indistinctly luminous, the shape of the sea more visible than the land. Blumenthal was muttering in his confiding manner into the radio close to his face. Caldy nudged Miller sitting behind him and then nodded out into the surrounding sky. The pattern of planes was all around them. 'All going in the same direction,' said the young pilot. 'Everything's going to plan. So far.'

'No fighter escort,' said Miller, regretting immediately that he had said it. But Caldy only shrugged. 'The sky is too crowded anyway,' he said. 'It's better those guys operate in daylight.'

Far ahead, where there was only darkness, the horizon was suddenly bruised by a warm, brief glow. Then another, erupting in a half-orange shape, then dying at once. No sound reached them. 'Bombing,' said Caldy. 'They're dropping the big stuff. That should wise them up, tell them we're on the way.'

Miller detected the nervous inflection in his voice. 'They're strafing the anti-aircraft guns,' he said.

'Could be,' said Caldy.

They were well over the sea now and Blumenthal looked downwards for the ships but saw nothing. Caldy suddenly said: 'Let's get this thing over with.'

He leaned over the controls as if he wanted to press an accelerator and send the plane forward like a fast car. Then to himself he muttered: 'Anti-aircraft fire.'

They could see the flash of the guns and the explosions in the sky. 'Way below,' said Caldy. 'They won't hit a God-dam thing like that.' He laughed tautly. 'They must be crazy.'

They saw the Dakotas in front begin to gain height. 'Don't forget us,' said Caldy. Blumenthal spoke to him and he said: 'Glad they remembered,' and eased the labouring plane to a higher altitude. 'Can't go too high,' he called to Miller as if he might not know. 'Those guys in the back don't like to have to fall too far.'

A silence fell between them as they crossed the French coast. Blumenthal was keeping up what seemed to be his private conversation, occasionally leaning towards Caldy so that he could make a terse comment. Miller observed that the anti-aircraft fire was thickening ahead. Caldy saw it too. 'We have to get through that?'

'Right through it,' confirmed Miller. 'Then we go straight ahead to the dropping zone.'

There was another silence. The coloured shell-bursts were directly in front. The Dakota began to bounce with the impact of the explosions.

Suddenly Caldy said: 'I can't go through with this.' His voice was just pitched above the din of the engines but it was a statement, he did not shout.

'You're going through with it,' Miller told him stonily. 'We all are. That's why we came.'

Blumenthal was muttering swiftly either to himself or into his mouthpiece. He glanced up once, sideways at Caldy.

'I can't do it,' said Caldy with a choking sound. 'I'm not letting myself die up here in this fucking crate.'

'Nobody is going to die,' Miller told him, leaning over from behind. He found himself undoing the flap of his revolver holster and laying his palm on the butt of the Smith and Wesson. 'We're going to drop these guys. They'll have to float down through that flak. When we've dropped them we'll turn around and go home. Got it?'

Caldy nodded sharply but he was weeping with fear. 'No,' he stumbled. 'I can't do it.' Then, with an odd kind of hope: 'I'll be saving the lives of these guys behind too if we go back. You've got to let me go back, captain.'

His voice rose over the close thunder of an explosion below the plane. The Dakota bounced in the sky. The door opened to the rear compartment and the loadmaster stood there. 'How long?' he said. 'My guys want to get out of this thing soon.'

Miller answered. 'Soon. Very soon.'

'Three minutes to dropping zone,' said Blumenthal.

'Okay. Make it a quick three minutes, will you.' The sergeant shut the door.

Caldy said tersely: 'Tell 'em to jump now. What difference will it make, captain? For Christ-sake.'

'Keep going,' Miller ordered him grimly. 'Quit and I'll have you court-martialled.' He touched his revolver again. 'Or I'll shoot you, son.'

'Then we'll all die.'

Miller said: 'Blumenthal can fly the plane.'

Blumenthal regarded them mildly. 'I can fly the plane,' he said.

'Okay, okay, okay,' sniffed Caldy in a shamed way. 'Since you're going to shoot me anyway I'll do it. But I want to go home.'

'Drop the 'chutes in the right area and then we can all go home,' said Miller. 'Two more minutes.'

'One and a half,' said Blumenthal quietly.

Now they seemed to be bouncing on a carpet of exploding lights. It was like a frightening fairground ride. High explosive burst below the wings and directly ahead of the cockpit, shaking the screen. Caldy was shivering. But then Blumenthal said something to him, almost confiding, and the young pilot steadied himself and his voice and said: 'Dropping zone below.' The only way now was back.

He fumbled for a button at the side of his seat. Miller guided his hand to it. He pressed and they heard the urgent buzzer sound behind them. The door opened.

'Okay, they're going,' said the loadmaster.

Miller wished them good luck.

'You got us here anyway,' responded the loadmaster. 'For my guys' sake I hope the flak on the ground is less than the flak up here.'

To Miller's amazement Caldy said: 'They'll be fine. Nothing to it.'

The loadmaster closed the door. The paratroopers began to jump. Miller stretched to see them flying away like butterflies through the pale night. Caldy was crouched across the controls. Coloured explosions erupted around them.

It took less than three minutes. 'Gone,' said Blumenthal then. 'Every one.'

The loadmaster opened the door again. 'Just fine,' he said. 'I'm going to have a cigar. Thanks, guys.' He closed the door behind him.

'Now we can go home,' said Miller.

'I'm sorry, captain,' said Caldy. 'I was scared.'

'So was I,' replied Miller. 'As shit. So was Blumenthal. So were the men in the back. But now it's okay, it's done.'

Caldy began to whoop and laugh. 'Let's go! Let's get out of this place!'

Blumenthal was leaning to look out. He said in his flat voice: 'The starboard engine's on fire.'

The Dakota began to descend in an orderly way, a long dive towards the sea. It was becoming daylight and as they crossed the French coast Blumenthal said calmly: 'There's all the ships. I never saw so many ships.'

There was nothing they could do. 'We're not going to make it,' said Caldy, oddly quiet now. 'Should we tell the guy in the back?'

'Let him enjoy his cigar,' said Miller.

Caldy half turned towards him. 'Captain . . .'

'Yes, son?'

'Will you hold my hand?'

'Sure. I need somebody to hold mine,' said Miller. He manoeuvred himself from the rear of the seats into a position wedged between them. He squatted across instruments that were now redundant. Caldy held out his hand and Miller took it.

Blumenthal said: 'Would you hold mine, too?' Miller did.

The plane, smoke and flames issuing in a plume from the starboard engine, came down at a steeper angle. It fell into the sea in mid-Channel.

There were no survivors.

Chapter Twenty-four

The D-Day landings on 6 June 1944 spread for almost a hundred miles from end to end. The Normandy invasion beaches had code-names from west to east: Utah, Omaha, Gold, Juno and Sword. There was also a phantom force moving towards the Straits of Dover to keep the Germans thinking that Hitler's arrogance was justified, that the strike would be in the Pas de Calais. The first news of the invasion was given to the world in an early-morning broadcast from Radio Berlin. The BBC continued to recite the words of Verlaine.

The American landings, at Omaha particularly, met murderous resistance and they suffered multiple casualties, including Private Benjamin Soroyan who was killed within his first few steps on the sand. Juno, Sword and Gold beaches were more readily, but not entirely easily, taken by the British force and by the Canadians and French.

Twenty miles inland from the desperate battles for a first foothold in Europe, the procession of Our Lady of the North was forming up for the third day of its creeping pilgrimage across upper France. Every day the religious people of the farms and villages, egged on by their priests, had joined it and by this morning it stretched for more than two miles from the plaster figure at the fore to the children lagging at the rear.

Antoinette Barre, in peasant dress, together with Gilbert and Paget who were wearing the French workman's *bleu de travail*, had joined it at early prayers in the village of St Jean des Eaux. There the church itself was filled with robed clergy and regional notables while the commonplace people sat on the churchyard walls and on the mossy and misshapen gravestones of their ancestors. Some would have to return that day to work in the fields but others stayed with the procession for, over the years, it had traditionally become something of a walking holiday. By now the pious crocodile numbered two thousand trudging souls.

Antoinette squatted on a tombstone near the church gate, her cigarette held down behind the crumbling slab. At a distance Paget observed her and Gilbert as they surveyed the walkers, the Englishman wondering at the bizarre occurrences that seemed to happen in occupied France as a matter of course. All three were armed and there were other resistance men and women among the pilgrims, singing the psalms and hymns, and responding to the incantations as they marched.

The local bishop walked before the better-class worshippers from the church, called a blessing across the tombs to the ordinary folks, and then went off convivially to breakfast with the priest and several ornately clad others. The start of the invasion had been mentioned but no more than that. There were more practical and immediate problems to be grasped as far as the procession of Our Lady of the North was concerned. The statue was several centuries old, and being borne about she was subject to wear and tear. The previous day her foot had fallen off. A man from St Nazaire, a specialist in the repair of relics, was to be summoned.

Once the leading clergy had drifted to breakfast a young, starved-looking priest, his skin drawn thinly over his facial bones, his ears almost transparent, his nose flushed, began taking fussy charge of getting the procession on the move again. The place where the statue's foot was missing had been covered with a piece of blue velvet, and the priest checked that it was secure, for the accident had been embarrassing for the clergy and distressing to the peasants who thought it might mean bad luck or terrible events. The thin young father then consulted a map and as he was doing so he was approached by Antoinette and Gilbert. Paget kept his distance. Antoinette enquired about that day's route and the priest brusquely jabbed his finger at the map and gabbled the names of villages.

'But, *mon père*, we should perhaps visit some other villages,' said Antoinette, pointing firmly at places on the map.

The priest was outraged at a woman making suggestions. His skinny eyebrows went up. 'Our Blessed Lady of the North has always gone by this way,' he almost snarled. 'There is no reason to change it. No authority.'

Antoinette shrugged and backed into the crowd. The priest stared after her uncomfortably and spotted the hard-eyed Gilbert who made the sign of the cross, then became immersed in the people, some of whom had started singing out of tune.

Standing on a grave the priest snapped some less than holy orders and the vanguard of the procession began to shuffle forward. Four strong men carried the platform on which Our Lady was borne. It was a subdued but fine morning and none of the sounds of battle carried to that distance although some who looked up noticed increased air activity.

Along the rural roads Our Lady was carried. The young priest trod anxiously and prayed that nothing disastrous would happen today as had happened yesterday; that the figure would arrive in one piece at the next night's stop. The bishop had not been pleased.

After two miles between strong hedgerows, the narrowing of the way making the procession even longer, they came to a village at a crossroads. The marked route was directly across the junction but Antoinette again approached the priest and this time pushed the muzzle of a Colt automatic pistol into his protruding ribs. He knew what it was. 'We will go to the right here,' she said quietly. '*Mon père*.'

'I cannot. The occupying forces forbid us to use the main roads.'

'We will march to the right,' she repeated flatly. 'It will take us to places that never see Our Lady.'

'I must ask the bishop,' said the priest.

Antoinette pointed: 'Here is a place. You can use the telephone.'

It was a dim, low-roofed, general store. They went in, the priest, Antoinette, Gilbert and Paget. The peasants waited outside, patient and puzzled. But what the priest did was never questioned.

The shop owner, a tiny man with a gnarled face, handed the telephone from under the counter. The priest looked frightened. 'Everything goes wrong,' he grumbled. He took up the trumpet earpiece from its cradle. At the same moment Gilbert reached across the counter and picked up a heavy pair of scissors lying next to a ball of thick string. As the priest said: '*L'opérateur*,' Gilbert chopped through the telephone wire.

Antoinette pushed the gun into the priest's waist again, deeper this time. She could feel his ribs. The shopkeeper watched unaffected, as if it happened every day. 'We turn right,' repeated Antoinette. 'I have no religious objection to killing you at this moment.'

The shopkeeper urged: 'Please go from the shop and do it.'

The priest shrugged: 'Of course we turn to the right.'

Our Lady of the North now floated above the hedgerows of the main road. The officer commanding a bicycle company of German troops heading for the invasion beaches, skidded to a stop.

Kapitän Franz Doller halted his men by shouting and holding up his hand. It was not easy because many of them were leaning earnestly over their handlebars, looking below the rims of their helmets, their equipment and rifles piled on their bent backs. The German Army was noted for its bicycle troops who could sometimes react to situations more quickly than motorised infantry or tanks, and certainly faster than men on foot.

Now the sudden halt caused collisions and a pile-up of laden soldiers behind him. Doller could not credit what he saw. The white-and-blue-robed figure was bouncing along above the hedged skyline. Cursing and pushing forward a few turns of his front wheel, he came upon the whole devout procession jammed in the confines of the high-banked road.

Doller hated the French, their perversity, their stupidity, their lack of fair play and their arrogance. Now all these emotions rose up in him at once. He almost threw his bicycle at his second in command and ran towards the crushed and bemused peasants. Antoinette, Gilbert and Paget left through the gate of a farm.

'Halt! No further! Stop! What is this?' demanded the kapitän.

The priest regarded him defeatedly. Surely nothing more could go wrong that day. 'It is the annual procession of Our Lady of the North,' he replied.

'Get these pumpkins off the road!' demanded the German. 'This is an emergency! Don't you know there has been an invasion?'

'There *was* some talk,' confessed the priest. He looked at the officer as if appealing to his better nature. 'It will take a long time to disperse these people,' he said. 'I must contact the bishop.'

'Bollocks to the bishop!' shouted Doller. 'Get them off the road. Over the hedges into the fields. I will make my soldiers clear a way. You French are mad.'

His second in command approached, balancing on his bicycle like an errand boy. He had news that he was hesitant about imparting. 'What? What?' demanded Doller.

'There is an armoured column coming behind us, sir. Panzers,' said the lieutenant. 'They order us to get out of their way.'

Paget knew nothing about the house except that it was an hour's drive away and that they said it was safe. Just in case it was not, they showed him the back staircase. As far as he could see through the ragged drawn curtains it was in open country, probably a farmhouse. When they arrived, they found that some bread and cheese and ham and several dusty bottles of red wine had been placed on the heavy kitchen table.

None of the group seemed to live there. Gilbert asked the way to the lavatory and then had to go and find it himself. Nobody said much and Gilbert and two of the others finally went away. A tall, slow man, who had been at the house when they arrived, said there was a room upstairs where Paget could rest. It was going to be a busy night. The man was not sure which door gave into the room but Paget soon found it. It was bare apart from two single beds with children's counterpanes of cartoon ducks and rabbits, and a pair of similar curtains which sagged woefully.

He took his French labourer's boots off gratefully and stretched on one of the beds. It just fitted him, his head and feet touching each end. Antoinette came through the planked door carrying her wineglass and a half-full bottle. 'We must share,' she shrugged. 'The other rooms are busy.'

She sat on the bed opposite. She was wearing the peasant dress, none too clean. 'Where is this place?' he asked.

Again she shrugged. 'A house. Somewhere. We will only be here a few hours.'

She began to laugh, something he had not seen her do before. She had fine teeth in a handsome mouth. 'That German officer today. The one with the bicycles. Nothing is so ridiculous as soldiers on bicycles.'

Paget smiled from his stretched-out position. 'It certainly worked. I wonder how long they were delayed?'

'Not long enough,' she said seriously. 'I hate those bastards, you know. I hate them with everything I have. For me there is no difference between those who say they are Nazis and those who say they are only Germans. They are the same. I hate them all.'

'What about your husband?'

Looking aggrieved, she said sulkily: 'He is not my husband. He is just useful.'

She poured some wine into her glass. 'You have no glass,' she said. 'You must share mine.' She handed it to him and he drank and then handed it back. He lay down again. She leaned a little towards him. 'These men, the Boche, you can see what they have done to my country. They have been raping this country since 1940.' She looked at him steadily. 'Since the British ran away and left us.'

'You think we ran away?'

323

'Where were you hiding then? The beach at Dunkirk was empty when the Boche arrived. The British had gone.'

'It's just as well,' he argued. 'Or we would all be under the Nazis now.'

She put the glass on the floor and held up her hands. 'Don't let us have a small war between ourselves. Not now. Now the invasion has happened.'

He had asked as soon as they had reached the house if there was any news. No one knew. Now he asked again.

'We have some,' she said. 'But it is too early. The Americans have suffered many dead on the beaches, but they won't lose. They are too strong.'

'What about the British?'

'Nothing of the British,' she said. Then with a surprising smile she added: 'Except for you. And you are here.'

She moved across to his bedside and studied his rough working clothes. 'The *bleu de travail* does not suit you. You still look English.'

Almost as if her mind was far away, she began casually to undo the metal buttons on the front of the rough blue trousers, tut-tutting like a mother when one proved difficult. She did not look at him but seemed to find something interesting in the pattern of the bedspread. '*Canard et lapin*,' she muttered dreamily. Paget lay back and watched her.

Still as though she was not following what she was doing, she opened the front of the trousers and pushed in her long fingers and then her hand. She went down to his groin and cupped him in her hand. She lifted her peasant skirt and grubby white petticoat, pulled away a pair of cotton drawers, and climbed on top of him.

Not a word came from either of them. It was as though there was nothing to say. She manoeuvred and slid him inside her and eased herself to and fro, her eyelids drooping as though she were going to sleep. Finally they closed altogether.

She had remained sitting on him, thighs spread, but after it was done, she fell forward across his chest, her heavy breasts below her country blouse lying on him. They had not even kissed. Then she mumbled: 'We must sleep now for a little, Monsieur *Anglais*. We have Germans to kill tonight.'

By nine thirty that evening she had shot two German soldiers dead. They were guarding a signal-box and when the French party moved in along the hedgerows in the dusk they caught them having a sly smoke. Antoinette shot them without pausing. The cigarettes were still smouldering as they lay on the ground.

A frightened Frenchman appeared at the top of the ladder to the signal-box, his railway hat hastily donned for recognition. '*Français*,' he told them, to make sure. A companion peered fearfully around the door of the box. There were three other men in the attacking group, but Antoinette was in command. She told the signalmen to come down the steps and go to a safe distance and remain there. They did so, looking doubtfully over their shoulders.

The resistance men disabled the signal-box controls. 'To blow it up would be nice,' said Antoinette. 'But it would be heard several kilometres away.'

She said to Paget: 'Come with me, now.' She looked at home, happy, carrying the sub-machine-gun.

Between the railway line and the road where he guessed they would pick up their next transport, was a building that looked like a school. 'Two more targets,' said Antoinette as she pointed towards the road. He could see the excitement bubbling in her. She would miss the war when it was over. 'The next in only half an hour,' she said.

As they approached the school building they heard the surprising sound of a brass band. Both halted in the shadows. Antoinette slid to a window and cautiously looked in through an aperture in the curtain. 'Germans,' she said with a warm smile.

Paget followed her to the window and looked in. There were a dozen bandsmen and their instruments grouped in a circle with a rotund bandmaster in a grey uniform. He was speaking to them with his baton raised. Paget had a view of several of them. They were all youths, little more than boys, some bespectacled, intent on their sheets of music.

Antoinette crooked her finger. With deepening dread he realised what she was going to do. He touched, then lightly held her arm but she shook him off fiercely. The first exterior door she tried opened. He felt his body trembling. They were in a corridor. The sound of the brass music came to them more loudly. Now they were outside the room. She put her hand in her bag and brought out a grenade. Paget, almost sick with horror, whispered: 'No. No.'

She had a wild look and she turned it on him. 'Go,' she snarled. 'Get out.'

Then she opened the door of the classroom. He had a moment's glimpse of the musicians in their circle, then she pulled the pin, shouted: '*Bonsoir,*' tossed in the grenade and closed the door. In seconds there was a shattering explosion. The door bulged and splintered, a window along the corridor fell in. Calmly Antoinette produced another grenade.

'No!' Paget shouted at her. 'They're boys! Just children!'

She glared and said: 'Nazis.'

She pulled the pin from the second grenade and dragged the damaged door half open. Paget attempted to stop her and his intervention caused the grenade to hit the door and bounce like a ball back into the corridor. He tried to fall away from it. She staggered in the other direction. It ignited with a massive flash and an explosion that seemed to burst his ears. Choking smoke filled the corridor. He realised his arm was hanging off. Blood was spurting on the floor. The arm was almost separated from his body. 'Antoinette!' he cried.

His eyes went blank. His head was full of smoke. He heard voices, French voices, and then knew nothing until he woke briefly in the back of a speeding car. 'Antoinette,' he repeated. There was blood all over him, blood-soaked towels on his shoulder.

'*Elle est morte,*' said a casual voice. 'We can get you to help. Do you want us to keep your arm, monsieur?'

Chapter Twenty-five

That same night Harris and his men rested in a farmyard after the longest day any of them had ever known. Guns still sounded not far away and they heard planes shuttling overhead, but their battle seemed to have ended for the day, as work does, and they could rest. On the five invasion beaches 2,500 Allied soldiers had been killed.

'Oi never want to do that again,' said Blackie profoundly. 'That coming up that beach. Better goin' over the bloody hill than that.'

Warren said tiredly: 'Which 'ill be that?'

'Desertin', I mean,' said Blackie. 'Goin' over the 'ill, loike they Yanks say. It were scareful, Bunny, weren't it?'

'None of us got ourselves shot,' muttered Warren. 'Jerry kept missin' us.'

'They 'it some blokes just up the beach,' put in Treadwell. 'Dropped as soon as they jumped ashore, poor buggers. All that trainin', then gettin' your lot like that.'

There were rumours reaching the farmyard. There was a German armoured division straight ahead at Caen, the Canadians were halfway to Paris, the French were fighting the French.

'The Yanks got a pounding, lots killed,' said an artilleryman from the next field. 'We got off light.' He asked if they knew where they could buy some eggs. He had some francs.

It was the run-in to the beach that had been so terrifying. Hardly a word had been spoken among the men going to the shore as the landing-craft had moved away from the troop transport. It was five miles and it took almost an hour. They were cold and wet and some were seasick; few said anything. Blackie had begun to whistle in a thin, irritating manner, but he was told to shut up. 'Bad luck whistling in boats,' Gordon pointed out. 'In Scotland, anyway.'

Because of the high sides of the vessel they could not see what was happening around them, only guess. As the dawn widened above their heads the noise of the invasion fleet filled the air, the pounding engines, the wash of the craft, then the shuddering big guns of the British heavy warships far out to sea.

'I 'ope they navy blokes got their range right,' grunted Warren. 'Don't fancy that lot comin' down on my 'ead 'afore we even get on the sands.'

They heard the high-explosive shells whistle and whoosh above them and the landing-craft seemed to stagger through the choppy water. Explosions echoed from the land. They could see some of the Allied planes as they roared across the visible patch of sky.

'No sign of Jerry,' said Harris, looking up.

There was a steel-helmeted man in the bow, staring out towards the shore.

'What's it like, mate?' somebody among the crowded men called to him.

'Gettin' lighter,' said the man.

'I meant what's going on, not a weather report. We can all see the bloody sky. It's about all we can see.'

'All right, all right,' said the bowman. 'Don't take offence.'

'Don't take offence,' whispered a soldier crouching next to Harris. 'That's what we're supposed to bleedin' do, take offence. For Christ's sake, that's why we're here.'

The bowman called back: 'Well, from 'ere I can see mostly barrage balloons,' he related loudly. 'All over the ships. 'Undreds of the buggers. Then there's 'undreds of boats, landing-craft like this and bigger jobs, all over the place. And right back you can see the guns flashing. No sign of Jerry, though. Keeping 'is 'ead down, I 'spect. Maybe 'e's gone 'ome.'

He had scarcely spoken when there was an explosion to one side of the craft and then another, even closer, which sent cascades of sea water flying over the sides. The men were thrown sideways as the helmsman at the back tried to turn the ungainly boat.

'Now Jerry can see us,' said Treadwell.

They heard orders crackling over the air waves to the helmsman. Abruptly the barrage from the shore increased. The boat rocked and shuddered. They could hear the small-arms fire hitting the side of the landing-craft as they crouched, faces taut, holding their rifles, ready to jump.

'Come on, come on,' Gordon kept saying. 'Let's get there. Stuck out here like sitting ducks.'

'Three 'undred yards . . . two fifty . . . two 'undred,' called the man at the bow.

With a big jerk the craft slewed, then came back on course. 'This beach is mined,' an officer somewhere shouted reassuringly. 'Follow the red markers the advance engineers are putting down. I hope.'

'There's a lot of guesswork,' muttered Treadwell. 'I thought they had it all worked out. I'm going to write and complain.'

'You do that, Treadie,' said May. His face was grey.

Gannick was chewing the stem of his pipe. Peters was trying not to cry.

The landing-craft abruptly slid up the beach, jolting and slewing again, sending the men off balance, backing off with the waves and finally being almost flung on the shore.

'Everybody out!' shouted the bowman. 'Any more for the Skylark?'

'That's what they used to shout on the beach at Southsea,' mumbled Harris irrationally. 'When I was a kid. "Any more for the Skylark?"'

The ramp at the front of the craft clanged down. The first man jumped and then they all disgorged from the vessel. It was swiftly and well done but it seemed as though it took an eternity. Harris was praying his ankle would not collapse and he lowered himself to the shore in an almost elderly, careful way.

It was bedlam all along the beach. In the early light he was aware of the boats, hundreds of boats, on the shoreline and those still coming in. One was on fire and going madly around in circles. Men were jumping into the sea. Another had run over its own troops as they landed. There were bodies in the water. Smoke rolled over the morning sky. And all to the chorus of the guns of the big ships out at sea. Men were running, or trying to run, under various burdens up the crumbling beach towards the shelter of the first sand-dunes. There were soldiers carrying guns and bicycles. Harris saw Treadwell pause to wipe the sand from his glasses. What the hell was a man who wore glasses doing there?

It was difficult to spot any others of his own squad among the confusion. There was some small-arms fire throwing up the sand to his left and then some bigger explosions erupted on the waterline. Bodies were lying in the shallows and more halfway to the sand-dunes. Suddenly Blackie appeared at his side.

'All right, son?'

'Just about, sarge. 'Cept I've just crapped.'

'Don't do it again. Where's the others?'

'Bunny is just over there and so are the rest,' Blackie pointed through the smoke. 'Oi reckon they're all right. We just got to get to those sand 'ills.'

'Here we must be just out of Jerry's line of fire. Once we make a dash for it we may be exposed. So make it fast. Tell the others.'

'Won't need to, sarge.'

He went like a monkey across the sand. Harris waved to his men and then shouted for them to go forward. They all ran madly to the cover of the dunes. The German machine-gun fire was late and they got there, panting, heaving, lying against the tussocks of grass, keeping their heads down.

'Good,' said Harris. 'So far.'

'Where's their big guns?' said Gordon. 'I thought we'd be for it.'

Harris said: 'That's what I was afraid of but they're not playing. The Airborne boys may have targeted them. Overrun them from the rear.'

'Up their arses,' said Treadwell.

They inched their way up the sand bank and spread out, crawling low. Blackie was pushing his rifle over the top and firing blindly, keeping his head down below his helmet and the dune. 'You ain't ever goin' to shoot any bugger loike that,' said Warren. 'You got to aim at 'em proper.'

Blackie held his rifle up and took another random shot. 'You never know when you moight be lucky,' he said.

Harris was conscious of a forward movement from the beach and all along the sand-dunes. Someone fired a red Very light and the flare hung eerily above the long, grey confusion. Harris had no idea what the signal meant but he moved forward through the dunes, calling the others to follow him. Behind them one of the landing-craft struck a mine and flew bodily in the air. Once the explosion and the smoke had cleared he could see and hear men shouting desperately in the water.

He turned away and urged his squad on. May lay still but he said he only had cramp. Peters was staring as if he were in a dream. Treadwell wiped his glasses, Chaffey his nose. They had gone about three hundred yards when firing began ahead. The sandy undulations of the land gave them cover and looking left and right Harris could see other troops pinned down under the machine-gun attack. They waited, keeping below the level of the marram grass. A burst of fire ruffled the ground ahead and they flattened themselves into the sand. When it had finished Blackie whispered, the only time anyone had heard him speak so low: 'Look 'ere, see what Oi found.'

He held up a sand-covered doll, a ragged little thing but with eyes apparently bright with gratitude. 'Lost,' he said.

Warren said: 'Keep un, take un 'ome for youm kids.'

Blackie grinned and nodded. Then he said: 'Oi ain't got no kids.'

A scarlet-faced officer crawled towards them from the right. 'Sergeant,' he said to Harris. 'Any chance of your lads dealing with these bastards? They're holding us up and you're nearest.'

'Yes, sir,' answered Harris, wondering how.

'Advance twenty yards,' said the officer, 'and you'll be in grenade range, just about.' He moved on saying vaguely: 'Well done.'

Harris was still not sure how it could be done. The enemy had them covered. 'Ask them ta surrender, sarge,' suggested Gordon.

'Thanks,' grunted Harris. 'We'll go around the flanks. Maybe their field of fire is restricted. When we open fire,' he pointed to Warren, 'let them have the grenade. You're the cricket-ball-throwing champion.'

Warren said: 'I were only second.'

Harris took Treadwell to the right, Gordon went left with Blackie, wriggling through the tough grass and sharp sand. The Germans were in a hollow and had stopped firing. Warren, with his considerable bulk only just below the top of the grass, rolled forward. He stripped off his pack and ammunition pouches. You were not supposed to do that. He was sure they would see him but the Germans remained quiet until they began firing towards the far right.

Harris realised that any covering fire from them would bring the enemy's attention back. 'Hold your fire,' he said and raised his finger above the grass. Warren saw it. The West Countryman took a breath, rose to his knees and then to his big feet. Cursing to himself, he ran forward like a half-crouching rugby player over the soft ground, pulled the pin from the grenade and tossed it overarm towards the middle of the German position. Then he threw himself down, knocking all the breath from his body.

The Mills bomb exploded among the Germans and Harris gave the order to open fire. They swept the position with rifle fire from both flanks. Harris got to his feet and ran while firing the Sten gun from his hip. There was no need. There were five dead Germans lying in the saucer of sand.

'Good throw, Bunny,' said Harris. Warren had got on his feet but now sank to the ground as if exhausted. The sergeant patted him on his sweating head. 'You'll be getting the Victoria Cross if you're not careful.'

'Oi not be goin' to do that any more,' vowed Warren. They saw that he was weeping down his big cheeks. 'Some other bugger can do it next time.'

When it was evening they rested in the farmyard. The farmer's wife came out and collected all their boots and socks and took them inside the house to dry by a fire. Then a field kitchen caught up with them and ladled out hot stew, jam roll and custard and cups of tea. They began to feel better.

There was an artillery battery of twenty-five-pounders in the field next to the walled farm. 'I know you,' a sergeant said to Harris who had walked over to see if they had any spare cigarettes. 'You're a gunner. What you doing in this mob?' They strolled back to the farmyard together.

'Crawling on our bellies, mostly,' said Harris. 'We got transferred to the Hampshires. It was a bad swap.'

'Been wallowing in it, have you?' His name was Berry. Harris remembered him from the mess.

'All day. The boys are knackered.'

The artilleryman had fifty Craven 'A' cigarettes, advertised as being good for the throat. He handed them to Harris.

'Lost anybody?'

'No, thank God. They're all still here. Thanks for the fags.'

A boy of about five came from the farmhouse, shyly walked up to the two sergeants and said: '*Des Allemands.*'

They looked at each other. The artillery sergeant said: 'He wants almonds.' He started to say: 'We haven't got any . . .'

'*Des Boches,*' corrected the boy.

'*Action stations!*' bawled Harris. His barefooted men picked up their weapons and scattered. Berry ran across the farmyard while the small boy blinked with astonishment. Then, from the back door of the farm came *Wehrmacht* Sergeant Fred Weber and his friend Gino, also wearing a German Army tunic. They were coated with dust and both carried white flags attached to walking-sticks. Weber also bore a bottle of schnapps and Gino tentatively cradled a football-sized red cheese.

'*Kamerad*,' said Weber. 'I'm a cook.' As if he thought it might help, he held up the hand with the single finger.

'Yes,' confirmed Gino with a hopeful smile. 'I assist him.'

'At least they brought the cheese,' grinned Harris. The grin was relief. His men came a touch sheepishly from their concealment places. They put down their weapons and relieved the two men of the schnapps and the cheese and gave them what was left of the army stew. It was getting cold but they ate gratefully. Weber whispered to Gino: 'It could have done with some seasoning.'

Harris allowed each of his men a tot of schnapps and a slice of cheese. The boy came out of the house with some lumps of bread. Harris went in to thank the woman for drying the socks and boots. The farmer, who had appeared cautious, as if he was not sure who they should be helping, pointed to a battery wireless set which he took from the dresser and placed on the middle of the kitchen table. '*Londres*,' he said. He cupped his hand to his ear. Harris sat down and said: 'We might as well hear who's winning.'

He thought nothing else could surprise him that day but then a smart young German lieutenant came through the door, tall and sharply clean, escorted by a short, mangy-looking private in the South Lancashire Regiment. 'This Jerry lad says 'e wants to listen to t' news, sarge,' he said.

The officer clicked his heels and, Harris thought, just stopped himself saying: '*Heil Hitler.*' The sergeant indicated one of the chairs. The farmer brought a bottle of calvados and three glasses and put them on the table. He sat down with them. 'I wouldn't mind a sup o' that,' said the small escort infantryman. The farmer caught his eye and produced another glass. The soldier remained standing, not much taller than his rifle.

The farmer checked the murky wall clock. It was warm in the

room because the fire had been lit to dry the boots. 'Do you mind if we have the window open?' asked the German officer in perfect English.

'As long as you don't jump out of it,' retorted Harris.

The lieutenant laughed thinly. 'I will not escape, sergeant. It has taken me half the day to become captured.'

Harris glanced at him. The farmer switched on the wireless but only crackling noises came from it. He shrugged and waited. 'You've been trying to give yourself up?' Harris said to the German.

'It has not been easy,' replied the lieutenant. 'Getting shot is easy, but not being taken prisoner. But here I am, safe and sound, more or less.'

'Your English is very good,' said Harris.

'Better 'an mine,' put in the private from the South Lancashire Regiment. 'It's like they say about the Virgin Mary, innit, sarge. Like 'er conception. What is it? Immaculate, that's it, immaculate. That's 'is English.'

The German glanced at him disparagingly. 'I went to school in England.'

'So did I. 'Oly Trinity, Birken'ead,' said the soldier.

'Please,' admonished the German officer. He turned to Harris. 'In Sussex, in fact. That is where I would like to go now, Sussex, green and pleasant Sussex.'

'Maybe we'll build you a special prison camp there,' said Harris.

'Don't take offence, sergeant. I'm glad to be in this situation. I'm probably the first German officer to throw in the towel in Europe. You'll ship me to England where I shall spend the rest of the conflict in some little discomfort, but not much. Far better than being dead, don't you think? While you will all be marching on with the war.' He smiled at their faces. The wireless set came to life.

'This is the BBC in London. Mr Winston Churchill, the prime minister, has told the House of Commons that all the invasion beaches in northern France have been secured and that American, British and Allied troops are pushing inland.'

The German officer raised his calvados glass to the farmer and to Harris, but he ignored the small Liverpudlian. 'To victory,' he said.

The following morning they moved ahead to a red-roofed village, Colomb, which had already been cleared by British paratroops. It was a pleasant walk in the sun after the noise and danger of the previous day. They could still hear the distant uproar of guns along the coast and several times low-flying planes crossed above them, making them dive into the hedgerows. But they had British or American markings. The *Luftwaffe* was still absent.

They approached the village cautiously in single file at one side of the road, the whole platoon stretched out over two hundred yards. Harris was in the lead of his section and they were the first into the cobbled square.

A group of paratroopers was resting by a small fountain, with the inhabitants in their best clothes standing around them. Two young women had brought trays of coffee and the grimed airborne soldiers were accepting the mugs gladly. 'Looks like the job's been done already,' said Harris.

Beyond the pleasant street and over the roofs of the houses they could see a meadow heavy with buttercups and poppies, and beyond that a church spire. Harris deployed his men along one side of the street, looking over the field through the gaps in the buildings. 'Bit late, boys,' said one of the Airborne men. 'Jerry's been kicked out of here.'

'Trust the infantry,' said another. 'Oversleeping.'

'We had to walk,' pointed out Harris good-humouredly. He remained conscious of his transfer to a foot-slogging regiment. One of the twenty-five-pounders from the artillery battery, which had been in the field next to the farm, was coming into the village pulled by a fifteen-hundredweight. Berry, the sergeant he had recognised, was in the seat beside the driver.

The young women, in their bright peasant skirts and white blouses, asked with polite eagerness if the squad would like some coffee and they went to get it. One of them in a blue apron and white blouse came from a house first, holding a round tray and six mugs. Harris took his first and then Treadwell.

As Treadwell moved to take the coffee and he and the girl stood facing each other, a single, concise shot came echoing from the distance. The bullet went through the girl's neck and hit Treadwell in the chest. The two strangers fell forward, the soldier lying across the young woman as though to protect her. His glasses fell unbroken to the cobbles. The round coffee tray rolled like a noisy wheel across the street; the cups smashed.

Nobody moved, nobody could take it in. Then Harris shouted: 'Action! Action!' and the soldiers ran to cover by the houses and the garden walls on the side of the village over which the shot had come. The paratroops flattened. The villagers screamed and ran. One hysterical woman tried to reach the shot girl but she was held back. A medical orderly with the Airborne men ran at a crouch towards the two young people prostrate in a square of sunshine. Harris shouted to Blackie, his nearest soldier, and sheltered by a wall. Blackie scuttled across the street to the pair. 'Treadie,' he choked. Harris crawled to his side. 'Christ . . . come on, Treadie!' Blackie sobbed. 'You'll be all right.' They knew he was not. When the medical orderly turned him over there was a blunt and bloody hole in his chest and no life in his face. The men were looking over their shoulders, trying to see. Blackie spread his hands speechlessly and picked up Treadwell's glasses.

'That spire,' said Harris. 'That's where the bastard is. Up in the spire.'

A paratroop sergeant on hands and knees arrived alongside him. 'My boys will flush him out,' he said. He looked at the group crouching over the two bodies. The village women were screaming the girl's name: 'Marie! Marie!' but being restrained on the pavement. 'Hard luck losing one of your lads just like that,' said the paratrooper.

Harris stared towards the church spire and said: 'I think *we'll* want to get him.' The sergeant looked at their rifles and Harris's Sten gun. 'You'll have to get a bit closer,' he said. 'That's all of five hundred yards.'

'We won't use the rifles,' said Harris. He strode past the sheltering houses towards Sergeant Berry and the twenty-five-pounder. 'That one of your boys?' said Berry. 'Bad luck, mate.'

'We'll get him,' said Harris grimly. 'He's up in that church bloody spire.' He looked the other sergeant in the face. 'Can we borrow the gun?'

Berry looked astonished. 'Borrow it? But we can . . .' He realised. 'Oh, I see.'

Harris said: 'We'll look after it. Remember, we're really gunners.'

'All right, why not,' said Berry. He looked over his shoulder. 'Our officer is still back by the farm. One of the guns got stuck in the ditch. Nobody will notice.'

'Good. Thanks.'

Harris called to his squad. They ran along under cover of the houses. As they did so another shot sounded. There was a small puff of smoke from the spire, from a single, dark window. 'Fixed you,' said Harris.

The men realised what he was doing. They hurried to get the gun prepared for action. Berry's men watched, astonished. The field gun was swung and trundled to a position at the side of the square, partly concealed but from which they had a clear view of the church. They were swiftly ready.

Then an old Frenchman strolled calmly along the cobbles. 'Our church is a little old,' he pointed out.

'Our comrade was a little young,' said Harris. 'They shouldn't use churches for sniping.'

The old man smiled in a thoughtful way. 'The priest is still in bed in his house. He goes back after morning prayers.'

'This will wake him up,' said Harris.

The crew were ready. The four crouching men had rehearsed

it so many times. 'Ready . . . load . . .' he recited, returning to the gun. His breath came thickly. Berry was standing under cover, hands in pockets, nodding approval, his men watching near him. Harris snapped orders. The muzzle of the weapon rose, the range was shouted, the aim was sure. 'Fire!'

The shattering explosion sent pigeons flying and squawking from the village housetops. The sniper had barely disturbed them. A sign outside a shop fell down. People crouched and clutched their ears. The shell struck three quarters of the way up the spire, hitting the single dark window. The top of the spire disappeared in an eruption of smoke and debris and toppled, falling down in three directions.

'I reckon you got the bugger there, sergeant,' said Berry. His men began to cheer.

'I reckon so too,' said Harris. 'You can have your gun back now. Thanks.'

He turned and went, with a military stride, to where the dead Treadwell and the girl were lying in the street.

Chapter Twenty-six

By mid-August the battles, still fierce, had moved south, east and west. The Germans had suffered 200,000 dead since D-Day on 6 June, the Allies half that number. Fifteen thousand civilians had died. Paris was liberated on 25 August but there were still nine months of the war to go before the Allied victory.

Summer lay heavily on the station yard, the big trees folding above it. The rooks sounded. Bees and flies buzzed. The yard was empty and dusty when Paget walked out from the station. He was the only passenger to have left the train at Crockbourne.

Wilks brought the taxi creaking around the corner by the loaded horse chestnuts. He stopped. 'Good morning, Mr Paget, let me take that.'

He picked up Paget's single case but made no comment about the empty sleeve of his air force tunic, if he saw it at all.

Paget was about to climb into the taxi when he saw Margaret waiting amid the deepest shadows of the horse chestnut trees. He stood still, almost transfixed, in the afternoon sunshine. The train hooted a cloud of steam and began to pull away.

He saw her smile as she stepped carefully towards him. She was wearing a summer dress, green and white. 'Your mother told me which train you'd be on,' she said.

Now they were face to face. 'Thanks for coming,' he said inadequately. They kissed lightly and she fell against him, crying on to his uniform. 'Oh, Martin,' she said. Then: 'Put your arm round me.'

He held her with his one arm and felt how much she was trembling. 'It's all finished now,' she said. 'The bloody lot.'

'It's all done,' he replied.

Wilks, showing no surprise, opened the rear door and they climbed into the taxi. They held on to each other.

'You been busy, I expect, sir,' Wilks said as he got into the driving seat. The ancient leather squeaked. He looked very old now. Even his fine grey hair was almost gone.

'Quite busy,' agreed Paget. 'Everybody has.'

'It's quiet here,' said Wilks. 'Nothing much ever seems to happen.'

The old handbrake creaked as he released it. Paget sat back, touching with his hand the linen of Margaret's sleeve. The taxi went forward, out of the empty station yard and along the village road towards his home.

As they neared, he saw his father clipping the privet hedge.

What Happened to . . .

Martin Paget and **Margaret Carne** married in 1947. They had a son and daughter to add to the two sons from Margaret's first marriage. Paget continued as an estate and land agent until 1952 when the couple bought a hotel in France, at St Vaast-la-Hougue, Normandy, which they ran for thirty years. In 1982 they retired and returned to England.

Harris took his squad right through Europe in late 1944 and early 1945. Both Blackie and Warren were wounded in Germany, and May died of illness. But the rest of the squad returned home to demobilisation when hostilities ended. After the war, Harris remained in the army as a regular soldier. Enid had their baby girl and continued to enjoy life in Southampton. Harris died of wounds at the Battle of the Imjin River in Korea in 1951. Enid remarried the following year.

Fred and Gino's dream of a restaurant in Jersey was never realised. Fred became a chef in Düsseldorf, and Gino returned to London to work at the Dorchester. They exchanged Christmas cards for many years but never met again.

Acknowledgements

My thanks are due to Lt.-Col. (Retd.) C. D. Darroch, Honorary Archivist of the Royal Hampshire Regiment, Winchester; the Imperial War Museum; the *Daily Mail*; the Southampton *Daily Echo*; to Michael Mellor and Michael Schanze, both of Munich (although they are strangers to each other). Also to my cousin Major (Retd.) Alan Graham who, as a nineteen-year-old, parachuted into France on the night before D-Day. To Denis Donovan, former BBC television newsman, for his great assistance in research; to my friend Andrew Millington for sharing his knowledge of pre-war cars; and to Sheila Perrett of Lymington who not only word-processed the manuscript (many times!) but also added her own small but astute input to the story.

Thanks must also go to my publishers Andy McKillop of William Heinemann, and Susan Sandon of Arrow, who gave me great encouragement; and to Mary Chamberlain who, once again, edited my manuscript.

Finally, as always, thanks to my wife Diana who read the story as it grew and came up with her own advice, suggestions and judgement.

Waiting for the Day is fiction set against the background of real events. Some of these events have been taken slightly out of context in order to fit the story, and I have changed other aspects of the six months leading to D-Day on 6 June 1944 but not, I hope, to the extent of distorting what happened in those astonishing times.

Much has been written in the past sixty years on the unfolding of the invasion of Europe. I am indebted to the following sources:

Chester Wilmot, *The Struggle for Europe* (Collins, 1952)

Dwight D. Eisenhower, *Crusade in Europe* (William Heinemann, 1948)

Max Hastings, *Overlord* (Michael Joseph, 1984)

M. R. D. Foot, *SOE in France* (HM Stationery Office, 1966)

Norman Longmate, *The G.I.s: The Americans in Britain 1942–45* (Hutchinson, 1975)

Neil Barber, *The Day the Devils Dropped In* (Leo Cooper, 2002)

Angus Calder, *The People's War 1939–45* (Cape, 1969)

John Strawson, *Gentlemen in Khaki: The British Army 1890–1990* (Secker & Warburg, 1989)

Charles Cruikshank/Imperial War Museum, *The German Occupation of the Channel Islands* (Oxford University Press, 1975)

Philip Ziegler, *London at War 1939–1945* (Sinclair-Stevenson, 1995)

N. D. G. James, *Plain Soldiering* (The Hobnob Press, Salisbury, 1987)

George Forty, *U.S. Army Handbook 1939–1945* (Ian Allan Ltd, 1979)

Robert Goralski, *World War II Almanac 1931–1945* (Hamish Hamilton, 1981)

Stephen Badsey, *D-Day* (Tiger Books International, 1993)

Norman Longmate, *How We Lived Then* (Hutchinson, 1971)

Robert Gildea, *Marianne in Chains: The German Occupation of France 1940–45* (Macmillan, 2002)

David Scott Daniell, *The Royal Hampshire Regiment in World War II* (Gale and Polden, 1955)

Henry Stanhope, *The Soldiers: An Anatomy of the British Army* (Hamish Hamilton, 1979)

David Chandler, ed., *The Oxford Illustrated History of the British Army* (Oxford University Press, 1994)

Leslie Thomas
Lymington, Hampshire
June 2003